FANTASTIC 4

A Novelization by
Peter David

Written by
Mark Frost and Michael France

Based on the Marvel Comic Book

POCKET
BOOKS

LONDON • SYDNEY • NEW YORK • TORONTO

An *Original* Publication of POCKET BOOKS, a division of Simon & Schuster, Ltd. Africa House, 64–78 Kingsway, London WC2B 6AH

ISBN: 1-4165-1104-0

First Pocket Books printing June 2005

10 9 8 7 6 5 4 3 2 1

Printed and bound in Great Britain

A CIP catalogue record for this book is available from the British Library.

FANTASTIC 4

1

BEN GRIMM LOOKED WITH OBVIOUS CONCERN AT HIS best friend, who was leaning back in the taxicab seat and apparently doing everything he could not to fall asleep. "You okay, Reed?" he asked. "If you ask me, you been stretchin' yourself kinda thin lately."

Reed forced a wan smile. "I'm fine, Ben. I'm fine."

"Just fine?"

"That's not enough?" Reed said. Instead of looking over at Ben, he closed his eyes and rubbed his temples to ease the pounding within his head. "All right, Ben, you win. I'm more than fine. I'm superb. I'm fantastic. Will that do?"

"I guess it'll have to," Ben said sourly.

Ben's face was set in something of a permanent scowl. His face was round, his head shaved, his voice gruff and annoyed. He had an air of strength about him that derived from his steely gaze and impressive musculature. He was the sort of man who, when he strode down the street, women would give him appraising glances while

1

men sensed that this was not someone with whom they'd want to pick a fight.

He could not have been more of a contrast to Reed Richards. Reed was thin, with the perpetually distracted attitude typical of the academic. His hair was black and straight, and he rarely looked anyone in the eye. It wasn't that he was being impolite so much as his mind tended to wander into realms that no one else could follow. A single word, a passing phrase, even an idly hummed tune could trigger his astounding imagination, and the next thing anyone knew, Reed was no longer looking outward, but inward, developing some new and elaborate scientific construct that might end up feeding millions of starving people . . . or have no practical application whatsoever. It was all much the same to Reed. The result was of little consequence; it was the conception and subsequent experimentation that held the true thrill.

There was nothing thrilling in his current situation, however. Crammed into the back of a slow-moving taxicab, balancing books, charts, and assorted presentation materials on his lap, Reed was trying to think what his next move would be should things not pan out at this next meeting. Nothing was readily coming to mind, and that alone was enough to concern him. Reed Richards was not the type to run out of ideas under any circumstance.

"It's just that I think you've been working yerself too hard," Ben said abruptly, clearly not taking Reed's dismissal of the notion at all seriously.

2

"I've been working myself exactly as hard as I need to. No more, no less." Reed pulled out a paper at random and started reading it. There was no reason for him to do so other than to try and shut down the conversation.

Unfortunately, Ben knew him all too well. "Reed, ya know everything that's on that sheet of paper. Every word."

"What makes you say that?"

"Because you wrote it, and you remember everything you've ever written. Seriously. You could quote word problems off your second grade math papers."

"You're exaggerating, Ben."

"Yeah?" He snatched the paper out of Reed's hand. "Fifth line, third word."

"'The,'" said Reed in exasperation. "Happy now?"

"Ecstatic," said Ben, flipping the paper back to Reed and chuckling. Then his face grew somber. "Reed, it's gonna be fine. It's all gonna be fine. I'm bettin' that this . . . whattaya call it? VDI?" Reed nodded and Ben continued, "That this VDI outfit is gonna come through. I got a feeling about it. A hunch. And you know about my hunches. They're always right."

"I certainly hope this is another one of those times."

Ben frowned, scratching under his chin. "Why's that sound familiar? 'VDI'? What is that, a phone company or something?"

"No, not exactly . . ."

"R&D?"

"Yes, very much into research and development," Reed assured him.

3

"Well, what's it stand for?"

"Stand for?"

Ben's eyes narrowed, an abrupt surge of suspicion rattling around in his brain. "Reed . . . ya think I don't know when yer hidin' something? You think you can pull somethin' over on me? Is that what'cha think? What are you hiding?"

"What in the world makes you think I'm hiding something."

"Your eyes spin counterclockwise."

"Ben, honestly, there's . . ." Then he stopped and let out a slow breath. "Look, at least let's get there before—"

Ben Grimm might not have been—definitely wasn't, in fact, no "might not have been" about it—on Reed's level when it came to reasoning and intelligence. He did, however, have enough canniness and smarts to make intuitive jumps at the most inopportune moments, at least insofar as Reed was concerned. This was one of those moments, as Ben growled, "The 'V' in VDI wouldn't stand for 'Von' by any chance, would it?"

"See, I knew you wouldn't have the desired reaction to—"

Ben leaned forward and thumped on the plastic. "Lemme out here."

"I can't," replied the cabbie.

"Yeah, y' can. Never mind, I'll get out myself . . ."

"Ben, you're overreacting," Reed said.

Ben Grimm wasn't hearing any of it. Instead he was pulling in frustration at the door handle. "Damned door's locked."

"Of course it is," the cabbie said. "I keep it locked from up here. What, you think I want fares jumping out before they can pay?"

"Look," and Ben leaned forward to see the cabbie's name on his hack license. "Look, Lockley . . . I'm the customer. I'm the one who's always right."

"And I'm the cab driver," replied Lockley, "and I'm the one who gets a huge fine and loses his license if I let somebody out in the middle of traffic. Besides, we're a block-and-a-half away. Let me get you where you're going, bring you to curbside, and then you can get out and stomp around and show your friend here, who you could probably break in half, what a tough guy you are."

Ben took this in, and then said, "You got no idea how much I wish I could rip this door off at the hinges right now."

"I'm getting the idea, yeah," said Lockley. "You know the old Chinese curse: Be careful what you wish for. You may get it."

"Not really seein' a downside."

"Ben," Reed started.

But Ben just shook his head in obvious disappointment and annoyance. "Yer hittin' up Von Doom for the money? Von Doom?"

"It's not as bad as all that . . ."

"His name's Von Doom! That alone—"

"Now you're just being ridiculous."

"His name was Van Daam, y' know. He changed it to Von Doom just t' scare the crap outta people."

"You're not amusing, Ben. Not remotely."

5

"I think it's kind of funny," Lockley volunteered.

Reed scowled. "Did anyone even ask you?"

"No. Just figured I'd throw it in for free."

"He's bad news, Reed," Ben continued. "You know it and I know it, and the history we all got together . . ."

"Is just that, Ben. History. I'm trying to build a future for humanity, and I can't let myself be dragged down by the past in pursuing that endeavor."

"Wow," said Lockley, sounding impressed. "Your friend can be rather pompous when the mood calls for it, can't he."

"You must really not wanna get a tip," Ben said.

The cabbie snorted. "I wasn't holding my breath on that score for a while now." He turned the steering wheel and guided it toward curbside. "We're here."

Ben looked out the window on his side and grunted, "Really? Y' think?"

Craning his neck to see what Ben was staring at, Reed immediately saw the reason for Ben's sarcasm. It was impossible to make a mistake as to what building they were pulling up in front of.

A twenty-foot statue was in the process of being constructed in the courtyard directly outside the towering building. Passersby were stopping to stare at it as Reed and Ben eased out of the cab and Reed dug through his wallet to find the fare. The air was filled with the sound of a welder's torch, hard at work on the statue's gleaming metal exterior. Sparks ricocheted, the welder protecting his face via a clear plastic shield, and the smell of burning metal wafted toward them. Ben's nose wrinkled in

6

disgust, but that wasn't the only thing to be disgusted about by what he was witnessing. "And that cabbie thought Reed was pompous?" Ben muttered as he rocked back on his heels to see the statue more clearly.

The metal display was Victor Von Doom, all right. His chiseled features—angular, perfect (almost too perfect)—his determined and no-nonsense stare, the extraordinary arrogance that self-sufficiency oftentimes breeds . . . it was all there. The statue's hands, already completed, extended some feet away from the twenty-foot-high "masterpiece." Situated between his hands were two intertwined columns of DNA. As far as Ben was concerned, a representation of Von Doom holding the keys of life in his hands certainly played to the god-like attitude he had toward himself.

"I wonder how long it takes to create something like that," Reed said as he watched the sculptor meticulously pursuing his craft.

"Don't see why it should need any more than a day," replied Ben. "After all, Von Doom made the whole world in six days, right? So one statue shouldn't take more than twenty-four hours."

Reed stared at him blankly for a moment, and then forced a smile. "Oh. Yes, all right. A reference to the Book of Genesis. Following through on the concept that Victor Von Doom has aspirations to . . . godhood, for lack of a better term."

"That ain't a lack. That's the term exactly."

"Very droll, Ben. If making jokes is how you keep your confidence up, then go right ahead."

7

"I keep my confidence up 'cause I'm confident. Ain't any more complicated than that." He shook his head, troubled over the direction that their endeavors were taking them, but unable to think of anything to say to Reed to discourage him. So instead he simply gestured for Reed to proceed him.

The two of them approached the soaring glass box atrium of VDI headquarters. Sun glinted off the glass, occasionally obscured by passing clouds that likewise reflected off the tower. It made it seem to Ben as if this was more than just the literal definition of a skyscraper. It was as if Von Doom had created a tower that purported to be the home of gods . . . with its creator, naturally, as the main deity in residence.

"Awe inspiring, isn't it," murmured Reed.

"Awwwww," Ben replied.

Naturally the joke, such as it was, went right past Reed. He was too busy analyzing the building that soared skyward before him. That was Reed's way. He analyzed everything he encountered, oftentimes practically to death. It was one of the things that Ben used to find unspeakably annoying, but he had long since become accustomed to it.

"High open space, exposed structural elements," Reed said appraisingly. "Obviously aimed at first-time visitors to create feelings of . . ." He cleared his throat and continued uncomfortably, ". . . smallness . . . inadequacy."

Ben looked him up and down, saw the small bead of sweat forming on Reed's upper lip. "Good thing it ain't workin'," he said dryly. When he saw that, yet again, his attempts at humor had done a complete flyby, he sighed inwardly and took one more stab at talking his friend out of what he was positive was a destructive course. "Reed, what are we doing here? This guy's fast-food. Strip-mall science . . ."

"This wasn't our first step, in case you forgot NASA."

Naturally, Ben hadn't. It had been one of the most humiliating meetings of his life. Sitting there with men, researchers, pilots whom Ben had known all his life, had come up through the ranks with. He felt as if they'd been looking at him in judgment, condemning him with their eyes. When they'd slunk out, one of them had come over to him and spoken in a soft, amused voice. The words still rang in Ben's memory: *Coming up short again, Grimm. Hanging out with losers. It's become your regular thing, hasn't it.*

Your regular thing.

Ben didn't know what a "regular thing" was, but he despised the notion of having it or being it.

Seeing his friend's discomfort, Reed was clearly sorry he had brought the ill-fated NASA meeting up at all. He rested a hand on Ben's shoulder and said hopefully, "And Victor's not that bad. He's just a little . . ." Reed glanced up at the statue and finished, ". . . larger than life."

Ben afforded a slight chuckle. It wasn't exactly brilliant comedy stylings, but that was about as close to humor as Reed was ever going to get. Ben felt he should, at the very least, support the attempt. He nodded briefly and they walked past the statue, heading into the sprawling atrium.

"He's financed some of the biggest breakthroughs of this century," Reed continued.

"You'd never know it," Ben said sarcastically, and he pointed. Hanging in the middle of the atrium was a high-tech, projecting orb, displaying footage of Von Doom's many "accomplishments." Anyone who'd read a newspaper in the past several years recognized them almost instantly as one image dissolved into another: the safe, clean nuclear facility that had replaced the antiquated, dangerous one at Indian Point; the prototype car powered by a fusion engine; the world's first privately owned space station, hanging high above the Earth against a starry background.

These accomplishments—so indisputable that even Ben Grimm had to grudgingly acknowledge them—were interspersed with photos depicting Victor Von Doom front and center with all sorts of movers and shakers. There he was, glad-handing the President on the occasion of VDI developing artificial stem cells for research purposes; now he had his arm draped around the Queen, after the miniature tracing devices that Von Doom had placed within the crown jewels had retrieved them within half an hour of a daring and politically calamitous robbery. There he was, side-by-side with other assorted international leaders, any number of whom Ben was sure would just as gladly destroy America as visit it. As if that association wasn't disturbing enough for Ben, the image of Victor Von Doom triumphantly hoisting the America's Cup above his head was enough to cause Ben to shake his head and mutter, "Jesus. That, too?"

At the far end of the atrium was a large, rounded marble structure that served as the reception area . . . or guard stand, depending upon how you chose to look at it. Three receptionists, two male and one female, were waiting there. Again, "receptionist" might have been too delicate a term since they were uniformed and had—if not guns—at least Tasers hanging on their belts. Even the female looked like she could probably take Ben apart, and as for Reed, forget about it. She'd probably kill him by spitting on him.

Trying to look undaunted and failing miserably at it, Reed, his voice cracking, said "Reed Rich—" He stopped, took a breath, and started over. "Reed Richards and Ben Grimm to see—"

It seemed the receptionist was not interested in learning whether Reed could get through the entire sentence successfully. She interrupted him, holding up a pass for each of them. "Executive elevator, top floor." Von Doom had obviously told her they were coming. Ben wished he could have felt good about that. But he didn't. Instead he was reminded that the spider was always warned when prey was being drawn into its web through the shaking of a few strands. Ben didn't know whether they were welcome guests, or had simply shaken the web so that they'd been noticed.

"What's the price for a smile round here?" Ben asked, trying to look ingratiating. It didn't work. She just stared at him. At least she was merely staring; the guards on either side of her positively glowered. Reed had already taken his pass and, black box filled with

11

presentation materials tucked securely under his arm, was heading for the elevator bank. Ben gulped, forced a token smile, and took the other pass as he hurried past the guard station.

The elevator doors were cold and shiny, similar to the statue. Ben was fanciful enough to imagine them as Von Doom's jaws slamming shut upon them.

No words passed between the two old friends. Ben couldn't even begin to imagine what must have been going through Reed's mind. Actually, that wasn't true. Now that he'd had a little time to "digest" the notion that they were going on hands and knees to Victor Von Doom for aid, he realized how paltry his own sense of frustration had to be compared to Reed's. Reed was ten times—hell, a hundred times—the scientist that Victor Von Doom would ever be. But Von Doom was the shrewder businessman by far, and that was what had made all the difference. That was why Victor was surrounded by endless luxury and testimony after testimony to his greatness, while Reed was swallowing what little pride he must have had left and seeking Von Doom's assistance.

Ben remembered how he'd once made a passing reference to Thomas Edison being a scientific genius on a par with Reed, and Reed had just shaken his head and smiled sadly. "Edison's strength wasn't only science, Ben. It was identifying brilliant scientists with tremendous potential. The Wizard of Menlo Park is a figure for the ages, while the great minds who helped develop the ideas are forgotten and gone to dust."

That had been several years ago, before they'd reach this point of frustration. He wondered if Reed remembered it. Then he wondered why he wondered, because Reed Richards was the type of guy who remembered the marks he got in fifth grade social studies. Not that that would have presented any sort of challenge; the odds were huge that all his grades had been "A+" throughout school.

He became aware that Reed was looking at him, and met his gaze questioningly. With a slightly arched eyebrow, Reed said, "Thinking about Edison, right?"

"Awright," Ben growled, "now yer just freakin' me out."

The freaking out of Ben Grimm was not about to stop anytime soon, for the elevator doors slid open and all that met them was blackness.

"So this is what dyin' and going to hell is like," said Ben.

Suddenly some sort of lights began to gather in the middle of the darkness. Reed stepped out, rapt attention upon the glowing, amorphous mass that was coalescing in the middle of a room so dark that it was impossible to get any sense of just how big it was. Filled with curiosity, Ben followed him. He was dimly aware of the elevator door sliding shut behind him, and tried not to dwell on bizarre possibilities such as the floor suddenly dropping open beneath them, all to satisfy whatever perverse notions passed as Von Doom's sense of humor these days.

Suddenly the coruscating light pulsed, drew together as if imploding, and then blew forth in all directions at once. Ben flinched, half-expecting some sort of ear-shattering explosion. Instead it all transpired in eerie silence, which Ben supposed made sense. After all, if this was happening in the depths of space, as the imagery suggested, there wouldn't be any air to carry the noise.

The holographic bits of what would be planets flew past Ben and Reed, and began to settle into orbit. Millions of years passed in seconds, and Ben could pick out the familiar worlds of the solar system as they cooled and revolved around the sun. He put his hand through Jupiter as it whirled past, no bigger than the tip of his finger.

"So tell me, Vic," Ben called out into the darkness, "did it take ya six days to create the universe, like the Bible says, or did ya work on the Sabbath, too?"

"Ben," Reed snapped at him in annoyance.

That was when a familiar voice boomed from the darkness. He did not sound particularly perturbed. He spoke with the easy confidence of someone who did not have to care about anything that anyone said, much less an out-of-work test pilot. "Actually, Ben," came Von Doom's voice with an easy familiarity, "I like to watch the work of a true master every now and then. Helps keep me humble."

"Kinda late for that, don't'cha think."

Reed closed his eyes in pain, not even bothering to remonstrate Ben, since he likely (and wisely) figured it wouldn't do much good.

"Your associate," Von Doom said silkily once more from the darkness, "seems to be doing the talking for you, Reed. Does he do the thinking as well?"

"Reed does more thinking, Vic, than you and me and all the—"

"Ben," Reed put up a hand and said, not ungently, "perhaps I could take it from here . . . ?"

"Oh! Right, sure," Ben bobbed his head and stepped back, reflexively ducking as Neptune cruised past.

"All right. Well . . ." Reed took several steps forward, squinting slightly in the vain hope of picking Von Doom out from wherever he was in the gloom. "First of all, Victor, I want to thank you for giving me this time . . ."

"If you really want to thank me for my time, Reed," Von Doom interjected, "you won't take up needless amounts of it. I read the basic prospectus. I know the fundamentals of what you're interested in. Now . . . impress me. I'd think that shouldn't present a problem. After all, you always presented yourself as my equal back in the day."

"I don't remember presenting myself one way or the other, Victor," said Reed. As he spoke, he removed a smaller black box from the case he was carrying and set it down. He produced a remote control from his pocket. "I did, however, recall your flair for the dramatic. 'Back in the day' was when you first cooked up this little holo-demonstration, and I know you're not one to waste anything. So I thought you might still be using it . . . and therefore felt it wouldn't be out of line to utilize it for my own purposes."

The black box flared to life and immediately Reed's own holograms superimposed themselves upon Von

Doom's, matching up with them perfectly. Standing off to the side, leaning against a corner, it was all Ben could do not to laugh. That was Reed all over: three steps ahead of whatever somebody else was coming up with, and trumping them at their own game.

There, moving across the revised hologram, was the slow, drifting cloud of a cosmic storm. It surged with unaccountable, formidable energy, undulating its way across the solar system, the edges crackling.

The additional illumination from the hologram was helping Ben's eyes adjust to the darkness. He was finally able to make out a large desk at one end of the table, with a man's silhouette positioned behind it. The elbows rested casually on the desk, fingers steepled. Ben felt his hackles begin to rise in a sort of warning, but he kept a remarkable poker face, as if Von Doom's presence was neither here nor there.

"My research suggests," Reed was saying, "that exposure to a high-energy cosmic storm borne on solar winds might have triggered the evolution of early planetary life."

The storm had continued on its way and now intercepted Earth's orbit with an almost sentient precision. "In six weeks," Reed continued, "another cloud with the same elemental profile will pass Earth's orbit." His voice grew more forceful, more excited, as he contemplated the possibilities of the things he was suggesting. "A study in space could advance our knowledge about the structure of the human genome, and help cure countless diseases, extend human life . . ."

Von Doom cleared his throat loudly. The implication was unspoken but clear: Reed was taking way too long with his presentation. Ben's face flushed with unspoken embarrassment for his friend, but Reed obediently sped up. In doing so, his voice rose, became more emotional due to his pure passion for the topic at hand. "Give kids the chance to be stronger, healthier, less prone to—"

"Turn it off, please," said Von Doom. As opposed to the casual flippancy of earlier, his tone sounded firm, commanding, even slightly annoyed.

"But I haven't fully explained my . . ."

"Yes, you have. Imagination. Creativity. Passion. Those were always your trademarks."

The lights abruptly came up, and Ben squinted against the sudden illumination. There was Von Doom, looking just like his pictures. Thirty-five, handsome, commanding, his hair black and curly, his stern jaw set in a slight grimace that bore a faint resemblance to a smile. His face looked more crafted by design than anything that had developed organically, as if it had been airbrushed onto the front of his head.

The office was ornately decorated, filled with trophies and memorabilia from Von Doom's globe-trotting successful career. The piece that leaped out most conspicuously to Ben was a full-size display of ancient armor that stood with a faint air of menace against the wall, like some sort of mute guard. Ben gazed into its empty eye sockets and could almost imagine someone—or something—glaring back at him. There was also a huge sculpture of the letter "V" on the far wall, presumably standing for "Victor," although Ben didn't rule out that it might be for "villain." Or just "vile."

Victor was holding a copy of *Wired* magazine, and he tossed it casually onto the desk. Ben knew what it was before he even looked at it: the copy that had Reed's picture on it and the words RICHARDS BANKRUPT? ANNOUNCES GRANT CUTBACKS plastered on it in forty-eight-point type. Ben couldn't help but recall that, when *Wired* had first covered Reed several years earlier for his brilliance and innovations, the typeface had been a lot smaller. Nothing made good headlines quite like failure.

"But dreams don't pay the bills, do they?" Von Doom added unnecessarily. He gave a damnably condescending smirk that Ben wanted to walk over and wipe off his face. Why not? What'd they have to lose? Victor Von Doom wasn't going to help them any more than anyone else was. He was just going to go out of his way to make them feel even more humiliated, that was all. "Same old Reed," Von Doom went on. "The hopeless optimist. Still reaching for the stars, with the world on your back."

"You remember in school we talked about working together," Reed said. "That's what I was about to explain." He pressed another button on his remote control, and a new hologram was added to the others. It was a space shuttle, gliding from Earth toward its obvious destination: an orbiting space satellite. Both the shuttle and the space station bore the logo of Von Doom Industries.

In spite of himself, Von Doom—who had risen from

18

behind his desk as an obvious way of signaling that the meeting was over—slowly sat back down. Clearly he was intrigued by the notion. The sight made Ben smile. Whereas others to whom Reed had gone had been nothing but representatives of soulless corporations, Von Doom had an ego the size of space itself. Appeal to that, and perhaps there was a shot to be had after all.

Then Victor's eyes narrowed, as if he realized that he was being played. "So it's not my money you want," he said understandingly. "It's my toys." He rapped his knuckles thoughtfully on his desk. "Tell me: If NASA doesn't trust you, why should I?"

Reed was clearly taken aback, and Ben couldn't blame him. Here Ben had been mentally patting Reed on the back for out-clevering Von Doom with the hologram, and meanwhile Von Doom held the trump card. How the hell had he found out about Reed's being casually dismissed by the NASA reps? Obviously Von Doom had some sort of mole in NASA. For all Ben knew, Victor had eyes and ears in every major corporation and government agency in the country.

"That's my job," Von Doom said in response to Ben's unspoken thoughts. "To stay a step ahead. To know what other men don't."

Ben had heard more than enough. He stepped in close to his friend and said in a low, angry voice, "I can't take this."

He didn't mean it on behalf of himself. He meant he couldn't take seeing poor Reed just standing there, being

19

handed this sort of abuse from such a smug so-and-so as Victor Von Doom.

But for all the physical strength that Ben Grimm possessed, Reed had as much and perhaps even more in strength of character. "Ben," he cautioned in a low voice. "This is business. Just work."

Von Doom looked Reed up and down, as if trying to take the measure of him, and then grinned broadly. It all seemed a game to him somehow. It was becoming clear to Ben, however, that Reed was more than capable of playing that same game if need be.

It was at that moment, with tension hanging thick in the air, that an unexpected female voice cut through it with a cavalier, "He's right, Ben. It's just business."

Ben had not heard the voice in years, and yet he knew it instantly, before turning to see the speaker. Even as he turned around to see her, he was hoping that she had lost her looks or put on a hundred pounds or something, but no, she was as beautiful as Ben had remembered her. Statuesque, blonde, with the sort of blue eyes that a man could lose himself in. She radiated confidence and coolness and . . . and . . .

. . . and once upon a time, a sweetness that Ben had quietly found irresistible . . . except he had resisted it, because his best friend had longed for her with a sort of quiet desperation, and there was simply no way Ben was getting in the middle of it. The best friend who, as it so happened, was standing right next to Ben, gaping in bewilderment.

The planet Venus swung between them and then departed, there and gone again. *Doesn't get more symbolic than that*, Ben mused.

Von Doom gestured toward the woman with the air of a magician waving grandly at the rabbit he'd just produced from his hat. "I think you both know my director of genetic research, Susan Storm."

"Heya, Susie," Ben said, tossing off a mock salute, even as he said in a low voice to Reed, "One *more* thing he's got."

Sue seemed to glide across the office as she walked. She never took her eyes off Reed except when she warmly hugged Ben by way of greeting. That made perfect sense to Ben. Unlike most every other man she'd ever met, Ben had never done anything to pursue her. For that reason, she had always regarded him as a friend, knowing where he stood and taking comfort that he would never try to turn that friendship into something else. "Ben, it's been too long."

Then she turned and gave Reed a polite handshake. Reed's gaze was fixed upon her, as if concerned that— should he look away—she would vanish into thin air. He shook her hand without realizing he was holding it, then he looked down at it in surprise. He looked back up at her and stammered out, "You're . . . you've . . . I mean . . ." He took a breath and, trying to come across as casual but only succeeding in sounding forced, he asked, "How have you been?"

"Never better."

Von Doom appeared to be sizing up the two of them.

Then he stepped forward and put a hand on Sue's shoulder. She promptly released Reed's hand. "This isn't going to be a problem, is it?" he asked, obviously referring to their possible working relationship.

"Not at all," Reed said.

Sue's response overlapped his. "Ancient history," she assured him.

"Good," Von Doom said, sounding satisfied. "Then you're just in time to hear the great Reed Richards ask me for help."

Once again Ben was seized with that same impulse to put his fist in Von Doom's face, but he controlled himself, taking his cue from Reed's impassive stare. If he was letting any of this bother him, Ben couldn't tell.

"You know," went on Von Doom, "you made a lot of folks at MIT feel like they were at a junior high science fair. So you'll excuse me if I savor the moment."

Ben wasn't inclined to excuse him. Ben's impulse was to wipe that smug look off his face. But Reed merely shrugged indifferently, as if to say that this issue was wholly Von Doom's and of no consequence to Reed at all. "You back up this mission," Reed assured him, "and I'll sign over a fair percentage of any applications or—"

"The number's seventy-five," said Von Doom. "And it's applications *and* patents."

"What about his firstborn!" demanded Ben, unable to contain himself. He took a step toward Von Doom, but Reed put out a hand without even looking at Ben and placed it on his chest, keeping him where he was.

22

"Ben," he said softly, "the money's not important. We could save *lives*."

Ben was about to say, *The heck with other people's lives! What'd they ever do for us?* But then he saw that Sue, just for the briefest flash of a moment, was looking at Reed in that way. That old way, from the old days, in a manner that spoke volumes of possibilities. She covered it deftly enough, but Ben knew that he hadn't been imagining it.

Von Doom didn't seem to notice it. He was still busy negotiating . . . if one could call mauling an opponent who wouldn't fight back "negotiating." "Twenty-five percent of a billion is enough to keep the lights on for a while, isn't it? Maybe even pay off your fourth mortgage on the Baxter Building . . ."

Unbelievable. Von Doom being up on the NASA meeting was bad enough, but when had Reed's personal finances become fodder for him? Before Ben could recover from the realization that there was seemingly nothing Von Doom didn't know about Reed, Victor held out a hand and said, with just a touch of challenge, "Deal?"

Reed looked at Ben, who softly shook his head *no*. This was the first person who had been willing to come through for Reed, but Ben was certain that Reed should simply walk away from it. Every fiber of his being was telling him that—best-case scenario—Reed would live to regret it. He didn't even want to consider the worst-case scenario.

But Reed nodded to Victor, which somehow was exactly what Ben had known he was going to do. He reached out and gripped his hand firmly as Von Doom said, "Well then! To our future, together!" Reed winced slightly in pain at the strength of Von Doom's grip, but that didn't seem to hurt him nearly as much as when Victor once again put his hand warmly on Sue's shoulder. "Funny how things turn out, isn't it?"

"Hilarious," said Reed with a deadpan.

As much as Reed's thoughts were roiling in conflict where Victor Von Doom was concerned, even he had to admit that Von Doom had a way of cutting right through the red tape when he was so inclined. They'd gone from an oral agreement in principle to a letter of agreement drawn up by Von Doom's director of communications, Leonard Kirk, within half an hour. It wasn't a full contract, but it set out the basic terms plainly and completely. Small wonder. Von Doom probably wanted to lock things up before Reed "came to his senses."

Reed felt bad about ignoring Ben's well-meaning advice. He knew, from a business point of view, that Ben was right to want to walk away from the lopsided deal. But Reed tended to never take the business point of view when there were lives to be saved and the betterment of humanity to be pursued. Which, Reed grimly allowed, was probably why his business had gone belly-up.

As they stepped into the elevator to head back downstairs, Ben was saying, "He knew about NASA! What if he made the call to shut us down—!"

Reed had to admit to himself that it wasn't outside the realm of possibility. NASA had, at first, been supportive of Reed's endeavors. But suddenly promised monies got sandbagged in committee, and Reed and Ben had been dragged back in front of a whole new array of people who had treated the two of them as if they were red-headed stepchildren. So maybe it wasn't just that Von Doom had good intelligence sources. Perhaps he had indeed orchestrated the entire thing. Nevertheless, Reed couldn't dwell on it. He prayed it wasn't true, and if it was, it wasn't as if he could do a whole lot about it now. "Ben," he pleaded, "think about all the people we can help if this works . . ."

"Maybe you should think about helping yourself for once!" retorted Ben. "You always let this guy push you around—"

Reed didn't really believe that to be true, but he wasn't about to get into a shouting match with his best friend about it. "We got what we wanted. That's enough."

He had spoken with an air of finality that he hoped would terminate the discussion, and it seemed to be effective as Ben said, "I know, I know." He paused, and then added, "I'm just worried about what he wants. Speaking of which—"

Not knowing what it was that Ben was referring to, Reed's gaze followed his friend's and then he comprehended as Sue Storm walked toward them, catching them just before the elevator doors closed. She stepped sideways and slid right though the closing doors, which slid shut behind her. "Reed," she said, "you should know, those solar winds are picking up speed in the—"

He knew instantly what she was talking about. That the incoming storm, thanks to recent sunspot activity that had generated more solar winds than usual, was heading toward Earth faster than originally thought. "I factored them into my coordinates," he said, trying to sound confident. Truth was, he was confident. He just had trouble being that way for Sue.

"Of course you did," said Sue, which sounded to Reed as if she trusted him implicitly. "In theory," she added, which instantly came across as patronizing. Reed forced himself to find some degree of mental equilibrium. Otherwise his mind was going to become a ping-pong ball if this kept up. "But it's a little different up there. And it's been a while since we . . . worked together."

There was an unspoken challenge in that comment. Reed knew this mostly from the way Ben reacted to it. But Reed chose to ignore it, determined to focus on making his and Sue's relationship a straightforward, smoothly functioning, working one. That was going to be best for all concerned, and certainly what Sue wanted from their mutual assignment. "So you'll handle biogenetics," he said, "and I'll handle molecular physics. Or maybe I'll take biotech, and you'll work astrophysics, since you have experience with the electroscopes."

She stared at him for a long moment, and then said curtly, "Right. Whatever you say."

Instantly Reed knew he'd said something wrong. He didn't know it thanks to any great insight on his part, because when it came to women in general and Sue Storm in particular, he had none to offer. Instead he knew it from the way that Ben looked at him, slowly shaking his head in pity. "Way to not overthink, slick." Ben then turned to Sue, as if to try and prevent any further conversation between her and Reed, presumably for Reed's own good. "So when do we leave?"

"I'll schedule the launch," said Sue. "Call me in the morning to talk about resources and crew."

She produced a business card and offered it to Reed. He made no move to take it, instead saying, "I, uh, think I remember the number."

"It's been changed," she said.

Ben looked abashed at that, and even Reed knew why. Sue had gone to great effort to get the specially requested phone number years ago: (212) 555-REED.

Obviously that was no longer the case.

Reed took the card, his eyes downcast. "As far as crew," he said, without meeting her gaze, "I was hoping Ben could pilot the mission . . ."

"Well, he's welcome to ride shotgun," Sue said, "but we already have a pilot on our payroll. You remember my brother Johnny . . ."

Reed certainly did . . . and Ben smiling with the sincerity of curdled milk confirmed for Reed that, yes, Ben certainly did as well.

Bad enough this deal had cost him money, pride, and dignity. He wondered whether his friendship with Ben was next on the list.

In Leonard Kirk's office, Von Doom looked over the letter of agreement with satisfaction. Kirk entered, flipping through some file folders as he did so. Without even glancing up at him, Von Doom said, "If Reed's right, then this little trip will double our stock offering."

"And if he's not?" Kirk asked cautiously.

Von Doom smiled that million-dollar smile. "Reed's always right. Good thing he doesn't always know what he's got."

2

BY ALL RIGHTS, THIS WAS REED RICHARDS' FIRST FLIGHT into space. Yet, in many ways, that was not at all the case.

Reed had made the trip numerous times in the past. The circumstances, the reasons for it, had changed from one time to the next . . . which was not at all unnatural, since all the previous occasions had been in his dreams.

The most vivid of them, curiously enough, had featured some of the same players who would be making the genuine liftoff with him this time around. In a frequently recurring dream, he saw himself dashing across an uneven, fantastic landscape that purported to be a secret military base. By his side was Sue Storm, as if she was always meant to be at his side and the fact that she wasn't during his waking hours was a mere aberration. Just ahead of him was the determined Ben, and just behind them was Sue's kid brother, Johnny. Even in his dream state, Reed knew that Johnny brought nothing to the party. But Sue couldn't be convinced to leave him behind, and so there he was. Nothing to be done for it, really.

They made it to the rocket ship for reasons that continued to vary. Sometimes it was just to beat the Russians into space, which was certainly one of the more dated dreams that Reed's sleeping mind indulged in. Other times it was to get to the moon, and still others it was something as nebulous and impractical as "the stars." For whatever reason, they strapped themselves in, and the rockets beneath them roared to life. Reed's body would shake violently, his teeth chattering, and the blast of the engine would drown out the scream that was inevitably torn from his throat as the unknown reached out toward him and prepared to drag him to its bosom.

Inevitably he would wake up with cold sweat pouring down his face. He would shake his head, lean forward, wipe the perspiration from his forehead and cheeks, and wonder yet again whether the dreams were serving to guide him down a path . . . or warn him off it.

If it was the latter, then they hadn't done an especially good job. For here he was now, looking up in wonderment at the spacecraft that loomed high above him. The rocket looked surreally out of place, with vast stretches of pure unsullied timberland stretching in all directions nearby. The gantry was constructed so that the flames generated by the rocket's ignition would be contained upon being unleashed. Von Doom had double-checked that, but Reed had triple-checked it. He had absolutely no intention of being hurtled skyward while leaving a raging forest fire in his wake.

Nearby was a peaceful lake, ducks and geese cruising across the surface. Whereas Victor Von Doom had to whip up hologram re-creations of creation in order to attain some perspective, Reed needed to look no further than those simple birds. All the work that humans had to go to in order to hurl themselves into the air, and birds could take flight with simple thought and a flap of their wings, courtesy of evolution. On the other hand, Reed reasoned, it wasn't as if a bird could turn around and drive a car or write a sonata, so maybe he didn't have anything to be envious of at that.

As he approached the spaceship on foot, his gaze caressed it with his customary scrutiny. It might well have been the best thing that NASA had turned up its collective nose at him. The ship he was looking at had taken the basic design of the shuttle merely as a starting point, and made advancements upon it in terms of aerodynamics, propulsion, and safety that NASA couldn't begin to touch either in ingenuity or affordability. The nose of the craft, two hundred feet high, was pointed straight up, pointing toward the sky as if to say, "I'm coming for you. So don't get too comfortable." There were men in jumpsuits crawling all over the gantry, running last-minute checks, like determined and highly trained ants.

Ben was waiting for him at the gantry overlook, just as they had prearranged. He was studying the hive of activity that was the rocket through a pair of binoculars. But he was shaking his head, which Reed did not see as an especially good sign. Was he seeing something wrong, some potential malfunction that had gone past everyone else? Reed stepped up next to Ben, raising his own binoculars and peering through them to try and determine what it was that Ben had spotted.

"Can't do it," Ben said without even lowering his binoculars. "I cannot do it."

Reed started rattling off a litany of potential stumbling blocks which had already been attended to. "External SRBs, orbital system engines. It's just like the shuttles you flew in—"

"No," Ben cut him off. "I cannot take orders from that underwear model."

Reed wanted to laugh, except he knew how serious Ben was about this. "Ben, I thought there was something wrong with the rocket!"

"There is! The hotshot is piloting it! That wingnut washed out of NASA for sneaking two Victoria's Secret wannabes into a flight simulator."

"Youthful high spirits," Reed said dismissively, lowering the binocs. He was curious to see that Ben was still gazing through his.

"They crashed it into a wall. A flight *simulator*."

"I'm sure he's matured since then."

Still without looking in Reed's direction, Ben reached over, took Reed's binoculars, and held them up to indicate that Reed should look through them once more. Confused but cooperative, Reed peered through them at the rocket, until Ben gripped Reed's shoulder and angled his torso so that the lean scientist was focused in another direction. Then he saw it and his heart sank.

There was Johnny Storm, perched atop a red Victory motorcycle with a license plate that said REDHOT. He was leaning over and planting a prolonged and smoky kiss on the lips of a drop-dead gorgeous redhead in the driver's seat of a vintage black Corvette convertible. Her license plate read FRANKIE.

Reed moaned inwardly, but tried to maintain a positive attitude for Ben's sake, if nothing else. "When have I asked you to do something you absolutely said you could not do?"

"Five times," Ben said instantly.

Reed glanced out the side of the binocs at his oldest friend. "I had it at four."

Returning the sidelong glance, Ben replied, "This makes five."

Reed lowered the binocs and breathed a sigh of relief. "You had me going there for a moment, Ben."

Ben started heading down toward the locker room facilities, Reed falling into step behind him. "If you think I'm gonna count on that wannabe jet jockey to get you back down here in one piece, then yer not the big brain I always thought y' were."

"I wouldn't ever want to chance letting you down."

"Just one thing . . ."

"Name it."

"If the kid turns us into a blazing fireball, then the second before we blow up, you gotta say, 'Ben, you were right about everything.' That's the deal. Take it or leave it."

"Everything?" Reed was a bit distressed about that. "I

don't know, Ben. I mean, there's been some things you've said that turned out to be—"

"Take it. Or leave it."

"Would you want my last words to be a lie?"

"I got no problem with that," Ben assured him.

"Fine," Reed sighed. "Should it come to that, I'll accommodate."

"Loud enough so I can hear you 'cause, y' know, a ship blowin' up can get pretty noisy."

"I'll shout it at the top of my lungs."

"Good. 'Cause it won't happen, but if it does, I'll be listening."

Once they'd gotten down into the locker room, they were busy unpacking their gear and going over some final flight check routines. Actually, Reed was busy doing that. Ben was busy shifting uncomfortably in the formfitting blue jumpsuit, which seemed determined to give him as little flexibility in his shoulders as possible. Then a brash voice called out, "Captain on the bridge!"

Muscle memory was a powerful thing. That much was evident as, on the strength of the commanding tone alone, Ben snapped to attention on reflex. The instant that he did so, there was a click accompanied by a flash. Reed shook his head. Whatever illusion he might have had that Johnny Storm had become remotely more professional in the past few years was being thoroughly dashed.

Johnny, gleefully grinning from ear to ear, shared his sister's striking blonde hair and snapping blue eyes.

And he was nearly as intelligent, as Reed knew for a fact since in the old days, Sue delighted in boasting about her brother's impressive test scores. Even then, though, Reed had known there was trouble in Johnny's future. Good grades came to him so easily that he never developed the discipline required to get ahead in life. So when he finally did encounter things that required serious work, he didn't have the focus or determination to stick with them. It was this lack of focus that had held him back, and also tended to put Ben Grimm's teeth on edge.

Already attired in the blue jumpsuit that was obviously the outfit of choice for the mission, Johnny held up the camera he'd just used to photograph Ben standing at attention. "Digital camera: Two hundred and fifty-four dollars. Memory stick: Fifty-nine dollars." He took a step closer and continued, "The look on your hard-ass former CO's grill when he finds out he's your *junior* officer: *Priceless!*"

Ben eyeballed him silently for a moment, and then his hand thrust forward with such speed and force that Reed was sure Ben was about to put his fist directly through Johnny's head. Even Johnny flinched, stepping back, and there was a flash of fear in his eye.

But all Ben did was grip the zipper on the front of Johnny's uniform and adjust it so that it was up on the collar and flat. "I can handle the ship," Ben said with remarkable control. "I can even handle Mr. Blonde Ambition." He released the zipper and looked with disgust toward Reed. "But I don't know if I should be flying or playing Vegas with these suits. Who the hell came up with them?"

"Victor did."

Sue had seemingly appeared out of nowhere; she might have been invisible for all that Reed had seen her coming. She was wearing the same suit as they, except it was clinging to her so tightly that it left almost nothing to the imagination. She had a sack of flight suits draped over her arm as she handed them out to the men. "The synthetics act as a second skin," she said, touching the top of the outfit. "Adapting to our individual needs to . . ."

"Keep the hot side hot and the cool side cool!" Johnny finished cheerfully, although he still looked slightly rattled from earlier when he'd thought Ben was about to cave in his face.

"Wow. Fantastic," Reed said, making sure to sound duly impressed. He was studying the way the uniform hugged Sue's body, marveling at its flexibility. "Material made from self-regulating, unstable molecules. I've been working on a formula for this."

For no reason he could determine, Sue looked slightly crestfallen. He wasn't sure why she would be. He was, after all, paying due compliments to her boss. What more could she want from him? "Great minds think alike," was all she said.

Victor chose that moment to make his entrance with a smug, "Guess some think faster than others." Reed wondered whether Von Doom had been lurking there the entire time, simply waiting for a proper moment to make his entrance, or if he just had good timing. Von Doom was already attired in the flight suit that Sue had entered with. He paused a moment and stood with hands on his hips in mimicry of a model on a runway. "I hired Armani to design the pattern. These colors will look great on camera."

"Well, good," Ben said. "It's nice t' know that ya haven't forgotten the important things."

"I haven't forgotten *any*thing, Ben," Von Doom informed him. "Important, trivial . . . it's all been attended to."

Reed knew that Ben was about to ask where in the grand scheme of importance being photogenic fell on the Von Doom scale, but Leonard Kirk selected that instant to walk in. In a sharp, charcoal gray suit, he was a stark contrast to the uniformed individuals in the locker room. "They're ready for you, sir," he said.

Victor grinned wickedly and said, "Showtime. Get into your flight suits and join me outside, folks. Wouldn't want to keep the press waiting."

He turned on his heel and headed out. The moment he was gone, Johnny said wryly, "Well? You heard the man."

"Yeah," Ben noted, "and what I heard was a guy who wanted to make damned sure that he got solo time with the press before we made it out there."

"Didn't know you cared," said Johnny, stepping into the flight suit and pulling it up over his shoulders.

"I don't, squirt," replied Ben. "The point is . . . he does."

As Von Doom walked briskly through the corridor, he made certain to check his appearance in every reflected surface that he passed. If Leonard noticed this, he made it a point to studiously avoid mentioning it. Instead he was reading some notes off a handheld organizer that he was sure Von Doom was going to want to be apprised of. "Our numbers are through the roof," he said. "The IPO's tracking at fifty, sixty a share. The bank's five times oversubscribed . . ."

Victor waved him off as if Leonard was giving him the weather report in Iceland. "It's not just the money. I can make money in my sleep."

This was news to Leonard. Not that Von Doom could make money in his sleep, but that he cared about anything else while he was awake. "Then what is it?" he asked.

"History, Leonard. History," he emphasized. "Everything else is conversation." His mind had already departed from the status of their stocks and moved on to weightier considerations. "How's the other matter?"

Leonard promptly reached into his jacket pocket and pulled out a black ring box. He flipped it open to reveal a ten-karat diamond ring. This was enough to bring even Victor Von Doom to a halt for a heartbeat as he gazed upon something that was more beautiful than he himself . . . at least marginally so. His breath caught as he stared at the tiny flames that seemed to dance within each facet. "Harry Winston sends his regards," Leonard added.

Von Doom smiled approvingly, then hurriedly gestured for Leonard to shove the ring back in his pocket. Leonard did so, then Victor turned to face the large double doors through which he was about to make his entrance. He glanced one final time at his reflection on the metallic wall, adjusted one last errant strand of hair that didn't seem to know its place, and then shoved through the doors to greet his public.

A barrage of camera flashes went off in his face as reporters shouted, "There he is!" and "Look this way, Victor!"

The perfect smile came easily to him, so naturally that one would have thought it truly was natural. He remembered when he had first begun the meticulous process of creating his public persona. Imagination, as was so often the case in matters of invention, became actualization. He had determined what he wanted the public Victor Von Doom to be: the stirring orator, the visionary, with the sparkling looks and easy, scintillating wit. He had cloaked himself within Von Doom, created a metaphorical mask behind which he had hidden the true Victor. The irony of it was that he had been sporting the mask for so long that whatever the "true" Victor was—what merits or foibles he might have had—were long gone and forgotten. The mask was permanent now, fitting him as easily as if it was the face he was born with.

He spread his arms, taking in the entirety of the makeshift press area with one, grand gesture. "Today we stand on the edge of the new frontier!" he called out. "In the furthest depths of outer space . . . we will find the secrets to *inner* space. The final key to unlocking our genetic code lies in a cosmic storm . . ."

Ben was mouthing the words along with Von Doom as he, Reed, Sue, and Johnny made their way past the podium upon which Von Doom was standing. He certainly knew the words well enough, having heard Reed say them plenty of times. Reed was pointedly not looking in Von Doom's direction, clearly trying to screen out what Ben knew to be the truth. He had no desire to rub Reed's nose in it, and yet he felt the need to underscore for his friend what a duplicitous creep Von Doom could be . . . just in case Reed made the mistake of trusting him. "Isn't that your speech?" he asked with feigned innocence.

"He's made a few changes," Reed said unconvincingly.

Ben shook his head. He knew what Reed's priorities were, knew that his interest was the betterment of mankind, not the betterment of Reed Richards. Still, it gnawed at Ben, and he couldn't understand how it wasn't bothering Reed on some level at least. "This is your dream, Reed. You should be the one up there."

Reed shrugged. "Victor's better at these things."

That hardly seemed like a reason to shun the spotlight as far as Ben was concerned, but then he spotted something just beyond the press area that made his conversation with Reed take a distant second in importance. It was the one thing in the world that could prompt him not to live up to his surname of "Grimm."

It was Debbie Sohn, Ben's fiancée. There was something about the odd-yet-attractive arrangement of her features that prompted Ben to smile just looking at the sweet-faced blonde. Indeed, that was what attracted him to her in the first place when they'd initially encountered each other in passing at a bookstore. Reed had been with him, and when he'd seen Ben smiling, he'd been so thunderstruck that he thought Ben was in massive amounts of pain and grimacing in order to cover it. Upon learning that a girl was causing that response in Ben, Reed had insisted that Ben approach her immediately, get to know her, and if at all possible, never let her go. Since Ben never questioned the fact that Reed was far smarter than he, he had taken Richards up on his advice and hadn't regretted it since.

Ben walked over toward Debbie, embraced her, kissed her tenderly. Johnny slowed down, and Ben noticed out the corner of his eye that Johnny was giving Debbie the appraising once-over. A single raised eyebrow told Ben all he needed to know: that Johnny was impressed, and probably even wondering what in the world a looker like Debbie saw in Ben Grimm. Ben would have been offended by the attitude except that he'd wondered much the same thing practically every day of their relationship.

He also saw Reed looking at the two of them, and then glancing over toward Sue. Sue walked right past without even looking their way or, more significantly, Reed's way. *Aw, Reed, ya dumb-ass, what's it gonna take, huh? Gonna wait until Sue's beyond yer reach forever?* He didn't say it aloud, though, since he suspected he knew the answer.

41

Debbie slipped a photo of herself into Ben's flightsuit. He patted it lightly for safekeeping. "I'll be watching over you," he told her.

"Just get back soon," she replied. "Or I start looking for a new groom."

He looked at the small engagement ring on her finger. "Soon as I'm back," he assured her, "I'm gonna trade that in for a bigger rock."

"I don't care about rocks. I care about you." She called after Reed, "You bring him back in one piece, or you can forget being best man."

Reed nodded and smiled, giving her an optimistic thumbs-up. Debbie gave Ben a last quick kiss, and he turned away from her only to see Johnny was now standing practically in his face. Johnny had that insufferably cocky grin that Ben had long come to know and loathe.

"What the hell you smiling at?" Ben demanded. "Just keep your mouth shut and your mind on those SMBs . . ."

"Actually," Johnny interrupted him, "the engines are SMEs. Hydrogen-base, carbon propellant. Couple generations past your last ride." He raised an eyebrow and added, "I'm not as dumb as you look."

He walked away, heading toward the gantry entrance of the shuttle. Reed hung back, looking toward Ben with a faintly guilty manner. Well . . . that was good as far as Ben was concerned. If it weren't for Reed, he wouldn't have to be putting up with this abuse.

He saw that Victor was still on stage, and Reed's hologram—the one that was an improvement upon Von

Doom's own—had been appropriated as part of the presentation. The pulsing red cloud of the storm was approaching, and Victor was saying, "Think of a world without genetic flaws . . . no asthma, allergies, baldness, breast cancer . . ."

Ben bristled at that. "What's wrong with being bald . . . ?" he asked rhetorically.

Still, Ben had to admit that Reed was definitely right about one thing: Von Doom was damned good at this stuff. He could see the faces of experienced reporters watching with rapt attention, even wide-eyed wonderment.

"Darwin discovered evolution," continued Victor. "Now we . . . *I* . . . will define it."

"Yeah?" muttered Ben. "Let's see him pilot the freakin' shuttle, if he's such a one-man band . . ."

"Let it go, Ben," sighed Reed. "Let it go."

They headed to the gantry elevator with Victor Von Doom's words ringing in their ears: "Only in America could a little country boy from Latveria build one of the biggest companies in the world, and truly reach the stars. Now, if you'll excuse me, history awaits . . ."

Minutes later, once Von Doom had boarded the shuttle—taking care to do so while hundreds of cameras were flashing, and having taken further care to make sure none of those cameras were snapping away when Reed and the others had been getting on board—the shuttle blasted free of Earth's gravity and sped toward the space station high in orbit above.

3

"HE LOOKS RIGHT THROUGH ME. LIKE I'M NOT EVEN there."

It was two days before the shuttle launch, and Sue Storm was meeting her brother for drinks at one of their favorite watering holes, Diablo's. She was staring at her scotch, neat, while Johnny kept pointedly checking his watch. Not pointedly enough, though, to garner Sue's attention.

"You have no idea how frustrating it is," Sue continued, slurring her words slightly. "We're supposed to be working together on this project, preparing for the launch, side by side. And I'm sending out signals. Definite, unmistakable signals."

"What kind?" asked Johnny.

"Mixed," she admitted. "I suppose that could be the problem right there."

"Y' think?" He paused, and then said, "Look, Sue . . . you know my thoughts about the guy. They haven't changed. But your life is your life. And have you considered that you might be . . . I dunno . . . putting up shields? I mean, let's face it, the guy hurt you pretty badly last time. And maybe you just don't want to get hurt again. Maybe he looks through you because you don't want him to notice you, and maybe you're doing whatever you can to keep him away in the first place."

"So you're saying it's all my fault. Some brother . . ."

"Sue," Johnny assured her, putting a hand on hers, "I have enough ex-girlfriends on my résumé to tell you that if I never hear anything having to do with concepts like assigning blame, I'll be a happy camper. I'm not saying anything is your fault, because fault means that there's wrongdoing. No one's doing anything wrong here. Reed is what he is, and you are what you are. However far the two of you can come to accommodating whatever screwed-up notions are ping-ponging around in your head, the better off you're both gonna be."

Much of her discussion that she'd had with Johnny—or at least, as much as she was capable of remembering through the haze of that evening—had come back to her. Although her professional demeanor aboard the shuttle would never have revealed it, she kept glancing over at Reed the entire time and wondering what he was thinking. Whether he was thinking about her. What precisely was going through that mind of his.

And as she did so, she felt nothing but growing annoyance with herself. There was no reason for her to be attaching this much importance to what Reed thought, or how Reed felt, or to Reed at all. He should be the one who was coming to her, presuming he was interested. Even if he was, who was to say *she* was?

Well, that was the problem at its core, wasn't it? She wasn't sure how she felt, and the issue now was that Johnny was, just perhaps, a small bit right. She hadn't been putting up shields, exactly, but she certainly hadn't been giving Reed the slightest indication that she was remotely interested or even receptive. Reed was rather clueless when it came to such matters even under the best of circumstances, and these certainly weren't those.

It made her smile inwardly. Some people might change, mature, polish up their act over the years. Not Reed. He was pretty much exactly as she remembered him when she'd first approached him as a young grad student, at the Hayden Planetarium. She'd noticed him sitting in the planetarium's auditorium, long after the show was over, just staring and staring at where the stars had been. She knew who he was, of course. Everyone did. She'd come out and spoken to him, which was a major thing for Sue, because he intimidated the hell out of her. She got the sense, though, that it was a far more level playing field than she'd expected: She was daunted by his intellect, whereas he was daunted by the fact that she was a female.

Still, he spoke to her in such a pedantic manner that, by the time the maintenance staff was shooing them away, she'd figured this had been a huge mistake . . . right up to the point where he'd looked at her in a hopeful, puppy-dog manner and asked in a whispered voice devoid of the pedant, "Am I impressing you?" She'd realized then that he'd been eager to please her, and yet clueless how to go about doing so. When they'd gone on their actual first date, naturally they'd gone back to the planetarium . . . although she did some prep work first, just in case. If he went back into pedant mode, she wanted to be able to keep up with him.

How in the world had things gone so remarkably downhill from there?

All this tumbled through Sue's head as the shuttle docked with the space station.

It wasn't long before they were moving through the narrow corridors of the space station with bouncing ease, thanks to the slightly lower gravity. Victor Von Doom was by her side, as he always seemed to be whenever they were working on a project.

They were heading toward the command center, and she winced inwardly as she heard Johnny speaking to Ben Grimm in the tone of voice that a father would use to an annoying child.

"If you behave," he told Ben, "maybe next time Daddy'll let you drive."

"Keep talking," Ben shot back, "there won't be a next time."

Johnny, don't go looking for trouble. It never has problems finding you even under the best of circumstances. As she silently begged him for restraint, Sue suspected that she'd have had the exact same luck with getting him to display it whether she spoke or just thought hard at him. Then, as she glanced around, she noticed that they had lost Reed. He was lagging behind, staring in silent wonderment out a viewing port at the Earth, hanging there against the darkness of space and turning in its orbit.

She stepped beside him, wondering if he'd notice she was there. Naturally not. *Ah well. If I'm going to be a secondary female in his life, at least I'm second to Mother Earth. Who could reasonably deal with that kind of competition?*

"Long way from the projection booth at the Hayden Planetarium, isn't it?" she asked.

Reed jumped slightly, startled by her presence since his thoughts had so obviously been elsewhere. Once he realized she was there, though, he looked genuinely flattered that she'd brought up the place that had such fond memories for the both of them. Could it be that he was honestly surprised to discover that she had any fond memories of him at all? Could he think that she despised him that much? Well, hell . . . it wasn't as if cold-shouldering him or adopting an icy professional demeanor in working with him was going to lead him to any other conclusion, right? Maybe Johnny had had a valid point when he'd been talking about her putting up shields.

Gently, hesitantly—as he so often was with her—he said, "Yes. Yes, it is."

Johnny Storm, watching his sister talking with Reed Richards, wanted nothing so much but for Victor Von Doom to build a time machine so that he, Johnny, could go whirling back to the past, find himself in the bar doling out advice to Sue, and beat himself around the head and shoulders.

He tossed an exasperated glance in Ben Grimm's direction as they made their way to the command center and observation deck. Ben shrugged in an infuriating *what-can-you-do?* manner. Well, Johnny knew exactly what he could have done. He could have been much firmer with Sue. He should have told her to keep those shields up. Instead he'd been dumb enough to keep in mind some of the stuff that Frankie had been pounding into his head about things that women *needed* to hear rather than stuff that men thought they *should* hear. So there had been Sue moaning in her cups about Reed, and instead of saying what she should have heard, which was that she and Reed were a lousy match and better quit of each other, he'd been dumb as a box of rocks and focused on her emotions.

As he tried to shift his concerns to matters of greater consequence—and certainly just about anything was of greater consequence than Reed Richards and the love life of Johnny's sister—he noticed that calling it the observation deck was at the moment something of a misnomer. There wasn't a good deal of observing going on since metal shutters were covering the windows. Victor was leaning over a computer console, speaking to ground control via a comm link. "Leonard, how's the feed?" he was asking.

Leonard Kirk's voice came over the comm-link. It was a startlingly clear signal. If Johnny hadn't known better, he'd have thought the guy was in the next room instead of thousands of miles below. *"Recording, sir. We see you perfectly."*

Victor Von Doom glanced up at a camera mounted into the console. Johnny was sure he saw the guy adjust his hair out of reflex. Sue, meanwhile, was busy checking over the computer banks with her customary confidence and precision. Johnny hadn't been privy to the remainder of her "dicussion" with Reed, but hoped rather mean-spiritedly that it had not gone well. "We can monitor the cloud's approach," Sue told Victor, "and observe the tests from here."

Ben Grimm, mighty pilot, sounded positively nervous as he asked, "Is it safe?"

Tell him, hell no, we're probably all going down in flames, Johnny begged his sister.

But she ignored, or simply didn't know about, his silent entreaty. It was Reed who spoke up. Fortunately for Johnny, he did so with one of his famed explanations that always made things sound worse. "The shields on the station should protect us," he said with an air of confidence that didn't seem quite in line with the actual words he was saying.

Ben naturally picked up on the discrepancy. *"Should?"*

Just as naturally, Von Doom couldn't allow even the slightest degree of discomfort on Grimm's part to pass unremarked. Oozing false joviality, he clapped a hand on Ben's shoulder and asked, "What's wrong, Ben? Eighty million dollars worth of equipment not enough for you?"

Whatever humor Victor was seeing in the moment was obviously eluding Ben Grimm. Johnny had never seen two people both looking at each other as if they were each bugs they would just as soon step on, but there it was. It was different frames of mind, though. Ben wanted to step on Victor in anger, whereas Victor would just as soon have stepped on Ben just to show that he could.

Before the tension could escalate into a relative bug-squishing contest, however, Reed intervened. He didn't exactly change the subject so much as move the same subject further along. "Let's start loading those samples. Get your suit ready, Ben."

Von Doom clearly wasn't ready to let it go. "So you still do all the heavy lifting?" he asked Ben with a tone that suggested he was prepared to recommend a good chiropractor if the strain on Grimm was too great.

Ben could have been carved from stone for all the response he made. Obviously he knew that Von Doom was just trying to get a rise out of him.

If Victor was dissatisfied that Ben wasn't reacting in the desired manner, he didn't show it. Ben may well have been stone, but Victor's face was a mask. He turned to Reed, patting him patronizingly, and said, "Maybe you should have stayed back in the lab. Fieldwork never suited you."

Defending Reed in a way he hadn't been willing to for himself, Ben Grimm said, "He does the talking, I do the walking. Got it?"

Victor's smile never flinched, even though Ben was clearly seething. Why should he? What was Ben going to do, really? Knock his face in? Von Doom was holding all the cards. "Got it," he said coolly. "So take a walk, Ben." Having lost interest in the conversation, Von Doom said to no one in particular, "I'm going to borrow Susan for a second."

"Sure," said Reed.

Johnny watched Reed for some small reaction as Victor Von Doom walked out with Sue, one arm draped around her shoulder in an affectionate—even slightly intimate—fashion. But there was nothing.

Well, really, why should there be? After all, Reed was only interested in his great scientific ambitions. Everyone—Ben Grimm, Victor Von Doom, Johnny Storm—they were all just a means to that end.

Minutes later, Johnny was standing near the air lock, watching Ben putting on a helmet and boots, preparing for a space walk. Johnny was busy unloading a set of clear sample boxes from a cart, each containing a variety of plants.

"Why do you stick with him?" Johnny asked.

Ben disdained to look at him. "Because he's the real deal."

"I don't know what you mean."

"Yeah. You do," said Ben, and this time he did afford Johnny a brief glance. "And you know he is, and you know you're not."

"I'm not?" Johnny said derisively. "How do you know I'm not?"

" 'Cause if ya were, you wouldn't have to ask."

Johnny bristled, but kept his smug calm in place.

"Please tell me your dawg's not trying to rekindle things with my sister."

"My 'dawg' was named Mickey, after Mantle, and he died way too young when a jerk just like you—not *you*, but you're a dime-a-dozen—hit him with his motorcycle. So that was it for my 'dawg.' If ya mean Reed, who ain't a dawg or dog or whatever slang makes ya sound cool, the answer is, 'Course not. Strictly business.'"

"Yeah, well, his eyes say different."

"Hey, two hearts got busted last time," Ben reminded him with a shrug. "Maybe she's not over it either."

"Let's see," said Johnny, holding out both hands as if they were two sides of a scale. "You got Victor, stud of the year, more coin than God." He dipped his right hand down to reflect the weight of Victor Von Doom. "Or Reed, the word's dumbest smart guy worth less than a postage stamp." The left hand, representing Reed, naturally was on eye level. He "weighed" the two hands and said sarcastically, "Hmmm. It's a toss-up."

"Put your tiny little mind at ease," said Ben. He placed the helmet over his head, the discussion clearly over, and clicked it into place.

"Don't you wander off, boy," Johnny cautioned him, as if Ben could hear him. Ben wasn't paying any attention to him, though. Instead he was facing the air lock door that would be opening within moments, allowing him to step out into space and do his job.

Ben moved out of the air lock and shut the door behind him. Through a small window, Johnny watched. Ben still wasn't looking at him, but obviously he'd been able to hear the door shut, because with his back turned he gave a confident thumbs-up. Johnny triggered the exterior air lock hatch, and it irised open. The void of space laid out before him, Ben Grimm confidently strode out into it.

Johnny Storm would never, ever have admitted it, but he couldn't have done it. He knew that EVA was going to be required, the boxes with the experimental plants having to be placed outside the space station. And the prospect of being out there, in space, on his own, unenclosed in a vehicle, was something Johnny simply couldn't handle. The very thought of it gave him the shakes.

But he wasn't about to tell Von Doom that, of course, when the subject was broached. So instead, Johnny had simply affected a confident smirk and said, "Aah, let Grimm do it. Why pass up the chance to give him a hard time, along with his buddy?"

Von Doom had laughed at that. It was a disturbing sound and Johnny hoped he wouldn't hear it again anytime soon.

Victor Von Doom, standing on the observation deck next to Sue, laughed in a disturbing manner that prompted Sue Storm to hope she wouldn't hear it again anytime soon.

It was in response to Sue's staggeringly poor attempt to cover her own bewilderment when he'd asked, "Bet you're wondering what the hell we're doing up here, aren't you," to which Sue had replied, "Nooo, no, never gave it a moment's thought."

"Come now, Susan," he chided her, once he'd recovered from his laughing fit, "you must have wondered just a little bit? Honestly?" When she made a noncommittal hemming-and-hawing noise, he pushed, "Certainly you're surprised I agreed to Reed's proposal."

"I understand the *business* reasons," she said cautiously.

"Well," he said, and he cleared his throat. There was something in his tone that changed, and Sue wasn't sure what it was. "When you're looking at your future, it never hurts to find closure about the past."

Her eyes narrowed. There was something else going on here, some subtext she wasn't getting. She was tempted to ask Victor what he was talking about, but she figured it wasn't necessary since Victor had this funny habit of saying exactly what was on his mind. Why not? A man in his position could pretty much say anything he wanted to anyone he wanted. If he'd ever developed the habit of watching his words, he was long out of it.

"Susan," he continued, "every man dreams that he'll meet some woman he can give the world to."

He pressed a button and the observation deck's outer windows opened wide, revealed a spectacular and—dare she think so—romantic view of the Earth. "In my case," Victor said, "it's not just metaphor."

She stared at the Earth, and it was at that moment that Von Doom's subtext became far more text than sub to her. She gasped inwardly, suddenly aware of where he was going with this, but before she could interrupt she saw that he was holding a small, black ring box in his hand. She didn't have to sport an IQ on Reed Richards' level to figure out what was in it.

"You've been with me two years now," said Victor. His eyes were glittering in a manner reflecting the stars that hung in the blackness of space.

"It's . . . been a good two years, Victor," she said hesitantly. "The company's accomplished so much."

Sue knew all too well that his business meant everything to him, so it was with a distant sense of shock that she heard him say, "Right, of course, the company," in an utterly dismissive manner. "But you see . . . I've come to realize all the accomplishments in the world mean nothing without someone to share them with—"

Oh my God oh my God tell me Johnny put him up to this that it's a gag omigodomigod . . .

"Sue," Victor continued, oblivious to the fact that there was a deer cringing in the headlights of Sue Storm's mind pleading, *Just run me over and be done with it.* "I've lived my life unafraid of taking big steps. And this is the biggest step yet. If it helps, think of this as a *promotion.* A merger of sorts . . ." He stepped closer to her and said, "Four little words that can change our lives . . ."

And with supernatural timing, Reed Richards burst in and shouted, *"The cloud is accelerating!"*

Of all the four words that could have changed her life, at that moment, Reed's were far preferable to her than any that Victor was about to say.

4

REED RICHARDS SAT AT HIS WORK STATION, RUNNING HIS interaction with Sue through his mind, and trying to find a solid, sensible, scientific basis to explain the mixed signals that she seemed to be sending.

Ultimately he decided that she was, in her own way, engaging in a sort of testing ritual. That she had been treating him coldly and distantly to see what manner of reaction that could provoke, and now she was actually being attentive and even warm in order to determine . . . what? Which attitude facilitated the working relationship? Or could it be that she was just involved in some minor psychological study of her own and was using Reed as a convenient lab rat?

Oddly, Reed realized that—if that was indeed the case—it didn't particularly bother him. In fact, he could respect it. Scientific inquiry and all that.

After all, people were truly scientists from the moment they were born. He'd heard frustrated parents complaining about their infants and not understanding what in the world possessed them to stuff macaroni into a DVD player or drop toy soldiers down the toilet. And Reed would dutifully explain that, well, babies are just miniature scientists. Since they know nothing of the world, they perform experiments. They stuff macaroni into the DVD player specifically to see what would happen to both ingredients when combined. They tossed toy soldiers into the toilet to see if they would float or sink. And if they sank, would building blocks also sink? How about wads of paper? How about rocks? Little scientists, every one of us, from birth. And some people never stopped viewing the world as their own personal vehicle for experimentation (which would explain, among other things, MIT students turning the Charles River into gelatin just to see if they could).

To Reed's mind, that's what Sue was doing. She was just manufacturing positive stimulus so she could compare it to negative stimulus and draw some sort of conclusion that might or might not be related to their time together. He could appreciate it in a clinical, detached way.

So . . . why was he feeling some degree of . . . disappointment? Why was it that something was missing? Why was it that the event threshold was at T-minus 10:00 . . . ?

Reed's mind slammed to a halt, did a one-eighty, and vaulted back to the readouts which were not remotely in keeping with the calculations he'd made up until this point. He knew perfectly well that, no matter how much one tried to predict environmental conditions, nature had a way of throwing in monkey wrenches that not even the most gifted mind could anticipate. Any weatherman who'd ever predicted light overnight flurries and woken up to two feet of snow could attest to that. But the vacuum of space should have minimized any possible variance to his predictions for the rate and speed of the cosmic storm's approach.

Yet there it was: event threshold in ten minutes and counting down. "No," Reed whispered. "No . . . impossible. It's . . . too fast."

His mind was racing ahead of his feet as he sprinted out of the room, through the corridors of the space station. Solar winds. That had to be it. Solar wind activity. Perhaps there had been unexpected sunspot activity that had generated more intense solar winds. He'd tried to take that into account in his calculations, had been sure that he had allowed for it. But how could any human being possibly predict sunspots to the fifteenth decimal point with hyperaccuracy? If there was even the slightest . . .

Dear lord, Ben was out there . . .

Reed burst into the observation deck, and Sue and Victor were there. His mind would take a mental snapshot of the two of them stepping back from each other quickly, as if caught guiltily in some sort of intimate moment. And the nature of that intimacy would be further evident when Reed realized that Victor had quickly tucked something into his pocket upon Reed's unannounced arrival . . . something that was shaped an awful lot like a box containing a ring. But he wouldn't "develop" the picture until much later, at which point it would be more or less irrelevant.

"The cloud is accelerating!" he cried out.

Sue quickly moved to a nearby control panel, intent on verifying Reed's claim. Part of him was slightly annoyed that she simply wasn't taking his word for it, but he knew that any scientific observation—even the most trivial—called for independent verification. Emotions and hurt feelings had no place in the process. Still, he wasn't waiting around for Sue to reiterate what he already knew as fact. "We've got minutes until it hits, not hours," he said. "Victor . . . that storm's *deadly*. The radiation's lethal. We need to abort!"

Victor wasn't looking at Reed, but at Sue. She looked up from the tracking station and gave a curt nod. Even upon receiving this verification, however, Von Doom didn't flinch. "Get a grip, Reed," he said calmly, as if Reed had merely delivered the news that Victor's shoes had just gone out of style. "We didn't come all this way to lose our nerve at the first little glitch. Just close the shields . . ."

"Ben's still out there—!"

"So reel him in," said Victor. "But we came here to do a job. So let's do it. *Quickly.*"

Later, Reed wouldn't even remember leaving the room. He would only remember being in the observation bay and then, suddenly, he was at the air lock. His mind was in such turmoil, such bouts of second-guessing and mental self-flagellation, that he would have no recollection of sprinting from point A to point B. All he knew was that Johnny Storm was standing there, watching Ben performing his EVA exactly as scheduled. There was, naturally, an umbilical tether that was keeping Ben anchored to the space station. His suit was equipped with small jet-spray propulsion devices that enabled him to move around with elegant confidence, if not great speed. Speed, however, was what the moment called for.

"Hey, big brain . . ." Johnny began.

"Not now, Johnny. Where's the comm-link?" Reed said, scanning the surrounding panels.

"What's so important that—"

"Where's the damned link?!"

Johnny, stunned, mutely pointed toward one switch. Reed would have spotted it instantly himself if he hadn't been so agitated. He tried to keep his voice calm, but his bubbling fear caused him practically to shout, "Ben, we need you back inside!"

Ben, for his part, was busy sliding the boxes of plants into pre-constructed brackets on the outside of the space station, and was so startled by Reed's voice suddenly breaking in to his comm-link that—even from a distance—Reed could see him jump slightly in response. He turned and looked at Reed and Johnny staring at him.

"I ain't done arranging your flowers, egghead."

"Ben, this is serious! Turn around!"

Johnny had been so focused on Reed's worried demeanor that he hadn't actually taken the time to see what it was that was causing it. But now he looked in the general direction that Reed was indicating, and his eyes widened. "Holy . . ." he breathed, and then he started gesturing and pointing alongside Reed.

From his angle, Ben was partially blocked out of a clear view by the curves of the space station itself. He jetted his way a few feet to the right, and suddenly he was able to make out the source of Reed's concern. The cosmic storm, red and undulating and crackling with power. It wasn't right on top of them, but it was heading their way, and Ben didn't need a degree in galactic physics to know that it was coming far faster than anyone's comfort zone would allow for.

"Roger that," Ben said quickly. *"On my way."*

Using the jet sprays in his EVA suit, he started moving as quickly as he could toward the air lock.

To Reed Richards, time seemed to stretch nearly unto infinity. He knew Ben was moving as fast as he could, but even so it was excruciatingly slow.

Johnny was watching worriedly. "How much chance does he have out there if he doesn't make it in before—"

"He'll make it in."

"I was just wondering . . ."

"He'll *make*. It *in*."

Ben, of course, couldn't see the speed with which the storm was bearing down on him. His back was now to it, and if he'd tried to turn around to look, the motion would have sent him heading off in another direction entirely. All he could do was remain focused with laser beam intensity on the safe haven of the air lock. Reed remembered all the times that Ben had talked to him about "actualizing." Of seeing things a certain way and convincing yourself that that's how it was going to turn out. He'd told Reed that that was how he'd gotten himself out of more than one scrape as a test pilot. When things had gone wrong, he'd just pictured himself making a safe landing with such fervency that he was convinced thinking it had made it so. Reed tried to do it, but all he could dwell on was worst-case scenarios. He imagined Ben enveloped in the cosmic storm, screaming in the silence of space, being reduced to an irradiated, ossified mass of what had once been flesh and bone.

"Come on, Ben, come on," Reed urged, even though the comm-link was off.

Abruptly an automated voice sounded throughout the space station. *"Event threshold in two minutes,"* it said in its calm, emotionless tone.

Then it was replaced with Victor's voice, no doubt coming from the command center. He might have seemed unflappable when Reed first delivered the news, but there was undeniable anxiety in his tone now. *"Reed, we're running out of time."*

Seconds later, the truth of Victor's words was brutally illuminated, as stray tendrils from the cosmic storm lanced out due to the cloud's inner turbulence. They snaked not only toward Ben, but toward the space station itself. The air lock corridor began to rumble, lights flickering and sparking from the sudden energy surges. All Reed and Johnny could do was watch in frustrated helplessness.

Victor Von Doom had been many things in his life. Peasant. Beggar. A student, receiving withering glances from the other kids over his shabby dress and pauper appearance. Inventor, entrepreneur, building himself an image, an empire, through sheer force of will.

But the one thing that he had never, ever been, was helpless. Even as a beggar, he'd had his pride, his determination that he wasn't simply going to stand by and allow the unfolding of fate to overwhelm him. And he sure as hell wasn't about to start now.

From the command center, he saw that Ben Grimm was still at least twenty yards away from safety. His mind, however, was racing, calculating the approach of the cosmic storm, and he had come to the regrettable, but inevitable, conclusion that Grimm simply wasn't going to make it. Oh well. Too bad. An unfortunate loss, at least insofar as Reed Richards was going to be concerned. But Grimm knew the odds when he'd first embarked on his rather hazardous occupation. In some respects, all test pilots and space jockeys such as Ben Grimm were living on borrowed time. If his time was now up, the lender demanding payment, that's the way it went. Victor Von Doom had no intention of cashing out along with him.

Sue was watching Ben on the monitor, having taken Victor's place at the main intercom. He expected her to make the tough call, issue the hard decisions. If nothing else, it would probably go down easier with Richards and Johnny if the order came from her rather than him. However, Sue appeared flustered, indecisive. "Johnny . . . Reed," she said in a fluttery voice that sickened Von Doom. He thought she was made of sterner stuff than that. Perhaps the abrupt arrival of the cosmic storm was more than just unfortunate happenstance. Von Doom wasn't the most theologically oriented of men, but still . . . maybe this was divine intervention to prevent him from making a proposal to a woman who was less than he'd thought and not truly worthy of him. It was something he'd have to consider after the emergency had passed.

He strode over to Sue and pushed her unceremoniously out of the way. She looked at him in shock, but he paid her no mind. He had more immediate concerns than putting Sue Storm's nose out of joint. "Reed," he said brusquely into the intercom, "you need to get up here so we can close the shields. Now!"

"Not until Ben is back inside," Richard's voice returned.

"Reed, in case you've forgotten, only the command center has full shielding. You won't be insulated from the radiation where you are, and whatever happens is on your own head."

Sue turned and looked at him with clear shock. "What are you, assigning liability in case Reed sues you? Making yourself judgment-proof? There are lives on the line, Victor!"

Von Doom snapped off the intercom for a moment and said sharply, "Yes . . . first and foremost, mine. And yours. I'm not throwing ours away because some people are afraid to make the tough decisions."

Having usurped Sue's station, he started entering command controls. "What are you doing!" Sue exclaimed.

How many times are we going to have to cover this? His relief over not having presented her the ring was growing exponentially. "Raising the shields," he said self-evidently.

"You can't leave them out there!"

There was contempt on Sue's face, but it was nothing compared to the contempt Von Doom was feeling inwardly over her insistence on belaboring not only the obvious, but that which had clearly already been decided. "Watch me," he said icily. "Reed had his chance. You can't help them any more than I can."

He expected more hesitation, more uncertainty, followed by the inevitable realization that he was one hundred percent right and knew exactly what he was talking about.

Instead, with one final defiant glare, Sue snapped, "I can try," and bolted from the command center before Von Doom could say anything to stop her.

Then again, considering the only thing he could think of to say was, "You're an idiot!" probably would not have been the best way to make her reconsider her course of action. And he found himself caring less and less the closer and closer the cosmic storm got to him.

It left him with a simple truth: Some people just didn't have the ability to surround themselves with the sort of hard shell required to make difficult choices. Sue was obviously one of them. But Victor Von Doom was made of iron, and if Sue Storm couldn't handle that—if she found that iron exterior to be too much to deal with—then better to know that now before it was too late.

Too late, Reed's mind was screaming. Peering out the air lock door in agonized frustration, thumping his hand impotently against the window, Reed had performed the same mental calculations that Von Doom had, and come to the same conclusion as to Ben's fate. The only question on the table, the only difference between the two, was whether they had any intention of sharing it. Von Doom had already made his decision, and now Reed was faced with his.

"Victor's right. Johnny, get to the command center. Close the shields," he said heavily, unaware that Victor was already in the process of doing just that.

"What about you?"

Reed's gaze flickered from Johnny to Ben and back. The message was unspoken but clear: He wasn't going to cut and run and abandon his friend to a hideous fate.

Johnny processed that, nodded . . . and then stayed right where he was. Reed's eyes widened. "Johnny, didn't you hear me?"

"Yeah, I heard you."

"So . . ." He gestured that Johnny should get going. When Johnny still didn't budge, he said, "Johnny . . . what do you think you're doing? Look, cards on the table. We both know perfectly well you don't like Ben, and you think little of me, so who do you think you're impressing by—?"

"Don't even start," Johnny said hotly. "I mean, maybe you know everything there is to know about a cosmic storm, but you know nothing about this Storm," and he thumped himself on the chest. "Understand?"

"I . . . believe I'm beginning to," Reed said.

Johnny nodded and then added, "Besides, if you think I'm going to give him," and he chucked a thumb in Ben's direction, "the satisfaction of knowing I cut and run, you can just freakin' forget it." As if Reed no longer factored into the equation, he turned and said tensely through the window, even though Ben couldn't hear him, "Come on, big guy, you can do it."

Victor Von Doom could see them in his mind's eye.

He could see Reed and Johnny, still down by the air lock, ready to throw their lives away needlessly simply because one of their associates had the bad luck to be in the wrong place at the wrong time.

He could see Sue heading down a corridor toward them. She wouldn't be panicked, not her. Angry, yes. Frustrated over what she perceived as failings on Von Doom's part. Determined to find a way to help even though there was nothing she could do. But not panicked.

Then she began to fade from his consciousness, as did Reed and Johnny. The shields were sliding into place around the command center, isolating Victor Von Doom within a cocoon of metal. Despite the sentiments of John Donne, Von Doom was indeed an island, entire of itself. The continent of which he was alleged to be a piece had drifted away, to sink on its own while he swam and survived.

"Event threshold in thirty seconds," the automated voice said to him. It was the only voice he took comfort in, because it assured him in its nonjudgmental fashion that he was in the right. If only humans could be equally so.

Then again . . . who were others to judge him? He remembered Sue saying he was acting as if he was concerned over Reed suing him, and he was trying to make himself judgment proof. Judgment proof? He was Victor Von Doom. That was sufficient armor against any such opinion.

Ain't no thing . . .

In agonizing, weightless slow motion, Ben drew closer and closer to the air lock. It was going to be tight, but he'd lost count of the number of times in his career when death had been breathing hotly on the back of his neck. In every single one of those instances, the same words had gone through his mind: *Ain't no thing.* Ship's engine overheating? Ain't no thing. Landing gear not deploying? Ain't no thing.

So his endeavor to reach the air lock which had become a real-life example of Zeno's Paradox, where he seemed perpetually to be halving the remaining distance but still unable to arrive at his destination, while at the same time, a cosmic storm was hammering right toward him, certain to envelop him with seconds?

Ain't no thing.

Then he was there, at the air lock, the ancient Greek Zeno thwarted once more. The outer door was waiting for him, open and inviting, like a return to Mother's womb. He started to haul himself in, chuckling at Death missing its chance at him yet again, congratulating himself on not panicking in the face of odds that might well have paralyzed others.

Ain't no thing was his last coherent thought as the leading edge of the cloud hit him. He felt as if he were being stoned to death, small but lethal impacts slamming through his body. His suit was pelted with orange stains from the hissing mass of space dust, and then smaller particles, and then larger, like rocks, or "space hail." He lost all sense of direction, the jet-spray propulsion device hanging useless, and he reached out for the tether, his lifeline, his umbilical cord. Nothing had penetrated his suit—nothing concrete, at any rate, although who knew what kind of radiation was coursing through him—but nevertheless he felt as if the blood in his body had turned to acid. His muscles wanted to shut down, to just leave him hanging in space, and there were no longer any coherent thoughts in his head. Just a determined, unassailable need to survive.

That, and to live long enough to pummel Reed Richards for getting him into this fix in the first place.

"Event threshold in ten seconds," the automated voice calmly informed Reed and Johnny, as Johnny punched the controls to close the exterior air lock door.

70

Too long . . . too slow . . . too long, Reed kept thinking, feeling as if time itself had distended as if it were elastic. Moving in what felt like slow motion, he grabbed a first-aid kit and yanked a thermo-elastic blanket from it. It was both warm and stretchable, capable of creating a full-body "cast" of sorts that they could wrap Ben in from head to toe.

He's going to want to beat the crap out of me for getting him into this, thought Reed. *Please let him live long enough to do it . . .*

Victor Von Doom pulled the engagement ring box from his pocket, and flipped it open to gaze at the diamond ring within. Hard. Perfect. Flawless. Like Sue . . . or at least that's what he'd thought when he purchased it. Now he realized that he had seen in it instead a reflection of himself.

Well . . . fine.

Her loss.

Clutching the ring tightly, he stepped over to a control panel to study the readouts that the exterior sensors would provide from the cosmic storm. Even if things weren't going precisely according to plan, at least there would still be enough information salvageable that this entire misbegotten enterprise wouldn't be a total loss.

The space station shook, but Victor remained confident in the shielding and his own imperviousness, right up until the moment when lights began exploding over his head. He stepped back, looking up in shock, and equipment was sent crashing out of its fixtures or moorings, clattering all around him like a fatal rainstorm of metal. He dodged this way and that, managing to stay clear, and staggered to the control panel to try and get an idea of what level of intensity the storm had reached and how much longer it was going to last.

The control panel exploded in his face just as he got there.

Von Doom let out a scream, throwing his arms up in front of his face to shield himself, and reflexively stumbled backward. Unable to watch where he was going, he tripped over some debris, fell, and then consoles came ripping right out of the wall and toppled upon him.

Although he would not remember doing so later, the last thing he shouted before blackness claimed him was "*Sue!*"

"Johnny! Reed!"

Sue was rounding the corner as the apathetic voice continued the countdown, *"Six . . . five . . ."* Seeing Johnny and Reed at the air lock, preparing to haul in Ben, she wanted to cry out a warning that the cosmic storm was nearly upon them even though every bit of her rational mind told her that they were well aware of it. She was so focused upon them that she didn't see the steam pipe gasket ahead of her just about to rupture.

She did, however, see the control panel just to Johnny's right that was suddenly sparking from overloads, but her voice was drowned out by the droning countdown of the automated voice.

The voice that said . . .
". . . *four* . . ."

Four . . .

A split second before the exterior air lock door closed, a single particle of orange matter streaked through and ripped into and through Ben Grimm's suit. Once, long ago, Ben had gone hunting with friends and he'd been struck by a bullet fired from the rifle of some other idiot hunter in another party. He'd never found the moron who'd missed the deer he'd been aiming at by a country mile, but he still carried the scar from the bullet, and he remembered the searing pain of it as it had thudded into his chest and grazed his rib cage. That pain was as nothing compared to what he was feeling now. It was as if his entire nervous system was being ripped out and then stuffed back in sideways. It was so overwhelming, so comprehensive, that he couldn't remember a time when he hadn't been in agony.

Four . . .

Johnny Storm heard his sister's cry and afforded a quick glance toward her. She was pointing at a control panel to his right. In the half-second he had to react, he made the wrong decision and, instead of ducking away from it, turned and faced it to see what she was trying to point out. As a result, he was hit square on when the panel was blown off the wall and sparks of flame leaped out at him, striking him in the face, the hands. He felt as if his blood was literally on fire.

Four . . .

Reed Richards, typically aware of everything that was going on around him during any time of scientific crisis, was paying attention to everything except himself. As he stretched the blanket toward the lurching figure of Ben Grimm, cosmic rays, swirling through the air lock, permeated the blanket and then Reed himself. He would feel a distant tingling, but he gave it no mind. After all, how important could it possibly be?

Four . . .

The reason Sue didn't see the vapor blasting directly in front of her was because it was practically invisible. But she felt it as she moved through it, and staggered, clutching at her chest, suddenly unable to breathe. Then, just as suddenly as the feeling had come upon her, it was gone, and she felt light-headed. Light as air, with about as much substance. Sue could no longer see herself, and for an instant she thought she had vanished. Then she realized that, no, that was ridiculous. The lights had gone out. Power all over the station had died. The cosmic storm was upon them. The one mercy was that, since there was no power throughout the station, at least that damnable warning voice had gone off.

Then, just like that . . .

. . . the cosmic storm was gone.

There was no reason for it not to be, after all. It wasn't as if it was a malicious or intelligent entity that was going to envelop the space station and pummel it within an inch of its metal life. It was just a force of nature, not sentient, and it kept right on going, unknowing and un-caring of the chaos it had left in its wake.

As it so happened, the people upon whom the chaos had been inflicted had no genuine comprehension of what had just occurred. The moment had come, the moment had gone. The people in the space station were concerned over far more mundane matters, such as whether they were still alive, and their curiously timed interaction with various parts of the besieged station made only the most passing of impressions upon their memories.

In the area of the air lock, Johnny, Reed, and Sue were hauling the unconscious Ben Grimm into the comparative safety of the space station. Johnny was shouting Ben's name over and over, as Reed cried out "He's not responsive!" even as they tried to remove Ben's helmet.

Meanwhile, in the station's command center, a pile of rubble remained unmoving for long moments. Then it stirred ever so slightly, rattled around a bit . . . and then pieces of equipment began to fall away, pushed to one side and another by the individual buried beneath.

Slowly, evoking mythical memories of vampires clawing from beneath the ground to arise, haggard and hungry, from their burial sites, Victor Von Doom emerged from beneath his premature entombment, making a mental note to fire the asses of everyone in-volved in constructing the station's shielding. It might well have protected Victor from the radiation effects of the storm, but it left a hell of a lot to be desired when it came to sheer endurance under the hammering of outer space phenomena. There was just no way that piles of metal and equipment should be able to come pouring down upon the head of Von Doom Industries during a time of crisis. What kind of planning was that?

The only explanation as to why Von Doom waited so long to process the information that he should be battered, bruised, and bleeding from multiple wounds, had to be that he was in shock. With the sort of determination that had gotten him to where he was in business today, Von Doom dispelled the fog that threatened to settle upon his brain and checked himself over. He examined his body, found a piece of metal that would give him a reflection of his face.

Victor realized that he had been unspeakably lucky. He'd sustained a few scrapes, but nothing serious. A tumble he'd taken down a hill when he was nine had left more profound contusions than anything he'd sustained in the space station. He narrowed his eyes and saw a throbbing cut on his forehead. He reached up, touched it gingerly and then with more assurance when he discovered it wasn't bleeding. That, he thought, was a bit odd. A fresh cut that didn't bleed? *Ah well. Always was a quick healer*, he thought.

A full thirty seconds had passed since he'd regained consciousness and proceeded to inspect himself. Another thirty would pass before it would even occur to him to check on the welfare of the others, including the woman to whom he'd only minutes before intended to propose marriage. That was to be expected. When a group of people embark on suicidal behavior against Victor Von Doom's explicit instructions, then they were dead to him until they took the time to "resurrect" themselves back into his good graces.

And Reed Richards, Johnny Storm, and Ben Grimm were going to have to do a considerable amount of resurrecting, that was for damned sure.

But Susan . . .

. . . well, she was a woman, after all. Women, reasoned Von Doom, flush with confidence over having survived a brush with death, deserve extra latitude. Particularly if they were worth the having. And if he had been harsh in his attitude toward Susan just prior to the crisis, well, the crisis being passed certainly triggered room for understanding on his part. All women were limited in their way, and was it not unreasonable to expect Sue to be exempt from those limitations?

Besides, he had invested a good deal of time, money, and energy in cultivating her. It would have been bad business to cut her loose, rather than try to pluck her.

5

THERE WERE ANY NUMBER OF PEOPLE THAT BEN GRIMM might have expected to see staring down at him in a scenario that involved him waking up in a hospital bed after a near-death experience. Johnny Storm was at the very bottom of that list. Actually, he wasn't on it at all. He was on the runner-up list of people so unlikely that they didn't make the initial list . . . and on that runner-up list, he was close to the bottom.

Yet here was Johnny Storm, leaning over him, calling, "Ben, wake up! Wake up!"

He had trouble trusting his belief that it was Johnny's voice, and his vision was so blurry that it was nearly impossible to verify it visually. Then, ever so slowly, his eyes began to snap back into focus. Sure enough, there was young Storm, looking down at him with actual, genuine, honest-to-Aunt Petunia concern on his face. The surroundings behind Johnny's head made it quite clear that Ben was in a hospital room. Johnny was wearing the sort of puke-green, loose-fitting ensemble that was typical of someone signed in for a stay in a medical facility. This stemmed from the apparent fact that, whatever illness may be responsible for hospitalizing you, the very first thing to go was always going to be your fashion sense.

"Where . . . where am I?" Ben asked, having mentally determined the self-evident fact that they were in a hospital, but still in a quandary as to which one or where.

"Back on Earth," Johnny told him. "Victor's medical facility in upstate New York. We're in quarantine."

Naturally. That made perfect sense. Once upon a time they'd regularly quarantined astronauts to make sure they hadn't picked up some sort of unknown contaminant, and they'd been subjected to far less dangerous conditions than Ben had, along with—

"Reed? Sue?" He was shocked at how much his own voice sounded like a croaking noise.

"They're fine," Johnny assured him. "Everybody *else* . . . is fine."

Naturally the way he'd stressed the word caught Ben's attention. He tried to study Johnny's eyes for some hint of what was wrong, but Johnny couldn't even bear to look at him. He turned away, his hand over his mouth as if he were trying with all his will not to be sick.

"What's wrong with me?" Ben demanded.

Johnny took a deep breath, then let it out to steady himself. "I swear to you, they've done everything humanly possible. The best plastic surgeons in the world, Ben. You had the best—"

There was a hand mirror sitting on the bed table next

to him. "Give me a mirror," Ben said hoarsely, reaching for it. But Johnny moved faster, snatching the mirror up before Ben could reach it.

"They said that's not such a good idea." Johnny was holding the mirror flat against his chest so that Ben couldn't possibly catch even the slightest glimpse of himself. "The shock alone could—"

"Gimme the goddamn mirror!"

Ben reached up, grabbed at it. Johnny struggled briefly, then let it go with a strangled cry, obviously realizing that Ben wasn't going to take "no" for an answer and was going to have to deal with the calamity sooner or later. Ben steeled himself, preparing for the worst even though he had no idea what that would be . . . and then held it up and let out a sob . . .

. . . which quickly morphed into more of a confused choking noise as he found his own, normal reflection looking back at him with a quizzical expression upon it. He had some serious beard stubble, reflecting that he'd been out for a time, but otherwise, there was nothing different.

"Unfortunately," Johnny said with the exaggerated dismal air of an Elizabethan era tragedian, "the doctors just couldn't do anything to fix your face!"

He cackled hysterically at his own joke as Ben fought to have the pounding of his heart reduced to something approximating normal. "Get out," he growled.

"Seriously, did you know you look kinda like John Belushi, except before he died? Or maybe after, now I think about it—"

"Get out!" roared Ben, slinging the mirror back and then forward. It spun through the air after Johnny's retreating back, crashing against the wall just as Johnny ducked out of the room to safety. Only temporary safety, though. It was going to last only as long as it took for Ben to get his hands on Johnny Storm and rearrange *his* face better than any cosmic storm ever could.

He saw the picture of his fiancée, Debbie, on the side table. It looked battered, with the edges ragged and the picture itself nearly folded in half, but it was intact. He picked it up, cradling it with a gentleness that was stark contrast to his outer appearance, and held it tightly against himself.

Nothing Johnny Storm did or said mattered. That was what Ben kept telling himself. Only surviving to get back to Debbie was the important thing. And he had done that. Johnny Storm could go hang for all Ben cared. Johnny, Victor Von Doom, Sue . . .

Even Reed?

"Yeah," he said to Debbie's photo. "Even Reed."

Reed had been out and about . . . at least, as far out and about as the quarantined section of the hospital would allow him to meander. Even so, he'd managed to get a good feeling for the impressive modern facility of glass and stone, tucked away in the forest for maximum privacy. As Reed walked down the hall, he touched the hair on the sides of his head for what had to be the hundredth time in the past half hour.

"Nice do," said a grinning Johnny Storm, who

seemed unaccountably amused about something. Reed didn't know what had struck Johnny as so entertaining, but he could take a guess. "Going for the 'grandpa' look?"

Reed honestly couldn't blame Johnny for the comment. It was tactless and immature, but it was also valid. Reed's temples had acquired streaks of gray on either side. It made him look twenty, thirty years older. It was unquestionably a side effect of the minimal radiation they'd endured in the space station, and Reed had every suspicion that it was permanent. Although naturally he was concerned about it, he also told himself that if the greatest damage any of them sustained was a few gray hairs, then he was perfectly willing to take their "punishment" to himself and spare the others.

He continued down the hallway, contemplating the situation. The things that had transpired made him think about those old cheesy, black-and-white science fiction films that had been so popular in the 1950s. The ones that always had the eager-beaver scientist who wound up in mortal danger and, more often than not, dead. This demise would be followed by someone with a deep voice shaking his head slowly and intoning, "There are some things that man is just not meant to know."

Ludicrous, to be sure . . . and yet several people had come perilously close to dying thanks to the eager-beaver scientist with the gray-streaked hair. Perhaps there really were some things man wasn't meant to know, and he would be reminded of that every time he looked in a mirror.

He passed a vase of lilies in the hallway at the nurse's station, just across from Sue's room. Reed pulled a couple of the flowers from the vase, doing it so deftly that the nurse at the station — nose buried in work — didn't notice. He smiled to himself at his cleverness, then headed over toward Sue's room. He caught a glimpse of her through the door, saw that she was sleeping. But that was all right. He actually didn't need to have a conversation with her. He was more than content simply to sit in Sue's room and watch her sleep. In fact, for some reason, merely contemplating the concept made him inexplicably happy. This was doubly odd for Reed, considering he was not accustomed to something being inexplicable, nor was he in the habit of being happy.

Of course, there were still his concerns about Ben to consider, but at least he had stabilized and the doctors were positive he was going to be waking up just about any time now. Heck, he might be awake already. Still, it was Sue who was occupying Reed's mind at that moment, and he had to think that Ben would have understood. He would have liked to think that. Actually, he knew he was kidding himself: Ben wouldn't have understood at all. But he wasn't going to let it bother him. Nothing was going to bother him when it came to Sue . . .

He stepped into Sue's room, clutching his handful of purloined lilies, and was instantly bothered by the sight that confronted him.

Flowers. Lots of flowers. Tons of flowers. It looked like someone had defoliated a section of the Amazon rain forest in order to acquire enough blossoms for this display, and Reed knew without question or hesitation who the "someone" was.

That someone was, at that very moment, plastered across the screen of the television sitting on a rolling cart opposite Sue. Obviously she had drifted to sleep watching TV. Her loss, that she was missing a live press conference with America's premier adventurer, scientific developer, and—apparently—florist. Reed stood there, stone-faced, as a doctor stepped past him to look over Sue's chart and jot down a few notes. He didn't even really register that the doctor was there, since his attention was upon what was transpiring on the television.

There was Victor, standing at what was clearly a makeshift press conference site just outside the facility. He looked a bit the worse for wear than he usually did, but not by much. Considering it hadn't been all that long since he'd been residing in a space station that was being pummeled by the solar equivalent of a hurricane, he could have been considered lucky to have gotten away with what he had: a few hairs out of place, a small bandage on his face covering what must have been only the slimmest of wounds.

Reporters were shouting out questions one atop another, but Victor's steely gaze was unfazed by the verbal barrage. He wasn't making any gestures for them to settle down, wasn't trying to call out above them to make his voice heard. He simply surveyed the horde and then pointed to one of them like a monarch selecting a foot soldier.

"You've been accused in the past of moving science a little too fast—" the selected reporter began.

Von Doom interrupted him peremptorily. "Accused by whom?" he demanded with a tone that indicated the unnamed accusers were beneath contempt, not even worth acknowledging. "My . . . competitors?" he asked, the word dripping disdain.

"But surely this accident gives you pause—"

Reed shook his head upon hearing this. It wasn't a press conference. It was an attempt at a video lynching.

He had to admit, though, that Victor was handling the assault with aplomb. Whereas Reed knew he would have been on the defensive, Von Doom went into quiet but firm offense. "Danger is *always* part of discovery. What would have happened if Ben Franklin never went out in a storm? Without risk, there's no reward."

Reed found himself nodding in mute agreement. It was true. For that matter, if all pioneers in space exploration had folded their collective tents due to mishaps and tragic accidents, the know-how would never have existed for space shuttle voyages and the space station . . .

. . . and Ben and Sue would never have been injured . . .

Immediately Reed shut down that train of thought, knowing that in that direction lay madness. It did, however, prompt him to look back to Sue and note with some surprise that a doctor was in the room, even though he'd been in there for more than a minute.

The reporters, meanwhile, were unrelenting in their

interrogation as another called out, "So where's the reward? You promised a cure-all."

Victor paused, and Reed could see—for the first time—the slightest hesitation in his normally confident mien. Then, the edges of his mouth upturning ever so slightly, Von Doom said, "And you'll have it. I've never come up short, and I'm not going to start now."

Let me know how that works out for you, Victor, Reed thought grimly, since he was naturally the one who was supposed to come up with the alleged "cure-all." Yet at that moment he couldn't even be one hundred percent sure that his friends, his nearest and dearest, were going to be all right.

One of the reporters was asking about Victor taking VDI public, and Von Doom was saying with certainty, "Yes, of course. I've never been more confident in the compan—" At that point, Reed had had enough. He picked up the remote control and hit the mute button. Von Doom's mouth continued to move, but no words were emerging. *Would that it could work in real life,* he thought as he turned to the doctor and said, "How's she doing?"

The doctor looked at him guardedly for a moment, clearly not sure how much he should share of his patient's condition. He knew who Reed was, knew his reputation, knew that Reed potentially shared Sue's medical fate. But Reed wasn't a family member and there were such things as doctor/patient confidentiality. After silently weighing his options, the doctor said, "Stable. Vitals are strong."

To the physician's clear annoyance, Reed took the clipboard with Sue's chart on it out of the man's hands. He didn't notice the glare the doctor was giving him, however, for he was much too focused on its observations. "Blood panels show no irradiation. Good. You'll step up this protocol, every—"

In his own way, Reed could be as overbearing as Victor. The difference was, if nothing else, that he didn't own the building they were in or the company that had built it. Victor did, and although the doctor might have had to take such behavior from Victor Von Doom, he saw no reason to tolerate it from Reed Richards. "Four hours," he replied sharply. "We know what we're doing. One more day of observation, then you're all cleared."

As he spoke he took back the clipboard that Reed had been studying. He tucked it under his arm and walked out, giving Reed an annoyed glance as he did so. Reed didn't notice it, though, since his focus was entirely on the sleeping Sue. He approached her, drooping flowers in his hand, and said quietly, "Sue . . . I want to tell you . . . I'm . . ."

There was a burst of noise at the door and Reed turned, thinking for one awful moment that a silent signal had been buzzed at the desk because Sue had taken some turn for the worse that he wasn't perceiving. But no, it was a nurse rolling in with a tray bearing several more extravagant bouquets. Reed stared at them with the steady, distant sinking feeling of one who knows that he's utterly outgunned.

"She's allergic to orchids," he told the nurse. She

87

regarded him with an upraised eyebrow, then looked nervously at the bouquets on the rolling tray. Reed could tell from her bewilderment that she knew nothing about flowers, and couldn't tell an orchid from a daffodil. He walked over toward her and picked out one of the bouquets, a combination of blue and white lilies. "Put that *Amaryllis Agapanthus* by her bed. The African lilies. They're her favorites."

She nodded gratefully and set the selected flowers close to the unconscious Sue. She didn't even notice when Reed walked out of the room, dropping the two wilted lilies he'd been holding into the trash.

Nor did Reed notice Sue opening one eye as the large lilies were set by her bed. An eye that caught a glimpse of his departing form. Even if he had seen it, he never would have known the thought going through her head that accompanied the slight welling up of a single tear: *He remembered.*

Johnny Storm had never felt more invigorated. If he'd known the incredible buzz that came with being in the path of a deadly cosmic storm, he'd not only have done it years ago, he'd have recommended it to all his friends. He felt more alive, more on fire, than ever before.

A hospital room was the last place for someone who felt as far away from sick as one could possibly be. So Johnny was preparing to vacate his as soon as possible. Stripped to his underwear, he was busy donning his ski outfit when he heard a throat being loudly cleared near the door. He turned to see a rather remarkable looking brunette nurse who appeared more likely to have come out of a Victoria's Secret catalog than a nursing academy. Her name badge read MARIE CARTER, R.N. She had a rolling testing station with her that was designed to measure a variety of vital statistics.

"And where do we think we're going?" asked Nurse Carter.

"I don't know if 'we've' noticed," Johnny said, "but the slickest runs this side of the Alps are *right outside that window . . .*"

"I've noticed," said Carter patiently. "But doctor's orders, you're not allowed to leave until we . . ."

"Finish the tests, I know." Having pulled on his ski suit, he turned his back to her and asked, "Could you give me a hand with this zipper?"

She ignored the request. Instead she pushed the station over toward him, shaking her head in a resigned fashion, like a substitute teacher who knows the class is going to make her life miserable just because they can. "You know this is not a ski resort."

"Not *yet.*"

He dropped to his knees, reached down under his hospital bed, and pulled out a cardboard box. He flipped it up onto the bed and, as Nurse Carter watched in bemusement, he pulled out from it a colorful fiberglass object about the size of a briefcase. With quick, efficient, confident movements, he unfolded it into a long snowboard. "Luckily Grandma still sends care packages," he chortled.

He turned around to ask her what she thought of it,

and was surprised to get a thermometer shoved in his mouth. Although he had to admit it beat the alternative, it wasn't the most encouraging reaction a woman had ever had to him.

"You," Nurse Carter informed him as if he didn't know, "are trouble."

"Brubbles my triddle name," he told her, then finished zipping up his outfit.

Nurse Carter sighed wearily and, worried that Johnny looked flushed, felt his forehead. "You're hot," she said in surprise.

"So are you." Johnny had rolled the thermometer around to the side of his mouth so that his ability to talk was less impeded.

"I mean you feel a little feverish." Her eyebrows knit, out of the habit that comes when encountering a patient who might be ill, she reached around for the purpose of feeling his forehead again.

Johnny brushed it away before she could place her palm firmly against his skin. "I've never felt better in my life," he told her, and then, as if to prove he was up for anything, asked, "When do you get off work?"

"My shift ends at four," said Carter. "But I couldn't . . ."

He pulled the thermometer out of his mouth. "Meet me at 4:01, top of the run. That'll give you a minute to freshen up." He flipped the thermometer to her, gave her a fast kiss before she even knew what he was about, and then bolted out the door. Carter was left shaking her head, and then the beeping from the machine alerted her as she glanced over and saw the thermometer's analysis. Her eyes widened, and then she grunted in exasperation. This blasted hospital was supposed to be state-of-the-art, and here something as simple as the thermometer was screwed up. What other reasonable explanation could there be for a digital readout that indicated Johnny Storm had a body temperature of 209 degrees?

6

BEN WAS STILL WALKING TENTATIVELY, BUT WAS GAINING more confidence with every passing hour. Having hauled his butt out of bed after what seemed a short eternity, he had walked around every corner of the hospital compound until he was satisfied he'd seen everything inside the place there was to see. It wasn't much of an accomplishment, but it was something.

His next endeavor was to check if anything interesting was going on outside the compound. Besides, there was nothing like the sweet taste of fresh air, especially when you've just lucked your way through a situation that convinced you you'd never be breathing air within Earth's atmosphere again.

Ben found a hallway with neatly painted arrows that read PATIO, indicating that he should head down and to the right. Obediently, Ben headed in the path indicated, and moments later found himself stepping out onto a patio with a few benches, a small table that doubled as a chessboard, and a stunning panoramic view of the mountains and trees in the near distance. He sucked in lungfuls of air gratefully, reveling in the sharpness that came from the snow, and the scent that was courtesy of the evergreen trees.

Then he heard the steady tapping of fingers upon a computer keyboard, being done with such consistency and energy that he knew who it was before he even looked around the small dividing wall to see if he was correct.

Sure enough, there was Reed, pounding away on a laptop computer. He didn't even seem to notice the superb view they had from this vantage point. Obviously nothing was more important than whatever it was he was writing up on the screen.

He waited for some sort of acknowledgment. A relieved "Ben, thank God!" would have been nice. A hearty handshake. Even an acknowledging bow of the head. Nothing. Reed was completely focused on what he was doing. This annoyed Ben slightly, but really, what can you do when someone is so focused on trying to make life better for all mankind that he doesn't even stop to notice his best friend is up and around?

Skipping the salutations, Ben asked simply, "How long was I out?"

"Three days," Reed said as images flashed past on the computer screen. "I was worried about you." Ben knew he was going to have to take Reed's word for it, because he didn't actually seem all that perturbed. "How are you feeling?"

He gave it a moment's thought and then said, "Solid." He tilted his head slightly, looking Reed over. "How *you* doing?" he asked cautiously.

Reed sat back, rubbing his eyes with one hand while still tapping in notations on the keyboard. "I don't know," he said in clear frustration. "I just keep going over and over the numbers . . ."

"Reed, even you can't compute every little thing."

Reed looked at him in a way that indicated he was willing to allow that maybe, just maybe, Ben was right, but he wasn't entirely convinced. "I should have done more. Run more tests . . ."

Ben reached over and pushed down on Reed's computer screen, clicking the laptop shut. "It was a freak of nature," he said firmly. "Last I checked, you don't have a crystal ball. Let it go."

He was cheered that Reed looked to be genuinely considering what he was saying. But then Reed shook his head and opened the computer back up. Without a word he went back to work, and Ben Grimm, his best friend in the world, might not even have been there. Ben couldn't even say for sure that Reed remembered he was standing next to him.

Frustrated over his inability to get through to Reed, Ben looked out at the gorgeous vista, the wheels turning in his mind. Then, struck by a thought, he said, "You go through something like this . . . makes you appreciate having the right woman in your life."

"Yes, you and Debbie are perfect," Reed said offhandedly, not looking away from the computer.

Ben crouched next to Reed and said, "Reed, I'm not talking about Debbie."

He didn't process what Ben meant at first, but

fortunately Reed's mind was such that he could work on two or more problems at once. So he pursued for several more seconds his calculations that would absolutely determine his right to copious *mea culpas* before realizing what it was that Ben was referring to. Even then he didn't give it enough credence to look away from what he was doing. "What? Come on. She's got a good thing with Victor . . ."

"I'm sorry," Ben said with a snort, "did that cosmic bath loosen your screws?"

"He's smart, powerful, successful . . ."

"Wow. Smart, powerful, successful."

"That's right."

"Well, maybe *you* should date him."

It filtered into Reed's mind that Ben wasn't going to let it go. He looked at him, resigned, clearly pained that he had to spell it out since the truth of it—at least to him—was so painful to articulate. "Ben, he'll give her the life she deserves. She ended up with the right guy. Things worked out for the best."

"Reed . . ."

Reed wasn't going to hear it, and to underscore that, he closed his computer, tucked it under his arm, got up, and walked away. Ben was left there by himself, shaking his head in irritation.

And then perhaps all the head shaking caused something to jog loose in Ben's mind, because a thought suddenly struck him. Idea aborning, Ben grinned, even as he said in mock frustration, "Do I have to do *everything* myself?"

*　　　*　　　*

She won't be there. No way. No way will she be there.

That was what Johnny Storm kept telling himself, standing at the top of the run, waiting for Nurse Carter to show up. There was just no way that she was going to drop everything and head off to meet him for snowboarding. A woman as gorgeous as that probably had her dance card filled for the next year.

He heard the sound of a helicopter in the distance, but it didn't really register on him until he realized that it was heading right toward him. He looked up, taking a step back, as the powder sprayed lightly around him. The small chopper approached, hovered a short distance above him, and then the door of the chopper bay slid open. Johnny held his hand up over his eyebrows to shield his eyes. Then he saw something unfurling from the back and rolling down toward him. It was a rope ladder. He looked up in confusion and then grinned. Marie Carter, R.N., clad in as gorgeous a hot pink snow bunny outfit as he'd ever seen a woman fill out, was indicating that he should climb up the ladder.

He gestured for her to come down instead, but she shook her head. He felt a flash of disappointment. Obviously this was some trick to try and get him off the run. But then Carter started pointing into the distance. Johnny turned to see where she was indicating, and a smile split his face. A short distance away was an even more impressive, staggeringly high and challenging mountain, one with no ready means of access. Clearly she was saying that the copter was going to bring them over to that one instead.

It could still be a trick, of course, but Johnny decided to chance it. He folded up his snowboard for easier transport and then scrambled up the rope ladder as quickly as he could. When he got close to the top, Marie reached out and helped haul him in the rest of the way. She shouted above the noise of the chopper's rotors, "I thought you might be interested in something that was a bit more challenging than the kiddie course."

Johnny laughed, liking the way she thought. "Bring it on!" he called out. "But where'd you get the chopper?"

"Friend of mine offered to fly us over. Wyatt Wingfoot, this is Johnny, Johnny, Wyatt."

She indicated the pilot, a wide-shouldered, square-jawed Native American who looked like he could have played front line on any pro football team. Hearing his name mentioned, but not much else, Wyatt glanced back and gave Marie a questioning glance. Having just pulled the ladder up, she gave a circular motion with her right, indicating that they were ready to move. Wyatt nodded in understanding, then shouted to Johnny, *"I'm a big fan of yours!"*

"Who isn't?" Johnny called back, laughing.

The chopper moved up and away from the "kiddie course" toward the far more challenging mountain that Marie had indicated.

As Johnny unfolded his snowboard once more—a custom design filled with wild acrylic patterns—Marie prepped her skis. She snapped them on with clear expertise, and Johnny nodded approvingly. This girl wasn't amateur hour. She knew what she was about. He'd seriously lucked out with her. Then again, he was Johnny Storm, and he'd come to believe that a certain amount of luck was his natural-born right and heritage.

A chopper bay wasn't exactly the best place for chitchat, but Johnny and Marie managed well enough through the simple expedient of bringing their faces as close to each other as possible. The pleasure of their respective proximity was not lost on them. Johnny knew that his squeeze-du-jour, Frankie Raye, would kill him if this little expedition with the gorgeous nurse progressed to anything beyond a ski expedition. On the other hand, even this outing alone would be enough to ignite Frankie's wrath so, y' know . . . what the hell.

"So you only go for the big mountains?" Johnny asked.

She grinned impishly. "I'm a thrill junkie! What can I say? The bigger the danger, the better I like it."

"How's that match up with being a nurse? A saver of lives?"

"I try never to mix business with pleasure," she said, and then she winked and added, "Present company excepted, of course."

As the chopper approached the run, Marie gave him a quick précis of the ins and outs of the course they were about to run. Johnny nodded, although he was confident in his ability to handle whatever the course might have to throw at him. Then Marie slid forward, her skis dangling out the edge of the bay, preparing to make her vault onto the moutainside as soon as they drew within range. Johnny followed suit, their bodies close in a bit of competitive flirtation. Johnny leaned slightly forward, getting his first good look at the death-defying black diamond run.

"Me like-y," he said.

Pointing out the safer path, Marie told him, "Stay right. Left is trouble."

"I thought we went over this," he said impatiently.

Before he could offer further protest, she put a finger over his lips to quiet him. "Last one down," she said with a promise of great things to come, "springs for room service."

She pulled down her goggles over her eyes and vaulted out of the chopper, landing on the snow so smoothly that even the sound of it was almost inaudible. Johnny, meantime, was momentarily paralyzed, his imagination having leaped forward by hours to a scenario so pleasurable that he fancied smoke was coming out of his ears. *Memo to me: Never doubt yourself again. Women can't get enough of you.* Then, snapping out of his immobility, he dropped out of the chopper after Nurse Carter, landing squarely in the snowbank—far bumpier than he had anticipated, though. It was as if the snow was giving way beneath him. Fortunately his momentum was enough to carry him up and over the hump. His snowboard took him high into the air for a split second and he spread his arms wide, howling his infinite sense of superiority. Then he thudded down and out onto the mountain and kept on going, not taking his eyes off the prize . . . namely, Nurse Carter.

Johnny was not the type who looked back under most circumstances. Had he happened to look behind him in this instance, however, he would have noticed that the area of the mountain where he had landed was sizzling and starting to melt.

But he was far too attentive to every move that Marie was making to know or care about what had transpired behind him.

It was clear to Johnny that Marie knew every inch of the trail. She sliced deftly in and out of the trees through the deep powder, clearly enjoying the expertise required to maneuver the path ahead of her as gracefully and elegantly as she was doing. Johnny, however, didn't give a damn about expertise or deftness. Johnny was a speed freak. He knew it, loved that aspect of himself, embraced it, and gave it its head whenever possible. It was eminently possible now. Attaining maximum velocity, the world going past him so quickly that it was one large indiscernible blur, Johnny closed the gap between him and Marie. He was dimly aware that his hat was flying off, but didn't know why. Not only that, he felt a sudden looseness in his jacket, as if the back was tearing away. Considering what he'd paid for the outfit, he was shocked at the shoddy workmanship. But he wasn't about to worry about it. Not with Marie barely two feet in front of him.

Drawing effort and energy from resources he didn't even know he had, Johnny drew even with Marie. She tossed a glance his way, and suddenly her jaw dropped. "You're on fire!" she shouted.

"Not this again," he moaned, thinking she was making more noise about him running a fever when he'd never felt healthier.

"No! You're *on fire!*"

Johnny looked down in alarm and saw that his gloves were burning. He had not yet figured out that a blast of flame was what had launched his hat from his head, and another had ripped open the back of his jacket, but he would later. For the moment, his only concern was his hands. He threw the gloves off in alarm. As they rolled away on the snow, the snow melting beneath them, he barely had time to wonder what in the world could have caused it when the back of his ski suit erupted in flame. The abrupt explosion of fire caused the very air to combust behind him, propelling him forward like a rocket.

Marie screamed, completely losing her concentration and focus, and fell. She brought her legs up, keeping her skis in the air so that she wouldn't become entangled in them and break one or both of her legs. She slid out of control down the mountain, grabbing out with her gloved hands and leaving a long, dug-out trail in the snow until she finally slowed enough that she was able to stop herself. She twisted around, trying to find some sign of Johnny, but he was long gone.

Johnny, for his part, was fighting a curious combination of demented exhilaration and total panic. Panic, obviously, from the fact that his clothes were going up in flames for no apparent reason. And exhilaration for no reason that he could articulate. It was a force of nature being released within him that was making him . . . what? More than human? Something elemental? Godlike, even?

He was so busy trying to extinguish his flaming clothes

that he didn't notice until too late that he had veered off to the left, specifically in the direction that Marie had told him not to go. Seconds later, he learned why.

There was a chasm in front of him. It was far wider than anything he could possibly jump.

Johnny was no longer feeling godlike. He let out a bloodcurdling scream as he launched off the cliff, his legs flailing, trying to defy physics by being able to walk on air. Flames began to trail his body as he angled down, down, missing the opposite side by a good twenty feet. Fires licked his body, continuing to billow from his back as he plummeted toward rocks below. He twisted in midair as if, like some cartoon character, he could reverse his descent by sheer willpower and "run" back up toward the cliff's edge.

Then the very air in front of him was on fire. He couldn't see anything except flame. It was in front of his eyes, in his ears, in his mouth, everywhere—he was completely engulfed. He knew—every hotshot pilot knew—that the single most painful way to die was burning to death. It was the gamble they took each and every time they strapped themselves into vehicles that were being powered by the equivalent of a hundred tons of TNT.

Johnny Storm was completely ablaze, and at first he thought he wasn't feeling the certain unbearable pain because his mind had just shut down, being too overwhelmed by the unspeakable agony. But then he realized that, no, it was more than that. Stranger, more insane than that. He wasn't feeling anything because it wasn't hurting him.

He felt as if his mind was being shredded, pulled in so many directions that he didn't know where to look first. It was hard to believe that Johnny had completely forgotten about the fact that he was falling, but considering he was busy being astounded that he wasn't being reduced to cinders second by excruciating second, it was understandable that death by falling was taking second place in his attention to death by immolation.

But then he remembered the rocks that were coming up toward him, and he looked down, completely disoriented . . . because even though he thought he was looking down, he was surprised to discover that he was actually looking off to the side. It was then he realized that he wasn't falling so much as gently pirouetting through the air, slowing by the moment. His flaming body gave him a bizarre lift that made him lighter than air, and as he drew to within several feet of the rocks, he angled away in a ninety-degree turn.

His flight was by no means elegant. As he tried to process what was happening to him, panic resurged as every shred of common sense told him this was all impossible. He could not defy gravity. He could not survive being on fire.

His arms flailed about in a frenzy of hysteria, causing him to tumble end over end and crash hard into a snowbank. Because he was moving so fast, he went in deep, so deep that he was effectively immobilized beneath a mass of snow and ice.

For a moment the extreme cold caused his flame to flicker out and die, and Johnny was convinced that he was going to follow suit. He struggled but couldn't move, held down by the weight of the snow all around him. He had gone, within a matter of seconds, from worrying about burning to death and then falling to death to, now, freezing to death, buried alive.

He thrashed about, his fear escalating once more, his sense of self-preservation in overload. It was enough to reignite his sputtering flame and, moments later, he was at full blaze again. Undeterred by the snow, it proceeded to melt the entire snowbank around him.

Marie Carter, having seen the snowboard tracks that had propelled Johnny off to the left, knew all too well that he was heading straight toward a chasm. Kicking off her skis, she found the narrow path that she knew would bring her down safely to the bottom of the ravine. Her heart was pounding. The question wasn't whether she was going to find Johnny Storm in pieces, but rather how many pieces it was going to be.

She couldn't stop beating herself up mentally as she made her way through the ravine bottom. What had she been thinking, aiding and abetting Johnny Storm—who was supposed to be quarantined, for the love of God—on a spectacularly dangerous ski run.

There was steam up ahead, just around the corner. She didn't understand how that could be. It had to be connected with the bizarre phenomenon she had witnessed of Johnny somehow, incredibly catching fire. What in the world could have caused it? Was he actually insane enough to have been packing some sort of . . . of jet pack beneath his coat in order to increase his speed? It was a ridiculous notion. Then again, it was no more ridiculous than the idea that he had just somehow burst into flame for no reason. Even if she did find him, and even if he was in one piece, he'd be covered with burns on one hundred percent of his body. The odds of him surviving that degree of damage were simply nonexistent.

Having built up in her head the horror show that she expected to find, she was duly stunned to come upon what was, to all intents and purposes, an impromptu hot tub. Johnny Storm, needing only a martini in his hand, was sitting naked in a small natural hot spring that, by all rights, should not have been there. There was so much steam and so much warmth being generated that, even though they were in the midst of snow-capped mountains, the area around them was as balmy as the Bahamas.

"Care to join me?" Johnny called.

Marie knew that she was faced with something that just couldn't be. Johnny should be dead or dying. Snow should be surrounding him. Instead he was grinning like a loon and inviting her to hop into a bubbling warm pond that was situated where a snowbank had been minutes earlier.

She had no idea what she was faced with. The danger was, quite simply, immense.

Naturally she shimmied out of her clothes and was in the water with him within seconds.

7

IF THE FORCES OF GOD AND NATURE WERE GOING TO interrupt Victor Von Doom a second time, they were going to require more than a cosmic storm. It was going to take a half-dozen tornadoes with a hurricane and earthquake tossed in, and even then Von Doom was willing to wager that he would not be deterred from his course.

It had been one thing when he had simply been pulling a ring out of his pocket with the intention of presenting it to Sue. In retrospect—if he were going to be really self-obsessed about it—the storm's timing had been impeccable because such an understated attempt at the proposal simply wasn't good enough by half. It didn't suit him, wasn't worthy of him. Never mind her. Him. The faults that Sue had revealed in her character were excusable due to a woman's frail nature which always comes to the forefront in times of stress, of that Von Doom was certain. But a lack of imagination on the part of Victor Von Doom in asking Sue Storm to marry him? Inexcusable. What had he been thinking?

This time, Victor was taking no chances. This time, his staff was scurrying about his office like army ants, preparing a million-dollar meal to go with the billion-dollar view. Victor was standing on an expensive parapet that extended out from his office, providing a scenic vista that was a feast for the eyes. Accompanying that was a feast for the palate that his personnel was in the process of overseeing, and Victor in turn was overseeing it all. He was busy making sure that every piece of silver-ware, every plate, every scrap of linen, was positioned just so, and he was doing so with an energy that could only be described as slightly manic. Even as he was in-volved with culinary micromanagement, however, he wasn't losing sight of other considerations. Leonard Kirk was standing nearby, consulting reams of pages of infor-mation while Von Doom fired questions at him. "How's the IPO?" he asked.

"Stable," Leonard said confidently. "We're looking at low twenties. It's a good number, considering the fallout from—"

"Reed's disaster," Von Doom interrupted. He shook his head wearily with the air of someone who is made to suffer due to the vast inadequacies of others. "You know, I half-think he did this to me on purpose."

"Sir," said Leonard, "I'm sure he wouldn't put him-self—"

Yet again Victor Von Doom interrupted him. This time it was because he was on to something else entirely, giving Reed Richards no more thought since the un-trustworthy scientist obviously deserved none. Reed had caused the damage; now it was up to Von Doom to embark on the damage control. "Get me on the A.M. shows. Larry King, cover of the *Journal* . . ."

He stopped, his voice trailing off. He picked up a silver tray that was on the table and stared at his reflection in it. Slowly he brought a finger up and touched, ever so gingerly, the line of the wound upon his face. "I've got to do something about this scar," he said. "Make sure they only shoot my right side."

Leonard sounded as if he wanted to say something but was reluctant to do so. Von Doom caught the hesitation and turned toward him expectantly. Leonard cleared his throat and said, "Actually, uh . . . people seem to think the scar 'humanizes' you."

Von Doom stared at him incredulously. He couldn't believe that Leonard put enough stock in such an absurd notion even to think it, much less voice it. "And that's a *good* thing?" he demanded.

Leonard looked stunned at the response, but Von Doom didn't see it. He was back staring obsessively at the scar. He was so intent on every centimeter of it that he didn't even notice his eyes were bloodshot, his face wan.

"You know," Leonard said finally in a tentative manner, "maybe you should get some rest . . ."

"Later," was the curt response. "First, I've got some unfinished business. A deal that needs closing . . ."

Leonard was studying the lavish spread being laid out. "Sir . . . I've always wondered . . ." He hesitated again, clearly not wanting to say or do anything that would incense his boss. But Von Doom simply turned and looked at him expectantly, and Leonard pushed forward gamely. "Why *Sue?*" he asked. "You could have any woman in the world, but—"

"*That's* why," Von Doom replied, as if that should be all the explanation that was required. When he saw from Leonard's puzzled expression that he had not yet made it clear, he shook his head wearily in the manner of one who does not suffer fools gladly and said patiently, "Because I could have any *other* woman. You know, when they asked Caesar 'Why England?' he said, 'Because it's not *mine.*'"

Then he nodded in approval at the smile that reflected back at him. At least *that* was intact.

More human. What kind of nonsense was *that* all about?

Ben glanced around the dining hall in the VDI compound later that afternoon and was relieved to see no sign of Johnny. That was exceptionally fortunate, because he was not in the best of moods, and he really didn't want to have to worry about dealing with what passed for the renowned Johnny Storm wit.

And considering that Ben had entered with Sue, that alone would have been a lightning rod for attracting Johnny over there to find out what they were talking about. Naturally he would assume that Reed was going to be the subject of discussion. That annoyed the hell out of Ben. Especially considering that his plan was somewhat more sophisticated and manipulative than that.

There was a buffet laid out, and about two dozen employees were busy availing themselves of it. "I can only stay for one drink, Ben," Sue told him as they walked across the dining hall. "I've got to meet with Victor."

"Wouldn't want to keep Vic waiting," said Ben, with a tone that indicated he didn't especially care if "Vic" was kept waiting until the end of the world.

He made sure to guide Sue toward the far side, near the other entrance to the dining hall. He glanced at his watch and saw that it was 2:15 precisely. It never entered his mind that Reed would be anything other than punctual, practically to the second. He wasn't disappointed. Reed walked in exactly when Ben expected him to.

Reed's eyes widened when he saw Ben there with Sue, and he looked as if he wanted to back out of the room quickly in hopes he wouldn't be noticed. That hope died in no time as Ben said cheerfully, "Hey, Reed! What are you doing here?" Then, before Reed could say something useful such as *You told me to meet you here*, Ben continued, "Great, why don't you join us!"

He grabbed Reed by the arm as tight as he could. *Reed, buddy, you've gotta start working out* he thought, because it felt as if Reed had no muscles at all. Ben's hands were practically sinking into Reed's arms.

Ben quickly escorted Reed and Sue over to a quiet table. As he did so, his stomach began to growl so loudly that the three of them could hear it. He'd been planning to excuse himself to go get some food, but his stomach had been remarkably cooperative by providing convincing sound effects. "God, I'm starving," he said. "Gonna hit the buffet." His stomach growled once again, this time so noisily that he was sure they could hear it next door.

He got a plate of food and hurried back to Reed and Sue as quickly as he could, certain that if he left them alone, in short order either one of them or both of them would be gone. Ben then embarked upon a balancing act, keeping a chipper stream of chatter going between himself and the two of them, doing everything he could to relax them in each other's presence. Considering that neither Reed nor Sue were exactly dummies, there was every reason to assume that they knew perfectly well what he was up to. They were, however, gracious enough not to let on. Instead they went along with it, keeping up their ends of the conversation, talking about anything and everything except—curiously—their mutual experience on the space station. Most of their time was spent dwelling on good times in the past, and it was clear from both their reactions that Reed and Sue had forgotten just how many good times there were.

Time passed and the population of the dining hall thinned out. Yet Reed, Sue, and Ben remained, chatting and laughing like in times past. It was amazing how easily they fell into old rhythms and habits, Ben thought. Even he hadn't remembered that, once upon a time, they'd all really liked each other.

It was becoming apparent to Ben, however, that something he'd eaten hadn't liked him. He belched loudly and pushed away the last shrimp on his plate. "Pardon me," he mumbled.

Sue and Reed stared at him as his stomach rumbled

again. This time, however, it wasn't from hunger. This time it was as if his gastric juices were making a claim to burn their way out of his gut. "Are you all right?" Reed asked with obvious concern.

"I think I need to lie down," Ben muttered. "Bad shrimp."

The irony was that it had, in fact, been Ben's plan to make some sort of excuse and get out of there, once having broken the ice, so Reed and Sue could have time alone. But the excuse was all too real. He rose from the table, clutching his stomach. "*Really* bad shrimp."

Reed started to get up from the table to follow him, but Ben smiled gamely and waved for him to sit. "Worst comes to worst, I'll go back to the med center. Don't worry about it. I'll be fine."

"If you're sure," Reed said uncertainly.

"Born sure," Ben replied, and he headed out of the dining hall, shaking his head and thinking, *If it ain't one thing, it's another* . . .

The moment that Reed had seen Ben with Sue, he knew perfectly well that Ben had set them up. But Reed made no attempt to absent himself from the scene, mostly because he was touched that Ben had gone to the effort.

When Ben made his excuses for departure, Reed had been certain to play along for all it was worth. Act as if he was willing to go with Ben and make sure he was okay, even though naturally he knew that Ben was faking the "bad shrimp" ailment so that Reed and Sue could be alone. Some small part of him was pleased with the notion of spending extended time with Sue, even if he knew for a fact that she was lost to him. In his own mind, he likened it to astronauts who had had the opportunity to travel to the moon, now looking at each moonrise nostalgically while knowing they would never tread upon that distant sphere again.

A fireplace was lit nearby, and Sue looked gorgeous in the flickering light of it. She rested her chin on her palm and looked at Reed expectantly. For the first time it was just the two of them, and clearly she was waiting for Reed to say something. He shifted uncomfortably in his seat, not sure where to start.

"Feeling better?" he asked.

He knew the answer already. Not only was he aware she was feeling better, but he was familiar with every detail of her current medical condition. But it seemed a polite thing to ask, and besides, conventional wisdom was that people most enjoyed talking about themselves. Give someone an opportunity to make themselves the subject of conversation, and they'd happily chatter away for hours.

"Yes, thanks," said Sue, and proceeded to thwart conventional wisdom by not saying another word.

"That's good," Reed said, then pondered it, gave it even more thought, and continued, "That's, uh . . . good."

Another even more deathly silence followed, and then Sue said jokingly, "You always had a way with words."

Reed forced a smile. Inwardly, he was assessing all

sorts of things he could bring up to talk about. But he didn't know where to start. He began ordering potential topics mentally, first from most important to least, then alphabetically, then by timeliness in comparison to current events.

He had no idea for how long he did it, but however long it was, it was clearly longer than Sue was willing to wait. "I should be getting back," she said, looking and sounding a bit awkward.

She started to get up to leave, and Reed decided to toss aside all his attempts to organize his thoughts and grab literally the first thing that came into his head. Unfortunately, the choice he made was an abysmal one, and he knew it the moment he said it, but there was no way of retrieving it. "I'm happy for you and Victor," he said.

It stopped Sue dead in her tracks. She stared at him as if he were a form of bacteria. "You're happy for me and Victor," she repeated in a dead, faintly incredulous tone.

"I can tell you guys are enjoying what was the best part of our relationship."

"Which was?" Sue prompted, clearly curious as to what Reed would say next.

"Passion," he said, and when he saw the expression on her face, he realized she might have misinterpreted. "For science," he clarified.

He expected that she would say "thank you" or "it's good of you to say" or "how sweet" or something that was, at the very least, polite. Instead, disgust on her face and frustration in her voice, she said, "You are such a dork, Reed. You never get it, and never will unless it's explained to you in quantum physics!"

The flames in the fireplace flickered in a ghostly breeze, and Reed could have sworn—although obviously it was a passing optical illusion—that she wavered for a moment, as if the fireplace light had mysteriously bent around her. It was a curious scientific happenstance, but at the moment it drew less attention from him than the situation into which he'd been thrust.

"What?" asked Reed, feeling like he'd been dropped late into a conversation that he couldn't even begin to follow. "What did I say?"

Looking more disappointed than angry, she said, "It's never what you say. It's what you don't say. What you don't do . . ."

Her voice choked slightly on the last word, and she looked away from him. He felt the weight of their personal history upon them, so heavy as to threaten to break both their backs and spirits.

What does she want from me? Reed wondered. *Am I supposed to . . . what? Fight for her? Against Victor? I could bend over backward for her and it wouldn't begin to equal the opportunities he could provide her, the wealth he could lavish upon her. Romance is all well and good, but Sue has always been a smart, ambitious woman. Certainly she's figured out that her wisest, best path is with Victor. Why in the world should I try to thrust myself into the middle of it, endeavor to confuse matters? What sort of kindness would that be to show her after all this time?*

He tried to convey to her that he was simply being considerate of her feelings, and acknowledging that which, certainly, she had already concluded herself. Somehow, though, he couldn't form the words. "I . . . I . . . I just wanted to . . ."

Her emotions bubbling over, she started talking faster and faster. "It's been two years, and all you can say is you're happy for me and some other guy!" She'd been sitting, but now she stood. "You know, Victor may be a lot of things, but at least he's not afraid to fight for what he wants . . . !"

Reed looked down, stunned at her words. *My God . . . is she right? Am I really being a . . . a coward?* "And it's nice to be wanted sometimes," she continued. "To be heard . . . seen . . . Reed, look at me," she said impatiently.

Am I using logic, distance, to insulate myself against acknowledging the course I should be following? It's like she can see right through me . . .

Reed raised his head, fixed his gaze on her, and his eyes widened as he saw right through her.

Her clothes were still there, to be sure. But her face was almost entirely gone. The blush on her cheeks was floating, as were her bewitching eyes, giving her an almost Cheshire cat air.

"Uh . . . Sue . . . ? I *can't*."

"What?" Her blush twitched. "What do you mean you—?"

"Sue," he said. "*Look at your hands!*"

With an annoyed exhalation of air, she raised her hands, obviously certain that Reed was embarking on

116

some sort of delaying or distracting tactic. But then she gulped as she saw her medical wristband floating before her on one hand, her wristwatch on the other . . . and no wrist to accompany either.

Sue let out alarmed shriek, looking down at her feet, seeing the visible part of her legs were also gone. Reflexively she took a step toward Reed but, unaccustomed to moving without being able to see her body, and in the throes of a full-blown panic attack, she slammed into the table and sent a wine bottle tumbling off it.

Despite the far greater concern that Sue had practically vanished into thin air, Reed reached for the bottle to snag it. He realized it was beyond his reach, and then it wasn't, it was cradled in his hand. By the time Reed processed the information that his arm had just stretched two feet beyond the cuff of his shirt, he had already hauled the bottle back to the table and set it down lightly. His distended arm hung bonelessly for a moment, and then he flicked it like a whip and the hand snapped back into its proper place. He was sure he even heard a faint "twang" like a rubber band being distended and then abruptly returning to its normal shape.

Sue's eyes widened at what she had just witnessed. Reed saw her chest—or rather, the shirt covering it—rising and falling so rapidly that it looked like she was hyperventilating. He wanted to tell her to calm down, but if he'd had difficulty before in verbalizing his feelings for her, this new challenge was just far too much for him to undertake.

Fortunately, he didn't have to. Just as quickly as it had

disappeared, the rest of Sue Storm faded back into existence. They stared at each other in mutual alarm.

Suddenly a voice called out, "Hey!"

They looked up to see Johnny Storm standing in the doorway. Standing next to him was a young woman whom Reed instantly recognized as one of the floor nurses. A pink parka, which Reed safely assumed belonged to her, was wrapped around Johnny's midsection, providing the only article of clothing he was wearing.

"You guys will not believe what just happened!"

Reed and Sue exchanged glances, and then Reed cleared his throat loudly and said, "I think you'll be amazed what we'd be willing to believe just about now."

The romance was slowly being leeched out of the air in Victor Von Doom's office.

Sue was supposed to have been there half an hour ago, and the delay was not being lost on Victor. The candles were burning low to the table, and although the food was being kept warm, Victor was starting to lose patience. Patience with Sue, and patience with himself for allowing this. Granted, Sue's independent streak was one of the more attractive things about her . . . but the attraction lay in grinding it into a fine powder and making himself her first priority in the world. So how the devil was he supposed to accomplish that when she couldn't even keep a simple dinner date?

Victor strode toward the door, running his fingers distractedly through his hair . . . and then was astounded when a clump of it came out in his hand.

He stopped and stared at the hair as if it had fallen out of someone else's head. Pivoting, he walked instead over toward his private bathroom, where he snapped on the light so he could see his reflection.

Immediately the hair that had fallen from his hair became a secondary problem. Of far greater concern was his scar. It was now longer than the bandage that covered it, making it seem as if it had spread. But that didn't seem possible. The scar should have been limited by the size of the wound that had initially created it. It couldn't just . . . just spontaneously grow as if an invisible attacker was continuing to slice at it with an unseen knife.

His hands hesitated over the bandage for a moment. He took a deep breath, then reached up and peeled back the bandage. He winced from the pain as it pulled at his skin. Once it was clear, he gaped at it. The scar had become bluish-gray. It was deeper, unhealthy, maybe infected . . .

How was it possible? When they'd been hit by the radiation from the cosmic storm, he'd been where the shielding was at its thickest. Behind that armor, he should have been safe. Invulnerable. Invincible.

"This can't be happening," he whispered. "I . . . can beat this. Stop this. I will not fear my future. I will face it."

The face of his future spoke the words back to him, and for some reason, it had a chilling sound to it. . . .

8

REED, SUE, AND JOHNNY EMERGED FROM JOHNNY'S room, having paused there long enough for him to toss on something marginally more appropriate than a pink jacket. They moved with speed and purpose. "It has to be the cloud," Sue said. "It's fundamentally altered our DNA."

"Let's not jump to conclusions," Reed told her. "We need a massive amount of evidence before making this leap . . ."

Reed glanced over his shoulder to make sure that Johnny was keeping up with them. He stopped walking. Sue, impatient, turned to see what was keeping Reed, and then she saw what he was looking at.

Johnny's fingertips were on fire.

Sue's first instinct was to yank Johnny back into the dining room and throw water on his hand. But then she saw that he wasn't reacting in pain, and—despite the fact that it was her brother's welfare at stake—her scientific curiosity took over. She watched in mute amazement as Johnny, his fingers extended, waved his hand slowly forward and back, leaving flame trails in the air. Then he snapped his fingers and the flames went out. Sue saw that his fingertips were unscathed.

"Now what is up with that?" Johnny asked.

Reed looked at Sue and then, with a deadpan, intoned, "The cloud has fundamentally altered our DNA."

If Reed was expecting Johnny to be blown away by this revelation, he was going to be disappointed. "Cool," said Johnny as if he'd just been informed that his favorite TV program was coming on. He studied the two of them, eyebrow cocked. "What'd it do to you guys?"

"Apparently," said Sue, forcing herself to voice something so fundamentally preposterous she could scarcely contemplate it, "I can disappear."

"Works for me. I hardly notice when you're around as it is."

"Johnny—!"

"Please tell me you can go silent, too."

Sue turned to Reed and said, "Do you think there's any chance I can make my brother disappear?"

She realized that Reed wasn't even listening to her. "We have to find Ben," he told her, and she knew immediately that his priorities were right in order. They had at least had some small degree of shelter from the radiation of the cosmic storm. But Ben had practically been slapped up one side and down the other with it. If bizarre changes were manifesting in the three of them, what in God's name had happened to Ben?

All sorts of horrific possibilities occurred to her as

they sprinted toward Ben's room. Reed was obviously just as worried, and somehow all of Sue's concerns about their relationship seemed trivial compared to the possible biological catastrophe they were now facing. As for Johnny, he was totally disengaged from the gravity of the situation. Instead he was snapping his fingers, generating small explosive bursts of flame each time he did so. On and off, on and off. He began to singsong to the commercial jingle for the Clapper, that device for people who were enamored of turning their room lights on and off by clapping. "Flame on," he sang, "flame off. Flame on, flame off . . ."

"Johnny," Sue said sharply, her patience severely tested.

Like a misbehaving child who has to make one last bid to show his defiance, Johnny snapped the flames on and off one more time.

"Stop it!"

"Okay, 'Mom,'" he sighed.

They made it to Ben's room, and Reed was about to push open the door when they heard banging, moaning, and what even sounded like pleading from within. Johnny unaccountably smiled. "Oh, you dawg you." Then, abruptly, he looked annoyed as another thought hit him. "Better not be my nurse!"

Sue had no idea what Johnny was talking about, and was quite certain that she preferred to remain ignorant.

"Ben, are you there?" Reed called, his sense of discretion preventing him from simply bursting into Ben's room unannounced.

Sue pushed on the door and discovered that it was locked. She looked worriedly at Reed, and then tried to make herself heard over the sounds from within. "Open up, Ben! We need to talk."

The moaning became louder, and it was accompanied by something else . . . the creaking of metal. Sue couldn't figure out what it was at first, but then it occurred to her that it was the metal frame of Ben's bed. It was as if he were lying upon it and becoming heavier and heavier, causing the bed to groan beneath the escalating weight. Just as quickly she was ready to dismiss the notion out of hand as jumping to conclusions . . . until she heard the unmistakable noise of the bed giving way and crashing to the floor. Before they could move, Ben called out to them in a voice that was deeper, more gravelly than normal. He sounded like he was speaking from within his own coffin.

"Leave me alone!" he cried out.

That, of course, was the last thing they could do. Clearly having decided he'd had enough, unable to wait any longer, Reed knelt in front of the door.

"What, you going to pray for help to get in?" Johnny asked sarcastically.

Reed didn't even bother to look his way as Sue snapped, "Johnny, for God's sake . . ."

But Johnny wasn't listening to her, which in and of itself was nothing new. Instead he was staring fixedly in mute astonishment at Reed. He was distending his arm, making it so thin that he was able to make it creep under the doorjamb.

Sue waited for Ben to cry out from within in shock at the sight of Reed's stretching limb, or protest over this invasion of his privacy, but he was silent. She didn't know what to make of that cessation of sound, unable to decide whether it was a good thing or a bad thing.

Reed, meantime, was leaning against the door, his shoulder pushed against it. His face was a mask of concentration as he clearly felt around, trying to find the latch on the other side. There was a bit of thumping, and then he said softly, "Ah." A moment later there was the click of the lock being turned, unlatching the door. Then he closed his eyes, focused once more, and withdrew his arm from beneath the door. It slithered upwards, like a snake, the flesh and bones literally reforming before their eyes until his arm regained its normal appearance.

Johnny said nothing for a long, stunned moment. "Ewwww," he finally announced. "That is disgusting."

Sue was about to retort when they all heard a tremendous crashing from within the room. Reed quickly turned the knob and shoved the door open, yet Sue somehow had a feeling as to what they would find when they opened the door.

She was partly right.

The room was trashed. Every stick of furniture had been smashed to splinters, Ben apparently having been seized by some sort of uncontrollable rage. But what Sue had not been expecting was the huge, gaping hole in the wall where the window had been. They rushed to it and looked out into the distance. There was no sign of Ben.

124

There was, however, something else. Some sort of . . . of creature, lumpy and orange, like a bad child's statue made out of dried-out Play-Doh having come to life.

"What is that *thing?*" Johnny asked.

The horrific truth slowly dawned upon Sue. "I think," she said, "that thing is Ben."

She turned to Reed to ask his opinion, but his face was ashen. For the first time in all the years she'd known him, she thought Reed was about to be sick. He looked at her then, and there was more agony in his eyes than she had ever seen in a human being before.

Susan Storm felt ashamed. Until this very moment, she had thought of Reed as this . . . this automaton. Incapable of feeling, of any sort of emotion. But she saw not only the fear for Ben in Reed's face, she also saw the guilt he bore for having put Ben—put all of them—into harm's way.

She tried to figure out what she could say to him. Something, anything, that would quell the sense of culpability he clearly felt. But before she could, the commanding voice of Victor Von Doom broke into her thoughts. "What's going on?!" he demanded.

Sue turned and blinked in surprise. She thought she might be mistaken, but it seemed to her as if Victor's bandage was bigger than it had been before. It was probably nothing, but still . . .

"Victor, are you feeling all right?" she asked cautiously.

He appeared to hesitate, but then he replied with an indifferent shrug, "Couple scrapes. I'm fine. Why?"

Then he saw the interior of the room. "What the hell happened here?"

"Ben did this," Reed said. There was no tone to his voice at all. This wasn't scientific detachment. He was numb. "He's had some kind of . . . reaction to exposure from the cloud." He glanced significantly at Sue and Johnny. "And he's not the only one."

Johnny spoke for once without his customary smugness or air of infinite coolness. "Anybody know where the big guy's going?"

Sue didn't have the faintest idea, but then she saw that Reed was staring fixedly at something. She followed his gaze and saw it: A photograph of Debbie, Ben's fiancée.

"He's going home," said Reed.

9

HE CROUCHED IN THE DARKNESS WITHIN THE EMPTY cargo car, swaying back and forth slightly as the train moved along the track. It had not been a difficult endeavor for him to undertake. He had simply waited there in the shadows of the shipping yard when the train came in, waited until the cargo in one of the cars had been off-loaded, and then waited until the car was closed and locked up before approaching it. Getting past the lock was no problem: One quick twist of the wrist had snapped the padlock off, and he tossed it aside in disgust. *Shoddy workmanship* he thought, not wanting to acknowledge that mere hours earlier, the lock would have thwarted all his efforts to remove it short of taking a crowbar to it.

Sliding the door open, he clambered up into the car and closed the door once more. He breathed a sigh of relief as the darkness swallowed him. Darkness, at this particular moment, was the only place he felt safe. Prying eyes could not discern him there, could not perceive what he had become.

What he had become.

He was no longer a who. He was a what.

The train moved off, its destination New York City. He knew the line and all the routes quite well. He never thought, in years past, that his occasional tendency to run away from home in his youth would wind up serving him so much later in his life. What a stroke of luck, to have had an abusive father and an alcoholic mother to provide the kind of home life that he strived to distance himself from repeatedly.

The pain had largely subsided, but he had no idea what he'd been left with. As the train chugged along, the still of the night punctuated only by the occasional squealing of metal wheels on metal tracks, he thought about all the things that radiation could do to the human body. The sores and lesions, the slow poisoning, hair coming out in clumps . . .

He couldn't recall anything like this, though. He kept running his fingers over his bare arms, and couldn't comprehend what it was he was feeling. His very sense of touch had changed. His fingers were thick and callused, so much so that he had a hard time discerning what his skin must have been like. As near as he could determine, it was thick, bumpy . . . like elephantiasis, perhaps. That sickness where one's skin swells up to epidemic proportions. But this wasn't just swollen. He traced the lines of his skin with a single thick finger and felt that his epidermis had hardened to an almost rock-like state. Not that he was turning to rock, of course. Nothing that insane could be happening to him. Nevertheless, he would gently tap his limbs against hard surfaces around him and not feel a thing. Swollen skin should probably have been hypersensitive to any sort of pain. Here, he felt nothing. It was as if it was no longer skin, but some sort of concrete hide . . . and although he had not looked too closely at it for fear of, well, losing his mind . . . he had the distinct concern that the hide had turned orange.

An orange, rocky monster of some sort. That was what he had become. And when people saw him, they would quite simply go nuts. In terror, they would charge him, attack him, and . . . and . . .

And . . . four fingers on each hand? *Great. So much for my cashmere gloves.*

There was a squeaking by his foot. A rat had skittered up to him and, apparently ravenous or else spoiling for a fight, tried to sink its teeth into him. All it managed to do was snap off its incisors and let out a yelp to boot.

He knew he shouldn't feel sorry for the stupid thing, but he did. The dumb creature, having no idea what to do, sped back and forth across the wooden floor, squealing in protest over having sustained such misfortune. Ben watched it go, offering no apologies. "At least," he growled, his voice sounding like a small rock slide, "you know what you are."

He sat back and closed his eyes. Sleep did not come easily to him, and when it did, it was brutal. He was reliving the cosmic storm, except Reed and Johnny were standing there in the air lock, shoving him back out into space rather than letting him get to safety. Reed was grinning dementedly, and Johnny kept saying "Dawg! Dawg!" because not only did he want to see Ben die, but he wanted to annoy him to death before the storm could take him out.

When he did finally wake up, he wasn't startled to consciousness by the train's movement, but rather by its lack of it. He listened for some sound of the engine to determine if it was simply pausing for some reason, such as switching tracks or something. But he heard nothing. All was silent, save for the raspy breathing in his chest. Breathing had been even harder before, because he was carrying God-only-knew how many more pounds than he had been and his body was scrambling to adjust. It was getting easier, though, which indicated to him that whatever had happened to him, it was still happening. His internal organs were mutating somehow to keep up with what was occurring externally.

For one hopeful moment, he wondered if there was any chance that the mutation would continue all the way through and he would wind up back where he started. Then he dismissed the notion from his mind. The sooner he started accepting that he was only going to look worse, not better, the sooner he could . . .

Could . . .

Could adjust to the notion that his life was over.

That was all. It was just . . . just over.

Almost every fiber of his being wanted to quit. Just roll over and die. The only thing that was keeping him going was the minuscule part of his personality that refused to accept defeat. When he'd been hanging in the depths of space, pulling himself desperately along his tether, he'd known deep down that he wasn't going to be able to outspeed the cosmic storm once he'd seen how fast it was coming. But he hadn't given up then. Now, face to face with the aftermath of the storm's effects on him, he wasn't about to toss in the towel. Not quite yet.

But what if the worst should happen?

He stared at his orangy, rocky hands and wondered just how, precisely, he would know when the worst had occurred. What, this wasn't the worst? How much worse would it, could it get? People pointing, screaming, and running like something out of a 1950s horror film? Rejected by all who loved him? Maybe when army tanks were pursuing him and his only means of escape was into a boiling pit of lava . . . maybe that would be the hint that he was finally hitting bottom.

Morbid much? Except . . . what if you're not being morbid? What if you really, truly wind up with no reason to live?

He reached up and gripped the cargo door. "Having no reason to live is no reason not to live," he growled, and shoved it open. It slid wide noisily, and for a heartbeat he was concerned that the racket might bring someone. Then he realized, well, so what if it did? They'd take one look at him and run in the other direction.

Leaning forward, Ben glanced around. It was late at night, and there was no moon, which suited him just fine. Even moonless, he could see that he was in the right place. There, on the horizon, was the glorious

Manhattan skyline, and he could tell from the direction he was viewing it that he was in Brooklyn. Surrounded as he was by unmoving trains, he didn't exactly have to possess the observational skills of a Sherlock Holmes, or even a Reed Richards, to know that he was in the Brooklyn train yards.

He slid out of the car and thudded to the ground, which shook beneath him. Good thing he wasn't jumping out of a train in Los Angeles; he might have triggered the San Andreas Fault.

A short distance away, he saw several homeless men gathered around a metal ash can in which a warming fire was blazing. There were some blankets strewn around as well, and Ben was barely clad in a few hanging tatters . . . the remains of his hospital garb, since he'd ripped his way out of what he'd been wearing earlier. It was bad enough that his skin had erupted in rock-like orange scales; he didn't have to be walking around indecently while it was happening. Maybe one of the blankets would help.

He shambled toward them. At first they didn't notice him, but then they looked up, squinting into the shadows that were cloaking him. Finally he drew within range of them, and the crackling fire illuminated his features.

He started to open his mouth to say something, but he didn't have the time. With an almost uniform shriek, the men turned and ran from him.

Well . . . should've seen that coming.

Still, there was some small benefit. In their haste to vacate the area, they had left some things behind. A makeshift tent, Ben saw, was not simply a blanket, but actually an insanely oversize trench coat that had probably been provided by Goodwill, and whose previous owner had likely died from a heart attack.

"Super-size me," said Ben, as he took the coat and slid his arms into it. A coat large enough to provide a living space for several people fit him as if it was made for him. A hat had fallen as well, a battered fedora. Ben placed it atop his head and drew the brim down low.

Then he reached over and put his hands up in front of the fire for warmth, just out of habit. He realized that he wasn't feeling any warmth from the fire, and then further realized that he wasn't actually feeling cold either. He knew it was cold out because he saw his breath emerging from his mouth in mist, but the cold wasn't actually suffusing him. He simply hadn't noticed it.

"Great," he muttered, and then he heard shouts from the distance. Guards, perhaps, or patrolling policemen who had noticed screaming homeless guys sprinting out of the train yard and decided that it'd be wise to investigate.

Without hesitation he turned and ran. He moved slowly at first, but picked up speed. There was a fence ahead of him. He didn't slow at all, putting his hand on top of his hat to keep it in place and smashing right through. The mesh slammed to the ground and he crunched it beneath his feet as he kept on running toward his old stomping grounds of Brooklyn.

He knew every street, every alleyway of what he often referred to as "everyone's favorite borough." As a result, he was able to keep himself out of sight, even making his way down a subway tunnel at one point and ducking to one side when a train came rumbling through. Eventually he climbed up out of the subway and emerged just a few blocks from his destination.

His eyes widened as he saw a genuine break handed him. It was a men's big-and-tall shop . . . shuttered, of course, but this was an emergency. He'd get around to sending them money for whatever he took. Right now he had what any reasonable person would describe as extraordinary need, and he really wasn't caring about the niceties of the law.

Going around back, he pulled the rear door open as if it were unlocked. In case a silent alarm was going, he knew he had to move quickly. He grabbed the first clothes he found, doffing the coat and trying to pull on a shirt or jacket. They ripped wide open. "Terrific," he muttered, and—cutting to the chase—took the largest sizes he could find. He pulled his oversize coat back on, bundled up his clothes under his arm, and quickly got out of the store.

Finding a back alleyway, he dressed as fast as he could. The biggest problem was the shoes. Even in the hugely wide size that he'd taken with him, his feet still barely fit. But at least he'd be able to manage.

Now fully dressed, with his coat drawn around him and his hat still low, he made his way over to his destination. There, on a street corner, trying to stay outside of the pool of light showing down from the street light, he peered up toward a second-story window of a small row house he knew oh-so-well. There was no sign of life there, but considering the lateness of the evening, that wasn't surprising.

He stepped over toward a phone booth, picked up the phone, and then stared in frustration at the dial pad. Then he looked at his hands. His thick, clumsy, four-fingered hands. He touched several numbers experimentally and couldn't get his finger to press only one at a time. Finally, maneuvering his hand very carefully, he managed to press the "O" for operator with his little finger . . . if "little" could remotely be used to describe what his finger was at that moment.

The voice of James Earl Jones welcomed him and thanked him for using the equipment. "Don't mention it," said Ben, and then there was a click and the operator came on.

"I wanna make a collect call."

"You can do that by dialing 'O' followed by—"

"Yeah, it's the 'followed by' that's the problem, lady," Ben said.

"I don't understand, sir. Are you calling to report a broken phone . . . ?"

"Look," and Ben thought for a moment, and then said, "remember that movie with the guy who could only move his left foot? Well, that's kinda me. Getting you on the horn is about as much as I wanna push my luck."

"I'm very sorry, sir," said the operator, sounding contrite. "Tell me the number you want and I'll dial it for you."

"Yeah, okay, that'd be great." He rattled it off and then told her his name.

"Putting the call through now, sir. And sir, you might want to consider gargling with warm water or perhaps eating some chicken soup for that raspy throat."

"I'll get right on that."

He heard the phone ringing and looked up hopefully to the window. What if she slept through it? What if she was out for the evening? All sorts of possibilities occurred to him, and then he was gratified and relieved to see Debbie in the window, grabbing up the phone. He felt as if his heart was beating again for the first time in days.

"I have a collect call from 'Ben,' " the operator said. "Will you—"

"Yes, yes, oh God, yes!" Debbie said. "I accept!" The operator started to tell her to go ahead, but Debbie spoke right over her. "Ben! Baby . . . ?"

"Deb, it's me," he confirmed.

"I've been so worried! The news was all filled with these stories, and they were talking about accidents, and I haven't heard from you, and I didn't know what to think, and I've been praying and hoping and—"

"Look," he said firmly, trying to stem the torrent of words, "I need you to step out front."

"Out front?" It took a moment for what he was saying to fully register. "You home, baby? I got a surprise for you!"

He blinked hard, pushing away the stinging he felt in his eyes. Nice to know his tear ducts still worked, even if the timing couldn't be worse. "I got a surprise for you, too."

Debbie disappeared from the window. He could imagine her running down the stairs, and mentally counted off how long it would take her to get to the front door. He was more or less on target, for within a second of getting to "one," she threw open the door. She was wearing the blue silk robe he'd gotten her for her birthday, and was clutching a sign that read "Welcome Home." She looked right and left, trying to see where Ben was. Since he had stepped out of the phone booth and into the sheltering darkness, she wasn't spotting him at first. The chill air cut through her and she drew her robe tighter. "Ben?" she called. She turned and saw him then, a formless darkened mass standing under a tree. She squinted, trying to make out details. "Ben . . . ?" She took a step toward him.

"Don't come any closer for a sec," he said, and she obediently stopped where she was. "This is gonna be kind of a shock . . ." *Jeez, Grimm, could you understate it any more than that? Me gaining a hundred pounds would be a shock. Gaining a half a ton of rocky skin . . . that ain't a shock. That's full-blown cardiac arrest.* He paused, took a breath, and then said, "You remember when we said 'together forever no matter what'?"

She tried to force a smile, but it did not come easily. "Baby, you're scaring me."

He braced himself, realizing that to prolong the revelation would only get her more and more worked up, and not make the first sight of him any easier to take. He stepped forward, allowing the light of the nearest lamppost to bathe him.

All the blood drained from Deb's face as she stared

137

in horror at the rocky surface that covered his entire body. He was almost twice as big as he had been, hairless, his brow thick and distended, his eyes sunken. His craggy skin made him look like exactly what he was: one of the worst victims of radiation poisoning that had ever walked the earth. The fabric of his clothes was stretched to the limit to cover him, and his skin's rockiness was easily visible even through it. So it was painfully clear that his hideous condition was all over him.

Debbie stumbled back, not knowing what it was she was faced with. He couldn't blame her. He didn't know what he was either.

"Oh my G-G-G . . ." She couldn't even get the word "God" out. "What did you . . . do to Ben?"

He frowned, although his face was no longer capable of displaying such a subtle shift in expression. "Deb . . . it's me. It's still me."

Ben instinctively reached out toward her, wanting to quell her fears even though he was the one responsible for them. Just as instinctively, Debbie stumbled back, tears swelling in her eyes. She covered her mouth, trying to stifle the scream that was building within her.

He took a step toward her, desperate to make things better, but Debbie kept backing away. The "Welcome Home" sign had fallen from her grasp. She tripped over the trailing hem of her robe and stumbled into the street. A car bore down on her, and for an instant Ben stood paralyzed in horror. Fortunately enough, the car screeched to a halt several feet short of the fallen young woman. Ben moved toward her to help, but Deb scrambled to her feet, clutching her robe tightly around herself.

"Don't . . . don't . . . *don't touch me!*" she cried out.

And then she started to scream, and kept on screaming. Her shrieks awoke the neighbors, lights flickering on up and down the street, growing shouts and cries.

Ben looked at Debbie, and knew without a doubt that this had been a hideous mistake. Better that she had thought him dead. Better that he had died. She couldn't look at him without trembling.

"I love you, Deb," he whispered. With that, he turned away. The "Welcome Home" sign had blown around a bit to land right in front of him. He walked over it, nearly tearing it in half as he did so, and kept going without looking behind him. As he walked, for no reason that anyone could really articulate, every house he passed where people were looking out their windows or coming out onto their front stoops to determine what was what . . . all those people became very quiet. They couldn't see him clearly, they didn't completely understand what was happening. They simply fell silent in his presence, dimly aware that some great tragedy was right at their doorstep, but uncertain what it was or how to react.

10

THE SUN WAS RISING OVER THE VON DOOM COMPOUND, and Victor was not happy with the way matters were progressing.

He was busy packing his monogrammed Armani briefcase, and as he did so he made his displeasure evident to Leonard, standing nearby with a not-so-patient expression that he was careful to hide from Von Doom as much as possible.

"How the devil," Victor said, not for the first time, "did something matching the size and shape of Ben Grimm—as he was described to me when last seen— elude my supposedly crack search team?"

"He got lucky, sir," said Leonard.

Von Doom stopped what he was doing and looked over at Leonard with undisguised incredulity. "'Lucky'? That's it? That's the best you've got, is 'lucky'? Leonard, I don't pay my people what I pay them so that other people can be 'lucky.' I pay them to get the job done. If they can't, I get rid of them and bring in people who can get the job done. Is that going to be necessary here?"

"Absolutely not, sir," Leonard said stiffly.

"Good, I'm glad to hear that." Victor paused, touching the area that his bandage was covering. He was relieved to feel that the scar had not extended beyond the cover of the bandage. "Make sure you find Ben. Bring him back here, and keep it quiet. I don't need this to hit the press. I'm busy enough doing damage control over the things that have hit the press already. Speculation is already running rampant, but the fortunate thing is that speculation tends to burn itself out if additional fuel isn't provided for the fire. The last thing we need is for speculation to be ended and photographs of Ben . . . or whatever Ben's become to be splashed all over the tabloids. And speaking of damage control . . ."

"Yes, sir." He glanced at his organizer just to confirm. "You've got the mayor at eight, then a nine-thirty interview with the *Journal*—"

"Front page?" asked Victor.

"Top left, as you asked," Leonard assured him, and then he smiled. "Today, Wall Street. Tomorrow . . . who knows? Maybe Washington?"

Victor snapped shut his briefcase, preparing to head for conference room where the video conference with the mayor and telephone hookup with the *Journal* reporter would be held. He looked with faint disappointment at his aide. "Leonard," he said with a scolding tone, and then smiled thinly. "Think bigger."

* * *

Most of those driving along the Brooklyn Bridge that chilly morning didn't even think to glance upward, since they were naturally focused upon the road in front of them. For those who did happen to look up for some reason, there was an odd sight: a statue of some sort perched high atop one of the main towers. It looked like a grotesque distortion of *The Thinker*, carved in the same general shape but rocky and off-color. Most simply winced at the ugly, orange, garish object and looked away, wondering what genius in City Hall had commissioned such a monstrosity. Several vowed to write their congressmen, although interestingly none of them actually knew who that was. Some reckoned that it was one of those random art projects that occasionally surfaced around the city, such as when those oddly painted cows started cropping up all over the place. More than a few figured it was some sort of publicity stunt to promote a movie.

Exactly one person happened to get it right. It was a young boy named Collin, up from Florida visiting his Uncle Umar in Brooklyn. With his parents on the last leg of a sixteen-hour drive, it barely caught a flicker of attention when Collin stared up and out the back window and said, "There's a man up there."

His father rolled his eyes and his mother craned her neck to see where he was looking. "No, Collin," said his mother, mistaking it for a statue as others had, but not knowing what exactly it was intended to be a statue of. "That's not a man. It's some . . . thing."

The object of discussion and speculation, meanwhile, remained immobile on his perch, staring down at the water below, brooding, muttering. One of Ben Grimm's all-time favorite films was *Die Hard,* and he particularly loved the part where a beleaguered Bruce Willis, trapped within an air vent and surrounded by terrorists, echoes in sarcastic fashion his estranged wife's urgings to come out to Los Angeles and "have a few laughs". . . . advice that had, obviously, proven spectacularly awful.

Now Ben, who could completely sympathize, spoke in the same ironic singsong that Willis had adopted: "A few days in space, it'll be great, what's the worst that could happen?"

A pigeon who also apparently mistook Ben for a statue landed on his shoulder. Ben looked at the bird suspiciously and before he could say, "Don't you dare," the pigeon deposited a small white puddle of goo and then flapped away. He glanced heavenward at the pigeon cruising past and glared at it. "Perfect. Thanks," he said. The pigeon kept going, unconcerned.

It took a few minutes for Ben to notice a new sound, mixed in with the rolling of the river below and the general traffic noise. It was sobbing. Someone nearby was crying. Confused, Ben glanced down and saw, farther down on the curve of the main cable, a bald, bearded man in—of all things—a business suit. He was holding a briefcase so tightly that Ben thought for a moment he had his child stuffed in there. But then he tossed it out and away. It snapped open and various papers fluttered out, drifting in the wind while the briefcase splashed down, down into the water. It didn't sink, as Ben would have thought, but floated away.

Well, at least it wasn't his kid, Ben thought with dark amusement. Obviously this was some sort of symbolic gesture the guy was displaying . . . not that Ben knew, or cared, what he was intending to symbolize. But then he saw the guy slowly, wobblingly, get to his feet. Obviously he was preparing himself for something, and it wasn't difficult to guess what that might be. If he was planning to try and get back down to safety, he could just slide carefully on his belly along the length of the cable, down to the roadway. There could only be one reason why he was trying to stand, and that was that he was gathering his resolve to follow the untimely demise of his briefcase.

If he'd noticed Ben at all, he'd probably thought, as others had, that Ben was just some sort of weird statuary. When Ben spoke, he did it carefully, not wanting to be abrupt and startle the guy. "You think you got trouble? Take a good look, pal. How bad could it be?"

The man turned, confused, not sure where the voice had come from. He looked down, saw nothing there. Then he looked up and past Ben, as if someone were crouched behind what he perceived as a large, rocky orange statue and speaking to him from there. Then he chanced to look into Ben's eyes and realized that Ben was looking right back at him. Ben inclined his head slightly to acknowledge that he was, indeed, as alive as the man. "You had to choose my spot, didn't you," Ben grumbled.

The businessman stumbled, terrified. It was a measure of how deeply ingrained the survival instinct was in humans, that a man intending to throw himself off a bridge reflexively clutched for support to avoid falling because his focus had shifted.

Ben stood immediately. Despite how high up he was, it didn't bother him. One didn't become a test pilot if one was scared of heights. Besides, what could happen? He'd fall off and die? Wasn't the worst idea he'd heard. He wasn't actively courting Death; it was more like he'd drawn a circle around Death's ad in the Personals section and was considering dropping her a line and saying he was interested in getting together. Still, there was no reason to let some other guy jump if he could prevent it.

But events were rapidly outstripping Ben's ability to head them off. The man was scrambling backward as fast as he could down the cable, but he was so panicked that he lost his grip. Ben lunged for him, but he was too late. The businessman fell toward the street below. The only thing that prevented him from crashing heavily to the asphalt and dying from the impact was that he ricocheted off the support cables, grabbing at them, falling from one to the other like an incredibly clumsy Tarzan through the forest branches. The result was that he landed on the road below battered, bruised, and somewhat the worse for wear, but very much alive.

His condition was in serious danger of going in the opposite direction.

A truck was bearing down on him. It wasn't a full rig, but instead simply a cab without a trailer attached. But if it hit the businessman, it would leave him a smear on the road nevertheless. Although the screeching of brakes reached Ben's ears—or whatever it was in the side of his head that served as ears—it was clear that the truck wasn't going to be able to stop in time.

"This is *really* not my day," said Ben even as he vaulted off the main cable and landed squarely between the businessman and the speeding truck. The asphalt crumbled from the impact, his feet sinking in slightly, as he swept the guy out of the way of certain death with one arm.

In the split instant that Ben was about to try and get over to the pedestrian walkway and clear of the traffic, he realized he wasn't going to make it. He had no idea just how durable he was, or whether he could possibly survive the impact. The only thing he knew for sure was that he had time for nothing except to brace himself while shielding the businessman from the impact.

He twisted at the waist, holding the would-be suicide tightly against his chest, and presented his shoulder and upper back to the truck, like the world's toughest football blocker going up against a two-ton offensive line. He shut his eyes, not knowing what to expect. Every bit of common sense told him that the truck would run him over, or knock him on his ass, or kill him outright. No one with a lick of brains would have given him a chance in hell of surviving, and the notion that the truck would come out the worse for the collision was outright laughable.

Oddly, no one was laughing when that was exactly what happened.

The irresistible force slammed into the immovable

object, and this time around in that classic match-up, it was the force that gave way. The truck plowed into Ben, and Ben's feet skidded back maybe two inches, but no more than that. Instead the truck buckled, crumbled. The grillwork was an instant casualty, as was the bumper, and the entire front section of the cab was crushed all the way to the windshield, the rear tires snapping up and popping a wheelie. The truck hung there in midair for a moment, nose down, back up, looking as it had just been dropped headfirst from a great height, or perhaps sent through a car compactor.

Then centrifugal force and the driver's futile attempt to avoid the collision caught up with the proceedings, with the result that the truck fishtailed across several lanes of traffic. Other cars desperately tried to get out of the way and failed. One crashed into another, and yet another, and like a huge chain reaction of dominos, the Brooklyn Bridge quickly degenerated into total chaos.

As the taxicab sped toward the Brooklyn Bridge, Johnny and Sue were seated in the back while Reed was up front with the driver. Reed's mind was racing a mile a minute, trying to figure out what they would do when (not if, he kept telling himself, but when) they caught up with Ben. What could they possibly say that would be of comfort to him? Could Reed look him in the eye and tell him that everything was going to be all right, considering that Reed hadn't yet figured out what had happened to them, much less how to reverse it?

"What if he won't come with us?" Sue asked from the back.

"He will."

"What if you're wrong? What if he's not going to Brooklyn?"

"*I'm not wrong!*"

"Hey!" Johnny said sharply. "Don't yell at her. You don't have to be yelling at her!"

"I'm sorry," Reed said, and meant it. He rubbed the bridge of his nose, fighting off exhaustion. "I haven't slept . . ."

"Yeah, well it's not like *any* of us had an easy night last night, Reed," Johnny reminded him. "So just lighten up, okay?"

"Johnny, enough," Sue interrupted. "I think we should all just cut each other some slack right n— Why are we slowing down?"

"Looks like traffic . . ." said the cabbie, as the taxi rolled to a halt, surrounded by unmoving cars on all sides. He leaned forward and groaned. "Aw, nuts, just my luck. An accident. Big one, looks like . . ."

"Figures," Johnny said. "I always said Ben Grimm was an accident waiting to happen. So naturally it . . ." His voice trailed off as he saw Reed's and Sue's expressions. "Wait . . . you don't think he's actually involved in . . ."

"Reed . . . ?" Sue looked at him questioningly.

"Hold on," said Reed, rolling down the window.

"There's nothing to look at!" the cabbie warned him. "Just tons of cars! And even if the accident isn't in this lane, we're gonna be stuck behind all the frickin' rubberneckers! If there's one thing I can't stand, it's rubberneckers! You ain't one of those types, are you?"

"Funny you should ask," Johnny piped up.

Reed, ignoring the exchange, stuck his head out the window and extended his neck. His head rose to about a foot above the roof of the cab, and there he saw a gargantuan entanglement . . . and an orange-skinned behemoth squarely in the middle of the whole thing. He noticed that people in surrounding cars were gaping in open astonishment at him, but he couldn't be concerned about that. His only worry at that moment was Ben.

Ben's only worry at that moment was the truck driver.

There was the howling of a trapped police car a short distance away, but it was as immobilized in the traffic as everyone else was. The cops' siren was wailing in indignant impotence, and who knew when something really useful, such as an ambulance, might manage to make it through.

Moreover, just to make things as bad as they could possibly be, Ben spotted sparks flickering from the truck's battery box. Miraculously the fuel tank hadn't ruptured, but there was still enough spilled gas to present major problems if the sparks hit. The driver was sitting there looking dazed. The air bag had deflated, enabling him to survive the impact, but he was pinned inside since the cab had crunched inward on both sides. There was blood oozing from a large gash in his forehead, and his eyes were glazed.

"Aw, you gotta be kiddin' me," groaned Ben, and as he started forward, there was suddenly a sizzling rush of air, and flames sprang up. They were all around him, and they were spreading to other cars that had crashed up against the truck. The other drivers were, fortunately enough, conscious, and able to get clear. But now panic was beginning to build as the growing danger to all concerned became evident even to those drivers who weren't part of the accident, but merely stuck. Sooner or later, the licking flames would strike a leaking gas tank, at which point the whole place was going to become an inferno.

Ben simply couldn't allow himself to think that far ahead. Instead he focused on one calamity at a time. Drawing up next to the crushed truck cab, he swiped through the shattered window and punched the air bag. Despite the bag's endurance, he popped it as easily as one would a kid's balloon. The driver didn't scream upon seeing him, probably because he was too dazed to have the faintest idea where he was, much less what was going on.

Reaching down to unbuckle the seat belt, Ben once again found his fingers too large for the job. "A little help here!" he urged the driver. "You wanna hit that button, sir?"

The driver continued to be nonresponsive. Ben's frustration built and built . . .

. . . and then something clicked in his head. He realized that he was inside a body that could withstand high impact from a truck with no visible damage, but he was still thinking with the mind of someone who was limited to purely human strength. For an instant, the image of Alexander the Great flickered through his mind, famously solving the problem of untying the puzzling Gordian knot through the simple expedient of declaring, "What does it matter how I loose it?" yanking out his sword, and slicing the thing in half.

The same words occurred to Ben now, and although he didn't utter them, his solution to the problem of the jammed door and locked seat belt would have been applauded by Alexander.

With so little effort that it almost frightened him, Ben Grimm ripped the door clear of the cab. It offered token resistance and a squeal of protesting metal, but otherwise Ben had it out in an instant and flipped it aside like a poker chip. Then he gripped the entire seat and tore it clear of the cab, driver and all. The driver's head lolled about slightly like that of a drunken man, but if the guy's head wasn't coming off his neck, that was good enough for Ben.

"Freeze! Put the man and the seat down!"

Ben didn't move a muscle, but he did risk a slow turn of his head even though he pretty much knew what he was going to see before he saw it. Sure enough, a group of New York's finest were standing there with their guns out, and more were heading in their direction. Ben locked eyes with one so young that he had to be a rookie. The rookie's gun was trembling violently, as if it was everything he could do not to drop it.

Why shouldn't the kid be terrified? Why shouldn't all

of them? They go to cop school, they're trained to deal with junkies and pickpockets and muggers and murderers. What could possibly prepare them to face down what they were now seeing: an orange, stone-covered monster surrounded by carnage and flame, with a bloodied man being held over his head by one hand in a frightening display of strength.

When he was a kid, Ben had always loved Saturday afternoons, tuning in to the local TV station because they always ran grade-B monster movies, hosted by some pseudo-scary guy in monster makeup. And now here he was, living the horror, stepping out of one of those movies big as life and twice as ugly. The only thing missing was a frightened young woman, a wide-eyed kid, and an eggheaded scientist who wanted to stop the monster without killing it, all in the name of science.

Reed's main imperative was to find a way to stop this disaster from escalating before someone was killed . . . with the most likely someone being Ben.

He moved forward as quickly as he could, stepping through the halted traffic, moving against the stream of bodies that were trying to go in the opposite direction. He glanced behind himself to make sure that Sue and Johnny were still with him. They were, but Sue looked frightened at what she was seeing, while Johnny was wide-eyed with amazement.

He turned back and saw that the smoke had briefly cleared away, thanks to a steady wind, and he was able to see Ben clearly for the first time. Police officers had him surrounded, their guns out as if they were ready to form a firing squad and execute him right then and there. They weren't shooting, however, and it was entirely possible that the only reason they hadn't started doing so was that Ben was holding a man above his head who would likely be hit should a volley of bullets begin flying.

Seeing Ben so mutilated by the effects of the cosmic rays, Reed felt as if he'd been gut-punched. *Please don't let Johnny make it worse with smart-guy remarks,* he thought, and he was about to say as much to Sue's sibling. It turned out not to be necessary. Johnny was shaking his head and muttering, "Not even Ben deserves that."

Ben hadn't spotted his friends approaching. With all the smoke blowing around and the guns pointed at him, it was natural that his attention was elsewhere. Slowly Ben put the seat down with the driver still on it. Reed, assessing the situation, immediately realized that the man owed Ben his life, but obviously the police weren't seeing it that way. Apparently Ben figured it out as well, because the moment the driver was down and out of harm's way, Ben darted behind the truck. The cops tried to follow him, but flames pushed them back.

It was painfully obvious to Reed what was happening. Ben wasn't concerned about the police shooting at him. Reed had spotted the crushed truck with the Ben-shaped dent in it. If a speeding truck hadn't been able to injure Ben, the odds were that small flying metal pellets would not present a problem. No, Ben was trying to get away from them because he didn't want anyone to see him the way he was. He wasn't interested in taking credit for saving a man. He wanted to avoid the shame he felt in his physical appearance.

Then smoke obscured Reed's view of the scene once more. Before he and the others could get any closer, several bridge policemen appeared, herding the crowd away from the accident. They were drawing closer to Reed, Sue, and Johnny, clearly ready to send them in the same direction that the rest of the crowd was heading . . . namely, away from Ben.

"What now?" Sue asked. "Reed . . . what do we do?"

Reed stood there, paralyzed, wanting to lead, wanting to know what to do. But he had no idea. He already had a sense that he and the others had powers that would enable them to do pretty much whatever they wanted, regardless of policemen ordering them about. But he had such a deeply ingrained respect for authority that the notion of trying to override the orders of law enforcement was almost unthinkable. Besides, they already had enough problems; what good would getting arrested do . . . ?

Sue moved in closer to him and said in a low but firm voice, "Ben's out there. Let's go get him."

And that was all he really needed to hear. If Sue was in his corner, then he realized with a surge of confidence that he was more than capable of handling whatever else wound up being thrown at them.

So when an approaching bridge cop shouted at him, "Maybe you didn't hear me! Those cars are gonna blow sky-high any second—!" he was completely undaunted.

"Look," Reed said firmly, "we've got a friend out there in trouble. We need to get to him before—"

Another cop, bigger, wider, surlier, said with equal determination, "Nobody gets past this point."

Reed considered simply trying to overwhelm the police officers with the sheer force of his elastic body. But he wasn't sure exactly what he could do yet, how pliable he was, or whether he was bulletproof should it come to that. Besides, assaulting an officer was a crime. He wouldn't hesitate to do it if Ben's life was on the line and there was no other way. In this instance, though, there was indeed another way. Why go for force when subtlety would do just as well?

He turned to Sue and gave her a significant look. She returned it blankly. "What?"

"We need to get past them," he muttered.

It took a moment or two more for what he was saying to her to get through, and then it dawned on her. Her mouth puckered in an "ooooo" fashion, and then her face became a mask of concentration. Slowly but surely, she began to fade out.

"What the hell is this?" demanded the first cop. "A magic show?"

It was perfect. Sue, invisible, could maneuver past the police, get to Ben, let him know that help was here and guide him to where Reed and Johnny would be waiting for him. Together they could explain what happened, sort things out, and make people realize that they weren't dealing with some sort of bizarre monster but instead a horribly unfortunate man.

Except that Sue's clothes weren't turning invisible along with her. The cops were gaping, trying to figure out how she was pulling off the optical illusion. "Sue, your clothes," Reed said under his breath. "Lose them."

"What?" came her voice, and then she must have looked down and realized. "Oh . . . but Reed! It's freezing!"

"Sue, please, there's no time . . ."

"What a time not to be drunk," muttered Sue.

Reed had the distinct feeling from her tone of voice that she wasn't thrilled with the idea, but she was as determined to aid Ben as Reed was. Quickly she unbuttoned her blouse, and her pants dropped to a heap around her feet. Floating underwear hovered in midair, and then they suddenly lurched forward as Sue apparently lost her footing for a moment. She lost her concentration as well and suddenly Reed was greeted with the sight of Sue Storm, fully visible, in bra and panties. Her arm was around her back as she had been clearly about to undo the bra, and perhaps it was that daunting prospect of nudity that had caused her to lose focus.

Whatever the reason, she was now in full view of the police, Reed, passersby, and—most unfortunately— Johnny, whose face went the color of curdled milk. "This is so wrong in so many ways," he said.

Realizing that everyone could see her perfectly, Sue froze in place, mercifully not releasing the hooks on the bra. Reed's mind raced. *Say something appropriate and helpful.*

"You've been working out," he observed.

Sue glared at him. "Shut up."

Okay, that apparently wasn't it.

She took a deep breath, closed her eyes, focused, concentrated with all her will. Nothing happened. Embarrassed, furious, she looked daggers at him and said in a steadily rising voice, "Any more ideas, Reed? Maybe *you* should strip down next, see how it feels to have fifty people staring—"

And she disappeared entirely, leaving only floating underwear as a guide to her whereabouts. The collective gasp from everyone around her was all the cue she needed to realize what had happened. "Oh well then . . ."

An instant later, the underwear was on the ground and Sue Storm was nowhere to be seen. The cops turned and looked at Reed in complete astonishment. Reed shrugged as if he was just as surprised as anyone else. Johnny, for his part, still looked dazed and mumbled, "I'm gonna need *serious* therapy."

There was a cough from nearby, and the cops looked in its direction. There was the briefest glimpse of a female form outlined by wafting smoke and then it was gone again. The cops turned around back to start demanding answers of Reed and Johnny, but they were too slow. Reed and Johnny had also disappeared.

Ben wanted nothing but to get off the bridge, but that seemed to be problematic at best. He toyed with the idea of just jumping off, suspecting that the fall might not hurt him. On the other hand, he was so heavy that he might well sink into the riverbed and be completely unable to get back to the surface before he drowned.

Besides, he wanted to find a way to help the people all around him. Which sounded like a futile endeavor considering that when he came near them, they just ran screaming in the other direction from which he was trying to guide them. They were just as likely to charge into fire, flame, and death to get away from him as they were to appreciate whatever rescue efforts he might extend.

He crouched behind a truck, trying to decide what to do. He was extremely annoyed with himself because of what was going through his head at that moment, yet he couldn't help it. He kept thinking that if only Reed was there to do the thinking for him, he wouldn't have to deal with this mess. Reed would tell him what to do, and Ben would be just fine with that.

Except Reed wasn't there, and besides, Ben was only in this disaster because of Reed. In fact, if Reed did show his face here, Ben might just as likely try to break his scrawny neck.

Suddenly Reed's face was directly in front of him. Ben let out a startled yelp and cried out, "What the—!"

"Ben, are you okay?" Reed demanded.

Ben was about to reply, but his mind was still upon his desire to throttle Reed. That was why it took a moment to sink in that Reed's head was there, but his body was nowhere in the immediate vicinity.

He stepped back and gaped at Reed in bewilderment. He looked in the direction of where his neck was stretched and saw the rest of his body wrapped around a car, perhaps to provide counterweight so that his extended head wouldn't cause him to tip over. As if this bizarre sight wasn't enough, Reed appeared to have a bundle of woman's clothing wrapped up in one arm.

"Am *I* okay?" Ben demanded, trying to give a reasoned answer in the face of so inane a question. "You wanna explain that?" He gestured at Reed's elongated neck and body, although he didn't even want to begin to approach the woman's clothing issue. Then he pointed at himself. "Or this? What the hell am I? 'Cause I sure ain't Ben anymore!"

Reed opened his mouth, but it was obviously more out of an automatic reflex, for no answers were forthcoming.

"Reed!" came Sue Storm's voice. "Ben! Look out!"

Ben's head snapped around, his thoughts tumbling out of control. Sue was there? What the hell was Sue doing there? And where was she? Maybe it was just all the smoke and confusion, but he couldn't see her at all.

What he was able to see, however, was a car inches away with the gas tank flaming.

Aw, crap, thought Ben, just as the car exploded.

That was all that was needed, the final match thrown on the powder keg of destruction. Empty cars began to explode, one after the other in a thunderous chain reaction. Flames mushroomed high, the intensity of the heat growing exponentially.

Ben didn't know where to look first.

Reed was to his right, sweeping his arms out wide in either direction to shield screaming pedestrians. Ben could see their faces delineated against Reed's apparently pliable body, as if they were shoved up against the tight rubber of a balloon.

Off to the left, a pack of attractive young women were shrieking, their faces smeared with soot. They were so terrified that they had stopped moving altogether, instead clutching at one another in mutual fear as if that would do them one shred of good. Ben's instinct was to head toward them, but then he saw Johnny . . .

Johnny's here too? What is this, a freakin' family outing?

. . . and he was gliding toward them . . .

Gliding . . . ?

What the hell?

It was insane, but it was also true. Johnny wasn't simply leaping through the air. The arc of his jump was increasing beyond the point where gravity should have been working to pull him back down again. Instead he was gliding forward, maintaining a parallel course to the ground, his arms flung out in either direction as if he were walking on air, gaining lift with each passing moment.

The moment he drew within range of the women, he spun in midair, landed, throwing his arm around the women to shield them from a belch of flames heading right at them. It was a brave, hopeless, suicidal gesture, because he could shield the women all he wanted, but there was no one to shield him. Sure enough, the flames enveloped Johnny's back, and Ben cried out in alarm and terror. The kid had been obnoxious, a pest, a complete disrespectful smartass, but to be burned alive in a futile attempt to . . .

. . . to . . .

Now what the hell . . . ? Has the whole world gone nuts?!

The flame was not injuring Johnny. It scorched up the back of his shirt, but that was all. Instead the flames flared brightly upon his back for a few moments, and then . . . they didn't just go out. They dwindled and looked for all the world as if Johnny was absorbing them into his back. Within seconds they were gone completely, and Johnny gave the girls a cheesy smile as if this were the most normal thing that could possibly have happened.

Then he heard another cry and knew instantly that it was Sue. He looked in the direction of it just in time to see her buttoning the front of her shirt, as if she'd just finished getting dressed. The clothes looked familiar, and he realized it was the bundle that Reed had just been carrying. Why had Sue taken her clothes off? Why had Reed picked them up? Ben's mind raced with possibilities, some of them rather intriguing, despite the gravity of the situation.

Even as that happened, he started toward Sue. She threw her arms up instinctively, as if she could somehow ward off the ferocity of the explosions that were heading toward her. The air started rippling in front of her, and at first Ben thought it was some sort of effect caused by the escalating heat. Then he realized that the rippling was originating, not from the burning vehicles, but from Sue herself. The distortion spread, going further and wider, actually appearing to encompass the area of the explosions.

Sue looked just as surprised as Ben was. Whatever it was she was doing, it was causing her tremendous strain. Blood was trickling down her nose, and she was trembling. Ben was only a few feet away from her, blocked by a pile of abandoned vehicles. As he shoved them out of the way, he witnessed the incredible sight of Sue creating, out of thin air, some sort of . . . of force field. There was no other way to describe it. A sphere of pure energy, maybe even of sheer willpower, that contained the force of the blasts generated by the exploding cars, deflecting it and shoving it away from herself and the people . . .

We're freaks . . . we're all freaks . . .

Ben watched in alarm as Sue collapsed from the stress as the concussive force she'd contained rebounded off the street . . .

. . . and struck an oncoming fire engine.

Oh, better and better . . .

It was pick-your-poison day. If Sue hadn't somehow, amazingly, fantastically managed to deflect the force of the explosion, dozens of people would be lying around as little more than sacks of meat with shattered bone where their skeletons had been. But because she had accomplished the impossible, the resulting focused concussive blast had deflected the emergency vehicle that had managed to wend its way through the debacle to provide aid.

Slewing sideways, the fire engine's tail slammed through the bridge's guard rail, shredding it like paper. The entire rear section, the bed, swung out and around, carried by momentum. The firemen clung onto the sides like bats, for the bed was moving too quickly for them to leap off without risking being killed. Better that they had taken their chances since they now found themselves hanging high over the water, hundreds of feet above almost certain death.

The truck teetered as the fireman driving it raced the front wheels, desperately trying to find traction that would yank the entire vehicle forward. Give the man credit; he could have just leaped clear. Instead he gunned the engine again and again, the tires spinning helplessly, determined not to abandon his people.

Ben Grimm wasn't about to abandon them either.

He charged forward, this time an orange-skinned tackle. He grabbed at the chauffeur's cab, sank one fist into the metal and gripped the cab's undercarriage with the other, grasping onto a tow ring that was large enough for even his oversize fingers. Ben had no idea how much he weighed, but it was clear that the fire engine weighed more, because it started to drag him forward. He dug his heels into the pavement, but the dangling fire engine continued to pull on him, hauling him against his will. He had, however, copious amounts of will where that came from. He redoubled his efforts, his heels digging grooves into the street.

He saw desperate firemen on the truck trying to save themselves. They were gripping onto the boom of the

163

lowered tower ladder, hauling themselves up hand over hand. Storage compartments snapped open as the equipment within slammed against them. As a result, the firemen swung themselves this way and that to avoid falling axes, helmets, fire extinguishers . . . all items designed to aid them, and all now deadly dangerous. Horrifyingly, the tower ladder snapped free from its moorings, swinging away and to the side of the bed. The firemen who'd been clinging to the boom now found themselves even farther away from the bridge than when they'd started. One lost his grip completely, tumbling, almost falling off and into the river. At the last second, he grabbed the railing that extended from the bucket at the end and clung onto it, his legs pinwheeling in midair.

Ben screamed, both from the incredible strain that he was undertaking and from the thought that these men were about to plummet to their deaths and he couldn't do anything about it . . .

No. You don't get to freakin' admit that you can't do anything about it. You just get it done. You get the job done! Get it done, Grimm! Get it done!

Every shred of common sense told him that what he was undertaking simply couldn't be accomplished. But he pushed it all aside, dumped it from his mind. His muscles rippled. He gritted his teeth, closed his eyes, and envisioned himself pulling the fire engine back to safety. He played the scenario in his mind over and over even as firemen screamed for help, even as metal creaked, even as his feet were dragged inch by agonizing inch toward the edge of the bridge.

Then the drag ceased. Ben could scarcely believe it, but didn't take the time to dwell upon it. Instead he flexed his knees slightly, still using visualization to focus his mind, his muscles, his heart upon what needed to be done. He took a deep breath, let it out, and then pulled in the opposite direction. At first nothing happened. For half a heartbeat, the thought that he couldn't drag it back flittered through his consciousness. That all he could do was just keep the fire engine suspended for a short time before he would eventually lose his grip. Then he returned to visualizing what needed to be done, and took his first, agonizing step backward. He cried out at the strain but took a second step back as he did so. Then a third step, a fourth. He felt as if he were fighting an epic battle, sympathizing with Sisyphus pushing that damned rock or Hercules rerouting a river.

It might well have been that every step he took was the expected twelve inches one usually saw in a measured foot, yet paradoxically the fire engine moved merely an inch at a time. But move it did, and whether it was an inch or a centimeter, at least it was moving in the direction that Ben wanted it to go. His footsteps were no longer tentative. Instead each one was a solid *thud*, cracking the pavement with each downward thrust.

Then it happened all in a sudden rush as, with a final ear-shattering howl of agonized effort, Ben sensed the momentum shifting to his favor and undertook a final Hail Mary, all or nothing yank. The gamble paid off as the fire engine slid all the up and forward onto the bridge. It teetered on the edge and then the front section slammed down onto the road surface. Some firemen tumbled off the fire engine into the street, others rolled all the way from the top of the ladder down and over the front, even falling over Ben himself.

Ben released his grip, his arms and legs suddenly going numb from exhaustion. He stumbled back and fell to the ground, gasping for air. At that point he felt as if he could have just lain there for several days.

Then he heard one of the most distinctive sounds in the world: the hammer of a gun being cocked. More correctly, a large number of gun hammers. Slowly, with more effort than he would have thought necessary, he managed to raise his head and focus his blurring vision.

He was ringed by police officers who had their guns drawn, watching him warily. They had seen what he had just managed to do, but their perceptions of his accomplishments were no doubt filtered by what they were seeing in his monstrous form. Memory and belief were tricky things, and it was entirely possible that—in their minds—they had already convinced themselves that Ben had been the one who had nearly thrown the fire engine off the bridge in the first place.

Out the corner of his eye, he could see Reed just beyond the perimeter. Sue had fainted and Reed was supporting her, calling her name. Ben couldn't hear Reed, though. He saw his mouth moving but there was a rushing of air, a rising pounding within his head that drowned out everything else.

It seemed, in Ben's exhaustion, that all the barrels

of the guns aimed at him blended into one huge barrel the size of a howitzer. *Fine. Go ahead. Shoot. Probably won't do any good, but hey, maybe you'll get lucky,* Ben thought. A different noise was starting to make its presence known through the buzzing in his head. It sounded vaguely like running water and he thought at first that it had something to do with the river far below. Then his mind started to sort it out and he realized that it was the sound of . . .

No, that's too much, it couldn't be . . .

. . . hands banging together. Applause. Slow, steady, building. The gun muzzles receded from one large one back into an assortment of smaller ones, and then the guns were slowly put away as Ben saw the policemen staring at the firemen. The firemen were the ones who were applauding, approaching Ben with clear relief and gratitude. Taking their cue from New York's bravest, the bystanders joined in the impromptu ovation of support and appreciation.

Reed, Johnny, and Sue seemed surprised and appreciative of the reaction, even touched by it. Ben, on the other hand, was all too aware of the many eyes upon him. He didn't want applause. He wanted somewhere to hide.

The firemen were extending coats to Johnny and Sue, who took them gratefully and draped them over themselves in the cold morning air.

And then Ben saw something so unexpected, so insane, that he had to take a moment to make sure that it was genuine rather than some sort of hallucination caused by exhaustion or inhaling smoke or something else like that.

It was Debbie.

How the *hell* was it Debbie? What was she doing there?

Then, for the first time, he saw a news helicopter come swinging by, the cameras right on him. It was the traffic copter for that stupid morning news show. He had no idea how long it had been there, but if it had been for any length of time at all, then Ben's image had been out on the airwaves for who knew how many minutes? And since the house wasn't far from the Brooklyn Bridge, she could easily have arrived on foot to see . . .

. . . him?

Suddenly all his exhaustion was forgotten. Adrenaline surged through Ben with such ferocity that he felt as if he could have picked up three fire engines and juggled them. She was there. Debbie was there. She had come to him, sought him out. She had seen his heroism first-hand, had realized how wrong she had been. She had come to tell him that she was willing to look past the grotesque exterior he had acquired. That she was going to stick with him for better or worse, just as they'd intended.

Debbie was crouching for some reason. She seemed to be placing something on the ground. As he approached her, she backed away, blending in with the crowd and vanishing into it. He saw that she'd left something on the ground. It was glittering in the morning light, shining like a small sphere of fire.

Ben arrived where Debbie had been and looked down. Her engagement ring was at his feet.

Slowly he reached for it. He felt like a balloon that had just been blown up and was now deflating just as quickly. His massive fingers tried to pick the ring up. They couldn't. He felt hopeless and pathetic, and then his hand squeezed into a fist as he prepared to bring it smashing down onto the ring. Diamonds are one of the hardest substances on earth? He'd see just how easy it was to pulverize one.

Then a hand came out of nowhere and snatched the ring from under Ben's fist before it could slam down upon it. He looked up, his eyes mirrors of his misery. Reed wrapped his elastic fingers around the diamond ring and said, in a calm voice filled with conviction, "I swear to you . . . I will do everything in my power until there is not a breath left in me. You are going to be Ben again."

Ben Grimm had never wanted to believe something so much in his entire life . . . and had never had so much difficulty doing so.

Victor Von Doom was having serious trouble believing what he was seeing.

He sat in his office, staring at his big-screen plasma TV that was guaranteed—so it was said—to make him feel as if he were right there at the scene of whatever he might be watching. If Victor were at the scene of what he was watching right now, he'd strangle the lot of them with his bare hands.

There was a crowd of firemen applauding Reed, Ben, Johnny, and Sue. The four of them were standing there, making vaguely heroic poses, waving to the people, hogging the spotlight that should rightly and properly have been on the efforts of the man who was footing the bill for their shenanigans.

Victor didn't notice that Leonard had entered his office until he spoke up. His gaze flickering toward his aide, Victor saw that Leonard was holding a phone in his hand and looking as if he wished anyone else but himself was there. "Uh, sir . . ." he said tentatively. "Larry King called, to cancel." He glanced at the events being depicted on the television screen and nodded toward it in acknowledgment. "Apparently there's a bigger story."

Mouthing the words "a bigger story" in imitation of Leonard, Victor turned back to the TV screen just in time to see Reed draping his arm around Sue's shoulders. A cold, dark fury roiled within him and slowly, very slowly, he thumped his fist repeatedly on the desk. Who the hell did Reed Richards think he was? That . . . insect. That gnat. That nothing. Flaunting his obsession with Sue on television, seeking to humiliate Von Doom in front of millions of people. Of all the—

That was when he noticed that his fist was making an odd sound when it thudded against his desk . . . a sort of clacking noise. Slowly he raised his fist and stared at it.

Small shards of metal were poking through the flesh. For the first time since this entire insanity had begun,

Victor Von Doom gazed at the changes that cosmic radiation had wrought upon him and didn't mentally recoil.

Instead it began to occur to him that this could represent a major opportunity if only he opened his mind to it and accepted all the possibilities.

He looked back once more at Reed with his arm around Sue and decided that opening his mind might be far easier than he'd previously thought.

11

AN IMPROMPTU COMMAND CENTER HAD BEEN SET UP near the base of the bridge. There was a series of police tents, surrounded by emergency vehicles, news vans, and fire engines. It was sort of an emergency holding area, thrown together and surrounded by police officers who were primarily expending their energy in keeping crowds, curiosity seekers and, most important, the press away.

Reed felt exhausted even though the day was barely hours old. He and the others had been answering a nonstop barrage of questions from representatives of the police department and, once that was done, an entirely new round of questions from the fire department, and once they were done, the Bridge and Tunnel authority had had a few questions of their own. He could only feel a swell of relief that there hadn't been a sanitation truck involved in the mess. For a little while there, Reed had been worried they were going to be arrested. Fortunately enough the businessman whom Ben had rescued, inadvertently setting the entire chain of events into motion, had copped to his attempted suicide over—of all things—his wife leaving him because she complained he worked too hard. Reed wasn't a big fan of someone that pathetic being put under arrest, but hey, better him than Ben.

They'd just finished washing the smoke and dirt from themselves when Fire Chief Stan Lieber came over to them and said, "There's some folks outside, want to talk to you."

"We're not going public with this," Reed said firmly. "We're scientists, not celebrities."

Lieber just smiled at that, shaking his head. "Too late, son."

He flipped on a TV monitor to a station, seemingly at random. But as he turned from one channel to another, Reed quickly realized that randomness had nothing to do with it. Variations of the same news footage or commentators upon it were playing on every station. On one channel there was what appeared to be an editorial running. A man whom Reed recognized as the publisher of a major New York tabloid was thumping on a desk, his mustache bristling. The sound was off, but he clearly didn't look happy. Behind him was a graphic that featured the four of them moments after Ben had salvaged the fire engine, and a banner that read, "Fantastic Four: Threat or Menace?"

In answer to the unspoken question in Reed's mind, Lieber nodded in confirmation. "That's what they're calling you. The Fantastic Four."

"Nice!" said Johnny with more enthusiasm than Reed really wanted to hear.

Ben, off in the corner, just shook his head. "What, not the Fab Four? Or maybe the Doom Patrol?"

Johnny, for his part, headed straight for the exit. Before Reed could get to him, Sue fortunately enough stepped into his path and put a hand on his shoulder. "Johnny, slow down," she urged him. "Let's think this through a second."

Fortunately enough, this plea from his sister seemed to get through to him. Johnny stopped where he was, stroked his chin once . . . and then, exactly one second later, said briskly, "Okay. Done thinking." Whereupon he ran out before any of the others could stop him.

Reed exchanged glances with the others, each of them reaching the same conclusion immediately: Johnny could *not* be their spokesman. Not without healthy doses of Ritalin or something to rein him in.

They bolted from the tent as fast as they could to catch up with him, and were greeted with a barrage of cameras firing at them from all sides. Reed had known that there was press there. Certainly he'd seen scenes like this in movies and TV shows. But he had never experienced anything like this in real life, with reporters jockeying for position, shouting from all around, taking pictures from every direction.

Johnny stood in the forefront of the group with a lopsided grin, eating it up. His arms were spread wide, as if he were physically absorbing the attention. The others hung back a moment, daunted, and Lieber stepped in behind them. He was holding a cordless microphone in his hand. Obviously he'd taken steps in advance, realizing that he had an impromptu press conference on his hands and trying to do everything he could to keep matters in line. He asked, "So which one of you is the leader?"

Without hesitation, Johnny said, "That'd be me."

Lieber gave him a quick glance up and down, and then said, "No, seriously."

As Johnny looked crestfallen at the offhand dismissal, Sue and Ben—as one—turned to Reed. Reed took a step back, starting to shake his head, but the fire chief handed him the microphone without hesitation and said, "You're on, son. They'll want a statement."

Reed gulped hard. The reporters' shouting began to die down as, faced with the prospect of getting answers, they quieted and waited expectantly. Not wanting to look at them, he looked instead in Sue's direction. She nodded slowly, smiling, the confidence she had in Reed reflected in her eyes. The result was that a small bit of that confidence made its way over to Reed. Not much. Just enough for him to start speaking.

"Uh . . . during our recent mission to the Von Doom space station," he began, trying to prevent his voice from cracking, "we were exposed to as-yet-unidentified radioactive energy . . . most probably some kind of nucleotide compoun—"

Reed was just starting to get comfortable with the situation since he was on the verge of discussing the purely scientific considerations of their condition. But the reporters had not come for a science lecture, and Reed's knack for academia quickly became academic.

The crush of questions came from all directions as if a dam had just been kicked down. "What happened on the bridge?" "Does it hurt to stretch?" "Were you really on fire?" "Is it true that one of you can fly?"

Johnny seized upon the opportunity, calling out, "Working on it! And it's a lot harder—"

Obviously not wanting Johnny to seize control of the situation, Sue pulled the microphone over to herself, although she made sure it stayed in Reed's hand. "We don't know much more than you do at this point," she confessed. "Which is why we will be going directly to the lab, where we can diagnose our symptoms and—"

Reed winced inwardly, knowing that Sue had chosen the wrong word insofar as public perception was concerned. And he was right, because the reporters seized upon it like hounds on a steak. "Symptoms?" one called out, and another said, "So is this a disease?"

The subtext of the question was obvious: Can people catch it from being near you? Are we at risk? Is the general population of New York faced with an epidemic of being transformed into whatever-the-hell-you-are?

For his part, Reed was looking at Ben, guilt surging in him. Ben was lost in thought, staring at Deb's engagement ring glittering in his palm.

Ironically enough, it was Johnny who quelled the mood slightly. His enthusiasm was so boundless that it went a ways toward diminishing any notion that what had happened to them was unsafe or a threat in any way. "Symptoms?" he said dismissively. "If having powers is a disease, then yeah, we got it." He leaned forward, relishing the attention. "And we are gonna *blow your minds*. There's a new day dawning. The day of the *Fantastic Four!*"

The reporters, however, did not look entirely convinced that some sort of silver age had visited itself upon New York. One of them looked dubiously in Ben's direction and said, "That *thing* doesn't look too fantastic."

The comment didn't register on Ben at first, but the sudden silence that followed it allowed it to filter through. Slowly, like a rhino noticing something that he was considering charging at, Ben looked up at the reporter. His fists tightened and there was a sound like rocks crushing together. Reed felt his pain. Reporters felt the fear, and—collectively and unconsciously—they took a cautious step back.

A deep, abiding anger began to build in the pit of Reed's stomach, and he focused that controlled anger at the reporters. *That thing* indeed. "Ben Grimm," Reed said tightly, "is a genuine American hero who's been through a terrible ordea—"

Johnny stepped forward and said quickly, "What he's trying to say is, every team needs a mascot . . ."

Reed felt another quick flash of annoyance at Johnny, but then he saw the look in Johnny's eyes and realized that he wasn't endeavoring to be mean-spirited. He was just trying to deflect attention away from Ben's pain, to lighten the moment as best he could. It succeeded in that it made the reporters laugh, but failed miserably in that Reed could see it only made Ben feel worse about himself.

"Look," Reed said sharply, quelling the laughter instantly. "We went up to space to find a way to understand DNA, to cure disease, to save lives. Well, now it's *our* DNA, *our* disease, *our* lives on the line . . ." At which point Reed realized there was absolutely no point in continuing this exercise in spin control any longer. "Thank you, no more questions."

They headed back toward the tent, and the press, dissatisfied with the quick termination of the press conference, surged forward, shouting questions at the top of their lungs as if Reed hadn't announced that the session was over.

In response to the mass, Ben turned and held up one finger. Like a huge, rocky ET, he snarled, "Be nice."

It was enough to send the press backpedaling once more, but this time they weren't so deterred. They didn't hesitate to fire off as many photos as they could.

They retreated to the tent and Johnny said cheerfully, "That went well! Don't you think?"

The others glared at him.

"Or, y' know, maybe not," he amended.

Under ordinary circumstances, Victor Von Doom would sooner gouge out his eyes than waste a single optic nerve on perusing the *New York Post*. But it was hard to avoid doing so when it was being slid right under one's nose.

That was the case now in the conference room of AmerEuro Bank, Victor's largest and most dependable source of financial transactions. VDI and AEB had been "in bed" together for many years, and it had always been a most satisfying and profitable relationship all around.

Unfortunately, most—if not all—relationships run into problems every now and then, and as lead banker and powerbroker Ned Cecil was making clear, this was one of those times.

As the bankers and investors sat grouped around the conference table, their respective laptop computers humming in a way that made Von Doom briefly nostalgic for pads of legal paper, Cecil slid that day's edition of the *Post* over to Von Doom. Victor afforded it a perfunctory glance, staring at a black-and-white cover shot of "the Thing's" face that he had come to know all too well in the past twenty-four hours. He was waggling a finger in the direction of the camera. The headline read, FAN-TASTIC FOUR: NEW YORK'S NEWEST HEROES.

Von Doom had always known that Cecil wasn't wild about him as a person. But Victor had never given much of a damn about Cecil's personal likes and dislikes. As long as the association was mutually profitable, Cecil would just have to tolerate Von Doom's cockiness and perceived arrogance. The problem was that Von Doom knew that Cecil had always been sitting in the high grass, waiting, just *waiting*, for something to go wrong. Waiting for some slight weakness on Von Doom's part so that he could pounce with a mouth full of I-told-you-so's and claws poised to tear Victor down. Now he'd been handed that opportunity on a platter, thanks to Ben Grimm . . .

No. Thanks to Reed Freaking Richards, Victor thought dourly. He should never have gotten involved with Richards, not ever. When you start doing business with someone who has thoroughly screwed up their own life, it's only a matter of time before they screw yours up as well.

Of course, Victor knew the real truth of it. The main reason he'd given Reed Richards as much rope as he had was to underscore for Sue just how far he had come. He'd known that Reed represented a huge question mark in her life, and taking on Reed's project so that he could lord it over him, rub his nose in Victor's success, humiliate him in Sue's presence . . . it was all designed to drive a final nail into the coffin of their former relationship.

Instead it had backfired in every way that it possibly could. Reed's folly had created headline-grabbing superfreaks that were threatening Von Doom's empire, and it had brought Reed and Sue closer together than ever before. Supposedly to the victor go the spoils, but here everything that Victor had been left with was spoiled.

"Well, Victor," Cecil said, his sarcasm cutting through Von Doom's brief sojourn into his own thoughts and concerns. "The bank would like to congratulate you . . . on the fastest free-fall since the Depression. We can't even *give* your stock away."

The edges of Victor's mouth drooped a bit as he returned the sentiment. "Give it to me straight, Ned. Don't hold back."

Cecil waved unnecessarily at the newspaper. "You promised a cure-all, and came back with *this!* Who the hell wants to invest in a biotech company that turns its workers into *circus freaks!*"

All too aware of the subtle changes that had been working their way into his own physiology, Victor bridled inwardly at Cecil's unknowingly categorizing him as a "circus freak." He gripped the table tightly in order to steady himself, not wanting to lash out verbally nor snap and lose his temper in front of all these pencil-pushing money jockeys. As he did so, the laptops flickered suddenly, losing their feeds. The simultaneous reaction puzzled the bankers, but astounded Von Doom.

Victor released his grip on the table. Instantly the screens went back to normal. He looked at his hands. *Did I do that?* Von Doom wondered. It didn't seem possible. Some sort of magnetic burst . . . ?

Circus freak . . .

Once more he took a deep breath and steadied himself. He forced his smile to widen into something that looked vaguely sincere, even though it wasn't remotely. "Ned, you know I can turn this around . . ."

"You're going to have to," said Cecil, and the heads of the others bobbed up and down like so many bobble-headed toys. "Or we pull out. You've got the week, Victor. *One week . . .*"

Victor leaned toward him, his voice dripping with condescension. "You're enjoying this, aren't you."

For all that he considered Von Doom to be arrogant, Cecil wasn't above looking down his nose at Victor as he announced, "This meeting is over."

Von Doom glared at him, his blood boiling. Being dismissed out of hand by this . . . this nothing. This no one.

Yet he took it. He *had* to take it; he had no choice. Because the terrible truth was that he needed that week, and to lash out now would mean losing even that grace period . . . and possibly even losing far more.

Still, swallowing the attitude of Cecil and his cronies burned Victor like an open sore with acid poured on it, and as he strode away down the main corridor, Leonard following in his wake, Victor Von Doom was seething. "Goddamn bookkeeper doesn't know preferred stock from livestock," he snarled.

Leonard, for his part, never lost sight of business priorities. "Sir," he said, keeping his voice deferential as always, "Reed's comments at that press conference *killed* us. How are we going to turn this around?"

Victor's first instinct was to be angry at Leonard for even asking. It sounded as if Leonard doubted Von Doom's ability to bring this catastrophic state of affairs back to his favor, and Von Doom simply didn't tolerate such faithless attitudes from his subordinates. But even as he kept walking he realized that it was a legitimate question. Not "if" Von Doom could do it, but "how." Understandable. Victor Von Doom was the one with vision, not Leonard. And Victor's anger had made that vision remarkably clear.

"Very simple," he said. "I cure them. If I can cure

these . . . freaks," he stumbled over the word, still thinking of the personal application, and then kept going, "then I can cure anyone. What better way to restore my reputation?"

Leonard nodded in obvious approval, impressed by the simple elegance of the solution. Victor was as well. A man of action was Victor Von Doom, and no one was going to bring his empire crashing down around his ears. Not a bunch of bankers. Not Ned Cecil.

And certainly not Reed freaking Richards.

12

JOHNNY STORM COULDN'T BELIEVE THE NEGATIVITY HE was experiencing in the car as they rode in the police convoy toward Reed's research headquarters. It was *a police convoy*, for crying out loud! They were being treated as if they were the President, or top diplomats, or rock stars!

Yet everyone seemed pensive, afraid to say anything lest they somehow offend each other. Reed appeared even more lost in thought than he usually was, and Sue kept looking from one to the other, frustrated because of that helplessness. Ben wasn't in the car, but instead riding inside a police paddy wagon. Johnny had offered to ride in it with him, but Ben had simply glowered at him and growled, "Why? So you can make smart-mouth remarks about me the whole time?" The answer to which was, of course, "Well . . . yeah." Johnny didn't say that aloud though, but instead simply shrugged and said, "Have it your way."

Johnny's thoughts turned serious as he stared out the

smoked windows. If only Ben understood. If only he realized that Johnny cracked wise with him because he didn't know what else to say to him. That if he said what was really on his mind, he'd come across like a total lame-ass. It wouldn't be in keeping either with his self-image, or the image he liked to present for others. He brushed away the brief conflict in his heart and turned his focus to other, more egotistically uplifting matters.

It seemed as if the last eight blocks of Fifth Avenue between them and their destination were lined with fans, photographers, curiosity seekers, and gawkers. Johnny didn't know for sure how word had gotten out as to when they were going to be arriving. It was likely someone who worked in the police department. Whoever it was, the others would clearly have liked to kill him. Johnny wanted to shake his hand.

Police barricades had been set up just outside their destination: the towering facility known as the Baxter Building. The wooden barricades weren't enough; cops were lined up with arms linked, and there were more in evidence clad in riot gear. Johnny hated to think that pretty much anywhere in New York City at that moment, bad guys were getting away with anything they wanted, because every damned cop in Manhattan was here. It was particularly daunting when one considered that, even with the sizable turnout of police might, they were still outnumbered by the onlookers by about ten to one. If the crowd decided to make a real push for it, they'd break through the police ranks with ease.

That was a prospect that intimidated Johnny not a little. After all, Reed, Sue, even Ben, could use their abilities to defend themselves in a nonlethal fashion. What was Johnny supposed to do with overeager fans? Incinerate them? Oh yeah. Yeah, that would look great on the front page of the *New York Post*. It'd be doing Ben a favor, since Johnny would instantly displace "the Thing"—what some newspapers had dubbed him—as the new pariah in the group.

The police escort pulled up to the front of the building. The crowd roared its approval, people crying out their names with such high-volume enthusiasm that Johnny was worried he was going deaf from it. He saw Reed, no longer off in his little personal zone, wincing against the sound. Sue didn't look any happier. What good were words of love and adoration if the subjects of it weren't listening?

"Guys, they love us!" Johnny pointed out.

Reed stared at him blankly, clearly unable to comprehend the relevance. Sue was even more succinct: "So?"

Addressing Sue while pointing at Reed, Johnny said, "Y' know . . . whatever he's got, you caught it from him."

When it was clear that neither of them knew what he was talking about, he shook his head and gave up. Instead, the moment the car had glided to a halt—indeed, a second or two before that—Johnny bounded out of the car. The crowd noise hit him like a thing alive. He was like a sponge taking in water, except he had an endless capacity for absorbency. Sue and Reed followed him out. Reed was squinting as if staring into intense illumi-

186

nation, which was odd considering the sun was behind clouds. Then again, he was facing the harsh light of public scrutiny and adoration. Trust Reed Richards to be blinded by metaphor.

Johnny heard a squeaking of metal and springs, and turned to see that Ben was stepping out of the back of the paddy wagon. There were audible gasps from the crowd, and—astoundingly—a brief lull. Then the decibel level surged once more, although it didn't reach quite the same levels. People almost seemed hushed, relatively speaking, in Ben's presence.

As Ben joined the others, the press surged forward, screaming questions. Ben ignored them all while Reed and Sue displayed brief but forced smiles. For his part, Johnny was one vast ear-to-ear grin. He nearly gave himself whiplash, trying to look directly into as many cameras as were pointed at him.

He saw Ben scowling at everyone and called out, "Smile, Ben. They want to like you. Give 'em your good side." Then he paused and added, "Or your less bad side."

Ben appeared to consider that for a moment, then turned and looked at a group of small kids. Stiff, tentative, he leaned forward, paused for a moment in thought, and then said, "Don't do drugs."

The kids stepped back, looking utterly terrified. Johnny laughed to himself, thinking, *Talk about "scared straight."* There was one thing that Johnny was willing to bet on: If those kids thought that doing drugs meant you'd wind up looking like "the Thing," none of them would ever so much as smoke weed.

Johnny continued to work the crowd, holding up four fingers to symbolize the group, blowing kisses, winking, and generally having a ball. Several extremely attractive young women were gesturing to him wildly that he should come on over, and he headed straight toward them . . . until Sue snagged him by the elbow and dragged him toward the building. He started to protest, and Sue snapped at him, "Rein it in, hot pants."

They entered the lobby of the Baxter Building. It wasn't especially large, but it had very much of an old-time feel to it, an art deco style that would have been right at home in the 1930s. In keeping with the "old school" feel, a doorman approached them, and he was sporting a long red coat, epaulets, a hat, and a bristling mustache. He was wearing a small nameplate that read O'HOOLIHAN on it.

He smiled kindly and said, "Welcome back to the Baxter, Dr. Richards." He motioned toward the cameras and crush of people outside. Police were still striving to keep the mob back from pressing into the lobby.

Reed sighed and said, "I'm afraid so . . ." His voice trailed off and he looked both bewildered and slightly chagrined.

Johnny wasn't sure what the problem was, but Sue divined it immediately. "*Jimmy*," she said with a particular emphasis directed at Reed. "Good to see you again."

Then, of course, Johnny got it. Had to trust old Reed. Ask him to trot out *pi* to about a hundred decimal places, and he was your man. Ask him to remember something as mundane as the first name of the doorman, and he was in a fog. Sue, on the other hand, had a steel-trap memory for details, but couldn't begin to match Reed for arcane knowledge. That was probably why they made a good couple.

Stop that, Johnny almost shouted at himself. *They do not make a good couple. They make a lousy couple. Stop thinking about them as a couple. Bad, bad idea.*

O'Hoolihan, meantime, was grinning upon seeing Sue. "Good to see you, too," he said. Then, in a low voice, he winked to Reed and said, "Don't worry, sir. I know how crowded that head of yours is."

Reed looked grateful at that, and Johnny noticed that Reed then quickly muttered, "Jimmy," very, very softly five times. Obviously he was trying to force himself to remember for the future. Johnny gave it maybe fifty-fifty odds. Then he asked, "Any visitors while I was away?"

"Just the usual," Jimmy said with a shrug. "Told 'em you were circling 'round outer space."

He stepped over to the stand that the sign-in book was kept upon, then reached down and slid open a drawer. It was filled with letters from various banks. Reed looked sheepish, confronted with this indisputable evidence of his financial ineptitude. The identity of the "usual" visitors was now pretty evident: creditors.

Reed reached over and slid the drawer shut, then looked to Sue and Johnny to see if they'd spotted the drawer's contents.

Before they could react, Willie Lumpkin, the long-time U.S. Postal Service carrier for the Baxter Building, rounded the lobby corner and approached Reed, Johnny, Sue, and Ben, who were awaiting the private elevator car. Willie was his usual jovial self and reached into his mailbag to dutifully hand Reed his bundle.

"Welcome back to the Baxter Building, Dr. Richards," proclaimed Willie as Reed accepted the banded stack of business envelopes. Reed quickly glanced down, seeing the red FINAL NOTICE stamps on the envelopes as he thumbed the stack. He looked discreetly back up at Willie, who replied reassuringly, "Good to have you back, sir."

"Thanks, Willie," Reed kindly answered.

It was clear from their pained expressions—or Sue's, at least, since Johnny was actually a bit amused by the whole thing—that they had seen everything. "We had a tough year," Reed said by way of explanation.

"Yeah, nine years straight," said Ben.

Reed fired him a look that said *Thanks a lot.* Johnny put up a hand to cover his amused smile. It wasn't funny and he shouldn't be laughing . . . but it was, and he was trying not to.

A "ding" noise informed them that the elevator had arrived. Ignoring the continued shouts from the crowd outside, demanding that they answer just one more question, pose for one more picture or sign one more autograph, they stepped inside the car. Reed let out a visible sigh of relief, thrilled to leave the circus atmosphere of their arrival behind. He tapped the top button, the one for the twentieth floor.

"Twenty?" Johnny said in surprise, noticing its placement on the control panel. "From outside the place looks a lot taller."

"Oh, it is," Reed assured him.

The doors closed on Reed, Ben, Johnny, and Sue, but the elevator didn't move. Then a beeping sound alerted them to the fact that there was something wrong. Johnny said cautiously, "Either we're moving really fast . . . or not at all."

There was a digital weight readout on the panel. It read, EXCEEDS MAXIMUM WEIGHT. Next to the readout was a square brass plate engraved with the words, 2000 POUNDS MAXIMUM. The elevator was bouncing slightly, suspended only by the cables and pulley system, which seem wholly inadequate.

As one, they all turned to Ben with a shared look of mutual embarrassment. It barely seemed to register on him, though. Johnny was starting to think that Ben Grimm had maxed out on his ability to absorb humiliation, and everything else was being sloughed off like raindrops off Scotchguard.

"I'll take the stairs," he said, and he might have shrugged, but it was hard to know for sure. He stepped off and lumbered away. Just before the doors closed, however, his gaze locked with Reed's for barely a second. But it was enough time for Johnny to realize that— for Ben Grimm—the capacity for humiliation had been replaced by a deep-seated rage that burned with far greater intensity than anything Johnny Storm could produce.

And if Ben was a boundless producer of anger, then it

was clear from Reed's reaction that he had endless capacity for translating that anger into guilt. He sagged back against the wall, thumping his head slightly against it, as the elevator rose.

"How come Ben can't turn it on and off like us?" Sue ventured.

Reed just shook his head. Not knowing something must have been particularly galling for him. "That's what we're here to find out," he said.

"If it happened to him," Sue realized, "then it could . . ."

She didn't finish it. She didn't have to. *It could happen to all of them*.

Johnny's eyes widened at the thought. "Wait. You mean there's a chance we could be full-on-24-7 fantastic?"

Sue gave him a scornful look. "Grow up, Johnny. You want to run around *on fire* for the rest of your life?"

He smirked. "Is that a trick question?"

But then his initial enthusiasm for the notion began to dim. He considered the harsh realities of such a life: Sue perpetually invisible, so that even crossing a street became an adventure as cars wouldn't know to slow for her; Reed's body losing its elasticity so that he became a stretched out mass of flesh and bone; Johnny living a life of enforced chastity because no woman would dare draw close to him for fear of being incinerated.

Suddenly it didn't seem like such a keen idea after all. Johnny kept the ready grin on his face, but it didn't reflect the seeds of inner fear that his sister had sown.

The elevator slid to a halt and the door opened.

"Doesn't look like much," Johnny said as he stepped out, and then realized that his voice echoed when he spoke. He looked up in amazement.

The elevator might have stopped at the twentieth floor, but Johnny's instincts had been correct. The building was immensely higher than that, as high as sixty floors of . . . nothing. The result was a gargantuan atrium that could have accommodated Paul Bunyan and his ox to boot. Yet it was brightly lit, thanks to powerful skylights positioned far above.

Reed didn't even give the impressive view a glance. Johnny and Sue followed him as he guided them toward another area filled with individual living quarters. "We should stay here until we can define the extent of our changes."

Stuck for anything to say, Johnny naturally found something anyway. "You got cable?" he asked.

Reed didn't acknowledge that Johnny had spoken, for he was too busy listening to the steady *thump thump thump* that was the slow, ominous footfall of his best friend trudging up the stairs. "And figure out how to reverse them," he added.

The crush of the press and onlookers had mercifully thinned by the time Victor's Bentley sedan rolled up. He wasn't sure he could have tolerated the intrusion. Between the crush of negative publicity, the bankers' meeting that was only a few notches above a mugging, and the disturbing changes his body was being subjected to, Victor Von Doom felt like a walking, gaping sore. He stepped out of his limo, wearing sunglasses. Yes, there were far fewer reporters and such there, but there were still a few, and Victor braced himself for the inevitable flurry of picture taking and questions being hurled at him from every direction.

None came. Photographers and curiosity seekers didn't give him a glance, and no reporters floated so much as a single question. At first he was relieved . . . until annoyance began to pervade him. What, he wasn't good enough to be asked anything? Not pretty enough to be photographed? Ben Grimm's freakishly transformed mug was suitable for front page display, but Victor Von Doom wasn't worth so much as a single roll of film? Dammit, Victor Von Doom was supposed to be the story here, not Reed Richards and his pack of fantastic freak friends . . .

Including Sue? Was she part of Reed's pack?

No. Let the reporters rot. Let the photographers lose interest in me. But she is, and will be, mine. Reed doesn't get her. Not her.

That single thought fueled him as he took the elevator up to the twentieth floor. O'Hoolihan knew perfectly well who Von Doom was and didn't even attempt to question his heading to the upper floors.

Victor strode onto the twentieth floor as if he owned the place. Although he had no way of knowing for sure where he was, nevertheless something guided him to the room where Sue was unpacking her things. Perhaps it was because the need for her had become so primal that his instincts about her were unerring.

Her back was to him when he entered her doorway. For a time he simply stood there, watching her, admiring her figure. She had one suitcase on the bed, open, from which she was unpacking clothes. A second bag was sitting closed on the floor. She turned around to put something away into a drawer and jumped back slightly when she saw him. He chalked up her flinching to her being startled by him.

He smiled for what seemed the first time in ages. "God, I've been so worried about you."

"Victor," said Sue, "I'm sorry, I didn't get a chance—"

Von Doom waved off her concerns. "Please, no apologies," he said generously. "I've arranged for your things to be moved to one of my condos. You'll have round-the-clock care."

He stepped forward and reached for her bag. Then, to his utter astonishment, she put a hand on his and stopped him from lifting it. For half a beat he simply stared at her, thinking that she was merely being feminist and desiring to carry her bag herself . . . until he saw the look in her eye and realized how badly he had misjudged the situation.

"Thank you," Sue said. "That's generous. But I think I should say here with . . ." She paused and said, ". . . my brother. Until we get a handle on this."

With my brother. Like hell "with my brother," Von Doom thought fiercely. *She doesn't want to leave Richards.* The doubts ate at him even as he forced himself to maintain a concerned, noncommittal air, as if her welfare—and not his ego or her feelings for Reed—was the only consideration. "Sue . . . I think you should let my doctors have a look at you."

The air fairly crackled with tension then. He reminded himself that he had the power here. As her employer, he could give her an order. As a man who loved her, he could assert his authority, because what kind of relationship could they possibly have if it wasn't clear he was in charge? Sue looked set to defy him, and he was set to steamroll over her objections. That was when, with his usual remarkable timing, Reed approached with files in hand. "Victor! What are you doing here?"

It required physical effort for Von Doom to shift his attention from Sue to Reed. "I'm starting to wonder the same thing," he said, his forced smile covering gritted teeth. Endeavoring to sound businesslike, he asked, "How much do you know about what happened to you?"

"Not much," Reed admitted, tapping the files. "We need to run tests to see the extent of the damage."

Von Doom was tempted to continue matters with Sue, but he realized that the only thing more mortifying than having Sue refuse his wishes was to have her do so in front of Reed Richards. And if she did continue to defy him, then what was he supposed to do, really? Pick her up and sling her over his shoulder? Haul her out like a Cro-Magnon? Actually, the notion had some appeal to it, but there would then be those pesky kidnapping charges.

Deciding that discretion was the better part of valor in this case, Victor simply nodded and said, "Well, let me know if there is anything I can do. We're all in this to-gether now."

He reached out his hand and Reed shook it gamely. However, although Von Doom was managing to keep his tone moderate and his face inscrutable, the growing anger within him was reflected in the ferocity with which he gripped Reed's hand. He did it so tightly that Reed's rubbery hand oozed between his fingers like putty. Reed was clearly in no pain from it, looking down with an eyebrow cocked in scientific curiosity. Disgusted both by the sensation and his utter ineffectiveness at causing Richards any discomfort, Victor released his hand, and turned toward Sue to kiss her. She preempted the movement by sticking out her own hand. Victor's smile remained frozen on his face as he shook her hand with a good deal more delicacy than he had Richards', and headed out of the room.

He was halfway down the hallway, moving fast, as if he could outrace his anger. Behind him, Reed called out, "Victor, wait!" Victor took a deep breath, mentally counting to ten, as he turned to face Reed. Reed, for his part, was shaking his hand vigorously in order to snap the elastic member back to its normal shape. "I just wanted to say," he continued as his hand reformed to its proper proportions, "I'm sorry the mission didn't go as planned . . ."

Still counting to ten, Victor didn't make it past six. Seething, he allowed more of his ire to be on display than he would have liked as he snarled, "Didn't go as *planned*? It was a *catastrophe!* You ruined the lives of four people—!"

Reed was taken aback, both by the vehemence and also by the claim itself. "*I* ruined? With all due respect, I told you to abort . . ."

"*Abort?*" Victor could scarcely credit the level of stupidity he was having to deal with from someone allegedly so brilliant. "Reed, I put my company, my name, billions of dollars on the line, and I will *not* let you make me look like a fool . . ."

"Victor, if we could understand what happened to us—"

"I don't want to *understand* it!" Victor said, unable to believe that he had to spell it out. "This isn't one of your science projects. I just want to *fix* it. *Fast!*"

As he ranted, the lights around him began to flicker. Reed looked around in confusion, unable to understand what was causing the short. He looked back at Victor, clearly nonplussed, and then he cocked his head and stared in confusion at Victor's face. Victor put a hand to his cheek and realized that the scar had grown about another quarter inch. Not much, but certainly noticeable to someone as infuriatingly observant as Reed Richards.

In the dimness of the hallway, Reed's face was a question. Before he could frame it, however, an annoyingly familiar voice said from behind them, "There a problem, Vic?"

The words had been casual, but the tone was fraught with warning. Von Doom turned and saw Ben Grimm down the hall, leaning in a doorway, arms folded across his massive chest. Victor was about to snap out a sharp retort, but then he took a careful look at the mountainous, rock-hewn body he was facing. The pictures hadn't done him justice. He looked like he could rip Von Doom in half with his bare hands, and although Victor didn't think he'd have the nerve to commit such an assault, he wasn't exactly inclined to bet his life on it.

"No problem, Ben," he said tightly. He turned back to Reed, the lights continuing to flicker as if a play were about to return from intermission. "Just pay your goddamn electric bill and get to work on a cure," he warned Reed.

He walked away stiffly toward the elevator. Ben was blocking his path for a moment, but then he stepped aside and made a sweeping "be my guest" gesture. Victor moved past him and Ben waggled his fingers cheerily.

Victor reached over to the panel to touch the "Down" button. His fingertip drew to within a quarter inch of the button and then it lit up before he could touch it, as if the circuit itself had responded to him. He heard Reed behind him, exhaling in relief over . . . what? That Victor was leaving? That Grimm had shown up in time to act as his bodyguard? Von Doom didn't know and, more importantly, he didn't care all that much. All he cared about was getting out of Ben and Reed's sight before he completely lost control.

He made it, but just barely. The instant the elevator doors closed behind him, Victor snapped. He slammed his fist repeatedly into the steel wall of the elevator. Incredibly, the wall buckled beneath the pounding, denting from the punishment it was taking.

Pain shot through Von Doom's hand, but not as

much as he would have thought. He shook out his hand and realized he'd cut himself . . . and rather badly, it seemed. The skin was just hanging off there . . .

. . . and there was no blood.

That was the first thing he noticed.

The second thing he noticed was so horrifying that he couldn't even begin to comprehend it at first.

The epidermis had been torn away like rotting meat, and the dermis layer had been transformed into . . .

Oh my God.

. . . a metallic shell . . .

This can't be happening.

. . . its dark surface pulsing with electric energy.

Find a cure, Reed . . . find it fast . . . or I'm going to kill you with my bare hands . . . and it seems increasingly likely that I'll be able to do it.

13

Files of Reed Richards, Project F4, Day One. Measuring and testing equipment still being put into place and assembled, but am not willing to delay commencement of tests. Time of the essence. The longer our bodies are allowed to remain in this state, the greater the possibility that our DNA will permanently adapt to it and it will become the norm. This is particularly relevant insofar as Subject Ben Grimm is concerned. The possibility of his permanent imprisonment in a body that is a grotesque distortion of his own grows literally with every passing minute.

REED KNEW IT WAS GOING TO BE A DIFFICULT AND LONG day. But no matter how much he prepared himself for it, it couldn't begin to approach the reality of what he faced.

His lab was state-of-the-art, or at least as state-of-the-art as could be considering the financial difficulties he'd had lately. As he and Sue checked over the settings for his preliminary investigations, he found himself wondering what his parents would have said had they lived to see the use to which he'd put his inheritance. He could still see his father shaking his head in discouragement and saying, "Reed, we always warned you, if you don't learn how to handle funds, you're going to wind up without a cent to your name."

He'd been perilously close to correct. Reed had a few cents to his name, but not much. The bottom line was that Reed really could understand Victor Von Doom's frustration. Reed had let his obsession for scientific research without consideration for practicality send his business down the drain. And now he was on the verge of dragging Victor down with him.

For all that Reed saw their personal situation as an opportunity for greatness, it only made sense that Victor saw it as a disaster. He couldn't argue that Victor was wrong. The harsh truth was that the betterment of humanity was going to have to wait for another day. It was easy to point fingers. For Reed to say that it was Victor's fault, and vice versa, was a nice exercise in placing blame, but otherwise accomplished nothing. Ultimately, if Reed could find a cure for their condition, there was every reason to believe that he could build upon that research and produce something that would be of use to mankind. That was what mattered, and if it was going to be done on Victor's terms, then so be it.

Reed glanced over at Sue, who was checking the final power levels, and she nodded in confirming approval. Ben was seated in a large chair that creaked slightly under his weight every time he shifted in it. There were straps on the armrest, but they weren't large enough to fit around Ben's wrists. Nor would they hold him in any event, so they simply lay there limply.

Approaching Ben with an electrode needle, Reed smiled gamely and tried to look confident. Ben's face was immobile. He could literally have been carved from stone.

The needle was a simple tool, designed to produce DNA analysis. As carefully as he could, Reed tried to slide it between the rocky plates that constituted Ben's skin. It proved to be far more difficult than he'd anticipated as the needle refused to penetrate. Reed pushed harder and harder still, and the needle snapped clean off. He held it up, stared at it with a mixture of disappointment and frustration, and could only dwell on the fact that the needle alone had cost $1,500.

"You got a chisel round here?" Ben said, sounding more helpful than he actually was.

Reed sighed. "If we're going to identify the source of the mutation, we need to isolate your recombinant DNA so we can activate positional genomes."

Ben stared at Reed for a moment, and then looked to Sue in a silent plea for a translation. Sue obliged. "We need to give you a physical so we know what got zapped."

"Well why didn't you say so?" demanded Ben, much to Reed's annoyance considering he thought he *had* said so. "You want me to lift weights or something?"

Shaking his head, Reed reached upward and pulled

down an X-ray machine that was attached to a large overhead swivel crane . . . not unlike what might be found in a dentist's office, but bigger. "No, just sit back. We have a good sense of your strength from the fire truck. We need to find the source of your strength."

He reached for a lead apron to drape below Ben's waist, but Ben just gaped at him in a manner that said, *You're kidding, right?* Reed tossed the lead aside, then stepped back and away from the machine, joining Sue a safe distance away from the X-rays. Sue had the monitor up and running. Reed activated the X-ray machine, which came to life with a steady humming noise. Ben hummed along with it, which didn't help, but Reed chose not to call him on it. Instead he turned his attention to the monitor to try and determine just what Ben's skin was actually made of.

Which, as it turned out, was impossible.

Reed and Sue stared in astonishment at the monitor. "Is it working?" Reed asked in a low voice.

"You tell me," replied Sue.

It took him only moments to double-check the instrumentation and discover the answer that both of them really already knew. The machinery was working perfectly. It just wasn't working on Ben. Instead of anything internal, all they were seeing was his massive exterior. It was like trying to X-ray the Great Wall of China. Less successful, actually, since Reed had instrumentation at his disposal that would have penetrated the Great Wall. But it was getting nowhere with Ben's hide.

Ben, meantime, was somewhat concerned by the

consternation he was seeing in the other two. "How bad is it?" he called. "You know, I used to smoke."

Instead of replying, Reed snapped off the X-ray, then picked up a sphygmomanometer from a nearby table with the intention of using it to measure Ben's blood pressure. That, unfortunately, proved even more useless than the X-ray, as Reed quickly found the device's cuff couldn't wrap around Ben's arm. It was way too short. Reed would require a blood pressure machine that could be used to measure the BP of an elephant, and while he didn't doubt that such things existed, he didn't exactly have them at hand.

Putting the sphygmomanometer back on the table from where he'd gotten it, he stared at the remaining instruments thoughtfully. Stumped for anything better, he picked up a small triangular rubber hammer in order to test Ben's deep tendon reflex, or DTR. He held it up to Ben's knee, but the hammer looked minuscule in comparison and he didn't even bother to tap with it. The chances were sensational that Ben wouldn't even feel it.

Ben stared at him inquisitively but said nothing. That silence was the worst part of the whole exam. But Reed would not be daunted. He went to a drawer that was full of normal hardware tools and slid it open. Reaching in, he pulled out a normal ball-peen hammer. He approached Ben and said cautiously, "Okay, this might smart a little."

He tapped Ben's knee lightly with the hammer, hoping to see if there were hints of any impediments to

Ben's nervous system, as well as trying to get a feel for resistance to pain.

As it turned out, Reed got a serious feeling for it. Unfortunately, it wasn't in Ben, but in himself, as Ben's leg reflexively snapped upward and kicked directly between Reed's legs. Reed's entire upper torso snapped upward in response and his head thudded against the ceiling in the lab. At that moment Reed found himself wishing that he'd conducted the experiments in the atrium with its cavernous ceiling. Here it was low enough to add insult to injury.

Reed groaned as he snapped back to his normal form. He didn't want to comically grab at his crotch in pain, if for no other reason than that Sue was standing there and he wanted to maintain some measure of decorum, however pathetically small that decorum might be.

So instead he stood his ground but spoke in a high-pitched, pained voice. "We'll . . . continue this later," he announced.

Files of Reed Richards, Project F4, Day Two. Tests on Subject Grimm prove largely inconclusive, except for Subject Grimm's right leg, which seems extremely responsive and powerful. Am focusing on Subject Jonathan Storm. I have constructed a fireproof titanium chamber within which Subject Storm can be confined, with vents to provide a steady air flow in order to fuel the fire. Subject Storm will then be asked to ignite his flame to maximum capacity. In that way we can measure heat output, durability, intensity, etc. Susan and I will be observing from a

*second level control room for safety's sake. I am not ex-
pecting anything to go wrong with the measurement devices, but frankly, after all that's happened, I'd be a fool
not to anticipate the possibility.*

The camera positioned inside the containment cube
was secured behind triple-ply transparent aluminum
that, Reed hoped, would be able to withstand the heat
Johnny unleashed. He had no idea what to expect, and
was even a little afraid to explore Johnny's limits. But
there was no other choice for it. They had to find out
what Johnny's capabilities were . . . and, for that matter,
what they were all capable of.

In the control room, Sue was watching her brother
on the monitor screen and shaking her head in wonderment. He was completely enveloped in searing red
flame, top to bottom. By any sane measure of human endurance, he should be screaming in agony. Instead his
arms were outstretched and he was clearly reveling in
the power he was generating.

Reed, meantime, was monitoring the temperature
readout. He'd been expecting it to grow and then level
off, grow some more and then level off some more. That
wasn't happening. There was no curve to the mounting
intensity, but instead a straight diagonal as the measurement climbed steadily from 2,000 degrees Kelvin to
4,000 degrees in a matter of minutes.

"This isn't happening," Sue breathed. "It's like . . .
like . . ." She shook her head. "I don't know what it's like."

"That could well be the problem . . . uh oh," said Reed.

207

Not only was the temperature escalating, but Johnny's flame was changing from orange/red to blazing white. Sue, unable to endure looking at his image directly anymore, grabbed a pair of tinted goggles off the counter and put them on. Reed did likewise even as the interior of the chamber walls began to glow red. The picture was starting to fuzz out, the protection around the cameras reaching their capacity. If this kept up, they'd lose picture feed within seconds . . . and possibly communication with Johnny as well. That could well be catastrophic, especially considering that Johnny was now levitating a foot or two off the ground, and this discovery was only causing him to burn hotter still.

Reed flipped the comm switch and his voice echoed within the chamber. "Back it down, Johnny!"

Through some bizarre train of thought that probably made sense to Johnny Storm, but certainly no one else, Johnny took the admonition as some sort of challenge. "I can go hotter!" he called out.

Sue looked with concern, and even a bit apologetically, at Reed. Apologetic since Johnny was being an idiot and she felt responsible for her brother, and concerned because she perceived the same potential for disaster that Reed had. Fortunately enough, Reed had foreseen the possibility that Johnny might go out of control because, hell, everything about this insanity had thus far. This time, though, he was ready for it.

He hit a switch on the wall next to him, and although the picture on the viewscreen had been lost completely, the sounds he was hearing were more than enough to assure him that the extinguisher was working perfectly. Foam was pouring out of overhead nozzles . . . the exact same type of foam spread on runways to retard fires for crashing airplanes. It worked equally well upon Johnny, enveloping him and dousing his flames. There was a loud hissing noise and then rippling mist rolled out from all the vents. When Johnny next spoke, he didn't sound especially happy.

"You're really cramping my style here," he called.

Sue stepped over to the comm unit and informed him, "You were at 4,000 Kelvin. Any hotter, you're approaching supernova."

If Sue was expecting Johnny to acknowledge the gravity of that situation, she was going to be disappointed. "Sweeeet," was all Johnny said.

"That's the temperature of the sun . . . !" Sue said, and then mouthed the completion of the sentence, . . . *you idiot!* but didn't speak it aloud. Reed smiled at her restraint. At least one member of the Storm family *had* restraint.

Wishing to impress upon Johnny the level of danger they were dealing with, Reed added, "Not only could you kill yourself, but you could set fire to Earth's atmosphere and destroy all human life as we know it."

As if he'd just been reminded by a driving instructor that red meant "stop" and green meant "go," Johnny said, "Gotcha. Okay. Supernova bad," so indifferently that Reed wasn't sure it had truly registered on him.

Reed turned his attention to the readouts of all the

measurements he had expected to take, and found that none of them made any sense. Sue, looking over his shoulder, shook her head in dismay. "He cooked the equipment," she said.

"Of course he did," Reed sighed.

Files of Reed Richards, Project F4, Day Three. I have been frustrated in my attempts to acquire any true specifics as to the makeup or nature of our transformations. With the equipment thus far not meeting the demands put upon it by the subjects, I am taking a different approach and interviewing the subjects in depth. This will naturally provide data of far less reliability, leaning more toward the anecdotal, but at least it will provide me with some sort of baseline from which I can proceed. I will begin with Subject Grimm. I will simply inform Subject Grimm that I have drawn up these questions and need him to provide answers in as much detail as he can, despite the intensely personal nature of some of the questions. Due to our long-standing relationship, both personal and professional, and the fact that we are both adults and men of science, I anticipate nothing but cooperation.

Reed and Ben sat in chairs opposite each other, facing one another. Reed felt as if they'd been sitting there for half an hour, until he glanced at his watch to discover that thirty seconds had passed. Ben was staring at him with a complete deadpan as Reed squirmed uncomfortably in the chair, clutching his clipboard and making pointless little adjustments to the questions before he began. After a while, Ben began drumming his fingers on the chair, making small dents in it.

"Okay," Reed began, feeling far more awkward than he could possibly have thought. "I've, uh, got some questions . . ." He paused and then lied, ". . . from Sue. That she thought might be better coming from me."

Please don't let Sue have overheard that. She could be invisible, standing right over there, and I'd never know until she smacked me upside the head for passing the buck.

Fortunately no smack was forthcoming, although Ben continued to rap his fingers on the chair. Taking a deep breath, Reed pressed on, looking at his first question. It read, *Please describe the nature of your body's elimination of waste matter: whether it still occurs and, if so, the steps required in order to dispose of it.*

Somehow that didn't sound like something Sue would write.

"Can you . . ." Reed cleared his throat and then plunged in. ". . . you know . . . go to the bathroom . . . like normal . . ."

"Yeah," Ben said curtly, and then added, "You don't wanna know the details."

Reed forced a smile, trying to look and sound like a friend of many years rather than an intrusive scientist. "Ben, I'm afraid I've got to ask . . ."

Leaning forward menacingly, Ben said, "Not unless you want that clipboard stretched up your—"

"Ooookay," Reed said. "We'll skip that question."

The next questions, unfortunately, didn't get any better.

*   *   *

Files of Reed Richards, Project F4, Day Four. Subject Grimm was . . . not as cooperative as one would have hoped. Ideally, however, a means will be determined to reverse his cellular damage so that his human appearance will be restored. I expect at that point he will be more forthcoming since his condition will be moot. Admittedly that does little to aid me in solving the problem, but no one ever said the road to research was a smoothly paved one. I will be continuing the questioning process with Subject Jonathan Storm and expect far greater progress. If there is one thing that Subject Storm enjoys talking about, it's himself.

Johnny was jogging steadily on a treadmill in the gym as Reed continued to fire off questions. The positive aspect for Reed was that Johnny was far more forthcoming than Ben had been, talking at length and saying whatever was on his mind. The negative aspect was that what he had to say was almost completely useless. Somehow it seemed appropriate that Johnny was capable of getting hotter than the sun, because he was acting as if everything in and on the world revolved around him.

"Is there something about flames?" Reed asked. "About flaming, that you—"

Tapping the "Pause" button, Johnny turned and looked at Reed uncertainly. "What are you trying to say? Just because I dress well and like to dance . . ."

Reed not only had no clue as to what Johnny was talking about, but he would continue not to have until

Sue read his notes and explained it to him later. At the moment, all he could do was say, "What? No. I'm trying to figure out why we each ended up with different symptoms."

"Oh, well, that's easy!" said Johnny.

For a moment, Reed's spirits were buoyed by this. Johnny was, after all, not a complete moron. Self-obsessed perhaps, but he had a brain in his head and it was entirely possible that he had made some observations that had gone right past Reed . . . who, admittedly, sometimes couldn't see the forest for the trees. Eager to get Johnny's insight, he sat there with pen poised over his clipboard.

"I'm hot," Johnny said with a wry grin. "You're . . ." He paused, trying to find a delicate way to phrase it, and finally settled for indelicate. "Well, you're a little limp. Sue's easy to see through. And Ben's always been a hard-ass." He paused and then looked with interest at Reed's unmoving pen. "Why aren't you writing this down?"

Files of Reed Richards, Project F4, Day Five. Getting nowhere. If observation with Subject Susan Storm has the same lack of success, then in the words of George Washington, I'm going to seriously consider retiring to the back country and living in a wigwam.

Reed adjusted the prismatic viewer over his eyes and gazed through it at the point in the room where he knew Sue was standing, invisible. It wasn't hard to find her, considering that her clothes were floating there. Fortunately

213

the nature of the experiment and his observation didn't require her to denude herself. For that he was grateful. He had enough distractions to deal with.

Even so, it was difficult for him to focus on the matter at hand. The prismatic viewer enabled him to discern Sue, and measure the degree of light refraction accompanying her utilization of her powers. The problem was that, when he did so, she appeared to his eyes to look like some sort of celestial creature, a glowing angel on Earth. It was slightly disturbing seeing her that way, particularly because—deep down—that was how he saw her even when she was visible. But he wasn't about to tell her that. It was hardly scientific.

"So how am I turning invisible?" Sue inquired. "Personally, I was thinking it was magic."

He smiled indulgently. "There's no such thing as 'magic,' Sue. There's scientific explanations for everything."

"Really."

"Yes," he said firmly. "In your case, it's not 'invisibility' per se. You're bending the light around you with some kind of malleable force field."

"Is that what I'm doing?" she asked.

"Yes. At first I thought you were able to create in yourself the same refractive index as air," he said, warming to the topic. "That doesn't answer all the questions, however."

"And bending the light around me does?"

"Exactly," said Reed. "That's what you projected on the bridge."

"So the light just never gets to me."

214

"Correct. It curves around you, rendering you imperceptible to the human eye."

"All right," Sue said thoughtfully, reappearing. "Can I ask a question?"

"Of course you can," said Reed, leaning back and rubbing the bridge of his nose, feeling tired but satisfied with the way this aspect of the research was going, at least. "Anything you want to know."

"How do I see?"

He stopped rubbing and peered at her over his fingers. "Pardon? See? See what?"

"Anything. Think about it: Humans are able to see because light reaches their eyes. That's just basic optometry. So if I'm bending light around myself, then none is getting to my retinas or corneas. Which means that when I disappeared, on the bridge earlier or just now, I should be blind, the same as anyone else whose eyes can't receive light."

Reed stared at her for a long moment. "Technically . . . yes . . . that would be true."

"Technically?"

"That's true."

"Then how am I turning invisible?"

Spreading his hands wide, Reed said with an air of utter hopelessness, "At this point . . . I'm guessing magic."

Sue laughed sympathetically at Reed's frustration. Then her amusement changed into concern for him. "What about you?" she asked. "You haven't eaten in days. And come to think of it . . . how come you're never on this side of the microscope?"

Reed stiffened immediately. He was immensely un-comfortable at the prospect of being the center of attention. He felt he should be the observer, not the observed. Again, he was a scientist, not a refugee from one of those bad 1950s science fiction flicks in which movie scientists used themselves as guinea pigs to test some new and insanely dangerous procedure, with inevitable less-than-stellar results.

Yet here he was, and not only was he the subject of a project gone horrifically wrong, but he'd dragged his friends into it as well.

He looked at Sue with the same flash of guilt he had every time he glanced at Ben. Sue was reaching out for him, taking his hand in both of hers, and reflexively he pulled away from her. Naturally the movement caused his arm to stretch, emerging far beyond the cuff of his shirtsleeve. Sue's eyes widened as she stared at his arm, but it wasn't until Reed looked down at the elongated limb that he realized Sue was reacting to something other than the sheer strangeness of the stretching. Instead she was looking at several large bruises, black and purple and fierce, spotting the length of his arm.

"Bruises . . . from the bridge?" she asked slowly.

He nodded and, abashed, rolled his sleeves down. The fact was that the sheer act of stretching was causing bruises, hematomas, and the like. There had been no actual tearing or scarring of his skin; it appeared far too elastic for that. But the damage his body was sustaining was disturbing, not to mention broken capillaries by the carload, and that was where the bruises were coming from. Every time he stretched and then later snapped back into shape, all the injury seemed undone, but the bruising was physical evidence that it had been done in the first place.

Sue was about to keep inquiring after them, but he shook his head, clearly indicating that he had no desire to talk about it. Instead he turned the conversation back to where he felt more comfortable: anyone other than him. "Have you had any side effects, from your powers?" he asked.

She knew he was deliberately changing the subject, but chose not to make an issue of it. Instead she considered her own difficulties, and admitted with some reluctance—and not a little vulnerability—"I've had some headaches. Migraines."

Reed considered that a moment. Then he jotted down some notes to that effect. There was some small part of his mind that said, *Ask her how she's coping. Ask after her health. Express the kind of concern that one human being shows for another, instead of just being a scientific automaton.* But he ignored it all. He had to keep the clear mind of a researcher fixed upon his goals, or he would never reach them.

Reed leaned back, chewing on the clicking end of his pen. "You should be able to bend light around other subjects, even people. If you could control your emotional state better—"

"Excuse me?"

Oblivious to the clear annoyance in her tone, Reed continued, "I'm saying, if you had a little more self-control, you could locate the trigger. Can you remember your exact emotions when—"

"Anger," Sue said immediately and pointedly. "Rage. Frustration."

"Okay. Is there any way to duplicate that feeling? Some memory or . . ."

Staring at Reed with fixed intensity, she snapped, "I'm sure I can come up with *something*."

It took her only a few seconds of gazing at Reed to become invisible once more. Not only that, but moments later a small, clear force field enveloped the microscope, rendering it invisible.

Reed, meanwhile, was so lost in jotting down notes for his files that he wasn't even aware yet of what was happening . . . just as he didn't know that he was the reason that Sue was easily able to muster the anger required to trigger her abilities. "How's that coming—?" he began, and then realized that not only had Sue vanished, but so had his microscope. "Whoa," he said. He reached for the microscope, trying to touch it tentatively with his index finger. But he wasn't able to get anywhere near it. Instead it was blocked by a pulsing shield of invisible energy . . .

Pulsing? Reed thought.

It was at that moment that the force field shot out in all directions, knocking over everything in a fifteen-foot radius. That included, naturally, Reed himself, as he was thrown from his chair and sent skidding across the floor. Instantly Sue snapped back into visibility. She ran toward Reed, helping him to sit up, as she babbled, "I'm sorry . . . I'm sorry . . . I didn't mean to do that. You must think that was some kind of latent hostility or—"

Reed looked up at her in complete bewilderment. "What in the world would give me that idea?" he asked.

He studied her expression, the hurt in her eyes, the anger twitching at the edges of her mouth. He ran the details of the previous several minutes back through his mind, like a rewinding videotape, studying every moment of his discussion with Sue. Finally he came to the startling conclusion that she was referring, not to anything having to do with the research, but to their previous social life. And he could not for the life of him understand why that should be a sore subject with *her*. He was, after all, the injured party at the end of that unfortunate affair.

All of this observation went through his head in perhaps a second or two. To make certain that they were on the same page with it, he asked her, just to confirm his recollection, "I mean, *you* broke up with *me*, right?"

Sue's eyes were wide. "Are you kidding?"

"No," said Reed Richards, the picture of analytic calm. "I distinctly remember: *You* walked out *my* door. Ergo—"

Sue dropped her gaze, not wanting to get into a serious discussion of something she clearly considered so painful. "Reed . . . I was ready for the next step. You weren't. Ergo, I walked."

Reed said uncomfortably, "I think it was a little more complicated than—"

"I just wanted to share an apartment!" She was

219

standing on the opposite side of the table from him. It was becoming evident that, whether he was comfortable with it or not, Reed was going under the microscope, even if it was a metaphorical one. "What was so complicated about that?"

Suddenly he wanted to find somewhere, anywhere else to look except at her. He continued to struggle in the losing endeavor of applying scientific reasoning to something as wholly unscientific as relationships. "There were a lot of variables to consider," he began, and then winced at how completely lame that sounded. This was madness. He was trying to pursue a course of research that was critical to their well-beings, and here he was letting himself become embroiled in a discussion that would have been right at home in a high-school cafeteria. It was sophomoric, it was a waste of time when more pressing matters demanded their attention . . .

. . . and yet the pure, raw hurt that throbbed in Sue's voice was enough to strip away all his scientific pretension. "No. There weren't," she said sadly. She leaned over the table so they were almost nose to nose. "There was you. And me. No variables, no math. It was actually the simplest thing in the world. But your head got in the way . . . like it always does."

Her words penetrated. He tried to slough them off, to put his priorities back where they should belong, but he couldn't. He knew she was right. He'd always known it. She was just forcing him to face the truths he had long denied, to her, to Ben and Johnny . . . even to himself.

"Sue . . ." he said, feeling helpless and lost. Words, which usually came so easily to him, fought his attempts to summon them now. "I just . . . I thought . . ."

"Same old Reed," she said with a sad smile. "Too much thinking."

He opened his mouth, about to speak, and suddenly the doors to the lab were slammed open. Johnny stomped in, wearing the charred remains of what had once been his favorite shirt. He pointed at them angrily and somehow managed to sound as if he were accusing Reed of malfeasance as he snapped, "Okay, guys, we have a *serious* problem."

Files of Reed Richards, Project F4, Day Six. The time spent investigating Sue proved fruitful in terms of charting observations potentially applicable to all of us. However, the fact that our powers seem to be triggered by abrupt passions or emotions is proving problematic . . . particularly in the case of Subject Jonathan Storm, who apparently was preparing to go out on a date—against my recommendations—and the mere contemplation of said assignation was enough to trigger a flaming incident that cost him costly clothing. Snide remarks from Subject Grimm, jibing Subject Storm about "the tragedy of premature ignition," did not exactly help matters.

However I believe I have hit upon a notion that will solve a number of problems. Our uniforms were exposed to the storm, like us. So, if my guess is correct, they can transform like us, becoming invisible, changing size on demand, or remaining impervious to flame. I am informing

the others and we will be squeezing back into those curi-
ous dark blue outfits in order to test my hypothesis.

Reed, Sue, and Johnny stepped in front of a row of mirrors that Reed had set up. They studied the way they looked in the uniforms. As far as Reed was concerned, the garments were intended to be purely functional, and weren't designed to be fashion statements or normal street wear. As a result, it seemed a ridiculous prospect, walking around in the streets in the outfits simply because their normal clothes couldn't stand the wear and tear their altered bodies were putting them through. To say nothing of the fact that until they had a handle on their powers, they posed a serious threat to the public wherever they went.

Ben was seated on the sofa of the living quarters, studying them skeptically. "You look like an eighties rock band," he noted. Johnny, in response, played a few quick licks on air guitar. Ben actually chuckled at that, which was the most positive moment Reed had witnessed in the better part of a week.

Turning toward Ben, Sue said optimistically, "The suit will stretch. You should try it . . ."

Ben snorted. "I wouldn't be caught dead in that."

"He's right," Johnny said, which may well have been the first time Reed ever saw Johnny and Ben in accord on something. Touching the fabric, Johnny continued, "These costumes are . . . missing something. I can't put my finger on it . . ."

"They're not costumes," Reed said in annoyance.

Sue turned to her brother. "We're not taking them

out, Johnny. We need to stay here until we've stabilized."

Reed was relieved that Sue backed him up. He wasn't sure if there was anyone in the world capable of riding herd on Johnny, but if anyone could come close to accomplishing it, it was Sue.

But Johnny displayed the frustration with which, to Reed's mind, he was becoming increasingly identified. "I'm getting sick of being trapped here. Even NASA wasn't this strict!"

"We have to worry about the public good, Johnny," Sue told him. "With our powers so unpredictable, we pose a potential threat if we step outdoors."

"Great. We get this incredible gig with fantastic abilities, and it's like we're lepers with first-strike capability." He turned on his heel and marched out.

Sue looked helplessly at Reed, then shrugged and followed her brother out. Silence fell upon the room as Ben and Reed stared at each other.

"Maybe it's missing a utility belt," Ben suggested.

Files of Reed Richards, Project F4, Day Seven. Johnny Storm is right. We're lepers with first-strike capability . . . and we're dealing with creeping cabin fever as well. Something is going to break soon, and I have no idea if I'm going to be able to pick up the pieces. God only knows how Victor is going to react when that happens. He seems like he's barely keeping it together now. If things fall apart, who knows what he'll become?

14

"DOCTOR . . . DOOM?"

Doctor Weber stared at the scribbled message left on his desk by his nurse. He had just come back from lunch and stared at the note with furrowed brow. "Roz?" he called to his aide. "What's this note mean? 'Doctor . . . Doom. Immediately.'"

Roz stuck her head in. "That was a call from Von Doom Industries. Victor Von Doom's people said he needs to see you."

"Von Doom?" Weber scratched his chin thoughtfully. "His yearly physical isn't for another six months. Did he give any indication of what it's about?"

"Only that it was very important and you had to get over there immediately."

Weber laughed softly at that. "Victor Von Doom can make an appointment like everybody el—"

Suddenly his aide called out, "Excuse me! What do you think you're—"

There was the sound of heavy footfalls, and three extremely large men were standing in the doorway. Three men possessed of one huge scowl.

"Victor Von Doom wishes to see you now," the largest of them said.

Doctor Weber stared at them a moment, and then said, "I'll get my hat."

Victor stood behind Doctor Weber as Weber held X-ray photos up to the light. Von Doom remained grim-faced, silent, much as he had been through the majority of Weber's analysis. All of the medical equipment that Weber had used to examine him had been brought in especially by Von Doom and set up in his office. He wanted as few people as possible to know what was going on. He knew that it was probably getting some raised eyebrows and speculation from his chattier employees. That was fine with him. Let them speculate. Let them wonder. It was better than knowing the facts . . . the facts being, as the X-ray clearly revealed, that the metallic transformation was creeping higher up his arm. It had reached nearly to his biceps.

Weber was shaking his head. "Your tissue, your organs . . . your entire bio-physical structure is changing," he said in wonderment. "Every system is still functioning, somehow—"

Von Doom cut him off in impatience. "And they're changing into . . . ?" he prompted.

"I don't really know," Weber admitted. He lowered the X-rays and looked instead at the results from the metallurgy studies which Von Doom had just received back from his labs. "A compound organic-metallic alloy.

225

Stronger than titanium or carbon steel. Harder than diamonds . . ."

That was exactly what Von Doom had thought he would hear. "Like the shields *Reed* said would protect us," he said grimly. His voice was filled with cold fury. "How long?"

Weber shrugged. It was clear he was guessing at best. "At this rate, the infection should be complete in two, maybe three weeks . . ."

"What do you mean 'complete'?"

"I wish I could tell you," Weber said. "I can't pretend to know what we're dealing with here." He put the metallurgy report next to the X-rays. "I'll notify the CDC and—"

Von Doom's mind had wandered to thoughts of what he was going to do to Reed Richards for getting him into this fix, but the doctor's comment snapped him back to razor-sharp focus. "What?"

"The CDC. The Centers for Disease Control."

"You . . . you can't. We have doctor/patient confidentiality . . ."

"Which ends where the public good begins. I don't have a choice, Victor," Weber said, trying to sound reasonable. "If this thing is contagious . . ."

Von Doom gripped Weber firmly by the shoulders. "Look at me," he said intensely. "I'm the face of a billion-dollar company. We *need* to keep this confidential, understand?"

"But . . . this disease," Weber stammered out, ". . . is progressive . . . degenerative . . ."

At that moment, something in Von Doom snapped.

Broke. He envisioned the issue of *Wired* that had trumpeted Reed's failure, except it was his picture in lieu of Reed's, his downfall that was being written about. The public humiliation, the snickering and guffawing from all the enemies he'd made during his climb upward, rejoicing at how the mighty had fallen. All that while he was being transformed into something . . . else. Something inhuman. Something monstrous.

All right then. All right. That which was inhuman didn't need to live within society's rules. Monsters were above and beyond the law.

Let me be what the gods have made me.

"That's terrible news," Victor said with mock sympathy, and with one cobra-swift move, Victor thrust his metallic arm into the doctor's chest and through the other side. There was a nauseating *splutch* noise as Weber's eyes went wide with shock. He was dead before he could even register what had happened. The doctor's weight was entirely borne by Von Doom's metallic arm for a moment, and then he yanked it clear. Weber started to sink to the floor, but Von Doom grabbed him and swung him onto the desk so the copious amounts of blood wouldn't pour onto the carpet and ruin it.

"But I think I'll get a second opinion," finished Victor.

He stepped back and looked around the office as if seeing it for the first time. His gaze rested on his display of antique armor.

He smiled. *Look at that. Look how lesser men had to work so hard to make themselves what I'm becoming naturally. Poor fools. Poor, pathetic fools.*

227

15

Files of Reed Richards, Project F4: Supplemental. Preliminary investigations completed. Preparing final analysis of all data. Anticipate breakthrough any time now.

THE LIGHT FROM THE FULL MOON FILTERED THROUGH the window in Reed's office. He rubbed his eyes, unable to believe that they could feel any more tired than they did. He was seated in his lab coat, going over formulas, equations, all manner of free-form thought that had prompted scribblings from him over the past week. He looked up at a wall where slides with diagrams depicting Ben's anatomy—prior to the change and since—were projected via a slide projector situated on Reed's desk. It looked like some twisted "before and after" advertisement for a bizarro physical fitness program. He stared at them for a time, waiting for inspiration to hit him. After all, wasn't genius supposed to be one percent inspiration and ninety-nine percent perspiration? Well, Reed had put in enough perspiration time. Now was the time for inspiration. That quick flash, that mental leap that would carry him over to the promised land of break-through.

He continued to check his equations, making more notes upon more notes, waiting for something to hit him.

Nothing did.

"Nothing," he muttered. "Nothing . . . *nothing* . . ."

Days of bottling up his escalating frustration exploded from him, and Reed slammed his desk with such ferocity that he jolted the projector, causing Ben's pictures to be replaced with a large square of white light. In total aggravation and despair, Reed's head thudded down onto the desk. The impact caused something to fall off the end of the desk and hit the floor with a crash.

Slowly Reed lifted his head. The world looked distorted to him, and he realized it was because he had managed to smash his face flat when he'd struck the desk. But that wasn't of major interest to him at the moment. Instead he stepped over from behind his desk to see what it was that had fallen off and created yet another mess for him to clean up after . . . not counting the one that he had created for himself, namely this entire fiasco of a —

It was a plant sample. Specifically, it was one of the samples from space, contained in a glass box that was now shattered. The plant was long dead, placed in the vacuum-sealed box to help preserve it. Now, however, exposed to air, there were small red sparks swirling around it, similar to the cosmic storm itself.

Reed had no clue why the contribution of air should make a difference. There was, after all, no air in space, and yet the cosmic storm . . .

Had accelerated and strengthened.

When drawing nearer to Earth.

Which had an atmosphere.

And now there it was, the cosmic storm in miniature, swirling around the plant. It wasn't growing any larger, for which Reed was grateful, but there it was, just the same. "Of course," Reed whispered, ". . . of *course* . . . the cloud . . ."

Files of Reed Richards, Project F4: Supplemental. Inspiration. Realization. Of course, of course. The storm that got us into this situation may be exactly what is needed to get us out of it.

I have designed a computer-image re-creation of the storm, based not only upon my first-person observations, but on extrapolations based upon the plant sample. I've covered six chalkboards worth of space with calculations and equations, drawing closer with each one, although I think I have chalk dust permanently under my fingernails. I'm also beginning designs on a machine that may serve to cure us of this condition permanently or, even better, enable us to control it once and for all.

It all comes down to the plants, from space. Their particles are still charged. With the right amount of energy, those ions could create the elemental profile of the cosmic storm.

*   *   *

"Are you joking, Reed?"

Sue was following him briskly down a hallway in the Baxter Building. Reed was busy flipping through his files, pausing only to ask, "When have I ever joked, Sue?"

"Fair point."

He went back to his notes with growing excitement. "If we can build a machine to re-create the storm, we can reverse the polarity . . ."

"And reverse the mutations," Sue said, the light dawning.

Reed was talking more to himself than to Sue. "Curing countless diseases, not just ours."

"But *we're* the focus, right, Reed?" asked Sue, and when she didn't get an answer, repeated, "*Reed?*"

"Of course, of course," he said so briskly that Sue had the distinct feeling he hadn't heard her at all. In fact, he was probably only barely aware she was there.

Nevertheless, she felt she had to persist. "And you're sure you can control this thing? Last time didn't work out too well."

He nodded reflexively, at which point Sue was positive he wasn't listening. That last remark of hers, although phrased carefully, would certainly have brought up at least an attempt at protest from Reed over her description of how the previous experiment had gone. Instead he just remarked, more to himself than to her, "With the right energy, we can stabilize the storm. Maybe tie into the city grid . . ."

Sue wasn't liking the sound of that. City grid? What,

231

for an encore to the previous disaster, Reed was going to black out Manhattan?

She tried to say something, but Reed kept his head down like a determined pitbull terrier and barreled into the storeroom. Sue had to hurry to try and keep up with him. She entered the dimly lit storeroom, squinting to make out everything that was in there. It was amazing to look at. Every square inch of the place was crammed with gear, gadgets, blueprints, inventions. It was awe-inspiring, overflowing with tangible proof of Reed's constantly working mind. She wondered when he ever found the time to sleep.

"You *really* need to get a janitor," she said dubiously. Reed didn't reply as he was too busy digging through who-knew-where to find who-knew-what. Sue walked the length of one of the shelves, bristling with over-crowded clutter. "This must be what it looks like inside your head."

"There's a system to it," Reed informed her defensively, his back still to her. Sue, however, was studying the most curious little model. It looked like a bathtub with wings. She pulled it out to study it, and just as she did so, Reed cried out, *"Wait! Sue, don't touch tha-!"*

It was too late. Like pulling a single thread from a tapestry that caused it to become unwoven, so too had Susan managed to select exactly the one object that apparently every other object on the shelf was resting upon. With the shelf now off-balance, a wave of inventions came clattering down toward Sue.

Reed was standing clear around on the other side of

the shelving unit. That didn't slow him, however, as he stretched his arms around the shelf, yanking Sue out of the way and toward himself just as the devices smashed to the ground. The two of them tumbled to the floor clear of the pileup, Reed's arms cocooned around her so as to protect her from the impact. They even bounced slightly as they struck the ground before coming to a halt. Reed let out a sigh of relief, and Sue started to ask him if he was okay. She was concerned every time he used his stretching power that it was going to cause some sort of permanent damage to him. After all, look at what had happened to Ben. What would happen if Reed couldn't withdraw himself back to normal and he was stuck that way, with his arms long and dangling?

But the question died in her throat as she became very aware of the closeness they were sharing at that moment. They were lying face to face, and she was cognizant of the emotion passing between the two of them, the awareness of each other's physical proximity. All sorts of memories came back to her, pleasant memories long buried under a heap of unhappy recollections. Now, however, they were returning to her, and for all the frustration she'd known with Reed, for all the lost opportunities they'd experienced . . .

Damn, they'd felt good together.

She could tell from the expression on Reed's face that the exact same thoughts were going through his mind as well. She knew it because she felt a slight tightening of his arms around her, as if he just wanted to hold onto her forever.

"Sorry," she said softly. "My fault. I won't . . . touch anything."

Reed cleared his throat and managed a nod. Slowly he withdrew his arms from their embrace, and that was when Sue heard some sort of scraping noise from the doorway. She twisted her head around to look behind herself, but there was nothing there.

The wall in Victor Von Doom's office had slid aside to reveal a bank of videoscreens, and Victor stood there studying them intently. There was a variety of different views, different angles there, and every single one was from somewhere else in the Baxter Building.

There was very little that Victor Von Doom did not plan ahead for, and certainly the return of Reed Richards and associates to the Baxter Building was not among those things he'd failed to anticipate. At the moment, he was particularly intrigued by what was transpiring in Richards' storeroom, made clear to him courtesy of a video camera secreted within the grill covering an overhead vent.

The first thing that had caught his interest, naturally, was Sue completely wrapped up in Reed's arms. There was no question in his mind that this was far beyond happenstance. Reed hadn't needed to form a protective cocoon around Sue to save her from harm. He could have just pulled her to safety with a single hand, or perhaps gone at it from a different angle by using his malleable body to create a protective covering between Sue and the falling debris. But no. No, Reed had chosen the method that ensured the most physical contact with her. *What a startling coincidence that was,* Victor thought sarcastically. He wondered if the two of them were still trying to fool themselves that it was over between them. He certainly hoped they were, because if they were trying to fool him, they were failing spectacularly.

The second thing he noticed was even more intriguing. Ben Grimm, perhaps drawn over to the storeroom by the crashing of miscellaneous scientific bric-a-brac, stood in the doorway and saw Reed and Sue in what any reasonable person could only see as a romantic clinch (even though the two subjects involved would probably completely deny it). Ben stood there and watched, unaware that the watcher was himself being watched. Then he turned quickly away before Reed and Sue—busy in their own little world—could notice him. The sound of his heavy stone foot scraping on the floor was enough to catch Sue's attention, but by the time she turned to look, Ben was gone. It was an impressive display of speed for someone who looked like a walking mountain.

Victor considered all the possibilities of everything he had just witnessed. He was too deliberate, too methodical, to leap to any conclusions as to the best way to proceed. Which was fortunate, since at the moment he was fighting the impulse to storm over to the Baxter Building and find a way to break Reed's neck, elasticity or no.

The main door to his office opened and Leonard entered. He looked at the screens with curiosity and walked over to Von Doom's side. "Is Reed any closer to a cure?" he asked.

"The only thing he's closer to is Sue," said Victor with a light flippancy he didn't feel. Then something drew his attention and he reoriented the focus of the camera toward it. He leaned forward, his eyes narrowing. In reaching out to grab a quick opportunity for cuddling with Sue, Reed had dropped the files he'd been carrying. One of them had fallen open, and the contents had instantly caught his eye.

Victor Von Doom knew that he might not be a scientist on the level of Reed Richards, but he wasn't exactly a slouch either. The diagram that he saw on the floor, while it was rudimentary and only in the preliminary thinking stages, was nevertheless enough to make Victor's heart skip a beat.

It was a transformation chamber of some kind. Reed was developing a means of changing them back to the way they were.

But he knew Richards. Reed was going to be ultra-cautious now since his initial experimentation had resulted in the five of them having their lives turned inside out. It was the scientific equivalent of closing the barn door after the horses were off and sunning themselves in the Bahamas. The problem was, while Reed was busy taking extra care in his development of this potential cure, Victor Von Doom was on the clock. He had the bankers breathing down his neck and, oh yes . . . for all he knew, his neck was going to be the next thing turning into metal.

Even as his mind began to formulate a plan, he said in an offhand manner to Leonard, "Make me a reservation for two at Cipriani tonight."

He then walked over to a storage cabinet and slid open a drawer. In it were an assortment of Ben Grimm's personal effects. Ben's erstwhile fiancée had sent several large boxes over to his last-known employer, probably because she didn't want them around the house anymore, and Von Doom hadn't yet bothered to have any of them forwarded to the Baxter Building. If there was one thing he knew, it was an opportunity when it was dropped in his lap. After his little confrontation with Grimm at the Baxter Building, Von Doom had opted to sift through the objects first, at his leisure. He didn't know what he might find. What he did know was that Ben was Reed's good right arm, and might well be the key to keeping Richards in line. Which meant that Victor had to find a way to get to Ben.

Most of the stuff had been fairly useless, but a videotape had proven particularly interesting. Ben Grimm might have been nigh-unto-invulnerable on the outside, which meant that the trick to getting to him was from the inside. This tape represented the first step in that challenge. Von Doom had already had a copy of it made for his personal files, but there was no harm in returning this one to its previous owner. He held it up and said, "And get this over to Ben Grimm."

Leonard took the tape, nodded once, and headed out of the office. Victor, meantime, leaned closer in toward the machine, manipulating the controls to get an even better view of the files. Unfortunately, this action was counterproductive as his proximity caused the screens to become filled with static. He frowned and picked at his scar. This time, when skin peeled off, it barely even registered.

16

Ben had no clue what could be in the package that the messenger dropped off for him. Depressingly, the messenger's job was to hand-deliver it, and his reaction to seeing Ben was about what one could have expected. What was really frightening to Ben was that he was getting used to it. He was resigning himself to the idea that people would perpetually be flinching back in horror upon seeing him for—well, for the rest of his life. That fact alone was enough to drive him into even deeper depression.

He ripped open the package and his eyes widened beneath his rocky brow as he instantly recognized it. Suddenly the fact that he didn't know who had sent it over or why was secondary to the fact that he was holding it at all.

Ben looked right and left without really understanding why he was doing so. Then he headed over to the media room which was, fortunately enough, empty. The last thing he needed was to run into Johnny in the middle of watching yet more news coverage of them, timing with a stop-watch how much screen time he was getting.

He fired up the video system in the living quarters and popped the tape into the nearest deck. Then he dimmed the lights and leaned back onto the sofa, which then abruptly collapsed on his end under his enormous weight. He continued to stay seated as the opposite end of the sofa protruded upward awkwardly at nearly a forty-five degree angle.

The screen lit up and he sat there looking at himself. There was Ben Grimm, hale and hearty and not at all a monster. He was standing there with his eyes closed, literally blind to his surroundings and metaphorically blind to his future. There was a voice—Debbie's voice—from off-camera, saying, "Close your eyes, baby. Keep 'em closed. Okay? Okay, and . . ."

"*Surprise!*" voices chorused.

On the video, Ben opened his eyes and grinned even wider. Debbie stepped into the frame, draping her arms around him and laughing. "You surprised?" she asked.

"Yeah, I'm surprised," said the human Ben Grimm. "Surprised the fire department didn't shut this down."

Whoever was holding the video camera whipped it around to reveal the surprise party that was crowding in to celebrate Ben's fortieth birthday party at O'Donnel's Pub. The living room was packed with people, so many that Ben Grimm—since having been transformed into this misshapen thing—had almost forgotten just how many friends he used to have. Like those occasions where one has such a miserable head cold that one forgets what it's like to be able to breathe normally, Ben realized he'd had no recollection of being anything other than lonely and miserable. This video was like seeing a pinprick of light after a period of blindness.

On the screen, Reed stepped into frame and draped his arm around Ben's shoulders, posing for a picture. In the media room, Ben grunted, "God, I was good-looking."

Everyone was singing "Happy Birthday" while a cake was carted toward him with enough candles to ignite a city block. Debbie kissed Ben with such passion that whoops and shouts of "Whoooaaaa" and "Get a room!" and "This *is* their room!" rebounded. Then Ben stepped back, puffed up his cheeks, and blew out the candles.

"What did you wish for, honey?" chirped Debbie.

"I already got it," he grinned, hugging her tightly. "Everything I want."

The Ben of times long past kissed Debbie, while the Ben of the awful present sat there with tears running down his cheeks. He didn't even feel them, though. His skin was solid rock; he felt nothing. Nothing at all.

He sat in darkness, inside and out.

Minutes later, he was heading down the corridor, wearing a ragged trench coat. He caught a glimpse of Johnny Storm wandering around, staring at something, and kept going before Johnny spotted him. Soon he was out into the streets, enveloped in more darkness and feeling depressingly at home.

*   *   *

Johnny strolled down the hallways, wearing a robe and slippers, heading toward the kitchen. As he did so, he passed a case where their uniforms were hanging. He slowed, his eyes narrowing, as he looked them up and down, considering the possibilities.

He thought he spotted something off to his right, out the corner of his eye. But when he turned to look, there was nothing, and he decided it was just a reflection off the glass of the display case. He studied it a moment more, and then went to the kitchen, his thoughts floating about. He knew he had the germ of an idea in there, but wasn't quite sure what it was.

He opened a cupboard and pulled out some Jiffy Pop. Opening his right hand, he placed it in his palm and concentrated. His hand warmed up steadily and the popcorn obediently began to pop. Johnny grinned, remembering that movie where a kid with ice powers was able to chill a soda just by puffing on it. Hell, this was tons better.

With his free hand, Johnny picked up the remote, making sure to focus on keeping one hand hot and the other cool. The last thing he needed to do was turn the remote control into melted plastic. Flipping on the TV with it, he proceeded to channel surf while keeping the popcorn expanding. The Jiffy Pop swelled until the tin foil container looked ready to burst, at which point Johnny lowered the heat to body temperature. All the while he continued going through channels until he settled on the X Games.

Sue tended to rag on him for his viewing choices, but

she wasn't in the room. Besides, what wasn't to like? Cool stunts, hot girls. As far as Johnny Storm was concerned, this was what television had been invented for.

He flopped down onto the couch, tossed the remote onto the cushion beside him, and tore open the top of the Jiffy Pop container. As he proceeded to chow down on the perfectly popped contents, the thoughts and notions that had been skittering through his mind began to coalesce into a concrete idea. A mischievous smile played across his lips, and he nodded to himself.

Oh yeah . . . definitely, he thought. *That's the way to go.*

Even though it seemed a lifetime ago that he'd been there, Ben still remembered the way to go. Why shouldn't he? If the comfortable house he'd shared with Debbie had been his home, O'Donnel's Pub was his home away from home.

He walked the streets of Brooklyn, trench coat pulled up to his neck and a fedora pulled down low over his head. He felt like something out of a film noir detective story. Or, more correctly, a detective story combined with a horror film.

The lights of the street lamps flickered and buzzed, and steam rose from the gratings that covered the vents for the subway system. As he approached O'Donnel's, he suddenly thought he knew how Scrooge had felt in *A Christmas Carol.* Not the aspect of being a miser, but feeling like a visitor to his own past.

There, just ahead of him, was O'Donnel's. It was exactly as he remembered it, with a neon sign flashing the pub's name. The second "n" had been burned out but now it was intact again, so Ernie, the owner, had obviously had it fixed. It shone a bit more brightly than the others. Someone had put a song on the juke box, and Ben winced at the ironic appropriateness of it: "Shake Your Groove Thing." Well, he was a thing and he had grooves, but he didn't feel like shaking any of them at that moment. There were sounds of laughter, people living their normal lives, eating, drinking, socializing, hitting on each other. He wondered if any of them were thinking about him, or if he'd just been banished from the minds of man like a bad memory.

He stood just outside the door for a long time, wrestling with the prospect of going in or staying out. Finally it came down to a matter of time expended. He'd come all this way, suffering the stares and glances from the people in the subway, just so he could . . . what? Be too chickenhearted to go in? What was the worst that they were going to do, point and stare? Like he wasn't used to that by now.

Pulling his hat lower, turning up his collar, Ben stepped sideways through what was now, to him, a very narrow door. He wondered if anyone was going to notice him. He didn't need to for long. As if he were a feared gunman in some film about the Old West, conversation died out almost instantly the moment he entered the dim lighting of the bar.

There were people standing about, talking, a few dancing, in addition to the folks at the tables who had been in the midst of conversations before Ben entered.

As if the crowd was operating with a single mind, they cleared out of his way as he walked across the pub toward the bar.

He glanced automatically toward where Ernie had always kept that 8 x 10 photograph of Ben in his astronaut heyday. For some reason he'd just assumed that Ernie would have taken it down. After all, if one's own fiancée wants to divest herself of everything having to do with you, you just kind of assume that everyone else in your life will follow suit. So Ben was pleasantly surprised to see that the picture was still there. Ben in his flight suit from years back, with some hair and a bit less jowl. He had his helmet tucked under his left arm, and was saluting with his right. He'd even inscribed the words, "To Ernie—Keep em flying! Ben Grimm" on the photograph.

Ernie had been under the counter, probably going for the martini mix. He stood up upon realizing that the pub had fallen silent, and his eyes widened at seeing Ben. To Ben's amazement, there was no horror or even pity in Ernie's eyes. He just looked surprised to see Ben there. If anyone from George Bush to Thomas Jefferson had walked in, Ernie would likely have reacted in the exact same way.

Without thinking about what he was doing, Ben pulled out a bar stool to sit upon. The moment he did, the stool snapped like a toothpick, sending Ben crashing to the floor so hard that the glasses suspended in racks overhead shook violently.

There was faint laughter from several patrons behind

245

him. Ben lurched to his feet, spun to face them, and snarled, *"That's not funny!"*

Of course, he supposed that on some level it was funny. People falling down are always humorous, at least to the people who are watching and not falling. But Ben wasn't exactly in the mood for hilarity. Then again, he didn't really know what he was in the mood *for*. What had he expected? That everyone would wave, say "Hi, Ben, been a while," and then go back to business as usual? How unlikely was that?

The bar went silent once more, and then customers started dropping money onto their tables in order to cover their bills. They cleared out quickly, some of them unable to take their gazes from him as they went, others doing what they could to look anywhere else but at Ben Grimm.

Ernie called after them indignantly, "Hey, that's Ben Grimm there!" He pointed a trembling finger at Ben. "The first mook from Brooklyn to go to outer space! So pay him some respect!"

They didn't listen. Instead, if anything, it made them clear out faster rather than stay and face the insensitivity of their own actions. Ben looked down, weary. "Sorry for killing your business, Ernie. I'll take the usual, then I'm out." He paused, then added, "Better make it a double."

Ernie went to pour Ben a scotch and soda, while Ben glanced at the last of the retreating figures and then shook his head sadly. Then he noticed, in the large mirror behind the bar, that there was a single young woman who had not fled the place. She was seated at a table behind and to the right of him. He turned slowly and looked at her, concerned that the moment she saw his face, she too would bolt.

She did not. Instead she simply sat there and stared into space. She had a drink in front of her which she appeared to be nursing. Ben felt as if she was the most serene-looking individual he'd ever seen. She was a young black woman, with delicate features and a mane of dark, curly hair. She reached for her drink, and to Ben's surprise she missed it. Not by a small margin, an inch or two at most. She recovered quickly and located it, but that was enough for Ben to realize what he hadn't at first. And he felt really dumb when he belatedly noticed the white cane against the other side of the table. She was blind.

"Who killed the party?" she asked in a curious and slightly musical voice.

"Every party needs a pooper, lady," Ben replied. "That's why they invited me."

No wonder she hadn't bolted. The only two people in the place that could stand to be with her were Ernie, who had known Ben since he was a teenage snot running with the Yancy Street Gang and trying to connive some drinks with painfully obvious fake IDs . . . and a woman who couldn't see him at all.

Sensing his mood, Ernie slid a drink in front of Ben and said, "Made it a triple. On the house, Benny."

Ben forced a smile as he reached for the drink, figuring that he couldn't possibly feel any lower. That turned

247

out to be optimistic as his grip shattered the glass, spilling it all over himself.

Ernie looked stricken, and at that moment Ben literally didn't know whether to laugh or cry. He settled for a depressed, even self-deprecating chuckle and announced, "If there's a God, She hates me."

"I don't think She's real big on hate," the blind girl said.

Ben had reached behind the bar, picked up a rag, and was busy drying himself off. "You wouldn't say that if you could see me," he replied.

"Hunh," said the blind girl. She knocked back her drink, settled the cup back down on the table, then reached out for her cane with unerring precision as she stood. She tilted her head slightly, like a dog listening carefully. "Can I . . . ? See you . . . ?"

She came slowly toward him as Ben exchanged nervous glances with Ernie. Ernie smiled gently and shrugged, and Ben had to wonder just what in the world he had to be nervous about. This was a slip of a blind girl, and he was built like the Hoover Dam. What could she possibly do to him? Hurt his feelings? So she'd head out the door just like the others. What was one more, really?

Noticing the prolonged silence, she smiled and said, "It's okay, I won't bite . . ." Her hand brushed against his arm and her face registered her surprise. "Not that I *could*."

That actually made Ben smile, and he couldn't readily remember the last time he'd done that. But then the smile faded as she raised her hand from his arm toward his face. He wanted to push her away, to tell her to keep her hands to herself. It was one thing when people took one look at him and bolted. But letting someone get this close . . . the horror that would inevitably be reflected in her expression, the hurried excuses that would be offered as she fled the pub. Hell, she might dart directly in front of a speeding car, she'll be so anxious to get out.

She touched his extended brow, his nose, brought up her other hand, and rested both hands on either side of his face. She slid her right hand under his chin and her left hand ran gently across his mouth. Her head was tilted upward, her eyes remaining blank, although they fluttered slightly as her hands moved around the entirety of his features. Ben realized he wasn't breathing, but continued not to exhale. Even Ernie was fascinated watching her trying to get a grasp of Ben's countenance.

"Such a sad face," she said at last, sounding wistful. "You know . . . sometimes being different isn't a bad thing."

"Trust me, this ain't one of those times," was all Ben said.

She withdrew her hands then and picked up her cane. Ben watched her face carefully, waiting for some sign of her revulsion to register. Instead she simply smiled and, as she headed for the door, said, "See you round, Benny." She paused once more and then added, "I'm Alicia, by the way."

She walked out, her cane tapping on the sidewalk.

Ben noticed there were a few people still outside on the sidewalk, looking in puzzlement at Alicia and then in silent wonder at Ben. One of them, a young guy, to Ben's amazement, gave him a thumbs-up.

Ben stared at them and tried to fathom what had just happened. Before he had the time to do so, however, a new drink was at his elbow. This one was in a sturdy steel martini shaker. Ben picked it up, holding it gingerly so that he wouldn't bend it, and knocked back the drink. It felt good going down . . . the best he'd felt in ages.

The lights at Cipriani were dimmed, as was customary for the evening meal in the upscale Central Park West restaurant. With small candlelit centerpieces in the middle of every table, it presented an effect that was almost stellar. It was like dining in the sky itself, surrounded by glittering stars.

Victor Von Doom, feeling quite at home in the darkness, sat patiently with his fingers interlaced and his face a mask. He was wearing thin white gloves that served to cover what he did not wish Susan to see. Granted, the gloves themselves might serve to attract her attention, but better a perceived affectation than a weakness actually seen.

Although . . . as he stared thoughtfully at his gloved hands . . . why was he thinking of it as a weakness? His skin wasn't peeling away to reveal marshmallow. It was metal beneath the flesh. Solid metal that served to underscore the type of man that Victor Von Doom was. Rather than hiding it, he should be putting it on display for everyone to see.

It was something he really should consider. But he wasn't going to do it now, because he needed to focus on the matter before him.

Sue Storm approached him, guided by the maître d'. It was clear that some people had either recognized her immediately and taken an interest in her, or else they had recognized Victor when he first sat down at his prime-spot table and were wondering who might be arriving to dine with him. Hopefully the arrival of Sue Storm of the newspaper-ballyhooed Fantastic Four would be sufficient to quell their infernal curiosity.

He did not allow his annoyance with his fellow diners to interfere. Instead he rose up, stepped around the table, and drew out the chair before the maître d' could do so. The maître d' bowed slightly in acknowledgment of the fact that Von Doom clearly had matters under control, and so absented himself from the table. Sue slid into the chair as smoothly as butter skidding across a heated griddle. "Thank you for coming out to see me," Victor said in a suave voice.

She nodded, a little self-conscious. The dress she was wearing wasn't quite formal wear, but it was an attractive enough off-the-shoulder ensemble. As she sat at the table, Victor eased her chair into place and came around the other side. As he did so, Sue asked with insistence, "You said it was urgent."

"It is," he said evenly. He returned to his chair and sat. "There's something we need to talk about. Something I need to ask you . . ."

"Victor, slow down," she said, raising a hand to halt him. "I want you to know I appreciate everything you've done for me . . ." She took a deep breath, let it out slowly, and continued, "But I just don't . . ."

"Susan . . . what are you doing?"

The words were cold as ice, as hard as metal, as sharp as a knife. Victor Von Doom was simply not someone who allowed his weaknesses, any weaknesses, to show. "You think I brought you here to talk about *us*? Please. This is *business*." He leaned forward, his voice low and intense to drive home the seriousness of his interest. "I need to know: How close is Reed to finding a cure?"

He watched her carefully, staring into her eyes, determined to act as a human lie detector who would be able to tell if she was being candid or not. "He's working round the clock," she said finally. "But the data needs to be tested, analyzed, before—"

It was exactly what he thought he would hear. He sat back, laughing with a bitter tinge to his voice. "Same old Reed. All analysis, no action." He hesitated just long enough for that to sink in and then, as if suddenly struck by a memory, asked, "Wasn't that the problem with you two?"

The remark got the desired reaction as Sue clearly had to fight to keep her cool. A Sue Storm who remained patient, analytical, distant, would be of no use to him. He needed a Sue Storm driven by the same urgency that drove him. "If these molecules . . . aren't stable," Sue told him slowly as she maintained a precarious grip on her patience, "they could make us *worse*. Maybe even kill us."

"Then why is Reed dragging his feet?" demanded Victor as if Sue's own words had just proven his point. His next words came across as if he were suddenly struck by the notion when, in fact, he'd been planning precisely what he was going to say, and was following a script which Sue was being cooperative, and predictable, enough to follow. "Maybe he *likes* having his prize specimen under glass. It's ironic, isn't it? You're finally the perfect woman for him . . . because you're his *science project*."

The words hit home, as he knew they would. She couldn't help but hear some truth in them. Hell, for all Von Doom knew, he was right. Sue lowered her gaze, unable to meet his, which was an additional signal to Victor that matters were going exactly in the direction he wanted them to. "Please don't make this personal," Sue asked with a touch of pleading in her voice.

"Oh, I think you already have," Victor said.

"Victor, we can't do anything until the research is ready . . ."

Despite his determination to remain as cold as the metal beneath his skin, Victor reacted to those words with a bit more intensity than he would have liked. He clenched his fist and, from beneath the glove, there was the sound of metal scraping against metal. "'We,' huh?"

He tried to rein himself in, dimly aware that he was losing it. He succeeded only to the degree that he did not reach across the table and throttle her. But he was still angry enough that he shoved the chair back, pushing against it so violently that he set the glasses rocking and water spilling from them. At the moment he didn't care about that, coming around the table quickly, getting uncomfortably close to her, and resting a hand on her shoulder. The eyes of everyone in the restaurant were upon him at that moment, and he couldn't have cared less.

"Don't forget who you work for, Susan," he said sharply. "So *get to work*. And *do your job*."

Then he turned and walked out. His hand was thrust deep into his pocket, and his fingers were wrapped around the diamond engagement ring within. Without even realizing he was doing it, he squeezed it, picturing his fingers around Sue's throat—Sue's and Reed's throats—and tighter and tighter went the squeezing. And then, impossibly but inevitably, he discovered that his hand had crushed the diamond ring into a fine powder.

He brushed off the dust into an ashtray as he went. As he did so, he heard some assorted gasps from behind him, and had a feeling that they weren't over his abrupt departure. He turned and saw exactly what he suspected he was going to see: Sue, steeped in embarrassment and humiliation, had vanished. Only her clothes were there, floating at the table.

Some businessman at another table muttered, "I wish

my wife would disappear." He'd had a few too many to drink and his voice carried more than he'd anticipated. Even so, ordinarily that wouldn't have presented a problem, but it did this time. The wine he had set down, and was now reaching for, suddenly eluded his grasp and tumbled forward into his lap. He yelped, staring at the spreading pool of liquid in his pants.

Von Doom smiled at that briefly, and then the smile disappeared. He'd had two plans for the evening. The "A" plan, the preferred plan, was to propose to Sue, make her his genuine ally through the bonds of matrimony, and use her in that capacity to exert pressure upon Richards.

But she had shot him down. The patronizing look she had given him, the cavalier dismissal of his intentions— intentions that he had quickly hidden under the guise of merely wanting to talk business—galled him beyond his ability to articulate. He had been forced to use plan "B," to retreat. And Victor Von Doom did not easily retreat. Nor did he ever forget those who forced him to do so.

No. Not ever.

17

THE NEW YORK CITY ARENA THAT SERVED AS THE HOME for the ESPN Moto X Games was alive with the sort of energy that can only be generated by a packed house enthusiastically watching a cavalcade of bike riders risking their lives in daring flips and acrobatics at insane speeds.

Every time another rider dodged death while performing a heart-stopping feat on his 250cc motorbike, the crowd roared with approval. The cyclists darted through a maze of mountainous dirt hills and ramps, while the announcer kept the crowd amped up anytime there was a danger of even the slightest diminishment of excitement.

"And now, ladies and gentlemen," boomed the announcer's voice to a crowd composed neither of ladies nor gentlemen, but twenty thousand screaming lunatics. "We have a special guest for you: Johnny Storm of the Fantastic Four!"

Johnny drank in the howls and cheers like an attention junkie. He was wearing his blue uniform, and he waved to the crowd as if he owned them. Remembering that film about a Roman gladiator, he swaggered forward with his arms spread, embracing the cheers as if they were physical things. It was possible that he heard a few catcalls and cries of "Freak!" mixed in with the shouts of approval, but he quickly dismissed them as the ravings of a handful of guys who'd had a few too many beers.

He stepped up to the pit where riders were prepping to head out on their bikes, and approached one in particular. "Hey, Ronnie Renner!" Johnny called out. "I'm a big fan!"

Renner, pulling on his helmet, gave a tight nod. It was clear from his attitude that he wasn't keen on being upstaged by anyone, much less some abnormal media curiosity who belonged on the front pages of *The National Enquirer.* But Johnny was oblivious to any lack of tolerance on Renner's part.

Other bikers were approaching with various degrees of curiosity mixed with amusement and even disdain. One of them, Kenny Bartram, said, "Heard you like to ride." He motioned to his own bike. "Wanna take her for a spin?"

Johnny thought he was joking at first. When Bartram nodded encouragingly and gestured that Johnny should feel free, Johnny tentatively, and then lovingly, caressed the mean machine's handlebars.

"Come on, bro," Renner said challengingly. "I'll teach you some tricks . . . *if* you can keep up."

Johnny Storm, who had flown a space shuttle,

experimental stealth planes, and ground vehicles that surpassed the speed of sound, had never felt so stoked in his life.

Minutes later, Ronnie Renner was barreling down the track, gunning his motor. Dirt spun through his wheels, kicking back at Johnny who was now wearing a motocross outfit over his uniform. He had the number "004" on the back, and a small "4" patch stitched over his heart.

Double-O 4. License to thrill, baby, Johnny thought deliriously as he opened up the throttle in order to keep up with Renner.

Ronnie Renner hit the first hill and, catching air, somersaulted high into the air as the announcer's voice blasted over the loudspeakers, "A rock-solid double-flip!"

The crowd went wild, even as Johnny thought *Piece o' cake.* He hit the hill at the same speed as Renner, but his angle was even more precise. The result was the exact same move with even more height. The achievement did not go unnoticed by either the crowd or the announcer who shouted, "Look at that lift, ladies and gentlemen!"

Johnny stuck the landing perfectly, and the swell of the audience roar grew. If Johnny could have seen Renner's face, he would have noticed a deepening scowl on the far more experienced biker who felt he was being shown up by this headline-grabbing upstart. Renner pulled harder on the throttle, taking the next jump and executing a stunning corkscrew motion in midair.

"Frontside 360!" the announcer called out, working the crowd into such a frenzy that it seemed they might spontaneously combust. "He's totally flat and whipped!"

Renner landed clean as the roar of the fans pounded through the stadium. Johnny revved his engine, his adrenaline running so hot that it was reflected in the steam beginning to rise from his body. He hit the hill and, incredibly, spun twice in the air, the spin taking so long that it seemed as if he hung there beyond the bounds of what gravity could possibly allow.

"Whoa!" said the announcer, clearly bewildered by what he was seeing. "That's a . . . what *is* that? A 720?"

Johnny landed as perfectly as Renner had, and the crowd went nuts. Ronnie didn't hesitate, bearing down toward the last hill and leaning over his handlebars, preparing a trick that was generally considered one of those reserved for the truly insane.

"He's going for a Kiss of Death!" the announcer warned, anticipating the move.

Sure enough, Ronnie hit the hill, performing a stunt that was a combination of the Fender Grab and the Hart Attack, only even more dangerous. While still in the air, Ronnie brought his bike as close to vertical as possible, and then kicked his legs up above his head while still gripping the handlebars. He froze there for a moment in the air, like something off a Motocross poster, and then shoved the front end down while bringing his legs back and down to the pegs. The crowd reaction was deafening as Ronnie landed, having flawlessly executed the dare-devil move.

Johnny was undaunted. He sped faster, and faster still, his heart pounding in his chest, moving so quickly that trails of flame began to streak off his back. He looked like a human rocket as he hurtled up the hill, jet trail behind him. He didn't leap into the air so much as launch, taking off like a missile, spinning at impossible heights, a flaming blur to all who saw him.

Seized with a heady, newfound sense of power and a confidence that he could accomplish anything he wanted simply by imagining it, Johnny released his hold on his bike. The second he parted contact with it, the crowd noise choked, as they anticipated Johnny going into a bone-crushing free fall.

He didn't. He did, in fact, the opposite. He kept rising, spiraling upward, and suddenly his body ignited head to toe. His eyes saw a world of flame before him, and right then, he was afraid of absolutely nothing.

The announcer couldn't begin to fathom what he was seeing. "Is he . . . flying?" he said half under his breath.

For that moment he was, and then the moment passed. The flame went out just as quickly as it had appeared, and Johnny fell back onto his still airborne bike, straddling it in midair. Motorbike and rider landed together, the wheels chewing up dirt. It was only upon receiving the jolt of the bike's landing that Johnny's mind snapped back to the reality of what he had just done. Even he couldn't quite believe it. *What the hell just happened?* Johnny wondered. While he had been in the moment, he had been seized with a sense of freedom, of power such as he'd never experienced. Now, after the fact, he could only look back at his accomplishments in wonderment.

Just in case Johnny had the slightest notion that what he'd just pulled off wasn't impressive, the announcer lay rest to that immediately over the spectators' ecstasy. "Unbelievable, ladies and gentlemen!" he said. "You've just seen the first . . . the first . . ." He was clearly searching for a lingo description of the stunt. Finally he settled on, ". . . the first . . . Torchflight! The McTorch!"

In the future, other riders would try to imitate the stunt, using everything from flash powder to gasoline and a match. But that was a long way away, and Johnny's only concern now was the wild praise of the crowd. That and earning the respect of the other cyclists.

They were approaching him now, riding toward him, their eyes wide in wonderment over the stunt that he had just pulled. The crowd was on its feet, cheering deliriously, not certain of what they'd witnessed but impressed nevertheless. Johnny vaulted off the bike, and Kenny Bartram was about to offer congratulations when the words froze in his mouth. He stared in shock at the seat of the motorbike he'd loaned Johnny.

The seat was melted. Not only that, but both wheels suddenly gave out, the tires having been melted right off. He looked back to Johnny for explanation.

"My bad," Johnny said with a shrug. "Sorry about that. Thanks for the lesson, bro."

He then turned away, arms still outstretched, to greet his adoring public that was overrunning the retaining wall and swarming toward him. There were some very attractive young women in the forefront. Johnny welcomed all his fans as they descended upon him, but he welcomed the girls most of all.

The following morning, Sue's mind kept returning to the uneasy and abortive dinner date she'd had with Victor. As she sifted through a mountain of mail that sat on the kitchen table, she kept glancing over at Reed, thinking about what Victor had said. Reed, for his part, wasn't giving her the slightest glance. Overworked, unshaven, he had walked in with his files under his arms, snagged some coffee out of the pot, and was seated at the table sifting through his notes and equations.

"Have you read these?" Sue asked, holding up letters at random. "From all over. People want us to fight crimes . . . save their kids . . . solve their problems . . ." When Reed didn't respond, she added ruefully and under her breath, ". . . when we can't even solve our own."

Naturally Reed didn't react to that comment either, caught up as he was in his own world of problems and considerations. Tossing the letters onto the pile, Sue wrestled with keeping the details of her dinner with Victor to herself, or letting Reed know of her concerns. She felt as if she were, in making that decision, choosing sides.

Oddly, it was a much easier decision to make than she'd originally thought, because once she framed her conundrum in terms of "Reed or Victor," it was a clear choice. Especially because she felt as if she and Reed— not to mention Johnny and Ben—were all in the same boat. Far better to operate as a unit rather than deal with divided loyalties.

"Reed," she said tentatively, but with resolve nevertheless. "I need to talk to you. About Victor." She paused, trying to figure the best way to put it without sounding alarmist. "Something's wrong. He seems off . . . strange . . . out of control."

It was those last three words that got a response from Reed, and Sue could easily understand why. Victor Von Doom was someone who loved being in control at all times, of everything. That most definitely included himself. So if Von Doom was acting out of control, that wasn't just strange. That was genuinely shocking.

But before Reed could respond, he was interrupted by an explosion of fury that consisted of Ben Grimm, down the hallway, bellowing, *"No! No! No freakin' way!"* There was a violent *thooom* sound that was no doubt Ben stomping around.

Sue knew instantly that whatever was bothering Ben, it had to take precedent, if for no other reason than that a truly enraged Ben Grimm might well be capable of bringing the entire building down around their ears.

Reed was on his feet, sprinting down the hallway, and Sue was right after him. They arrived in the media room to find Ben stalking it like an angry lion. An angry, rock-covered, dangerously superstrong lion. "Ben!" Reed cried out. "What? What's going on!"

The first thing that went through Sue's mind was that it was as simple as that Ben had gotten up that morning, looked in the mirror, and finally melted down. That was apparently not the case, though, because whatever was irritating Ben, it was on television. He was pointing at the wall-size TV.

A banner read "ESPN Moto X Games," and the word "Live" was slugged in. There was a cyclist hurtling through the air, and Sue frowned at the sight. "Oookay," she said slowly. "I can see that . . . that, uh, motocross being live first thing in the morning can be kind of upsetting. I think I read that this was some kind of marathon tournament. I'm sorry that, uh . . . that you wanted to go, I guess . . ." She looked to Reed, who nodded sympathetically, ". . . and I know that our having to stay put is—"

"Shuddup," Ben growled. "I did go out and that ain't the point. *Look*!"

The cyclist in the air suddenly burst into flame, hung in the air, and then landed on his motorcycle.

"Oh my God," breathed Reed. Sue felt all the blood draining from her face, and most of her body, and coagulating in her feet.

The image suddenly disappeared, to be replaced by a reporter standing there with a grinning Johnny Storm. "That was the scene earlier this evening," said the reporter, "when Johnny here introduced the 'McTorch,' exclusively here at the X Games." Johnny, meantime, was in the process of peeling off the burned remains of his motocross outfit, revealing his blue uniform which now had a stylized "4" stitched onto it. The reporter eyed it with interest. "So what can you tell us about the outfit?"

"Not too much," Johnny said. "But I will say it's all weather and no leather. Kind of Armani-meets-astronaut."

Sue stared at the screen with her mouth agape, matching the expressions of the others. "He didn't," she said.

"Oh, he did," Ben assured her.

The "4" seemed to leap out of the set at her. "*What* did he do to the uniform?" She turned to Reed to further express her annoyance with her brother, and then gazed in bewilderment at an identical emblem on Reed's own uniform, which had hitherto been hidden by his lab coat.

"He talked me into it," Reed said with a shrug.

"*How*? With blackmail photographs?"

"He said it would be an interesting experiment to see if it would provide us with a sense of unity . . ."

"You," said Ben, "would sell yer sister to gypsies if ya thought it would be an interesting experiment."

"Well, first, I don't have a sister, and second—"

"Our super hero names?"

It had been Johnny responding to the most recent

question from the reporter. He looked briefly confused, as if caught off guard. "Yes," prodded the reporter. "So what are your super hero names?"

"I go by the Human Torch," Johnny said after a moment, trying to act as if he'd spoken without hesitation. Then he added in a tone that he probably thought sounded macho, "The ladies call me Torch."

"What about the rest of the team?"

"Uh . . ." Johnny was clearly thinking as fast as he could. "We call my sister the invisible girl . . . the Invisible Girl."

"*Girl!*" sputtered Sue.

Ben leveled a look at her and said in mock sympathy, "I'm sure he meant it like, 'You go, girl.'"

"That's easy to remember!" said the reporter cheerfully, which was exactly what Sue didn't want to hear. If it was easy to remember, that probably meant it was already seared into the memories of everyone who was watching. "And Reed Richards? He's the leader. So what's he? *Mister* Fantastic?"

"Well, I wouldn't say he's the leader," Johnny said, clearly interested in discussing the question of who was in charge.

Reed looked at Ben and shrugged. Obviously he didn't hate the name, Sue thought. Mired in this stupidity generated by her brother, she nevertheless found some small measure of amusement in that. She didn't think Reed had any ego at all, much less enough to be accepting of the name "Mister Fantastic." For his part, Ben merely said, "Could be worse."

At which point the reporter held up a copy of the *New York Post*. The infamous one that had sold out in hours and was already, Sue had discovered, going for thirty dollars and up on eBay. He pointed at the photo of Ben and said, "What about this one? What do you call this thing?"

Johnny smiled and, looking right into the camera, said, "That's it. Just 'the Thing.' We would have gone with 'the Rock,' but that was taken. And 'Thing' pretty much sums it up."

Ben nodded, absorbing it, and then said matter-of-factly, "Okay. I'm gonna go kill him now."

He turned to leave. Before Sue could say anything to stop him, Reed had extended an arm and draped it around Ben's shoulders. "Ben! Slow down a second and—"

The reporter was holding up another photo, this one the cover of *Wired*, which featured a pre-change Reed. "Is it true," asked the reporter, "what they say? That he can expand *any* part of his anatomy?"

"Actually, between us, I think he's got some problems staying rigid," Johnny replied.

"—and wait for me," Reed said without missing a beat, his eyes hardening.

"Which may explain," said the reporter, now holding up a photo of Sue that had appeared on the cover of *People* magazine, "why *this* woman's not smiling."

Sue, who was about to rein in her associates, instantly announced, "I'm driving."

They headed out as Johnny, on TV, said with a distinct air of "ewww" in his voice, "Dude! That's my sister!"

Johnny Storm was having the time of his life.

A gorgeous girl was on his arm. He hadn't caught her name yet, but that was the last thing on his mind. He was living the life that he had aspired to for ages. Everything was up, up, up, and he was never going to have to worry about down again.

A line of enthusiastic fans were waiting for his autograph outside the exit, and he was perfectly happy to accommodate them. "You're wonderful!" one of them bubbled. "You're the greatest! You should be the leader of the Fantastic Four!"

"Preaching to the choir, babe," he said, as he finished signing. There were others clamoring for his attention, but he waved them off as the girl on his arm jostled him, clearly hankering for his attention.

He headed toward where he had valet parked his car, having called ahead to make sure it would be brought around and ready for him. The valet was standing there, looking surprisingly ill in the morning light. Johnny wondered why even as he displayed his claim ticket. The valet didn't bother to look at it, instead staring forlornly at Johnny in such a way that set off warning bells in Johnny's head. "Where's my ride?" Johnny asked cautiously. "The red Porsche? With the license plate that says TORCH'D?"

Looking like a man on death row, the valet blew his whistle in two short bursts. In response, a four-foot ball of red junk metal rolled down the street and stopped at the curb directly in front of Johnny.

The valet timidly proffered the keys.

"What the—?" Johnny looked at the ball of scrap, waiting for the practical joke to be revealed, and slowly realizing that he himself was the punch line. "Is that my . . . ?"

Something hard and metallic bounced off his head. He yelped, staggered, and looked at the flat piece of metal that had rebounded off him and clattered to the street. The word TORCH'D looked up at him from his license plate, the only noncrumbled remains of his car.

Rubbing the sting from his head, Johnny turned in the direction from which the remains of the car had rolled and saw Ben Grimm in the distance, dusting off his hands.

"You're gonna pay for that, Pebbles!" Johnny bellowed. The remaining fans, seeing the "Human Torch" about to square off against "the Thing," reacted in two ways: A handful remained to see what would happen. The rest bolted in the other direction.

Johnny felt himself starting to get steamed up, and welcomed the sensation. But then he spotted Sue heading toward him. "What?" he bellowed, not wanting his sister's presence to dampen his mounting anger and, thus, his flame capacity.

"You gave us *names*?" Sue demanded. "What are you, the 'face' of the Fantastic Four now?"

Ben, meantime, was drawing nearer, his hands balled into fists. "It's about to be a broken face," he said with a snarl.

Reed stepped in between, trying to be the voice of

reason, even though Johnny could see that even Reed was torqued with him. "This isn't permanent, Johnny," Reed said. "We need to be careful until we're normal again."

"What if some of us don't *want* to be 'normal again'?" Johnny demanded. He could see from Reed's reaction that the scientist had never considered that possibility. Well, now was the time to drive it home. "Some of us like the idea of 'fantastic' being the new 'normal'! We didn't all turn into monsters like—!"

He saw Ben lunging toward him, wielding a fist the size of an anvil. Johnny stepped back, trying to put enough distance between himself and Ben until he got his flame stoked. But Ben froze with his fist in the air, visibly struggling with his impulse to take a swing at Johnny . . . and obviously realizing that there would be nothing left of Johnny if he connected. Nothing except a blood-spattered corpse and a homicide charge left to be leveled at New York's premier monster.

Slowly he lowered his arm and turned away.

Johnny didn't care. Infuriated by the sight of his car transformed into a ball, and feeling humiliated in the eyes of the remaining fans who were looking on—not to mention the gorgeous girl who had taken a few steps back, uncertain of what she should do—Johnny held out his hand and watched with satisfaction as a fireball flamed into existence.

He swung his arm back with the precision of a baseball pitcher and hurled the fireball directly at Ben. It smacked him in the back of the head and brought him to a stop. Slowly Ben turned to look at him with in-credulity, more shocked than injured. Reed and Sue were standing there, paralyzed, like witnesses to a tractor trailer in the process of jackknifing, knowing that a major wreck was about to occur but unable to think of how to stop it.

"Did you just—?" Ben started to say, and then a sec-ond fireball hit him full in the face. That was it. What-ever concerns he'd had about consequences went out the window as Ben charged at Johnny like a taunted bull, bellowing, "Okay, that's it, Tinker Bell! You wanna fly? *Fly!*"

Reed lunged in between them, spreading his arms wide, and he shouted Ben's name. Ben either didn't hear or didn't care as his fist drove forward and slammed into Reed's chest. Reed's intervention slowed Ben's assault, but only to a minor degree. Ben's fist hammered right through Reed, indenting it, and Reed's back expanded with it, so that Ben's Reed-covered fist slammed into Johnny at slightly less speed than it had initially pos-sessed. The result was that Johnny survived the impact. But there was still enough power in it to send him hurtling off his feet. He didn't go far, as he crashed into the side of a Burger King billboard truck, a sponsor of the X Games. There was a large advertisement for the chain's "flame broiled Whopper" on the side where Johnny hit. He was flattened against it for a moment, and when he fell off, there was a flaming Johnny Storm–size imprint where the all-beef patty had been.

Cameras started snapping from every direction.

Johnny didn't notice. His focus was entirely upon Ben, standing several yards away, endeavoring to extricate his fist from Reed's chest. Johnny's body temperature spiked and kept going as, bruised face twisted in fury, he brought up both his hands, which were now crackling with flame.

"Let's see if we can get blood from a stone," he grated.

Ben shook off Reed as he and Johnny locked eyes. With a block of sidewalk between two men—one of them with fist of flame and the other with mallets of orange rock—they started toward each other in a dead-out run. Bystanders and onlookers screamed, some in fear, others in perverse joy over being witness to a serious super hero smackdown.

A heartbeat before they reached the point of no return, however, Sue stepped directly between the two of them. She did not even bother to bring her force field into effect. Instead she stopped each of them in their tracks with a single look, one so cold that it froze Johnny and so hard that Ben recoiled from it.

Like a mother scolding a couple of petulant five-year-olds, Sue informed them, "You two need a time-out."

"Blockhead started it!" Johnny said accusingly, pointing at Ben. Ben, in response, held up his fist and thrust it upward in such a way that—had he still had a middle finger to be upraised—would have been a rather crude gesture. Then he turned and stomped off, the crowd melting away from his path like the Red Sea before Moses. Cameras continued to click until Ben snatched one from the hands of a guy whom Johnny immediately recognized as a reporter, crushed it, then handed it back to him.

"Damn it, Johnny!" snapped Sue, although she looked more disappointed than angry. She was about to say something else, but then simply shook her head in frustration and headed off after Ben. Johnny saw Reed approaching him and rolled his eyes, wanting to do anything except have this conversation.

"You need to control yourself," Reed said curtly, "and *think* before you—"

"—act?" Johnny completed the sentence for him. He wanted to stay angry, but it was hard to remain that way with Reed. The guy was just so freaking clueless, being mad at him was like clubbing a baby seal. "See, that's your problem. You're *always* thinking, never *acting*. What if we got these gifts for a reason? What if we have some . . . you know . . . like, calling?"

"A higher calling. Like getting girls and making money?" asked Reed.

Johnny nodded, pleased that Reed was understanding it. "Is there any higher?" He turned to the crowd, igniting his hand so it was aflame. People shrieked in excitement and snapped more pictures. Johnny turned and smiled at Reed. "This is who we are, Reed. Accept it. Or, better yet . . . *enjoy* it."

Turning away from Reed, he stepped into the crowd of fans, who eagerly babbled questions to him like, "Were you scared?" and "That was so amazing! Did it hurt?" He fielded the questions, posed for more pictures, took down a few phone numbers from women who kept slipping them to him on pieces of paper. And it was only when he cast one final glance in Reed's direction and saw the disappointment on his face that he came to a realization: When Reed was talking about the higher calling of girls and money, he wasn't being understanding. He was being sarcastic.

Sue continued to sprint after Ben, wending her way through a crowd composed of a seemingly endless number of people who wanted her attention. She'd never have managed to catch up except that, where Ben walked, he got the opposite reaction: People continued to clear out of his way. Finally she managed to get into his wake and draw close enough so that the curiosity-seekers fell back and away from them, not wanting to get near Sue when she was in turn near Ben.

"Ben, slow down," she pleaded.

He cast a sideways glance at her but didn't stop moving. She managed to fall into step next to him, although she had to take insanely long strides to keep up with him. "He didn't mean it. You know Johnny. He's always been a hothead—"

To her surprise, Ben replied, "It's not him. It's them." He chucked a misshapen thumb in the direction of the people behind them. Even the slightest wave of his hand was enough to make them flinch back. "I can't live like this."

"Just give Reed a little more time. You know how he works . . . analyzing every little step before he takes one . . ."

274

"It's easy for you to be patient."

"No, it's not!" she snapped, feeling more irritated than she really felt she had any right to be. "I thought I was done waiting for Reed." He fired her a glance as she continued, "I know this whole thing is a nightmare, but we're all in this together now, Ben . . ."

He slowed, stopped, turned to her and said in a low, intense voice, *"Together?* Look at me, Susie. You got no idea what I'd give . . . to be invisible. Your nightmare . . . is my dream."

She opened her mouth, but had no ready response to that. The depth of pain in his eyes was almost more than she could bear. Ben grunted at her silence, then turned away and headed off into a nearby alley. This time she made no effort to follow him.

18

VICTOR DIDN'T KNOW FROM PERSONAL EXPERIENCE
what the inner circles of Hell were like, but he had a
sneaking suspicion that at least one of them bore a remarkable resemblance to the conference room of
AmerEuro Bank. Outside the day was dreary. The rain
had been coming down in torrents and was only just
now easing up.

As he stared at the television screen featuring CNN
footage that was courtesy of civilian videotapers . . . including prolonged, frame-by-frame replays of Johnny
Storm and Ben Grimm attempting to pound the snot
out of each other, while Reed Richards and Sue Storm
intervened to varying degrees of success . . . he decided
that, yes, this was definitely what Hell was like. Endless
CNN-viewing of the people who had ruined his life
while Ned Cecil and his assortment of identically
dressed-and-pressed corporate goons sat there and gave
him the fish eye.

Cecil was holding a remote and he chose to freeze-frame an image of the Thing snarling directly into the camera. Von Doom had once gone to a research base in the Arctic, and had to believe that that environment was less sterile and cold than the one he was facing at this moment.

"*This*," said Cecil, extending the "s" in the word into a sibilant hiss, "is how you 'turn things around'? These freaks are on the front page, and your company's in the obituaries."

Von Doom saw the others nodding in synch, like the good little sycophants they were. Victor, who had a larger bandage on his face than he did before, pulled together every fragment of self-control he had and said, his voice level, "I have a plan to *use* their publicity for—"

Putting up a hand, Cecil said, "Victor, stop." Von Doom ceased speaking, and waited expectantly, knowing exactly what Cecil was going to say before he spoke. "The bank's lost enough already. This isn't a negotiation. It's a notification. We're pulling out."

The words hung in the air for a moment like floating pieces of broken glass. Victor didn't blink. As cool, as collected as if he were offering the time of day, he replied, "You know . . . this is why I don't keep my money in the bank."

He rose from the chair, offered a curt nod and a dismissive, "Gentlemen," and walked out of the room.

And then he went downstairs, down to the parking garage. He studied the layout thoughtfully. Puddles everywhere due to the cars that had come in from the rain. Reasonably well-lit, but he could take care of that without much difficulty. Yes. Yes, here would do nicely.

He stepped off into the shadows, containing his anger, knowing it would be necessary to focus it instead.

He wondered if Cecil would be alone, and came to the realization that he didn't care all that much. Whoever was with him . . . well, they would be there for this private conference that Victor was planning.

As it happened, for the first time in a long time, luck was with him. An hour had passed, maybe two. It had been late in the day already and he'd been expecting people to come filing out. Sure enough, here came Cecil, stepping out of the elevator, heading toward his car. Von Doom had known the vehicle instantly upon seeing it. And why not? Back in happier days, when Cecil had first purchased the merlot-colored Aston Martin DB9—thanks to money generated by investments in VDI—he'd sent Von Doom a photograph of himself draped over the car with a hand-scribbled note saying, "It's all thanks to you, Victor!" Those days seemed very far away somehow.

Cecil approached and, as he did so, the lights within the parking structure began to flicker. He looked up in confusion and then watched in increasing bewilderment as the lights started to go out. It wasn't just that they were being extinguished; they were going out in a particular order. From the point farthest away from Cecil, one by one the lights blinked out, drawing closer and closer to him until the only light remaining was the one shining directly over his head. He glanced around, clearly unnerved. There was now nothing but darkness between himself and the car, and something—some primeval warning hardwired into human beings since the earliest days when they'd crouched around fires while fearing the eyes in the darkness—rooted him to the spot.

"Hello . . . ?" he called out nervously.

Victor let the single word hang there a moment, and then he walked forward, taking slow, deliberate steps. He savored the unease on Cecil's face, and even better . . . he knew that the moment Cecil recognized who it was, he would relax and think he was out of danger. It was the same perverse pleasure that small boys took in toying with wingless flies . . . except, in this case, Cecil was unaware that *his* wings were in danger.

Sure enough, as soon as Victor drew close enough for Cecil to make out his identity, he let out a sigh of relief. It was slightly guarded, because he wasn't sure what the hell Victor was doing down there. But clearly he thought there was no reason to fear. "Von Doom! Gave me a little shock. No hard feelings, right? Nothing personal."

Victor said nothing. He preferred to drag the moment out for as long as possible. Cecil, for his part, continued toward his car while saying with condescension lacing his voice, "You know, you could always move back to Latvura, start fresh. Maybe that's where you belong, back in the 'old country.'"

Von Doom didn't know whether Cecil had deliberately mispronounced the name of his mother country, or if he had simply spoken out of ignorance. Neither was an excuse.

He timed it perfectly. His eyes narrowed as Cecil approached a puddle of water, heedless of the threat, and just before Cecil stepped into it, Von Doom sent a surge of electricity coursing through himself, down his leg, and into the ground. The current hit the water near him, snaking across the garage like a high-voltage serpent and hitting the water puddle just as Ned Cecil's foot came into contact with it.

Victor supposed that Cecil never fully understood what happened to him. One minute he was walking and speaking with smug arrogance, and the next he had enough electricity jolting through him to drop an elephant. Cecil's body spasmed uncontrollably, a jumping marionette bereft of strings. His arms splayed about, his head snapped around, and he opened his mouth in a wordless scream.

Victor's power swelled even as Cecil collapsed, dead before he hit the floor. Had he lived—unlikely as that event would have been—he would have seen the scar on Von Doom's face split wide to reveal a metallic growth shining from beneath the skin. Victor wasn't paying any attention to it. The flapping skin was an inconvenience, nothing more. It was no more irritating than the extra skin a snake might shed. Instead he was focusing on continuing to keep his cool.

"It's pronounced *Latveria*," he corrected the corpse. Then he paused and added with infinite, smug satisfaction, "This meeting's over, Ned."

He turned and walked away, and the final lights in the parking garage extinguished themselves in his passing until the entirety of the place was in darkness. As far as Von Doom was concerned, it served to make him feel that much more at home.

Von Doom entered his office with a feeling of almost infinite power and endless confidence. Life was the most sacred gift that God could bestow, and Victor Von Doom was able to take it as if it were nothing. What did that say about the relationship between God and man? Who was proving himself to be the more powerful?

He approached the screens and simply gestured—they instantly glowed to life. All manner of televised events and shows played out across them, but on one of them—a news program—the images of Reed, Sue, Johnny, and Ben appeared. This naturally drew Victor's attention, and he leaned in closer as the volume automatically rose to accommodate him.

A local news broadcaster was informing his audience, ". . . the Fantastic Four put on quite a show last night. They landed on every major headline in the northern hemisphere. In related news," and an image of Victor himself appeared on the screen next to the others, "Reports have surfaced that Von Doom Industries may be filing for bankruptcy. You may remember that it was Victor Von Doom who—"

He stepped back from the screen, sending the volume down. His gaze never left the image of Reed Richards.

Von Doom heard a soft footfall at the door and knew instantly that it was Leonard. He said nothing, but instead simply continued to watch the screen. Sure enough, Leonard spoke up from the doorway, concern in his voice, "Sir . . . is everything okay? What happened to your—?"

Face, of course, was the word Leonard had been planning to say. Victor mentally finished the sentence for him. But he did not even deign to look in Leonard's direction, for he was far more interested by what he was gazing at upon the TV screen. "Reed . . . he got what he wanted," he said under his breath, seething with hatred. "*Everything* he wanted . . . he *took* from me." He leaned even closer to the screen and focused his hatred, which took the form of an intense barrage of static that wiped out Reed's face from the screen.

His head snapped around and slides of Reed's research began coming up on another monitor screen. Like the eye of a camera, he zoomed in onto certain key words: "Danger." "Unstable ions." "Mutation." "Overload."

Victor gave a slow, thin smile, his mind working toward a terrible but inevitable conclusion. "Now I'm going to take it back," he whispered. "Piece by bloody piece."

His fist clenched, making a metallic grinding noise as it did so.

19

REED WAS EXTREMELY PLEASED WITH THE WAY HIS CONstruction of the transformation chamber was going. Granted, it was only in the preliminary stages, and there was a long, long way to go on it. But that was how science operated, one step at a time. Science was a perpetual case of learning to walk, like a toddler. Watch a toddler struggle to take three steps at once, and naturally it will fall. One foot in front of the other: That was the scientific way.

These thoughts went through Reed's mind as he entered the transformation lab at the Baxter Building, carrying a stack of boxes that no normal man could possibly have balanced. He was, naturally enough, far from ordinary. His arms were wrapped around the boxes five times over, like human twine. But he stopped short and dropped everything when he saw Victor Von Doom and a virtual army of technicians, swarming over his work like ants at a picnic. No, not just swarming: The ants were making off with the sandwiches. Everything—

his files, his diagrams, the hardware of the transformation chamber itself—was in the process of being packed up.

Victor was overseeing it all. Practically one entire side of his face was bandaged up. He was starting to look like he should be skulking about in the sewers beneath the Paris Opera House. Despite the fact that Victor was attempting to abscond with all his work, Reed's first thought was for Von Doom's well-being. "Victor, are . . . are you okay?" he asked slowly, approaching him.

"Don't worry about me," Von Doom retorted. "Worry about *yourself*."

"What are you doing here?" Reed asked as he looked around his lab, watching it being turned upside down.

"What I should have done a long time ago," Von Doom said. "Applications and patents, Reed. This all belongs to me."

A technician was walking past with one box brimming with folders. Reed's arm snaked out and he snatched a folder out of it and held it up, waving it at Von Doom. "But I'm not done with the machine—!"

"Which is precisely the point," snapped Victor. "Analysis is over. It's time for action. My men could have mass-produced this by now."

Reed was in disbelief. "Mass-produced. This isn't a toaster! You have no idea how it works!"

Without hesitation, Von Doom reached into the folder file and whipped out an intricate diagram of the machine. He pointed to it as he spoke.

"Re-create the storm," he said sharply. "Invert the polarity *here*. Reverse the mutation *there*." His voice dropped in volume and rose in implied menace. "Don't talk to me like I'm some schoolboy. I've got the same Ph.D. you do."

Reed was more than a little surprised that Victor was so familiar with his machine, even as he pointed to a secure chamber on the blueprint. "The storm needs to be handled exactly right, or it could make our mutations worse. *Much* worse. Maybe even *kill* us . . ."

Something in Von Doom's face seemed to shift. His movements had been quick, precise, decisive. But now they slowed, as if some part of what Reed was saying was penetrating the anger-based shield that he'd erected. Was he actually getting through to Victor . . . ?

Or are you giving him ideas?

The stray thought occurred to Reed and he immediately dismissed it. This was Victor Von Doom, a man he'd known for years. They might have disagreements over how to go about things, but ultimately they were interested in the same thing: making the best of a bad situation.

"Victor," Reed said slowly, "please. We need time to verify the data. We can't afford any mistakes: There's only enough ions for two or three attempts."

Victor continued to consider Reed's words, and Reed really believed that Victor was finally seeing things his way . . . right up until the point where Von Doom said, "Reed . . . I'm not asking permission." He nodded to the files and said, in what sounded like a vague attempt at compromise, "Tell you what: Instead of relocating to another location, we'll do it here and keep you in the loop. We'll build it, while you check the specs."

He walked away, leaving a bewildered and frustrated Reed Richards behind him. Reed turned to leave, shaking his head . . . and saw Johnny Storm standing there, shaking his head as well. But he knew immediately that, whereas his own frustration was aimed at Victor, Johnny's was aimed at Reed. Johnny Storm, standing there in judgment of him.

Reed simply shrugged. What was he supposed to have done anyway?

He watched as Johnny headed away, and thought grimly, *Why do I have the feeling I'm going to hear from Sue on this?*

Sue Storm had taken some rare time off, spending a couple of days visiting with her and Johnny's dad in Cape Cod. After all the insane stories hitting the media, and the regular frantic phone calls she'd been getting from him, she'd felt the need to spend some time with Dad just to help settle him down. When she returned to the Baxter Building, Johnny was waiting for her, and filled her in on what was going on. Reed didn't exactly come out heroically in the retelling, which she supposed was typical enough for Johnny. Unfortunately, the rendition also sounded typical enough for Reed.

Sue headed straight down to the main lab to see for

herself if what Johnny had told her was true. On the one hand, she had trouble believing it . . . and on the other, it was unfortunately all too easy to believe.

She walked in and stood there, eyes wide. Technicians wearing Von Doom Industries jackets were all over the place, like insects. Once, long ago, she'd caught the eye of some hotshot movie star who'd invited her to spend the day on the set. Intrigued, she'd taken him up on it, and she'd been struck by the constant motion, commotion, and incessant hammering. That's what the lab reminded her of now: technicians hammering, drilling, materials being put up all over the place. Radiation shields were being lifted, and sparks were flying as beams were being welded into place, competing with the screaming of the drills to see which could be louder and more annoying.

She turned just in time to see Reed walking into the room, presumably to check out how things were going. But the instant he saw her, he rolled his eyes, pivoted, and headed out the way he'd come, clearly wanting to dodge the pending confrontation. Sometimes she thought the only thing that exceeded Reed's scientific know-how was his determination to avoid conflicts. She immediately headed out after him, calling over the howl of drills, "Can I talk to you?"

Reed slowed in the hallway as Sue caught up with him. Distanced from the racket of the power tools and hammers, she said in a low, tight voice, "You're letting Victor bully you again . . ."

"He was going to take away all my data, equipment . . ."

"Better than your *life*," she said, pointing back toward the lab. "Victor's not the one who has to get into that thing. *We* are."

He stood there for a moment, trying to compose himself . . . and then, for the first time that she could recall, he failed in that effort. His voice trembling with rage that threatened to slip its leash at any moment, he snapped, "Which is why I'm working twenty hours a day, checking every variable . . ."

"Every variable but yourself," Sue replied. "You can't live in your head like—"

Reed replied with such vehemence, such anger, that Sue took a step back, startled. "*I'm* not the only one in there!" He started ticking off names on his fingers. "I've got you, Vic, Ben, Johnny, rattling around. It's so crowded in there, I can't even hear myself *think* half the time!"

Sue was stunned at the outburst. She looked closely at him, wondering if during the four hours that he wasn't checking variables, he was lying awake in his room, staring at the ceiling and double-checking the figures by running them through his mind.

"It's crowded in there?" she said after a moment. "So clear it out." She paused, drew closer to him, and said quietly, "Remember where we used to go . . . to get away from everything . . . ?"

Clearly having readied himself for a long and bitter argument with Sue, Reed was caught off-guard by her response. When it finally sank in on him, however, he actually smiled.

She'd forgotten what a great smile he had. She had a feeling he'd forgotten it, too.

On his previous excursions to Brooklyn, Ben had shown up under cover of night, skulking around like a thief, clinging to the shadows.

Not this time. He'd had his frightening mug plastered across newspapers, on news organizations and, for all he knew by this point, *Starlog* magazine. *I'm here, I'm rocky, get used to it,* he thought as he stomped down the street, his very presence practically daring people to make an issue of it.

Naturally no one did. Instead people scrambled to get out of the way, pointing and staring. He found that it was starting to irritate him less. He remembered how his father used to say that once you were out in the rain for ten minutes, you were already soaked, so there was no reason to worry about it anymore. You could only get wetter.

People were going to gape or shrink back from him. He knew that going in. Once he had come to grips with that reality, then it was only a matter of degrees, of how many were going to be repulsed by him. When he thought of it that way, it stung a little less. A little.

Then, to his astonishment, a little girl and her friend ran straight toward him. He could only imagine the kids' parents having heart attacks, knowing that their children were approaching the dangerous, monstrous, frightful creature that everyone was calling—

"Mister! Mister!" the little girl cried out. "Please help me!"

Oh God . . . not a cat stuck in a tree. Not a freakin' cat. I hate freakin' cats.

"My kitty is stuck in a tree!"

Ben's eyes glazed over, and then he glanced around to see if someone from one of those TV shows who play practical jokes on people was nearby filming him. Nobody was, but that hardly mollified his mood.

Cats in trees. What the hell is it with cats and trees? Is this some sort of demented rite-of-passage for people with super powers? In the Superman *movie, he'd plucked a cat out of a tree. And that cartoon movie about super heroes a year ago, that guy had to get a cat out of a tree. The hell with 'em. Someone should just take a chain saw to all the trees. Or all the cats. Either way, problem solved.*

"Please!" said the little girl. "Save Miss Lucy!" She pointed and, sure enough, an orange cat was perched on a high branch in a nearby tree. Stupid thing was probably trying to climb up and kill some birds. Deserved what it got, as far as Ben was concerned, but the kid was gazing at him with such hope that Ben could only roll his eyes and walk toward the tree.

He considered climbing the tree, but quickly ruled out that notion. Instead he grabbed the tree with one hand and started shaking it as violently as he could. The cat let out an alarmed yowl, tried to hold on, and couldn't; the branch it was holding onto snapped off from the jostling. The cat couldn't maintain its grip. It slid off, tried to snag another branch, missed, bounced off, and plummeted to the ground . . . except, at the last moment, Ben stuck out his hand and Miss Lucy landed safely in his palm. Its eyes were still ricocheting around as he handed it to the girl.

"Thank you!" she said. "Thank you, thank you—!"

He ignored her and walked away. The only thing he took small pleasure in was that the now-nauseated cat made a deep retching noise and coughed up a hairball on the girl's blouse.

Ben continued to walk, heading in the general direction of O'Donnel's. It was early in the day and probably wouldn't be especially crowded, which was fine: fewer people to send stampeding toward the door. But something caught his attention as he walked, causing him to back up and gape in confusion through the window of an art gallery where a hanging sign read: KIRBY GALLERY.

He was looking at himself.

It was a bust of him, his head, neck, and upper shoulders, and it wasn't simply a replica of him. It . . . spoke to him somehow. Exquisitely rendered, it captured not only his brute physicality, but a sense of haunting anguish. It radiated strength that he was afraid to use lest he hurt someone, the sense of being isolated no matter how many people might be surrounding him. Nor was it made from clay; it was actually carved from solid stone, providing it an additional feel of authenticity. Ben was amazed, touched, impressed . . .

He leaned forward and spotted a small sign next to it

that read MASTERS. Then he touched his extended brow. "Eyebrows are a little big," he muttered. "Hell of a thing to put on display."

"I figured the only way to get you here was to stick that in the window."

He looked up and was astounded to see Alicia, the girl from the bar, standing there looking at him. Well, not at him. In his general direction. "How'd you know it was me?" he asked.

She laughed at that. "I'm blind, not deaf."

"You made it?" Ben asked. She nodded. "So you're a master artist?"

"What?" Her eyebrows knit.

"It says 'Masters' next to it. Masters is . . . what? A class of artist?"

"It's my last name, genius," she said matter-of-factly. "Masters. Alicia Masters."

"Oh. Okay, well . . . okay." He looked back at the bust. "I wondered who was masochistic and nuts enough to waste their time carving a statue of me." Then he saw her smile and continued, "Boy, I'm just saying one right thing after another, ain't I."

"Looks that way." She didn't appear to be upset, though. Indeed, it seemed to amuse her no end.

"Okay, well . . . why'd you put it up there? Up front, I mean. Aint'cha worried it's gonna scare customers away?"

"I figured it was worth the risk." She gestured behind herself. "Wanna come in?"

He shrugged in response, and then realized that she

292

couldn't see it. He started up the steps but then halted as the sounds of voices and laughter reached his ears. Ever on the defensive, he automatically thought that he was the target of the laughter. Then he realized that, no, there was just a party going on toward the back of the gallery.

He looked down at himself. At his bare chest and arms. "I'm not really dressed for a party."

"Relax, it's casual," said Alicia.

"No, I mean . . . I'm a little . . ." He hesitated, then said, ". . . dusty . . ."

Alicia smiled, an idea obviously occurring to her. "Go around back," she said. "You'll see a small structure. It's my studio. I'll meet you there."

"What about your party?"

"Never much liked parties," Alicia replied.

Several minutes later, Alicia had let Ben into the studio and flipped on a light. Ben looked around in amazement at statues in various degrees of completion, including a second bust of himself. There were also several oversize puppets hanging on strings in the corner.

She guided him over to the center of the room, then brought out a sculptor's hose and a couple of thin carving chisels. As Ben stood unmoving, she fired a steady, thin stream of water at him, cleaning off the dust and grime from him as if he were a statue. To be completely thorough, she used the chisels for the cracks in his skin where the water wasn't going. It was a sort of bizarre equivalent of a nurse giving a patient a sponge bath. It was intricate work, and more, there was a strange intimacy to it that Ben couldn't help but enjoy. There was just something about this woman that automatically relaxed him, even more than any time when he'd been with Debbie. It wasn't as if there could be any sort of future between him and Alicia, he told himself. She was still a beautiful woman, while he was this . . . thing. But he loved the attention she was paying him. Loved it so much that it started to make him a little nervous.

So he sought something else to discuss. Staring at the large puppets, he said, "Those yours, too?"

"'Those'?"

Right. She doesn't know where you're looking, genius.

"Those puppets," he said.

She nodded, understanding. "My stepdad's. I'm strictly into stone." She paused and then said, almost shyly, "I was wondering when you'd walk by."

Ben chuckled at that. "You know, you could'a run an ad in the personals."

"Sensual blind chick seeks three-ton, rock-hard he-man for deep spiritual relationship."

Ben laughed even more loudly then, but the laugh eventually died in his throat. "This ain't permanent," he said in a way that sounded more hopeful than realistic. "My friend Reed's working on a cure . . . I think."

She stepped in closer, running the chisel along the cracks in his arms. "Bennie . . . you feel pretty good *as is.*"

But he shook his head sadly, trying to get her to understand. "You don't know what it's like out there. Walking around like some kind of circus freak. People staring, whispering . . ."

"I wouldn't know anything about that," she said sarcastically.

Instantly contrite, Ben said, "I mean . . ."

She rested a hand along the side of his face, and her touch was enough to silence him. "Tell me," she said, "When you grew up in Brooklyn, how many astronauts did you know?"

The answer, of course, was none. Instead he'd grown up surrounded by people who had repeatedly told him that his aspirations for space flight were nonsense. Mooks from Brooklyn simply didn't go into that line of work. NASA wanted classy, well-to-do, cream-of-the-crop types, not a guy raised on the tough New York City streets. To Ben's knowledge, there had been exactly one astronaut in the history of the program, besides himself, who was born in Brooklyn, and that other guy actually grew up in Scarsdale. The tony streets of that upper-upper-class neighborhood were about as far from Brooklyn as one could get.

Alicia didn't need to hear the answer since she probably already knew it. "You went your own way then," she reminded him. "You didn't listen to people. So why start now?"

And that was true as well. Ben could still see them, the faces of all the guys who told him that people like him didn't get trusted with multibillion-dollar spacecraft. People like him were the ones who security guards

295

prevented from throwing eggs at multibillion-dollar spacecraft.

"Fer someone who can't see," Ben said after a time, "you got a pretty good bead on things."

"It's a knack," Alicia said with a shrug as she continued to clean the dirt from Ben's skin. "Oh, hey! I've got two tickets for the ballet tonight! A friend just canceled. You interested?"

"The ballet? But how do you . . . ?"

"See? I don't, obviously. I just like the music."

"Yeah, well . . . canceling for the ballet. Hard to imagine somebody doing that."

Teasingly, she sent a small jet of water into his face. "Tell me you'll think about it, at least."

"I'll think about it," he said, wiping the water from his eyes.

Johnny Storm remembered reading articles and interviews with famous people in which they complained about how difficult their lives were. How they couldn't go anywhere without hordes of people coming from all directions and asking for photographs, autographs, just a minute of their time, and so on. It all sounded like a colossal burden.

Johnny thought they were nuts.

It might be because it was all new to him, and there was still a good deal of novelty to it. Perhaps in two, three, four years he might grow tired of crowds forming wherever he went. But in the meantime, it was going to be a great few years.

In this case, he hadn't gone far at all. A crowd had materialized practically out of nowhere the moment he'd exited the lobby of the Baxter Building. Rather than thinning out, more people had shown up the longer he remained there. He continued to sign autographs as fast as he could, pose for pictures, and still the crowd wasn't thinning out. He was beginning to see the slightest glimmerings of the downside of his current life, since his intention to head over to a popular Manhattan night spot was being impeded by the massive lovefest he was encountering. Still, he couldn't be too upset about it.

An incredibly long stretch limo pulled up, honking loudly to get his attention. A tinted window rolled down and there, inside the vast vehicle, was Victor Von Doom peering out at him. "Need a ride, Johnny?"

Johnny hesitated. There were lots of people in the world that he didn't think very much of. In fact, several of them resided in the Baxter Building. With Von Doom, however, he was genuinely wary, distrustful. The guy had his own agenda and clearly regarded Johnny and the others as playthings in whatever game he was at. By stepping into the car, Johnny was practically hanging a sign on his back that said, "Kick me." To say nothing of the fact that Von Doom had treated Reed pretty shabbily. Granted, Reed brought it on himself with the way he let people walk all over him, but that didn't excuse the walkers either.

He was about to tell Von Doom to take a hike, and then caught a glimpse of several impossibly beautiful women in the car along with Victor . . . women whom Johnny instantly recognized from the pages of the *Sports*

Illustrated swimsuit edition. All else was forgotten as Johnny clambered into the open door of the limo.

"A few fans," Victor Von Doom said. "Hope you don't mind."

Johnny, ever the humanitarian, said, "Gotta take care of the fans, right?"

He sat down opposite Von Doom, and the girls shifted themselves over so that they were sitting on either side of him. The limo moved off from the Baxter Building. Johnny could hear the disappointed moans from the fans who hadn't had a chance with him, but at that moment he wasn't caring all that much.

"Look," said Victor, rubbing his gloved hands together, "I built my business knowing what people want. And right now," and he indicated with a wave the crowd they'd just left behind, "the people want *you*."

The models were eyeing Johnny hungrily. He was having trouble keeping himself focused on the subject at hand, which was impressive considering the subject at hand was him. "And we don't want to let the people down now, do we," said Johnny.

"No we don't. Which is why we need to strike while the iron's hot . . . no pun intended." Johnny looked at him with interest as Victor continued, "I'm talking action figures, video games, sponsors—"

A thought occurred to Johnny as he tried to think of things that were appropriate. "Maybe my own grill! Like George Foreman!"

Victor nodded, smiling, like a fisherman who knew

that he had a live one on the hook. Fortunately, or unfortunately, the simile didn't occur to Johnny.

Still, there was something about the timing of this, the way that it had all transpired, that was sufficient to pierce—at least for a brief time—the pleasant haze that had fallen upon Johnny in the midst of such female adoration. With a note of caution sounding in his head, he asked, "You talk to Reed and Sue about this?"

"Johnny!" Victor laughed, and then said, "Let's be honest here. Ben, Reed, Sue . . . good people, all. But . . . stars?" He shook his head. "I don't want to break up the band, but *you're* the one they want," he said, indicating the girls in the car with them. Girls who were, presumably, symbols of the wider-spread interest in him from all over America and even the world. "Don't you think it's time to go solo . . . ?"

Johnny didn't notice Victor subtly nodding to the models. If he had, though, he wouldn't have cared, as the three of them suddenly enveloped him from all sides. One remained on either side, while the third climbed into his lap.

Von Doom rapped on the side window and the driver promptly pulled over to the curb. "Take the car for a spin. Think about it. Is this the life you want? Or would you rather live in Reed's lab?"

Victor stepped out at curbside, swinging shut the door behind himself. As the car started to roll away, all the windows instantly began to steam up.

* * *

"People are occasionally stumped by the question, 'What is the closest star to Earth?' A few with a smattering of scientific knowledge might answer, 'Proxima Centauri.' The answer is, of course, the sun itself. The sun is a—"

In the Hayden Planetarium, with a vast field of stars projected overhead, a voice droned on about the sun, the stars, and the galaxy in general. There was only a handful of people in the theater at the moment, yet Reed and Sue had chosen to sit all the way in the last row. Reed's head was tilted back, and Sue thought for a moment that he was simply enjoying the view. She should have known better, for as she leaned closer to him, she heard him muttering, "I could get Ben to tap into the Baxter's main power to generate enough voltage—"

"Reed, shhh! Just be quiet and look up."

His gaze had actually been inward, but now he shifted it so that he was staring up at the stars. They seemed to have a calming effect on him, and he actually smiled.

"Remember our first date here . . . ?" she asked. "God, I was so nervous."

"You *were*?" Reed seemed thunderstruck by the notion.

"Of course I was," she replied, recalling the cramming session she'd done before that date, prepping for it in the way that someone might get ready for a final exam. "I'd read all your papers on bioethics. Some of them two times, just so I'd have something to say to you."

He smiled softly, thinking back to those days. "You know," he said conspiratorially, "I bribed the projectionist ten bucks to keep it open late."

Sue was taken aback. "I gave him twenty!" For an instant she actually felt some degree of retroactive annoyance that the projectionist had profiteered off both of them. But then Reed laughed, and so did she. This got them some annoyed looks from others in the room, and they promptly quieted down.

She looked up at the stars herself, and said very quietly, "I didn't want that night to end."

Reed gazed at her, and she felt as if she could see raw emotions battling his cold, hard logic behind his eyes. There were clearly things he wanted to say but was reluctant to, and was fraught with indecision over them. The struggle was his, though, and there was nothing she could do to help him. He had to win it or lose it on his own.

Finally, after what seemed an excruciatingly long time, Reed told her softly, "Sue . . . you were right."

"I know," she said. Then she paused and asked reluctantly, "About what?"

"It wasn't 'complicated.' Our breakup, I mean. You wanted to take the next step, and I . . . I just wasn't ready to be . . . to become . . ." He struggled to find the words, and then said, a hair defensively, "You can be a little intimidating."

"I know," she said again, and this time didn't need to ask for further clarification.

"You always talked about how you liked the kind of man who could approach you . . . speak his mind. One who wasn't afraid to tell you what he wanted."

"I did!" Sue said, raising her voice. "I did, Reed . . . but I wanted *you* to be that man."

301

This garnered them more irritated and louder shushing, and the two of them slumped further down into their respective chairs. They were extremely close to each other by that point, and Sue said, "When I walked out, I waited *ten minutes* outside your door. Ten. Waiting for you to come find me."

"Why didn't you say anything?"

Well, that was typical Reed, wasn't it? Approaching actions taken purely in the white heat of emotion and endeavoring to apply logic to them. To Reed, the logical thing would have been for Sue to stick her head in and say, "You know, Reed, I'm standing here outside waiting for you to come after me."

Sue realized right then that, in some ways, Reed was never going to change. She was thus left with a choice. She was going to have to allow herself to be driven away by it . . . or she was going to have to choose to find it charming.

For the time being, she was going to opt for the latter.

"That would have kinda defeated the purpose," she pointed out. "And Reed . . ." Her voice was deep and filled with emotion. "I'm saying it now."

Their eyes locked. There was a moment of genuine heat between them as all the demons of the past were laid to rest, all the little pointless secrets they'd kept now revealed. They drew closer to each other, closer . . .

And Sue vanished.

Reed, whose eyes had been half-lidded, was taken aback. Hushed, playful, Sue said, "Come find me."

Cautiously, Reed leaned in toward her, and Sue felt

his lips caressing her nostrils. "That's my nose, genius," she said, her voice nasal. She reached out toward him and Reed's face was mushed in on either side by her hands taking a firm grasp on it. "*These* are my lips." She pulled him into a deep, loving kiss, flattening his mouth as she did so, but neither of them cared. Above the stars twinkled, and people toward the front of the theater sighed in relief that the couple in the back had finally shut up.

20

Ben Grimm knew exactly what to expect when he and Alicia showed up at the party being held in the back of the gallery, and he wasn't disappointed. Or rather he was, but he'd come to expect disappointment.

The crowd, as anticipated, quieted when he entered. There were a few stray whispers from curious partygoers wondering what in the world he could possibly be doing there. He couldn't blame them; he was wondering much the same thing himself.

Then Alicia came up alongside him and wrapped her arm around his. The moment she did so, it was as if he had instant legitimacy. People began talking in normal tones again, and if a few of them kept glancing in his direction, so what. Let 'em.

"Look around," Alicia suggested. "I'll get us drinks." Anticipating his objection to her going to any trouble on his behalf, she added, "They always let blind girls cut the line."

He snorted at that as she turned and walked off. She

didn't even need her cane for this, since she knew the parameters of the gallery so well, and she was easily able to sense people in her way and step around them. Ben watched her and was amazed by the fluidity of her movements, the play of her legs beneath her loose-fitting skirt. The lines of her neck, the light on her skin . . . it was an astounding combination on an equally astounding woman.

And she seemed to be attracted to him. *To him.*

Part of him said that she wouldn't be at all if she could see him the way he really was. But then he glanced over at the bust that she had made of him, thought about the things she'd said, and came to the gradual conclusion that perhaps she was attracted to him specifically because she *could* see him the way he really was.

For that matter, other guests at the party were inclined to at least try to see him through her eyes, or through her inner eye, as it were. They weren't exactly flocking to him in droves to find out everything about him, but they offered strained smiles (which, by and large, was the only kind he received these days) and made polite small talk noises of "Glad you could make it" and "You're much handsomer in person." Ben would nod in response, not taking much of it seriously, but at least they were making the effort. If they could, so could he.

Alicia was approaching the bar, but several guests were chatting with her, smiling and laughing. Well, why shouldn't they be? They obviously had respect for her artistry. She was in her element, and not only that, but she was encouraging Ben to share it with her.

He stood there, immobile, fascinated by every little gesture, every movement. So he didn't notice the small group of latecomers who had arrived and were giving him a brisk—and very unimpressed—once-over. "I don't know about this one," a woman who looked like a dowager said. "It lacks a certain . . . realism."

Ben heard it and wondered what they were referring to. Before he could move, though, he overheard another couple of people who were with the woman. They were looking straight at him. He stared back, and one of them murmured, "It's one of those things where the eyes just follow you wherever you go. It's creepy."

"On every level," said a friend. "She's always had a thing for runaways and strays, but this is ridiculous."

"I know. Did she really think these sculptures would *sell?*"

"Like anybody would want this *thing* in their house. That girl's a one-woman charity."

In that one moment, with those few words, everything in Ben Grimm's carefully constructed house of cards that represented his ego came crashing down. He had convinced himself that what people said about him didn't mean anything to him. But what Alicia thought about him had come to mean a great deal.

Was it true? Was she into strays and charity cases and runaways? Is that how she saw him? Not as a man, or even a man with an unfortunate condition and a good soul, but instead merely some castoff of society that she could lend a hand to out of pity.

Scorn, ridicule, fear . . . these had become part of his

306

existence. But pity from Alicia? It was more than he could endure, more than anyone should have to.

He spotted her laughing and chatting with people again, but now his mind was writing in the words for her. *Oh heavens, yes, I know he's ghastly, but you know me, I felt I had to try and pitch in somehow. He reminded me ever so much of that pathetic mutt I took in last month, the one with the broken leg and mashed face who finally had to be put to sleep. But I'm hoping for better luck with this one.*

Well, that all made sense, didn't it? Certainly more sense than that Alicia felt drawn to him in some way.

People staring at him, laughing about this, that, or the other thing . . . except now he convinced himself that he was the thing being laughed at in every discussion with every person.

The people who had been commenting on the ugliness of the statuary that he represented had already moved on, and so didn't see when Ben turned away and headed for the door. He went out the door, down the steps of the front stoop, and out into the street, moving as quickly as he could.

Had he glanced behind himself, he would have seen Alicia returning to where he'd been standing, a glass of wine for her and a pitcher for Ben, so that it was easier for him to hold. She was smiling in anticipation of speaking to him once more, but quickly sensed he wasn't there. She spoke his name tentatively, then a bit more loudly when he didn't respond, hearing the steady thudding of his feet as he headed away.

Nor did he take notice of the man seated in a carefully nondescript manner who was watching him go. The man dialed a cell phone and waited two rings until someone picked up on the other end.

"Avalanche is moving again," Leonard Kirk said.

"*Stay on him,*" came the voice of Victor Von Doom. "*I'm already on my way out there. Tell me when he comes to rest again, and where. I'll take care of everything else.*"

"Yes, sir," said Leonard, snapping shut the telephone.

Rain was pouring down upon the fleabag diner in which Ben had taken refuge. His coat was drawn tight around himself, his hat pulled low. Even so he was becoming increasingly aware that his brilliant disguise was fooling exactly no one. He sat at the counter, sipping a cup of coffee that he'd requested be served to him in a metal mixing bowl. The other customers were giving him a wide berth. At least he was never going to have to worry about having enough elbow room again.

"This seat taken?" came a voice from nearby.

Ben turned and looked in astonishment to see Victor standing there, watching him with cold amusement. "How the hell did you find me?"

"You're not easy to miss, Ben," replied Victor. "If I need to locate you, it's not really that difficult for me."

He thought about questioning Von Doom more closely on that claim, but finally decided it wasn't worth it. He turned back to staring at the bowl full of coffee and grunted, "What are you doing here?"

"I'm worried about you."

Ben didn't believe that for a second. There was no one and nothing that Victor Von Doom worried about aside from Victor Von Doom. It was almost insulting that he would think Ben was so gullible. "About me. How sweet."

"Come on," replied Victor. "Let me buy you something to eat. Looks like you could use the company."

His first impulse was to tell Von Doom to take a hike. Then he remembered the old saying about keeping your friends close, but your enemies closer. Finally, he pictured Alicia—who, by this point in his recollections, was laughing at him and his gullibility—and came to the conclusion that he no longer had any clue who were his friends and who were his enemies. He could try to keep them all away . . . or he could let them get close enough to say what they had to say before sending them packing.

What the hell. He's buying and I'm hungry.

They moved over to a window booth, which Ben fit into only with difficulty. "Whatever my friend here wants," said Von Doom, "and keep it coming."

Ben decided to take Von Doom at his word and began ordering anything and everything off the menu that caught his fancy. He had to credit Victor: The guy didn't flinch. He made no effort to keep up Ben's pace, but he did all right for himself.

Even more startling, Von Doom started talking sports with him. As if they were just two guys hanging out at a bar, Victor asked him what he thought of the Yankees' chances this year, and it just went from there. He seemed to know everything about every major game played by every major New York team, with strong opinions on all of them. Plus he had some intriguing behind-the-scenes gossip since he was tight with the owners of several of the teams.

Ben became so engrossed in the discussion that he lost track of how much he'd eaten. The waitress was placing a foot-high stack of pancakes in front of him, removing the huge empty plates that he'd just finished with, when Ben let out a belch so loud that it rattled other people's china, not to mention the windows. Victor laughed while the waitress cleared out as quickly as she could.

Dabbing a napkin to his mouth, Ben muttered, "Scuse me."

Von Doom looked sympathetic. "I know it can't be easy. Life hasn't changed that much for Reed, Sue, and Johnny. At least they can go out in public. But for you? People staring, whispering behind your back . . ."

Ben sighed inwardly. He'd known that, sooner or later, conversation would swing around to this. His condition was the elephant in the room, the thing that people could pretend they were ignoring but really had to address sooner or later. "If you're trying to cheer me up, you're doing a helluva job—"

"I'm just saying . . . I know what it's like to lose something you love. To see it slip away, and know it's never coming back."

Picking up a slice of apple pie that had been brought out earlier, Ben shoved it into his mouth whole. "Reed's gonna fix me up," he said, juice from the pie trickling down the sides of his mouth.

"For your sake, I hope you're right." Victor paused, then said, "I'm sorry if that sounds a little skeptical."

"Skeptical?"

Despite Ben's general distrust of Von Doom, Victor was managing to hit all the things that Ben was most concerned about. Besides, trust didn't necessarily matter if the guy floating the points was making sense. Even a busted clock was right twice a day.

"Look," said Victor, leaning forward and lowering his voice. "He's a brilliant man. We should trust he's working as hard as he can. You're his best friend. So what possible reason could he have for taking his time?" Then he paused and said, in an offhand manner as if he'd just thought of it, "I mean . . . other than getting closer to Sue?"

Ben wanted to dismiss the notion out of hand. It was the most ridiculous thing he'd ever . . .

Except . . .

Maybe . . . maybe not so ridiculous.

After all . . . he knew how Reed felt about Sue. He knew how inept he felt about approaching her. But the longer she was bound to him while waiting for a cure, the longer he had time to . . .

But Reed wouldn't leave Ben out to dry that way, right? Ben was his best friend, right?

And how much time had he been spending with his best friend recently? Yes, granted, it wasn't like Ben had been the most sociable guy in the world lately. It wasn't as if he hadn't been pushing Reed away. But still, if Reed were really his friend, he would have overcome that. He would have pushed back. Instead, Reed was off doing . . . what?

And with whom?

Reed could not remember the last time he'd been this happy. Indeed, he didn't realize until that moment that he'd forgotten how to *be* happy. But Sue was reminding him, bringing it all home once again.

They stepped off the elevator, laughing quietly, their bodies close, and headed over to the lab. It was pitch-black, which surprised Reed. He'd have thought that Victor would have technicians working 24/7. Reed snapped on the lights, his arm still tightly around Sue, and then the two of them halted as if frozen to the spot. The laughter that had come so easily to them deserted them.

Ben was sitting in the middle of the room, scowling, like a disapproving parent catching the kids coming in way too late at night. "Yeah. I have that effect on people," he said in regard to their good humor dissipating.

The fact that Ben was lurking about in the darkness was disturbing enough to Reed. What surprised him even more was what was directly behind Ben: the completed transformation chamber. Reed couldn't believe it. How the hell had they finished it so fast?

"Ben . . ." Reed began.

"Oh, you remember my name, do you?" It was the most animated that Ben's voice had sounded in ages. Unfortunately it was laced with sarcasm, all directed at Reed. "You happen to remember what you *swore* to do with every breath in your body?"

"We're working as hard as we can . . ."

"Yeah," Ben said, looking at Reed oddly. "I can tell. Victor was right."

He tapped his own lips as a hint, and Reed reached up and touched his own. He felt a smear of Sue's lipstick against them. "That's nothing," he said quickly, and then winced as he saw Sue's reaction . . . which was, of course, the exact response one might expect from a woman who'd just been told that her affections were "nothing." This was not Reed's night. It was as if he couldn't say a single sentence without offending someone.

Ben wasn't inclined to let it go or make it any easier on him. "Glad 'nothing' could take you away from your work."

"Ben," Reed said, approaching him carefully. "I don't know if this thing'll change us back or make us worse. I need you to be patient for a little while long—"

Immediately Ben was on his feet and he met Reed partway. "Look at me, Reed," he said, poking his finger into Reed's chest, sinking in as if Reed were the Pillsbury Doughboy. "*Look* at me!"

He grabbed Reed's face hard, his fingers indenting the skin. Reed's face seemed almost to melt around it, and a disgusted Ben shoved Reed back. Reed slammed to the ground and Sue gasped at the ferocity of the impact.

"I am looking!" Reed gasped, more from shock over being tossed around by his best friend than any sort of pain. "That's why I can't make a mistake! I've got to get it right, and it's *not right yet!* We *need* to *test* this."

Ben shook his head, glaring down at Reed. His fists

were clenching and unclenching as he spoke. "I spent my whole life protecting you, from the schoolyard to the stars. For *what*? So you could play Twister with your girlfriend while I'm the freak of the week?"

Reed tried to stand, but Ben swept his arm around with a vicious backhand and caught him hard. Reed slammed into the wall and slumped to the ground, looking stunned.

"Ben!" Sue warned him angrily. "Stop it! Or *I'll* stop it!"

She brought up her hands, ready to summon a force field to drive him back. Ben stabbed a finger at her. "Stay out of this, Susie."

As the Thing turned toward her, Reed shook off the brief disorientation, and saw what appeared to be Ben threatening Susan. He reacted instantly and instinctively, leaping forward with his body stretching from the waist up. He completely encircled Ben, pinning his arms at his side, looking like a python as he whipped around Ben repeatedly to try and secure him. Ben let out a roar, trying to shake Reed off and failing. Without hesitation he ran backward into the wall, trying to slam Reed's head against it. He succeeded in smashing against the wall. However, Reed's neck extended around so that his face was right in Ben's, gritting his teeth and clearly straining in his endeavors to contain the Thing, but determined not to release him.

"Good thing you're flexible enough to watch your own back," Ben advised him. "Cause I won't be. Not anymore. You're on your own now."

Something in the way Ben said it made Reed realize that—for the moment—the conflict was over. Ben was no longer straining against the hold that Reed had on him. He knew that he was taking a chance, since Ben could continue the attack any moment. Nevertheless, Reed released Ben. As he retracted his body, Ben shook out his arms to restore circulation, and then turned and walked out without giving Reed so much as a backward glance.

Sue immediately came to Reed's side. His face was banged up and he was bleeding. But he waved Sue off, saying, "I'm okay. Just go. Go after him. Stop him."

Taking him at his word, she nodded and then ran out after Ben.

Slowly, Reed got to his feet, his mind reeling. He thought of what Ben had said, and how he had just come to grips with the way that his delays and uncertainties had made mincemeat of his and Sue's life together. Was he never going to learn? Did he literally have to have it beaten into him that sometimes one just has to take things on faith?

No. Not anymore.

He stared up at the machine, then walked over the control panel. Firing up the primary relays, he sent power flooding into the transformation chamber to begin its slow, steady build toward readiness. Then he stretched out his hand to the display case and pulled out his blue uniform with the number "4" stitched on it.

His infernal reluctance to take chances, to have faith, had cost him years off his relationship with Sue. Now it was going to lose him Ben? Not if he could help it, and he was positive that he could.

Johnny Storm, feeling pretty damned good about himself, if a little exhausted, strode into the lobby of the Baxter Building just in time to see Ben on his way out. Well, this was just perfect; the ideal time to show him a little item that Victor had left in the limo. "Christmas came early!" Johnny announced. "Check it out!"

He held up an action figure toy that was clearly supposed to be "The Thing." It was terribly off-model, with a remarkably bloated body topped by a tiny pinhead. Not that that bothered Johnny. Indeed, that was what made it all the better. Plus the hideous appearance wasn't even the best part. The capper came when he pushed a button on the back of the toy and, in a stilted, robotic voice, the toy announced, *"It's clobberin' time!"*

As it turned out, the action figure was remarkably prescient for a toy. With one hand Ben shoved Johnny up against the nearest wall, and with the other hand yanked the action figure out of his hand. He threw it toward Johnny as hard as he could. It smashed against the wall inches from Johnny's head, and did so with such force that it wound up sunk a foot into the plaster.

"Hey!" Johnny protested. "That's a *prototype!*"

"Go back to the drawing board," Ben suggested as he strode away.

With an annoyed sigh, Johnny tried to pry the action figure out of the wall. He had no success at all, and didn't want to try burning through the wall to get it because he'd just melt the plastic. He headed toward the elevator with the intention of going upstairs, borrowing a crowbar, and trying to lever it out that way. Just as he got to the elevator, however, Sue came barreling out.

"Johnny, did you see Ben?" she asked, looking out of breath.

"Yeah, for the last time, I hope," Johnny said. "I'm done with this freak show. I'm moving back to the real world."

"Is that what you call it?" Sue demanded. "With the fast cars and faster women, and the empty applause from audiences? That's 'real'?"

"At least it beats living in a lab like somebody's science project," Johnny shot back. "You know what? To hell with the crowbar, and to hell with the lot of you."

He turned to leave, and Sue wanted to stop him . . . but hesitated. Johnny reasoned that maybe, just maybe, she was starting to wise up. "You know," she said suddenly, "if Mom was here—"

Johnny vehemently shook his head. She might have used their departed mother to guilt Johnny before, but not this time. "Look around, sis!" he said angrily. "She's not here! So you can stop talking to me like I'm your little boy—"

"As soon as you stop *acting* like one!" Sue said angrily. Then she stopped, took a deep breath, and steadied herself. "Come on, Johnny," she continued, trying to sound as reasonable as she could, "you're smarter than this. You think those people out there care about you? You're just a . . . a fad to them."

He pulled away from her, taking a step out the door. "Let's try something new: You live *your* life, and I'll live *mine*." He paused and then added, "And just for the record: They *love* me."

He strode off into the night, knowing that Sue was going to stand there and watch him go. He didn't even glance behind himself. The night called to him, and it was his to light up as he saw fit.

He had been the one who had made the Fantastic Four a household name, and as far as he was concerned, if no one else ever mentioned the group to him again, it would be too soon.

Sue felt events were completely spiraling out of her control. She had no idea what was happening, why everything was falling apart. But she knew one thing for certain, and that was that her relationship with Johnny was one of the cores of her existence. She had to get him back, had to pull him back into the fold.

She started after him, and suddenly the lights flickered wildly in the Baxter Building lobby. From high above her, there was a jolt that she could feel all the way down here, and at that moment she knew something terrible had happened, and who it had happened to.

"Oh God. Reed," she said, and bolted for the stairs.

21

VICTOR VON DOOM HAD A SUDDEN DESIRE FOR POP-corn. Hunkered down in his office, the screens tied into the security system at the Baxter Building laid out before him, he felt as if he were watching the long-awaited climax of a movie he himself had scripted.

"I love it when a plan comes together," he said softly.

He kept getting so excited as he watched that he drew too close to the monitors, causing them to fuzz out. Then he had to pull back and make the effort of restraining himself.

There was Reed, having donned his uniform, and he had the transformation chamber up and running. It was counting down to full activation as Reed made last-minute adjustments to the power levels. Within the chamber, the re-created cosmic storm whirled and crackled: galactic energies brought down to Earth and harnessed, put at the disposal of Victor Von Doom and his cat's-paw, Reed Richards.

That's all Reed was, really. For all his intellect and

genius, he was nothing but Victor's chess piece to maneuver, to play . . . and, ultimately, to sacrifice as needed.

Victor was enthralled, leaning forward—but not too far forward—and breathless with anticipation. On the observation screen, Reed was drawing closer and closer to the door. He took a deep breath, then threw open the chamber and gazed with his own eyes upon the forces that had transformed his life. His face was flushed with excitement and not a little concern.

It was a moment of truth for both of them: Reed facing his fear of acting on impulse, of leaping rather than looking; and Victor, having worked behind the scenes to push matters forward over Reed's foot-dragging. There was still a chance it could fall apart. Reed might yet lose his nerve, pull back, shut things down . . . in which case, Victor was ready to head over there and throw Reed in headfirst himself.

It wasn't necessary. Reed stepped into the machine, closing the door behind him. Victor switched cameras to the one that was located within the transformation chamber itself. The cosmic storm was a virtual tornado, spinning and crackling dead center of the chamber.

Victor could only guess what was going through Reed's mind. Was his life flashing before his eyes? Was he bored out of his skull because of it? Victor wondered which Reed regretted more: letting Sue go, or his pathetically transparent efforts to get her back. Was it Ben or Sue who was more important to Reed in the grand scheme of things? All these and more were questions that Victor had and would likely never get answered. Fortunately enough, he was only interested in a vaguely intellectual way. In his down-to-earth reality, he was more than content to let Reed die with the questions left unanswered, if it should come to that.

Reed spread wide his arms as he approached. Victor sneered at that. Could Richards be any more melodramatic? He drew closer and closer to the center of the storm, and Victor kept wondering if Reed was going to lose his nerve. To Reed's credit, he didn't. In fact, with each step he seemed more resolute, more determined to see it through.

Reed paused at the periphery of the storm for half a heartbeat, took a final deep breath, and then thrust himself into the midst of the maelstrom. Victor lost sight of Reed as the storm swallowed him. He thought he caught brief glimpses of him being yanked around, staggering, jerking out of control, and then—

Nothing.

The screens went black. All of them. Victor briefly thought that he was responsible for it. That he'd gotten too excited at what he was seeing or had gotten too close again to the monitors. But then he looked out the window and saw a gargantuan flash atop the Baxter Building in the distance. The rest of the building, along with every structure in a two-block radius, was plunged into darkness. The very upper tip of it continued to glow, although in a flickering manner.

Victor spat out a curse. He'd never felt so helpless.

At least the power to the monitors hadn't gone out. It was just that the surge had overloaded the lights in the Baxter, and he was going to have to wait for the backups to kick in.

He hoped it wouldn't take too long. He hated the notion of missing the end of the show.

The lights were flickering in the Baxter Building as Sue stumbled into the transformation lab. She struck her shin on some piece of furniture in the dark and yelped, but quickly forgot the pain as her eyes widened with horror. Sue had known ahead of time what she was going to find, and yet being confronted with the reality of it was a brand-new shock. There was a thick, sickening smell of ozone in the air, and she heard a faint moaning from within.

She grabbed at the door, prepared to rip the thing off its hinges if it was locked. But it gave way immediately and she yanked it open, peering into the darkness within. It was thick with smoke, the air now so acrid that she was squinting and her eyes watering. Sparks darted about, the last remains of the power that had surged through the machinery. Then she was able to make out a form, slowly standing up and wavering in place. It was Reed. His back was to her. She whispered his name and he staggered like Frankenstein's monster, turning slowly in place to face her. He made it only halfway, though, and then collapsed to the floor. When he fell, it didn't sound like a human body hitting the ground, but rather a plastic bag filled with water.

Sue stumbled through the smoky environs toward him, dropping to his side and trying to lift him to a sitting position. It was an almost impossible task because everywhere she tried to pick him up, his body gave way. She remembered once years ago, when she and Johnny were both young and on vacation with their parents up at a lake. They'd discovered a long-drowned rabbit washed up on shore. It had been submerged for so long that every time Johnny tried to pick up any part of it, its skin had just peeled right off. Johnny had been endlessly fascinated while Sue had fought not to get sick.

That was almost the condition she was finding Reed in now. Half of his body was practically gelatinous, stretched out, devoid of any semblance of bone structure. Most hideously of all, one side of his face looked like it was melting off.

All my fault, my God, it's all my fault, I pushed him, I told him how he was always delaying things, afraid to commit to things, always overthinking, oh my God, he did this because of what I said, because of what Ben said, we've killed him, God in heaven . . .

To her utter shock, Reed was trying to talk. It was hard to understand him as his jaw almost detached from the upper portion of his head. "I can . . . make it work," he managed to say.

"Reed, stop," Sue begged him, not knowing where to hold him or what to do. "You need to rest your—"

"The power . . . I need . . . more power . . . to control . . . the storm . . ."

"You *need* a doctor," Sue said, although she couldn't

323

imagine what doctor could possibly address the catastrophe that had overtaken Reed's body.

At least the few passing minutes since this fiasco had served to make Reed's body slightly easier to manage. As Reed slipped into unconsciousness, Sue found some parts of Reed's nauseatingly gooey body had hardened enough that she could get a grip. Half lifting, half dragging, she pulled him out of the chamber, desperately trying to think of who could possibly help them.

"More *power* . . . ?"

Victor Von Doom, having witnessed the touching and faintly sickening reunion between Reed and Sue via his monitors, looked thoughtfully at his own hands as he repeated, "More power."

He reached for the phone on his desk with the intention of activating the speaker on it. As it turned out it wasn't necessary; the speaker phone snapped on in response to his merest gesture. He smiled briefly at that, then mentally "pushed" a number on his speed dial. It responded automatically and, seconds later, Leonard picked up.

"Leonard," Victor Von Doom instructed him. "Bring me our lab rat."

Ben Grimm sat alone beneath the Brooklyn Bridge. It seemed that solitude was becoming his natural state of being.

He could see the faces of all the people he had once considered friends, family, or loved ones floating before him, mocking him, tormenting him. He craned his neck and glanced upward at the high span of the bridge, and wondered if maybe that idiot business man—the one whose attempted suicide had precipitated the insane chain of events which had served to bring the Fantastic Four to national attention—maybe he hadn't had the right idea.

After all, they always referred to suicide as a permanent solution to a temporary problem. But if it wasn't temporary . . . then wouldn't a permanent solution, maybe, be called for?

Suddenly headlights slashed across Ben. *What now? Reporters? Thrill seekers? Hell, bring 'em on.*

The car pulled up and the door on the driver's side opened up. Ben squinted against the brightness of the light, and was surprised—but not too surprised, somehow—to see Von Doom's right-hand man, Leonard, standing there.

"Ben!" he called. "They need you back at the Baxter Building. It's . . ." He paused and then said, "It's Reed."

His first impulse was to ask, "What's Reed?" but then he realized. His gaze shifted automatically in the general direction of the Baxter Building. He thought he was able to vaguely make it out in the Manhattan skyline . . . or maybe not. It appeared darker over there than it should be, the lights of Manhattan providing illumination to everywhere except the general area of the Baxter. But he was probably imagining it . . .

What if you're not?

Seeking confirmation, Ben turned to Leonard and said, "The power? Is it—?"

Leonard simply nodded. There was something in his face that made it abundantly clear matters were far worse than Ben could be imagining, and somehow, Reed was involved. *Perhaps he's gotten himself killed* . . . and then Ben looked at his own rocky, malformed hands, and added mentally, *or worse*.

Well . . . so what? It didn't really matter anymore. Reed wasn't his problem . . .

Except . . . what if Reed had been injured, killed . . . because he still considered Ben Grimm to be *his* problem, even if Ben had practically disowned him. Even if the newspaper was busy dehumanizing Ben Grimm, calling him "the Thing." Even if . . .

"*Crap*," muttered Ben. "Guess Mister Rubber Baby Buggy Bumper still needs babysittin' even at this ripe age." He turned toward Leonard and said, "Take me to 'im."

The walls were vibrating in the Manhattan nightclub called "Waid's 54." The music was cranked to the max and the DJ was still trying to coax even more decibels from it, just to make sure that no one would have their proper hearing by morning. The pulsating lights added an eerie, disorienting feeling to the atmosphere . . . not that it bothered the people who were writhing to it in fits of primitive enthusiasm. Few of them noticed the streaks of flame that danced among the lights, and those that did simply assumed it was part of the light show. None thought to trace the flaming streaks back to their point of origin in the VIP section of one of the balconies.

Johnny Storm sat there, happily ensconced, surrounded by what was becoming a typical bevy of beauties. They were climbing over each other to try and get closer and see, firsthand and close up, his dazzling array of pyrokinetic parlor tricks. Johnny, as always, was grooving on the attention and adoration.

One young woman in particular caught his eye. She was not with his impromptu entourage, however, but instead seated at the next table. She appeared to be alone, gazing into a compact and doing some touchups on her makeup. The others grouped around Johnny were attractive enough, but this one was a full-on knockout. Johnny thought she might even be a starlet he'd seen profiled in *People* recently. Ignoring the other girls near him, he leaned in toward her, startling her slightly. The thick, round candle in the middle of her table began to melt, and beads of sweat started dripping down her face.

"What do you say we get out of here?" Johnny said softly.

She reacted in a way that Johnny wasn't accustomed to. She stared at him as if he were some new virus that was attempting to intrude on her system. Before she could say anything, a shadow threw itself over them. Johnny glanced up to see a very large man looming over them, and abruptly realized where he had in fact seen the girl's photograph. It wasn't that she was a starlet. It was the guy who'd been in *People*: He was a halfback for the Jets and this was his girlfriend.

Ah well. That just made it more interesting.

"This your boyfriend?" Johnny asked, eyes wide, voice innocent, already knowing the answer.

"Is that all you do?" asked the halfback in disdain. "Bar tricks and stealing chicks?"

Johnny saw the guy was holding a drink in his hand. "For my next trick," Johnny muttered, and he reached up and tapped the guy's drink. Instantly it ignited into flame.

With an alarmed yelp that was an ill-match with Johnny's peal of laughter, the halfback dropped the glass. It smashed to the ground and instantly the carpet caught fire. Fortunately enough it was a small flare-up, and he was quickly able to stomp it out.

As he was doing so, Johnny smirked at the halfback's antics, right up until the guy's girlfriend rounded on him and snapped, "What are you doing? You could have burned somebody!"

The fire out, the boyfriend turned toward Johnny, fists balled, clearly ready to take a swing at him. Johnny half-rose from the chair, his eyes narrowed, and there was enough danger in his eyes that the girl quickly stepped in between the two of them, clearly afraid for her boyfriend's safety. "You get your hands scalded, you can't play," she reminded him tightly. "Keep away from him. He's not normal."

Upon hearing that, Johnny's frustration about feeling like "a leper with first-strike capability" surged up. He said defensively, "I am so normal. I'm just . . . supernormal."

"Uh huh," said the girl, unimpressed. As she guided

her angered boyfriend away, she hurled back over her shoulder, "You know, if I had your power I'd be doing something with it. Not wasting my time doing cheap bar tricks, hitting on some other guy's girl." With that parting shot, the couple put as much distance between themselves and Johnny as they could.

Johnny had felt a swirl of what seemed like a hundred emotions since the accident that had changed his life. But he could never recall having felt embarrassed: not even when he was sitting buck-naked in a newly created hot tub in the snow. Now, however, that was exactly how he felt. It wasn't helped by the looks he was getting from his erstwhile fans. Whereas before they were vying for the opportunity to get into his face, now they didn't even seem to want to make eye contact with him.

He knew all the old saws, about how fame was fleeting and the public was fickle. But he'd never thought it possible that people could turn so quickly, and with so little provocation.

Or maybe the provocation wasn't that little.

For the first time, Johnny Storm experienced the sensation of what it was like to feel alone in a crowd . . . and it gave him just the slightest feeling of what it was like to be the Thing. He couldn't say he liked it all that much . . . nor was he enamored of his behavior toward the Thing in recalling it now.

"Ben," he said softly.

Leonard led Ben into the lab at the Baxter Building. Ben looked at the transformation chamber, unsure of what to think. He had a sense of what it was and what it was supposed to accomplish, but he couldn't imagine what it was doing there alone and unattended . . . or, specifically, where Reed was. Something about the entire situation just felt wrong to him.

Victor Von Doom was standing at the control station, presumably doing some last-minute checks. "Ben! Come in!" he said as if greeting his oldest friend in the world.

"What is this?" Ben asked suspiciously, looking at the chamber. His nostrils caught a faint whiff of something having been burning recently. "Where's Reed?"

Sniffing disdainfully, Von Doom said, "Where do you *think*? With *Sue*." He flipped some switches and lights began to illuminate around the sides of the chamber. As they flickered, Ben noticed that even Leonard looked a bit intimidated by the scene.

Apparently, so did Von Doom. "I'll take it from here, Leonard," he said softly.

Leonard nodded, said "Yes, sir," and got out of there so fast that it made Ben wonder if, maybe, Doom's assistant didn't have the right idea.

"What do you want, Vic?" Ben asked, his voice laced with distrust.

"To help you," Von Doom said soothingly. "I've run every test known to man. And they all yield the same result: *The machine is ready*."

Ben shook his head. He desperately wanted to believe what Von Doom was saying, but . . .

"Reed said it'd be weeks until—"

"He also said," Victor reminded him, "we'd avoid that storm in space. And we know how *that* turned out."

Slowly Ben went from shaking his head to nodding. That much was true. It wasn't as if Reed had a flawless track record. Every time Ben passed any kind of reflecting surface it was a reminder of just how flawed it was. He wanted to believe, so badly, that it was possible. That he could go back to normality just by stepping through that door. And what, really, did he have to lose?

Still . . .

"But why did Reed say it wouldn't be ready until—?"

Von Doom had the answer at the ready. "He couldn't generate enough power for the machine to reach critical mass. Yet another mistake for 'Mister Fantastic.'"

"And you can?" Ben asked. "Power it up?"

"Yes," said Victor firmly. "I've found a new energy source."

Ben looked back at the machine and, as a result, didn't see the slight crackling of energy that sparked around Von Doom. Victor was taking care to stand back in the shadows and, more, he was keeping his arm behind his back. "Tell me again," he said, as energy started to build around his arm. *"Do you want to be Ben Grimm again?"*

Ben didn't see the energy, didn't notice the warning signs. His world seemed to consist only of the massive chamber, beckoning him to enter.

"Let's do it," said Ben.

22

THE CHAMBER DOORS OPENED AS IF EXTENDING AN IN-
vitation. Having made up his mind, Ben walked inside,
fully resolved to see it through no matter what. After
all, what were the four possible outcomes? It cured
him. It didn't have any effect. It made him even uglier.
It killed him. There wasn't really a downside to any of
them. The cure was the ideal, of course. No effect was
no effect. He already repulsed people, so what difference did it make in terms of degrees? And if he died,
well . . . he'd risked death for far flimsier reasons every
time he'd climbed into the cockpit of an experimental
plane.

He looked around the sterile box of the chamber, the
faint ozone smell stronger in his nostrils now. It was
clear to him that it had already been activated, but it
might well have been as a result of Victor doing a test
run. The doors slowly closed behind him and he could
hear the sound of seals falling into place. He shut his
eyes, praying silently. Visualization. That was the key to

accomplishment. Visualize how you want things to turn out, do it fervently enough, and you can shape reality to your liking. He pictured himself as Ben Grimm, smiling, cocky, human.

He could hear the machine powering up.

Please, he thought. *Please.*

As the lights went on inside the chamber, they dimmed in the lab. Energy began to pump into the machine, and Von Doom could see through the small observation port that the cosmic storm had flared into existence. It was picking up in intensity and velocity, but the power wasn't going to be able to sustain it, just like last time.

Except this wasn't last time. This time, Victor Von Doom was there, and it was as if everything that had happened until now was making a strange kind of sense. Afflicted with his own version of the disease that beleaguered the Fantastic Four, simultaneously he had the key to the cure literally in the palm of his hand.

He walked over to the chamber, pulled open a panel that he himself had added. His own little improvement to Richard's designs. A special circuit that would enable him to both supply his own energy to the fuel the storm . . . and siphon off what the storm would generate as it increased in intensity, as well as the energies it would theoretically draw off Ben Grimm. It was like earning interest on an investment. He slid his hands into it and sent power surging from his body into the device. Over on the control panel, the countdown to full ignition began.

A movement over at the viewing port caught Von Doom's eye. It was the Thing. He was looking out the window, glancing around, perhaps trying to catch a glimpse of Von Doom. Maybe he was looking for some sort of final assurance, a thumbs-up. Something.

He wasn't going to get it.

The counter ticked down to zero.

The artificial, but all too real, cosmic storm roared to full life, striking with all its fury.

Within the chamber, Ben Grimm faced down the elemental powers that had ruined his life.

He had thought he was ready for anything. But when he saw it bearing down upon him, suddenly he was no longer this creature made of rock in a controlled situation, hoping for a cure. He was, instead, the helpless astronaut, clutching a safety tether and hauling himself hand over desperate hand toward safety, trying to make it, knowing he wouldn't. It was that Ben Grimm, with the simple human frame and the life of normality about to be cut short, who reacted now when the cosmic storm hammered through his body.

He twisted back to the window, his mouth open and screaming in silent agony. He staggered, tried to get to the door to slam it open, and collapsed before he could reach it, to lie writhing on the floor.

It was the energy surge that awoke Reed Richards.

It had seemed to take forever for his body to return to its previous form, and even then it wasn't completely healed. There were parts of his anatomy that just felt wrong, as if they were a few millimeters from where they were supposed to be. Reed lay in bed in his quarters, still recuperating, drifting in a near-dream state. But he snapped fully awake when the lights began to flicker wildly around him. He forced himself out of bed, straining with every muscle left in him. His body screamed for him to stay where he was, but his brain sent determined instructions that the situation demanded otherwise.

Somebody was screwing around with the transformation chamber, and there was no doubt in Reed's mind who it was.

Sue was in the medical supply room when the power went out around her. She'd been sifting through the medications, trying to find the right painkiller for Reed, and her first reaction to the diminishment of power was, *Damn, how am I going to be able to see which pills to bring him?*

But then the reasons behind the power outage became of greater concern to her. And when she felt the walls starting to shake, the rationale became horrifically clear. At first she thought that Reed had been insane enough to take another run at the cure. But she dismissed it just as quickly. Reed could barely stand up, much less operate heavy-duty machinery.

Somebody was screwing around with the transformation chamber, and there was no doubt in Sue's mind who it was.

*   *   *

Johnny Storm was alone, which was an odd sensation for him these days.

He was walking slowly down Fifth Avenue, heading in the general direction of the Baxter Building, his thoughts whirling. He kept returning to what that woman in the club had said to him, about how he was wasting his powers. He tried to tell himself that she didn't know what she was talking about. She, after all, wasn't living in his flaming hot skin. She was just some jock's main squeeze who had her picture in a magazine. She wasn't remotely on his level, and where the hell did she get off sitting in judgment on him? He thought he'd been putting his powers to pretty good use, thanks.

So why did he keep coming back to her? Why did he feel as if she had somehow made some sort of valid point?

Suddenly the lights in buildings all around him flickered and then went out. There was no illumination anywhere . . .

No. No, that wasn't true at all. There was a bright, almost blinding flash leaping from a window in the Baxter Building, the source of a wave of light spreading through the sky.

Johnny had no idea what was happening, what was causing it, what the ramifications were or what the outcome would be. But there was one thing he did know, with a clarity as blinding as the light that he had just seen erupting from the upper reaches of the Baxter.

Somebody was screwing around with the Fantastic

Four, and there was no doubt in Johnny's mind who it was.

Von Doom watched with distant fascination, like a god gazing down from Mount Olympus, as the red cloud within the machine swirled with debris, crackling with light. The chamber was rattling dangerously, the power being generated seeming to shake the very foundation of the building. He knew, however, that the process was in its final throes, and he was correct.

The light died down somewhat, although it was still pulsing along with the chamber. Then the chamber door slid open. A long moment passed, and then a form appeared in the doorway.

It was Ben Grimm.

Not the Thing.

Ben Grimm.

No longer covered with rocks, no longer a monster. A man. Naked. Tired. Wasted beyond belief. But a man.

He picked up the trench coat he'd left fallen outside the chamber and pulled it on. The slow, pained way in which he did so made it clear that he was in agony. It wound up overwhelming him and he collapsed to the floor, landing hard on his elbows. With all the discomfort he was suffering, however, it was likely he didn't even feel it.

He had other concerns. Practically swimming in a coat that was way too large for him, Ben was staring at his hands, his arms. Tentatively he brought them up to his face, ran them across his now-normal brow.

"Oh . . . my God," he whispered. "Th-thank you . . . *thank you! Vic—!*"

Sparks being generated over in the shadows caught his attention. Ben turned . . . and gaped.

He could see Victor's arm clearly in the darkness. It was a bizarre combination of flesh and metal, as if Victor had been transformed into a cyborg. Victor stepped forward from the shadows, flexing his arms, displaying the fact that his entire body now looked that way. Electricity pumped through his body, and his metal-and-flesh body glittered in the night.

"Vic . . ." whispered Ben. "What the . . . ?"

"Vic" spoke as if from a great distance, his thoughts whirling back to the space station. "Everyone thought I was safe behind those shields . . ."

"Victor," and Ben was staggering to his feet. "The machine worked for me. It can work for you—"

"It did, Ben," Von Doom informed him. "It *worked perfectly.*"

Von Doom thought it was almost comical, the expression on Ben's face as the dime dropped. "You *planned* this?"

Victor reached out his hand, rubbed his fingers together, and smiled at the sparks it generated. But he was far beyond such parlor tricks now. Electricity began to build in his shoulders, coursing down his arms toward his hands. "I've always wanted power. Now I've got an unlimited supply . . ."

"And no *Thing* to stand in your way," Ben said with harsh realization.

Von Doom smiled, nodded, and said, "Take a good look, Ben. This is what a man looks like who embraces his destiny."

It was Victor Von Doom who had spoken those final words, and Victor Von Doom who clenched his fist in preparation for his next move. But Victor Von Doom had been dying by slow degrees over the past weeks. When he finally, mercilessly, generated a massive burst of energy that slammed into Ben, sending him flying backward across the room, Victor Von Doom completely, irrevocably died. Instead he was replaced by someone completely confident in his power and ability to wipe out anyone and anything that dared to stand in his way.

Victor Von Doom had spoken to a conscious Ben Grimm of men embracing their destiny. But it was Doom who said to the now-insensate Ben Grimm as he lay sprawled upon the floor, "One down . . . three to go."

Adrenaline surging through him, Reed gained strength with every step as he pounded toward the lab. He was already running through all the possibilities of what he was going to see when he arrived, and yet nothing prepared him for the sight of Victor standing there wearing some sort of bizarre body armor while a half-naked man lay in the corner with a coat draped over him . . .

Then Reed realized two things almost at the same time, and he was unable to decide which was the more astonishing. The unconscious man on the floor was Ben. And Victor wasn't wearing body armor.

"Right on cue," said Victor.

Reed couldn't speak at first. Finally he managed to whisper, "What did you do . . . ?"

"*Exactly* what I *said* I would. I built a better, stronger being. And outsmarted the great Reed Richards."

"Victor, this isn't the way to—"

"Victor has left the building. I'm simply Doom now. Or," and he appeared to consider it. "No. 'Doom' . . . that's a video game, isn't it. It needs something more. *Doctor* Doom. What do you think? After all, you always know best." He smiled darkly. "So tell me: Chemistry 101, Part One. What happens when you superheat rubber?"

Before Reed could respond, Doctor Doom answered his own question as he brought up his hands and blasted Reed with an electrical bolt. Reed gasped as he was lifted off his feet. For an instant his heart actually stopped and Reed was unaware of anything around him, and then it miraculously restarted again. But he was disoriented, having no idea where he was, what was happening.

It was driven home to him with jarring finality as Reed crashed through a huge window with such force that—had he been normal—it would have shattered every bone in his body. As it was, Reed's body rubberbanded from the blast. Barely conscious, he managed to keep his body adhering to the exterior of the Baxter Building. He proceeded to "slinky" down the side of the Baxter Building, his skin rippling as he fought to remain awake.

* * *

Doctor Doom glanced out the window and smiled at the sight of his one-time rival flipping along the building like a child's toy.

Rival. What an odd word to apply to someone who, in the end, turned out to be so utterly inconsequential.

Doom headed over to the elevator and, this time, didn't even have to gesture in a perfunctory fashion. Instead the elevator responded to his thoughts alone, opening up for him and bringing him down to the lobby without any further prompting.

He stepped out into the lobby where the doorman, O'Hoolihan, was looking extremely jumpy over all the power flickering on and off. But if O'Hoolihan was nervous before, he was much more so upon seeing the frightening figure approaching him. "Mr. Von Doom . . . are you oka—?"

With a casual swipe of his hand, he send O'Hoolihan crashing through the revolving doors. "Never better, Jimmy." As he walked past the unconscious doorman, he added in an offhand manner, "And it's 'Doctor Doom' now."

Out on the sidewalk, he looked up and saw Reed practically melting down the sides of the awning, like something out of a Salvador Dali painting. As he started to drop down toward the street, he caught Reed's face and held it close.

"Who's going to walk the walk for you now?" he asked.

Reed's eyes rolled up into the top of his head and he blacked out. Doctor Doom laughed, then yanked Reed off the awning and stalked off into the night, dragging the elasticized body of Mister Fantastic behind him.

It had taken Sue forever to get from the Baxter Building's medical center to the lab where the transformation device was situated. There had been smoke everywhere, and when the lights had gone out, she'd stumbled around in the dark helplessly for what seemed like hours. Finally, however, she made it and raced in. In the dimness of the backup lighting, she was able to make out a scene of terrible devastation. Wreckage was strewn about, and one of the windows was shattered. She coughed as wisps of acrid smoke filtered into her lungs. She called out Reed's name, but got no response. Never had silence been such a terrible thing.

Then she noticed a pile of wreckage shifting, and she saw there was a man lying there beneath it. *Reed?* No, it was someone else, and a second later, she came to the shocked realization that it was . . .

"Ben!"

He had a tattered overcoat draped over himself, and he was badly banged up. She helped him to his feet, and at that moment she heard Johnny's voice calling out, "Sue!"

"In here! Johnny, in here!"

Johnny ran in and almost tripped over debris on the floor. He steadied himself and then squinted in the dimness, trying to make out what had happened. "I'm sorry, sis, for leaving you guys—!" he called as he carefully maneuvered his way through the wreckage.

"No, *I'm* sorry, for pushing you out," she said.

A moment passed between them, a bridging moment that ideally would heal the divide separating them. But Sue understood it was going to have to wait, for they had far more pressing matters to deal with. Johnny recognized that as well when he saw who was standing next to Sue. "Jesus! Ben!" He eyed him curiously and then, adopting an achingly bad Ricky Ricardo impression, said, "I go away, look what happens. You got a lot of splaining to do."

Ben motioned toward the wreckage. "The machine works. And Vic's gone 'Mister Hyde' on us . . ."

"Really," said Johnny in a voice tinged with irony. "With a name like Von *Doom?* Never saw *that* one coming."

At that moment, there was only one thing of interest to Sue. "Where is Reed?" she asked, looking around and getting no answer.

"Victor must've taken him," said Ben.

There was a moment of silence, and then Johnny said with unexpected vigor, "Then we take him back."

He put out a hand, palm down, in front of the others. Sue half-smiled, thinking of how childish a reaction it was . . . and yet somehow so right. She placed her hand palm down atop Johnny's, and they looked to Ben. Without hesitation, his hand came down on top of theirs.

"Ain't no thing," he said.

23

DOCTOR DOOM SAT AT THE HEAD OF THE TABLE IN HIS conference room. From this vantage point, he could look down upon the city with the air of superiority that he had come to feel was his birthright.

He was wearing a green cloak and hood (the only possession of his late father's that he still had from the old country). On his face, to cover his scarring, was a metal mask that he had appropriated from his armor collection. He felt fully alive for the first time in his life, and could only look back on his existence prior to this as some sort of lengthy dream from which he had finally, mercifully awoken.

Power had been restored to the city, and there were repair crews running hither and yon far below him in the streets, trying to figure out what had gone wrong and where. They were like ants to him and scarcely worth even a passing thought.

From gazing out the window, his eyes flickered toward the other end of the table. "Chemistry 101, Part

Two," he said. "What happens to rubber when it's super-*cooled*?"

Reed Richards was strapped to a chair at the table's far end. Ordinarily he could easily have slipped any such bonds simply through elasticizing his limbs. But that wasn't a possibility at the moment, for there were tubes inserted into his skin via specifically designed needles, pumping the biological equivalent of liquid nitrogen into him. Doom had specifically customized it so that it wouldn't poison Reed outright, but instead drop his body temperature to freezing and beyond. Any ordinary person would have been dead already despite the fact that it was nontoxic. But Reed was no ordinary person. Thus would his reward for his uniqueness be extended pain and suffering, as was often the fate of most extraordinary people who failed to outthink their opponents.

Ultracold vapor was coating Reed from head to toe as Doctor Doom stepped in closer, a sadistic smile barely visible through the mouth slit in his mask. Reed desperately tried to move, but couldn't so much as flex his fingers into a fist.

"Allow me," Doom said with a fake air of solicitousness. He pressed down on one of Reed's fingers, which made a horrific cracking sound. Reed's face twisted with agony. Doom pressed on a second of Reed's fingers. Reed clearly wanted to cry out, to achieve the release of screaming, but even that was denied him with his jaw frozen shut.

Doom leaned in closer and whispered, "Painful? You don't know the meaning of the word. But you will."

He was starting to become bored with tormenting Reed, though. Besides, he was expecting that there were other issues to attend to. Stepping away from the freezing scientist, Doom walked over to a crate and flipped open the top. He reached in and pulled out a military-issue rocket launcher, hefting it onto his shoulder with satisfaction.

He aimed over the city skyline, leveled it at the Baxter Building, seeking out a heat signature that he could lock onto. Serendipity was with him, for there—right on his screen—was an unmistakeable source of heat attraction: Johnny Storm. Obviously he had come running home when the problems had hit, which was extremely considerate of him. He was providing a perfect means of targeting, far more reliable than Sue or Ben would have been at this distance. The words TARGET ACQUIRED flashed onto a small computer screen.

"Flame off," said Doctor Doom, and he squeezed the trigger.

The missile leaped out of the rocket launcher like an unchained wild dog heading after a scampering rabbit. It roared off into the night, lighting up the darkened sky as it began its wide turn and headed toward its destination.

Through the shattered window, Johnny, Ben, and Sue all heard the distant sound of the missile being fired, but the significance of it didn't register immediately. Johnny was the first to cross to the window, and he let out a yelp of alarm. The others quickly joined him and saw the unmistakeable jet trail of a missile heading straight toward them.

On a hunch, Johnny ignited his right hand and waved it back and forth. He saw, ever so slightly, the nose of the missile matching the movement. "Great. Heat-seeker," he muttered.

He stepped to the edge of a broken window even as Sue cried out, "Johnny, what are you doing?"

"Sis, let *me* take care of *you* for once."

"Are you sure you can—?"

"Fly?" he finished the sentence. "If not, this is gonna be one hell of a base-jump."

Sue reached out to him, but before she could get to him, Johnny dove headfirst off the edge.

Time extended in that way it did when one was in truly dire circumstances. Johnny focused all his energy, all his will, and nothing happened. No flame anywhere, much less all over his body. He began to sweat furiously, and still nothing, and the street was coming up at him with horrific speed.

You're forcing it! You never forced anything in your life! That's how you operate, by just going with it! Do that now! Just let it happen!

Despite the fact that a violent and ugly death was seconds away, Johnny relaxed, letting the adrenaline wash over him rather than trying to compel it. Five seconds from impact, he focused his energy not on staving off death, but on pure bravado as he shouted at the top of his lungs, "*Flame on!*"

His entire body ignited, his clothes incinerating instantly, leaving him in his blue, skintight uniform. He veered up and away from the sidewalk, banking, swooping skyward, flying, leaving a blinding trail of flame behind him. The missile immediately followed his arc and zoomed off after him.

Ben could see the swell of pride in Susan's face at her brother's heroism. "That took guts," Ben admitted. Then, his voice hard, he said, "We need to help Reed . . ."

But Sue shook her head. She looked sympathetic but determined. "Ben, this fight's not for you." She rested a hand on his shoulder, squeezing the normal human flesh. "Not anymore."

He stood there, watching her go, feeling helpless. She was right. Doom had smacked him around without even touching him. As he was, he was useless. He looked back out the window, saw Johnny's flames streaking away across the city skyline, dodging the missile that was in hot pursuit.

All this because he'd provided himself as a guinea pig for Victor Von Doom.

"What . . . what have I done?" he whispered.

Doctor Doom watched from his vantage point as the Human Torch twisted and turned across the skies, trying to give the missile the slip or, failing that, finding something harmless he could send the thing crashing into. But nothing was presenting itself, nor was the missile slowing down in its pursuit.

Doom didn't even bother to glance in Reed's direction anymore. The so-called leader of the Fantastic Four was little more than a frozen dinner in a blue stretch suit. He wasn't exactly a factor in the outcome of things . . . not that the outcome was remotely in doubt.

Then his internal monitoring sensors warned him of the impending presence that he had been expecting. He stepped into the far corner of the darkened room and waited for what he knew he would inevitably see and hear.

Sure enough, the door at the far end of the room slowly, carefully opened all by itself. Just a little bit, just enough to admit a slender female figure. There was a series of soft creaking noises across the hardwood floor as Reed continued to sit helplessly. Doom wasn't even sure that Reed knew what was going on around him anymore.

One of the freezing tubes started to shift. It grew taut all by itself, clearly being manipulated by an unseen hand. Sue shimmered into existence next to Reed, obviously satisfied that they were unobserved. "What has he done to you?" she whispered.

"How romantic," said Doom, causing Sue to jump slightly in surprise. She turned and squinted in the darkness, trying to see him. Doom obliged her, moving far enough out into the room that Sue could make him out. She gasped, which was understandable. He knew he must have cut an imposing figure, in his metal mask and cloak, with electrodes throbbing all over his metal skin.

Sue licked her lips, trying to fight back nervousness (and who could blame her, really, for a case of nerves). "We know the machine works," she said, informing him of the obvious. "It worked on Ben, it'll work on you. We can turn you back—"

"Do you *really* think," he asked disdainfully, "fate turned us into gods so we could *refuse* these gifts?"

Her face hardened, and Doom could tell from the buildup of energy in the air molecules before him that Sue was conjuring up a force field. He smiled inwardly. As if such a quaint and limited display of energy could possibly be a threat to him. Why, he could beat her with one hand behind his back . . . which he was in the process of doing as his hand, hidden from view, began to generate the energy for a blast. "Sue, please," he said in sarcastically silky tones, "Let's not fight."

Darkly infuriated by what Doom had done to Reed, Sue shot back, "No, Victor . . . *let's.*"

She hurled a force field at him, obviously intended to contain him or, even better, knock him out. It connected, knocking him back all of a half-step. Then he simply shook it off, too powerful to be daunted by such an assault.

"Susan," he smiled beneath his mask, "you're fired."

He swung his hand around and threw at her an electric shock wave that slammed into her, launching her backward. She spiraled through the air and crashed into the far wall before thudding to the floor.

Valiantly, she gathered her strength, trying to fade

into invisibility. But she wasn't nearly fast enough, and even if she had been, it would have made little difference. Attuned as he was to energy sources, the field she generated that made her invisibility possible was like a beacon to Doctor Doom.

She disappeared from view, and Doom called out mockingly, "Marco," then waited for Sue to move so that she might actually think she had a chance. "Polo," he announced as he spun and grabbed for what seemed midair. What it was instead was her throat as he gripped her tightly, shaking her like a cat worrying a mouse. With a contemptuous laugh he threw her to the floor, where she faded back to visibility, lying helpless and beaten.

Johnny crisscrossed the city, looking for an out. He'd never really flown like this before, wasn't a hundred percent sure how he was doing it, and didn't have the slightest idea how long he could keep it up.

He also didn't understand why the city lights were going on and off again. What, more power surges from the Baxter Building? That made no sense. Was Von Doom up to something else now?

Then something caught his attention, out over the East River. He changed his angle and hurtled toward it, the missile only twenty feet behind him now and gaining steadily.

It was a docked garbage barge. The crew was still on the dock, sipping coffee, about to take the ship out on its run. They looked up as they saw Johnny dive bombing toward them, then saw the missile behind him. That was more than enough excuse for them to scatter in every direction.

Johnny hurled a fireball directly at the barge. It struck dead center and instantly the whole thing went up in flames. He looped back around and hovered behind the inferno as the missile drew in on him with breathtaking speed. Fifteen feet, ten . . .

Just as it was about to strike, Johnny extinguished his flame and dropped toward the water, disappearing through the smoke and fire.

Having lost its initial target, the missile instantly reacquired a far greater source of heat, and slammed into the barge at full speed. The garbage scow blew sky-high upon impact, rattling windows for blocks around.

In Doom's conference room, he watched with grim satisfaction as the missile exploded. Flames danced in the distance, and he turned toward Sue, staring at her with dispassionate eyes.

To think he'd once wanted to marry this creature. What the hell had been going through his mind?

Reed tried desperately to move, but was unable to do so. Doom almost felt sorry for him. Mister Fantastic managed to break the ice off his index finger, but that was about all. And somehow Doom didn't consider a single waggling index finger to be much of a threat.

"One more down," Doom said softly. "Now it's just the scientist and his specimen."

He wasn't sure if Sue had even heard him, for all her attention was focused on Reed. Reed was trying to move his mouth, to speak to her, get some sort of words out. Doom, who had been firing up his energy, tamped it for a moment as he listened with morbid curiosity.

"Sue," Reed managed to say, as if Doom wasn't standing mere feet away. "The only thing . . . I ever knew . . . without thinking was . . . I . . . love—"

His lips froze over before the next word could be uttered, which was of vast relief to Doom. Matters could not possibly become any more maudlin for his taste . . .

Oh, but wait! Yes they could. For he watched in vague disgust as Sue, like a romance novel heroine, whispered to him, "Me, too, Reed."

Filled with surging revulsion over what he saw as undistilled mawkishness, Doom stepped forward and said, cruelly, quietly, "And so four became none. It's *my* time now."

At that exact moment, a door torn off the outside hallway elevator came crashing into the room. Doctor Doom barely sidestepped it as the door flew into his desk, shattering it to splinters.

He gaped in astonishment and suddenly realized that maybe, just maybe, he should have either made sure Ben Grimm was dead, or else destroyed the transformation chamber before he'd left the Baxter Building.

Unfortunately he had done neither, and now the result of those oversights was standing ten feet away from him: a ton or so of pure rocky fury.

"Actually, Vic . . . *it's clobberin' time!*" bellowed the Thing.

*   *   *

Ben Grimm charged forward, leaving a stunned Doctor Doom no time to react. Ever since the first time he'd been altered into his monstrous form, he had been waiting for a target that he could unleash his strength upon. Somewhere that he could channel his unbridled fury.

That target presented itself now. Swinging his fist like lightning, he connected with Doom, hitting him so hard that—in Ben's mind—Doom's ancestors would die.

Doom soared through the air, careening into the massive "V" sculpture on the far side of the room. It snapped off, crashing down upon him with what must have been half a ton of weight. Electricity sparked and crackled around Doom and the sculpture for a moment, and then faded out. No movement from either.

Ben let out a sigh of relief and turned to Reed. "Damn, I've been wanting to do that." Singsonging his voice like something from *Sesame Street*, Ben added, "The clobbering of this bad guy is brought to you by the letter 'V' . . ."

"And the number 'Four,'" Sue added weakly.

Reed managed the thinnest of smiles as Bed started disconnecting the tubes from him. Mimicking Reed's comments from what seemed ages ago, Ben said, "Victor's 'not that bad,' huh? Just 'a little larger than life'? Maybe you'll listen to me next time before . . ."

The wreckage shifted. They turned and saw Doom emerging from it, shoving aside the weighty sculpture as if it were a paperclip. He stood, power surging through him.

"Uh oh," muttered Ben.

Doom lunged at Ben. Ben met the attack with equal

enthusiasm, and the two of them slammed into one another at full speed. The impact drove both of them off to the side, and the next thing Ben knew, they were treading on thin air.

Twisting, tangling in midair, Doom and Ben plummeted toward the ground, wrestling the entire time, jockeying for position even as gravity was determined to have the final say in their match. People saw the two of them falling and, screaming and running, ducked for cover.

The plunge took them spiraling toward Doom's office building and then they ricocheted off like a pinball from a bumper. The change in trajectory sent them tumbling at an angle toward a hotel across the street. The hotel had a swimming pool that was within a glass-covered atrium, and it was through that that Ben and Doom now crashed.

They hit the water and sank about as fast as a man made of rock and a man made of metal could possibly sink. Glass rained down from overhead, sending the few bathers who were there scattering in all directions. A young boy, snorkeling nearby, stayed put and watched in rapt fascination through his scuba mask.

Ben punched Doom as hard as he could in the face, smashing his mask. It split, shattered, and a terrifying visage of jagged flesh and twisted metal glared at him beneath the water. Ben swung again, and this time Doom just managed to yank his head out of the way. As a result, Ben drove his fist right through the lower wall of the pool, rupturing the structure of the entire area. Water gushed toward it and through, a sudden vortex having been created that was sucking everything above it.

The young boy just managed to get to the pool ladder, and he desperately clutched on with both arms as the water drained away at high speed.

The exterior wall of the hotel wasn't designed to withstand the unexpected battering of thousands of gallons of water, and it didn't manage to rise to the challenge. Instead it blasted outward, water cascading downward like a newly created waterfall. Ben Grimm and Doctor Doom tumbled out through the hole and down the deluge, into—of all things—a garbage truck that had just been passing through the adjoining alley.

Water flooded the entire area as people ran, stumbled and swam to get out of the way. As it continued to pour, the garbage truck rocked violently as Ben and Doom struggled within, dents appearing on all sides accompanied by grunts and growls and loud profanities.

Two police cars, with more certainly to come, pulled up to the scene across the street. The officers leaped out of the cars and were already knee-deep in water as they approached the scene of the shuddering truck. People were screaming all manner of conflicting reports as to what was going on, and the cops—their guns out—felt they had to be ready for anything from crazed drug addicts to attacking men from Mars. They passed a car that had stalled out thanks to the flood. Two old women were inside, one of them trying in vain to get the engine to turn over. But there was no time to try and help them out now.

The officers approached the shaking truck, and suddenly . . . with no warning . . . it stopped moving. The police looked at each other, trying to decide what to do, and suddenly a large orange shape exploded from within the truck, soaring through the air and landing atop the stalled car.

A man who appeared to be made out of metal stepped out of the garbage truck. "Don't move!" shouted the cops, but he advanced and they immediately opened fire. Bullets ricocheted off him, pinging off the walls and the garbage truck.

"We're gonna need bigger guns," said one of the cops as they backed up.

Meanwhile the two elderly women were shrieking, clambering out of the damaged vehicle as the roof creaked over their heads.

The Thing rolled off the top and landed on the street.

"Who are you?" hollered the woman who had been the passenger.

"I'm from the auto club. Excuse me, ma'am," he said to the driver. "Can I borrow your car?"

"All . . . all right," stammered the woman, "but I . . . I think it's flooded. And the transmission sticks a little."

"Not gonna be a problem," he assured her.

He lifted the car as if it weighed nothing and swung it squarely at the armored man approaching him. It struck him hard and sent him skidding across the street.

The Thing dropped the car back onto the street, albeit with a large Doom-shaped dent in the front, tipped an imaginary cap to the women, said, "Happy motoring," and charged off after his opponent.

How the hell does a guy in armor disappear?

That was the quandary saddling Ben Grimm as he sprinted around the corner, trying to determine where in the world Doom had gotten off to. Granted, his situation wasn't being made easier by the lights flickering on and off as the city's power grid struggled to recover from the evening's assaults upon it, but still . . .

He turned around, determined to retrace his steps, and thus was unprepared as Doom appeared seemingly out of nowhere and slammed his fist into him. Ben staggered, skidded on the slippery streets, and fell onto his back.

Doctor Doom grabbed onto a nearby street lamp and, with little effort, yanked it from the ground. He reached down, gripped the wiring that was hanging from beneath, and began to draw energy from it. One by one, the buildings around Doom, which had just gotten their lights back on, began to go out again. Every building as far as Ben could see was soon dark.

Still gripping the street lamp, Doom stalked toward Ben. A massive amount of power was surging through him, and as Ben tried to stand up, Doom swung hard, knocking him flat once more.

Taking a cab back from the ballet, Alicia sat in the back-seat, lost in thought. She had barely been able to concentrate on the music, consumed as she was with worry about Ben. What in the world had happened that had prompted him to take off like that? It made no sense. She kept running through her head everything that she'd said to him. What could possibly have . . .

"Holy crap!" said the cabbie as the car skidded to a halt so violently that Alicia was flung forward. She cracked her head on the clear plastic partition between the front and backseat. "Sorry, lady!" he called.

"What's wrong? Traffic?"

"I dunno! There's water, like, everywhere, and— *Jesus!*"

"Now what?" She was starting to feel exasperated. This whole day had been going downhill ever since—

"It's the Thing! That guy from the papers and TV. He's fighting some other dude, down the end of the block! Lemme back up, try to get away from—"

"The *Thing?* Ben?"

Instantly snapping out her white cane, Alicia clambered out of the car, ignoring the cabbie's warnings to get back in. She stood, trying to hear what was going on. "*Ben!*" she cried out.

Doom looked down at Ben Grimm in scorn. The acclaimed muscle man of the Fantastic Four, barely able to move. What a sight to see. Ben started to rise and Doom kicked him back down again with no trouble.

He brought the street lamp up, its jagged metal edges from where it had been torn up pointing straight down at Grimm. Doom wasn't entirely sure whether he could manage to penetrate the Thing's hide and impale him with this impromptu spear, but he was willing to give it a shot. He figured he had a good chance, especially as he continued to siphon energy from it so that he had enough strength to . . .

Suddenly the lamp began to flicker, and then without warning it went out. Doom turned around and saw the elongated arm of Reed Richards, and in its hand were the electrical cords dangling from the lamp, ripped out of the circuits that had been feeding it from the street.

Quickly Doom turned back to Ben, eager to dispatch one problem before dealing with the next. But there was no sign of him. Instead Reed was there, unfrozen, meeting Doom's gaze with cold, hard, barely contained fury. "No more analysis, Vic. It's time for some heavy lifting."

Before Doom could make a move, Reed drew back his fist and it unbelievably morphed into a massive anvil. He slugged Doom with earth-shattering impact, knocking him back a good ten feet. Doom landed with a thud, and then got to his feet as Reed advanced on him, a dark smile on his face. It was obvious that, after all this time, Reed Richards had finally decided to show some guts. How startlingly predictable that his timing was off, because at this point, Reed's display of nerve was irrelevant to the inevitable outcome. Totally unharmed and not at all intimidated, Doom grated, "You don't really think you can stop me, all alone?"

Reed smiled back, tough and fearless. "No. I don't."

And suddenly, out of nowhere, the Thing, the Human Torch, and the Invisible Girl all appeared standing right behind Reed. Obviously Sue had cloaked their presence so that they could perform some huge, dramatic reveal that would theoretically cow Doom into submission.

Doom laughed. "You expect me to tremble at the feet of circus freaks?"

"I only see one freak here," Johnny shot back.

"This is who we are," Ben told him. "We can accept it."

"And maybe even . . ." said Sue.

Completing her thought, Reed said, "*Enjoy* it."

Doom lunged at Reed, the nearest of them. But Reed's arms stretched out with blinding speed, wrapping Doom in a massive bear hug. Doom screamed as Reed's arms tightened their grip around him.

"Johnny!" Reed called out, struggling to hold Doom. "*Supernova!*"

Johnny gaped at him. "Superwha—?" He looked around. "But all these people . . . !"

"*Now! Do it!*"

Reed pulled his arms back in a sudden, whiplike motion, setting Doom spinning like a top. Doom tried to right himself and stopped the spinning, but couldn't keep his balance and fell. From the ground, he looked up just in time to see Johnny running toward him, flames on his body starting to build to a blinding white intensity, engulfing everything. Johnny threw himself upon Doom and, gripping him for all he was worth, shouted, "*Flame all the way on!*"

He ignited, white hot, and Reed and Sue looked away

as Johnny erupted into a blinding pulse of illumination. It started to heat up everything around it, the asphalt melting, the remains of the water instantly boiling away and becoming steam.

Over the screaming of onlookers, Reed shouted to Sue, "Sue! Remember all that murderous rage we talked about? Think you can keep it . . . *under control?*"

She nodded and focused all her energy, all her concentration, on the growing heat and light that was emanating from Johnny while Doom struggled to get out of his grasp. It built up within her, stronger and stronger, and then Reed nodded, signaling her.

"*Susan, no!*" screamed Doom, but she didn't even hear him over the roaring within her own head. Her arms spread wide, a giant force field exploded from her, a massive wave of energy unlike anything that she would have thought possible.

Everything in its path was contained and pulled back, and then it enveloped Johnny's supernova blast, containing it in a bright sphere of energy. The light increased to the point where it would have seared clean the corneas of anyone looking at it. People twisted away, shielding their eyes.

Finally, Johnny's supernova faded. He collapsed to the ground, exhausted, smoking. Sue exhaled, falling to her knees, her force field fading. There was steam and smoke everywhere.

Nothing moved for a time . . . and then came a steady clank . . . clank . . . clank . . .

Doctor Doom stepped forward, unharmed. His

metallic body glowed white, trailing molten metal. He turned to Sue, Ben, and Johnny, savoring the distressed looks of shock and disappointment on their faces. He gestured toward Reed mockingly.

"You really thought a little heat could stop me?"

And Reed Richards, unflappable, replied calmly, "See, Vic, that's your problem. You never studied. Chem 101, last class: What happens when you supercool hot metal?"

He stretched out his arm toward a nearby fire hydrant. Realizing what Reed was up to, Ben flipped open the hose nozzle cap with one hand while gripping the operating nut on top, ready to twist it. Reed morphed his arm into a long, blue hose, slamming it against the hydrant nozzle.

"No," gasped Doom, throwing up his arms as if he could ward off what was about to come.

"You'll excuse me if I savor the moment," said Reed, and Ben twisted the operating nut, unleashing the flow of water. It blasted out of the fireplug, gushing toward Doctor Doom under the careful guidance of Reed's hoselike arm. Steam filled the air in giant clouds as the cold water struck the superheated metal.

"Funny how things work out," continued Reed.

"Hilarious," affirmed Ben.

For long seconds the water kept coming, steam filling the air so that, once again, no one could see what was happening. Doom's screams also resounded before they finally, mercifully, stopped. The steam finally dissipated to reveal . . .

Doom. A true statue now, a hard, cold, solidified piece of metal, frozen forever. His arms outstretched in what would be an eternal gesture of supplication, destined never to be answered.

The Fantastic Four exhaled in relief, standing as one. "Simple math," intoned Reed. "Four is greater than one."

Aware that the danger was over, onlookers emerged from hiding. They applauded, cheered, honked their horns, going wild in their approbation.

Grinning, Johnny said, "Damn, I love this job."

Reed and Sue locked eyes, thinking the same thing. Ben, looking amused, said, "Job, huh . . . ?"

Johnny put out his hand as before, palm down. Sue promptly put hers atop his, and Ben his on top of theirs. They all waited to see what Reed would do.

He shrugged and, stretching his arm, placed his hand atop theirs. "We're super heroes, not scientists," he said.

"Always a way with words," laughed Sue

That was when a woman's cries of "Ben!" echoed above everything else.

Instantly Ben turned in the direction that the cries were coming from. An attractive young woman, waving a white cane, was trying to make her way toward them.

"Alicia!" he called, immediately moving away from his friends and toward her. He shoved several cars out of the way without giving them a second thought until he finally reached her and took her hands in his. "What're you *doin'* here?"

"The . . . the ballet," she said.

"Cripes!" he said, wide-eyed. "Okay, fine, if yer that determined to chase me down, I'll go!"

"It's over," laughed Alicia.

"Aw, thank God."

"Why did you go? Why did you run off?"

"Because . . ." he fished for an explanation, and then came up with one that seemed perfectly plausible, given the circumstances. "I hadda go off and become a hero."

Alicia smiled and said, "Ben . . . you were *always* a hero." And she put her arms around him as far as they would go.

Johnny sauntered up and said, with a rakish smile, "Hey, Miss. I'm—"

"Hit on her and you're a dead man," Ben said.

"Later," Johnny said quickly and headed off in the other direction.

24

THE PARTY WAS LONG IN COMING AND WELL DESERVED.

The Circle Line boat chugged slowly around New York City as Reed and Sue kissed in the banquet room of the specially rented boat. Festivities were going full blast, and yet Johnny still managed to drift over in time to say in good-natured disgust, "Dude, that's still my sister."

Among the crowd were O'Hoolihan, his arm in a cast, and everyone who had ever provided any service for any members of the Fantastic Four . . . up to and including their mailman, Willie Lumpkin, dazzling others with his remarkable ability to wiggle his ears. Ernie the bartender was serving drinks behind the bar. He'd been an invited guest, but decided he didn't like the way the Circle Line bartender was handling things and took command in the way that only someone from Brooklyn could.

Reed and Sue came up for air, and then Reed turned to Ben and said, "Ben, I've been crunching the numbers on the machine. I think if we can rework the power settings . . ."

"Forget it, egghead," Ben said casually. "I'm good as is."

"That's my Benny," Alicia said, approval in her voice. She handed Ben a large metal mug into which Ernie had poured a beer for him. She held up her own glass mug and they clinked glasses. Unfortunately, Ben shattered hers, leaving her standing there holding a grip and no drink.

"We're going to have to work on your touch," said Alicia.

"I like the sound of that," said Ben.

Reed looked at the closeness of Alicia and Ben. He suspected that Ben was just trying to spare Reed any further guilt, but chose to accept Ben's sentiments at face value . . . at least for the moment. Reed then turned to Sue and said, "Sue, can I talk to you for a second?"

She followed him out, looking puzzled but game. They stepped out onto the deck of the boat, taking in the romantic view of the cityscape. "I found a broken gasket, from space—" he began.

"A gasket?" Sue clearly couldn't believe he was talking shop now. "Reed, we're at a party. A party we used a good chunk of our savings to throw, I should add, so—"

Reed opened his hand, revealing a circular piece of metal that was just about the size of a ring. Sue stared at it, not entirely understanding, but the light was slowly dawning.

"If one of us were to *wear* it," said Reed.

Sue spotted Johnny and Ben inside, watching, obviously in on it. She turned and looked Reed square in the

367

eye and said, unflinching, "Reed . . . what are you doing?"

Reed slowly dropped to one knee . . . but his neck stretched so that his head remained at eye level with Sue. Sue gaped, emotion flooding through with such velocity that she started to disappear.

"No more thinking," said Reed. "No more variables. Sue Storm . . . will you . . ."

She vanished entirely.

"Sue?" Reed called out. "Sue? You there?"

Then the ring suddenly vanished from Reed's hand . . . because Sue had insinuated her finger through it.

"Yes," came Sue's voice. "Yes, I'm here, and yes to . . . the other."

Smiling, Reed leaned forward to kiss her. From the empty air, Sue's nasal voice said, "That's my nose, genius. *These* are my lips."

In a replay of their time in the planetarium, Sue squeezed the sides of his face together, drew his mouth to hers and kissed him passionately.

Word of the proposal, meantime, had spread throughout the party, and everyone was watching when they kissed. Instantly there was applause from all, including Alicia once Ben had filled her in on what happened. As the party moved outside to join the newly engaged couple, Ben said in a low voice to Johnny, "No more cracks about how I look."

"Hey, I'm Mr. Sensitivity now," Johnny protested, and then he called out, "Clear the way, wide load coming through!"

Ben glared, fists clenched, as Johnny grinned mischievously before hitting the outer deck. "Flame on!" he shouted and leaped skyward, taking off into the air. Everyone pointed, shouted, and clapped as Johnny went higher, higher, and then started twisting and turning around on his own flame trail. Seconds later there was a blazing number "4" hanging high over Manhattan in the night sky.

"Show-off," muttered Ben.

Ignoring the illumination overhead, Leonard supervised the proceedings with the utmost meticulousness down by the harbor.

The immobilized form of Doctor Doom was crated up while Leonard spoke into his cell phone, assuring the Latverian consulate that everything was proceeding precisely on schedule. Leonard had checked the shipping papers one more time to make certain all was in order for the crate's transportation to Victor Von Doom's mother country.

Just before the dock workers sealed the lid on the box, there was a crackling sound of electricity and Leonard's cell phone suddenly went dead. He stared at it in confusion, and then glanced over at the crate suspiciously.

"Naaah," he said, and then walked away a little faster than he had to as the crate was loaded onto the freighter bound for Latveria.

ABOUT THE AUTHOR

PETER DAVID is the *New York Times* bestselling author of numerous *Star Trek* novels, including *Imzadi*, *A Rock and a Hard Place*, and the incredibly popular *New Frontier* series. He is also the author of the bestselling movie novelizations for *Spider-Man*, *Spider-Man 2*, and *The Hulk*, and has written dozens of other books, including his acclaimed original novel, *Sir Apropos of Nothing*, and its sequels, *The Woad to Wuin* and *Tong Lashing*.

David is also well known for his comic book work, particularly his award-winning run on *The Incredible Hulk*, and has written for just about every famous comic book super hero.

He lives in New York with his wife and daughters.